THE GAVEL AND THE GUN

"Just how long have you been chasin' this story, Mister Breed?"

"Ten years."

"Jesus! I heard tell about the Widow Maker before Hornback walked in here. I saw a pulp or two about him. Never read any of it. Just what the hell is so special about J. D. Preacher that you'd chase him for ten years?"

Breed's eyebrows raised. "Why, Marshal, I'm surprised at that question. Given what he is, the very fact that he's stayed alive for ten years is quite a story."

THE LAST GUNFIGHT

Doc Holiday was about four feet from Preacher. He closed the distance to a foot. "Ya know somethin', bounty killer," Doc said, spitting the words out, "you've come to take your family name too serious. If I want preachin', I'll go to church. As to dyin', that's my business."

"Not if you try to get me to set it up for you."

"You scared o' dying, Preacher?"

"No, but I'm not ready yet."

THE GAVEL & THE GUN/
THE LAST GUNFIGHT

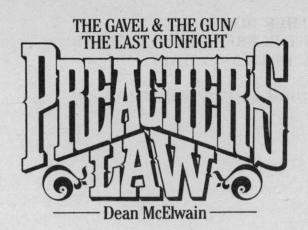

PREACHER'S LAW

— Dean McElwain —

Book Margins, Inc.

A BMI Edition

Published by special arrangement with Dorchester Publishing

THE GAVEL & THE GUN

Dedicated to:
The Wild Bunch*

Erickson Gang and Gardner Gang
Jessica	Sabrina
Andrea	Lucas
Sonja	Angela
Hillary	David

Mary Ella

*Apologies to "Butch and Sundance"

1

Texarkana, Texas, 6 March 1877

Jim Buck grabbed at the papers caught up by the gust of wind and looked toward the door of his office. A rotund little man, clutching at a derby, seemed locked in combat with the *norther* and the door. He finally prevailed. Just.

"What can I do for you, mister," Jim asked. The man smiled a nervous smile, rearranged his few remaining strands of hair and walked about half the distance from the door to the desk.

"My name is Caleb Hornback, sir. I am a purveyor of arms and ammunition of the very finest quality." He seemed to be expecting a response. He tugged at the ill-fitting suit, shifting the derby from hand to hand as the need arose.

Jim Buck considered him, rubbed the end of his nose and finally said, "A gun drummer." The little man looked insulted.

"Ahem!" Hornback pulled his shoulders back, swallowed and said, "I am considerably more than a mere salesman sir. I demonstrate weapons as well. Furthermore, if I may be so bold, I do so with considerable skill. I doubt that more than a dozen men now west of the Mississippi River know more about firearms than Caleb F. Hornback!"

7

"Mister Hornback, I'll be straight with you. I've got about the best gun I can afford. Besides that, I'm used to it." Jim Buck started to get up. Hornback's jaw dropped. Buck won. Hornback's jaw couldn't compete with six feet six inches. Quickly recognizing Hornback's discomfort at having to look up so far, Jim Buck settled on the edge of his desk.

"I'm not here to sell you anything," Hornback finally said. "You are the marshal, aren't you?"

"I am that."

"And your reputation, as I've heard tell, is untarnished and unbeatable."

"That aside, Mister Hornback, what exactly can I do for you?"

Hornback fished into his right hand coat pocket. He cleared his throat, shifted the derby to his other hand and fished into his left hand coat pocket. Again he came up empty.

He smiled, sheepishly. "It's here somewhere." He stepped forward and put his derby on Buck's desk. He retrieved a yellowed paper from inside his suit coat and handed it to the marshal. Big Jim opened it. It was badly worn, some of the folds perforated. The bottom half was water stained. It was a wanted poster.

"Is that still valid?" Hornback asked. Jim Buck didn't answer. Indeed, he went behind his desk and rifled through a stack of posters, finally extracting one. He put the one he found and the one Hornback had given him down on the desk top side by side.

"Only difference I see in them," Jim said, "is the bounty. It's higher by five hundred."

Hornback smiled. "Then sir, if—that is, if you captured this man because of me I'd get the reward?"

"Yes, sir. Actually," Jim said, "the court would pay you $2700. They'd take out ten percent for my wages."

"Yes. Of course."

Big Jim considered Hornback. He frowned. "You thinking of turning into a bounty hunter, Mister Hornback?"

Hornback's jaw dropped again. "Me? Oh my! No. No, Marshal. Why I'm a married man with children."

"Uh huh. Well, then, just what do you have in mind?"

"Like I said, just turning him in."

"That's a well worn dodger, Hornback. Why this particular fella?"

"Well, Marshal," Hornback said, sighing, "that's a rather long story. But I'll say this. There's probably some remuneration just for telling it. I've carried that poster ever since I rode out of my old sales territory near two years ago, I'd guess."

"And just where was that?"

"Up in the Dakota territory, Marshal. Deadwood was my last stop."

"Uh huh." Jim Buck had work to do and even he was running out of patience. "Mister Hornback, I don't mean to seem disrespectful to a law abiding citizen like yourself, but you do have a way of not getting right straight to the point."

"Oh yes. Goodness! I have taken up a great deal of your time, haven't I, Marshal?" He didn't wait for an answer. "Well, then, will you do it?"

Jim Buck's eyes got big. He leaned back, considered Hornback's question and then said, "Do what?"

"Why, arrest this fellow, of course."

Jim shook his head in despair, looked down at his boot tops, smiled a little and then looked into Hornback's face. "Sure will, Mister Hornback. You just tell me where he is."

"Across the street and down the block, Marshal, at the Gilded Lily Saloon." It was Jim's turn to be taken aback. He was. He stood up again, leaned forward and displayed a most intense countenance.

"Mister Hornback," he said, thrusting the dodger under the little drummer's nose, "this description could fit an awful lot of men. How can you be so certain that the fella at the saloon is this one? The one called the Widow Maker?"

It seemed to Caleb Hornback, for the first time, that Marshal Jim Buck was on the defensive. Besides that, the question was a leading one. It led Hornback right straight into familiar territory.

"Well, Marshal, of course you're right, absolutely right. A lot of men would fit his description." Hornback turned away, walked the width of the room, turned back and seemed to swell up a little. As much as a man like Hornback could swell. "Yes, sir! Looks can be similar." He jabbed nothingness with a stubby index finger. "But weapons? No, sir. That, Mister Marshal, is a different story.

"Weapons?"

"You bet! Now this gent, this Jeremy Preacher, well, he's about the most skilled shootist west of Saint Looie. One big reason for that is what he totes."

"And just what does he tote?"

"Matched, ivory gripped, customized forty-four forties. One in a vest holster just under his left armpit and the other on his right hip. Both were hand crafted for him by a highly skilled, German gunsmith, now deceased, in Denver."

"I don't think I've heard about pistols like that," Big Jim Buck commented.

"You haven't sir? You haven't?" Hornback smiled. A broad smile. A smile of satisfaction. "But you will. Soon I'd wager. Colt—Remington—Smith and Wesson—all of them will follow old Grinstadt's lead."

Jim Buck was studying the more recent of the two dodgers. He didn't hear all of Hornback's prediction. He looked up. "I've heard something about another gun this man is supposed to own. A damned nasty one."

"Indeed, Marshal, and that, sir, is the final proof. It is a fifty-eight calibre, pistol carbine. Originally a single shot, percussion weapon. It was re-tooled as well."

"By this old gunsmith."

"Quite. It is a lever action, seven shot gun now. Deadly! Yes, that's the only word for it. Deadly." Hornback was obviously thinking about the gun. He was staring into space. He blinked. "I saw it. It's in his room." Hornback suddenly looked concerned about his revelation. Perhaps he thought the marshal might take exception to his unlawful entry into another man's room. He saw no signs of disapproval and resumed his earlier confidence. "I went to his room for that specific purpose, Marshal. The gun is there. No doubt, sir, the man is the bounty hunter called Preacher."

"Mister Hornback, where are you staying?"

"One of the rooms at the Texas Hotel, sir, right next to the Gilded Lily there. That's how I came to . . ."

"Yes, sir. I understand, Mister Hornback. Now

I'll tell you what you do. You go back to that room and you wait there 'til I contact you.''

"But I wanted to see . . .''

"Until I contact you, Mister Hornback," Jim said, firmly.

"Yes, of course, Marshal.''

Jim Buck watched the little gun drummer until he saw him enter the hotel. Then, Jim went back to his desk, sat down and studied the dodger.

WANTED FOR MURDER

J.D. Preacher

also known as

Widow Maker

$3000 $3000
REWARD

The marshal read the physical description several times, noting that the bounty was to be paid by the authority of the nearest Federal court jurisdiction in which the man Preacher was taken into custody. Jim Buck gritted his teeth at the bottom line of the dodger.

Dead or Alive

"Damn," he mumbled to himself. "I could sure use a deputy now." He sighed and then began making preparations to attempt to arrest the most notorious bounty hunter in the country.

James Charles Buck was a rather gentle giant to those who knew him. He shunned public acclaim, although he could not always avoid it. He had been given the complimentary sobriquet, "The lawman's lawman." Indeed, many of his exploits easily rivaled those of some of his more notorious contemporaries. He thought them too swelled up, as he called it, on themselves.

After one particularly harrowing incident, in which Big Jim had emerged both victorious and unscathed, one Western journal bordered on elevating him to sainthood. A part of their effort read:

> "He stands like a great oak on the windswept prairie. He offers succor and security to the weary and fearful wayfarers. At the same time, he poses a mighty obstacle to those who would pursue their avarice outside the boundaries of civil tolerance."

If the prose was somewhat flowery, it was not that far removed from the facts. In just under two years, U.S. Marshal James Buck had become the figurative gun to Judge Isaac Parker's literal gavel.

The two men had been sworn into office on the same day. It was their first meeting. By no means was it their last. Parker, a 200 pound, broad straight, six-footer, was 36 years old when he volunteered to assume the federal judgeship in the Western District of Arkansas. It was the most violent in the country. He asked for a volunteer to assume the role of Chief Marshal to his court —but independent of his direct authority. Jim Buck answered the call.

Both assumed their official duties on the same day, May the second, 1875. Parker, his wife and their two sons arrived in Fort Smith. Mrs. Parker took one look at the surroundings and declared that her husband had made his first professional mistake. Jim Buck dined with the Parkers that evening and the next day rode on to Texarkana.

In the ensuing months, Jim Buck interviewed and helped to train—such as training was—several deputies to work out of Parker's court. While the court itself was limited by boundaries, that is it could not order a man hanged in Oklahoma, its lawmen could bring a man back from Oklahoma to hang in Arkansas.

Among Jim Buck's early students could be found such men as Chris Madsen, Billy Tilghman and the quiet and cool-headed Hec Thomas. By the beginning of 1877, Parker's deputies, answerable in the field to Jim Buck, numbered two score and growing.

Buck himself was 40, single and totally dedicated to law and order. He left justice to Judge Parker. In 12 months, Jim Buck rode after seven men. He brought four of them into Judge Parker's courtroom alive. It was, at the time, a record. Most such men appeared in the courtroom reposing in a pine box. While his detractors frowned on such a practice, it was nonetheless an edict of Parker's court. They *would* appear—one way or another.

While many of the most infamous characters ever to sit a saddle seemed to find a challenge in the commission of crimes within Parker and Buck's reach, many of the lesser men began to ride in wide berth by 1877.

Marshal Jim Buck was a mighty deterrent to such

saddle tramps. Few men would even consider facing him in a barroom brawl. Most underestimated him in a shootout. He carried two Colt's revolvers, one a Navy issue and one a standard Army pistol. They weren't matching and neither were the holsters in which they reposed. He wore them on his waist belt, slanted inward, cross-draw style and so close together their butts nearly touched. It was unorthodox but it was a style which Jim Buck had mastered. He usually went into an in-town arrest toting a shotgun. Where it was applicable, Marshal Buck was one of the best rifle shots aorund, once having bested Bill Cody in a target shoot.

Big Jim slipped on his battered stetson, buttoned the lone button on the front of his sheepskin coat, leaned over and blew out the coal oil lamp, picked up the scattergun and left his office. He gritted his teeth against the bite of the wind, pulled his collar closer to his neck, eyed the street ahead of him and then tucked his chin against his chest and headed for the Gilded Lily.

Texarkana, Texas, boasted fourteen saloons, a score of bawdy houses and two of the most colorful and unique characters west of St. Louis. In part, they were so rated due to an agreement between them.

The first was the proprietress of the Gilded Lily. She was a ravishing, raven haired, buxom, wasp-waisted firebrand named Corabelle Dancer. She hailed, so she said, from Falls Church, Virginia. She also said something else.

"I can ride any horse or tame any man in Texas." Having so stated her confidence, Corabelle would let go a hearty laugh and add, "Or the other way 'round if need be!''

Corabelle's intent, when she drifted into Tex-arkana in the high summer of 1874, had been to provide every need and fulfill every desire of her patrons. In the fall of 1875, Corabelle was reminded, none too kindly, that she had completely neglected her patron's spiritual requirements. Doubtless she would have thrown anyone else out of her place had they brought this shortcoming to her attention. But the individual who did so caught her fancy at once. Such was the cut of the man.

He was the Reverend Mr. Poole, Josephus Obidiah Ezekial Lounsdon Poole. The good Reverend was noted for several outstanding features. Perhaps the most obvious was his girth. A safe bet would have been that it made up at least one third of his mountainous structure, 300 pounds of structure. The weight was distributed, albeit none too evenly, on a frame which was just over six feet high and moved about on short, powerful legs. Most of the height was gained from girth to crown.

The good Reverend was usually decked out in bleached buckskins, moccasins, a black, wool shirt and a faded, red neckerchief which, it seemed to observers, he was always adjusting. Only on Sundays did his wardrobe change. A finely tailored black suit, white silk shirt, shiny black shoes with pearl-white spats, all of which he topped off with a beaverskin, plug hat.

Even on Sundays, the Reverend Mr. Poole toted a .44 calibre Remington revolver with a pearl grip. It was held neatly in place by his waist and against girth. And a few *permanents* in the border town could testify to his skill with it. During the remainder of the week, in addition to the six-gun, the Reverend Mr. Poole toted what appeared to be a Sioux or Crow Indian war club.

Poole hit Texarkana busted and feisty. After several days of trying to drum up interest in building the town's first church, Poole exerted a combination of efforts, thus displaying a combination of skills. He whipped two of Corabelle's best with what he called Greco-Roman wrestling holds. He then displayed an uncanny talent with cards and a more than novice understanding of other games of chance. Ultimately, he agreed to assume the duties of house manager at the Gilded Lily. As a part of his wage, he asked for the use of the casino, undisturbed and untainted, from sun-up Sundays until midnight Sundays. Church services would be offered.

Like his voluptuous business associate, the Reverend also lived by a credo.

"The Lord moves in strange ways, his wonders to perform. I'm about the damned strangest you'll find. In my church, no whiskey, no tobacco, no lust, no vulgarity. You got six days to do that. Them as abides is rewarded. Them as don't will feel the wrath. Mine first—the Lord's as he sees fit. He's got more time to ponder over it than I do."

Marshal Jim Buck stepped through the door and gingerly closed it behind him. Few noticed his entrance. One who did was Corabelle.

"Evenin' Jim," Corabelle's hardened exterior always softened considerably in the presence of Jim Buck. There was talk in Texarkana. Whispered talk, for Corabelle would have horse-whipped any gossiper spreading words about what she thought, privately, of Big Jim.

"Corabelle." She eyed the shotgun and frowned. Jim removed his sheepskin.

"Expectin' trouble, or is it already here?"

"That's what I've come to find out. You seen a rangy gent dressed in black? Moustache. Totes a custom pistol on his right hip. Another one like it in a vest holster, left side?"

"I haven't, but I've been upstairs most o' the day. Ask the Reverend. He's been here since 'bout ten this mornin'. Right now, he's housin' a high stakes poker game for me in the parlor room."

"Thanks, Corabelle."

"My pleasure, Marshal. Just try to keep my place intact."

Jim Buck nodded. The parlor room was an elegant and self contained addition to the Gilded Lily. It boasted its own bar. Only the best whiskey was served there, formal wear—at least suit and cravat—were required and no women were allowed. There was one other rule which put Jim Buck at a distinct advantage. Men could bring their guns into the parlor room, but they could not wear them. They were either placed on a table behind the house dealer or, still holstered, hung on pegs along the wall behind him.

Reverend Poole looked up, winced when he saw Jim Buck and said, "Gentlemen, forgive this untimely intrusion. I'll tend it as quickly as possible." He got to his feet, the only man toting a gun except for Jim Buck. He moved around the table and got to the marshal before he'd gained too much of an entry.

"I'm looking for a tall man. Moustache. Black out-fit."

"Toting a vest pistol and a match on his right hip?"

"Then he's here?" Jim Buck had no trouble looking over Poole's head toward the table.

"Not now he's not, but he was."

"When? How long did he stay?"

" 'Bout an hour ago Marshal, and he didn't stay at all. Wouldn't part with pistols. I've a grim feeling inside that I know the man, and he's trouble."

"Was he?"

"None. Just said he'd do his gambling in the main casino, table limits and all."

"I'd like you to point him out to me, Reverend."

"Can't do that, Marshal. He left the Lily about 20 minutes ago. He used the back door. I happened to see him when I was fetching a bottle."

"Thanks, Reverend, I'm obliged."

"Enough to tell me who he is, and what you want with him?" Jim Buck glanced toward the table. None of the others seemed interested in the conversation. Still, Jim motioned toward the door. Reverend Poole walked to it.

"Got a wanted on him. Gun drummer at the hotel thinks he recognized the man as a bounty hunter called the Widow Maker." Poole let out a long, low whistle. Jim Buck considered Poole. The wily card shark turned Christian usually didn't show much reaction to anything. "You know him, Reverend?"

"No." Poole looked up. "But I saw him in action once."

"I've heard stories."

"They're nowhere near the truth, Marshal. The man's no gunman. He's a prestidigitator."

"A *what?*"

"A magician, Marshal. He produces guns from thin air, fires them with an accuracy and speed faster than the eye can follow, shoots to kill, never misses and maintains control of his nerves about the same way a Bowie knife holds its edge."

"He broke the law. So reads the dodger on him. He's in my jurisdiction. Judge Parker can decide the rest."

"He'll kill you, Mister Buck."

"Mebbe."

"I'd badge a dozen men if I were you."

Jim Buck smiled a sardonic smile. "If he's all you claim, I couldn't find a dozen men who'd ride with me. Anyway," Jim Buck said, turning serious, "I don't want the word out around town. Keep this to yourself, least 'til I can verify it. If it is this fella Widow Maker, he'll draw ever' gunhand in the territory into Texarkana."

"Seems to me, Marshal," Reverend Poole said, looking straight into Jim Buck's eyes, "that you'd be wiser to get a pardon from good Judge Parker in exchange for the man's services."

"Judge Parker doesn't deal in pardons, Mister Poole. Gallows are more to his fancy."

"Well, good luck to you, Marshal Buck. I'll personally conduct the services without a fee on the day they hang the Widow Maker."

Jim headed back for the door but was cut off half way there by Corabelle.

"Jim . . ." The marshal waited for more words. None came. He looked quizzically at Corabelle. "One o' my girls just slipped a note to the barkeep. Bill Longley is upstairs."

"Damn! Cold as it's been, you'd think the snakes would stay to the rocks." Jim Buck shook his head. In 24 hours, Texarkana had gone from a relatively safe haven for law abiding citizens to a stopover point for two of the most skilled shootists ever to strap on a rig. Jim thought: Is J.D. Preacher

looking for Longley, or is it the other way 'round?
He smirked to himself. He knew it didn't make a hell
of a lot of difference. Either way spelled big trouble,
and any man caught in the crossfire would buy
himself a six by six plot of Texas soil.

The man known as the Tall Texan was, in fact,
barely more than a boy. Twenty-seven years old and
reputed to have killed at least that many men.
Among them, so Jim Buck had heard, were at least
three lawmen. One deputy sheriff, one city marshal
and one U.S. marshal. The last had been a personal
acquaintance of Jim Buck's. Frank Bisbee had been
one of the early arrivals in Texas and he had been as
smitten with the country as had men like Sam
Houston, Stephen Austin and the nine score and six
defenders of the Alamo. Like them, Frank died
defending his beliefs and the territory he had given
oath to protect.

Jim Buck headed for the door again. "Be careful,"
Corabelle said. Jim heard but he didn't respond and
he didn't stop. It was good advice, which he didn't
need. Corabelle hadn't given it as advice. Jim knew
it. She'd spoken as a woman who cared about him.
In his business he didn't need that either, at least
not just then.

What Jim did need was a damned good deputy.
One like young Conchudo, the half Mexican, half
Apache shotgun rider on the Red River Line. He'd
tried to employ the youngster a half a dozen times.
Conchudo wasn't interested in wearing a badge. He
wanted to be a lawyer. His dream was to help the
people—both sides of his heritage—with laws that
would outlive the gun. Jim's efforts to persuade him
that being a deputy U.S. marshal might open new

doors for him in his pursuit of a legal career had continued to fall on deaf ears. Conchudo's gun skills were already developed, and sometimes Jim Buck got angry with himself when he examined his own motives for trying to entice the young man into a deputy's badge.

Jim started toward his office. He was cold, tired, hungry, disgusted and angry. Most of the anger, he knew, had been smoldering in his gut for weeks. Repeatedly since he had assumed his position, he had requested additional funding. A handful of dedicated men were now faced with attempting to keep the peace in a territory which even the U.S. Army could not adequately patrol. His requests, at least two of them directed to—and seen by—President Grant, had been ignored. More recently, Jim Buck had received a personal letter from President-elect Rutherford B. Hayes. Hayes was now in office. Sworn in just two days ago. And his attitude had already softened on the issue of protection in the new, western territories. He had, in his inaugural address, issued a word of caution to those who would heed Horace Greeley's challenge.

Jim pulled up short. He had rounds to make. He was too old a horse to let a short fuse burn too long. It wasn't U.S. Grant's fault—or President Hayes' problem—that Jim Buck's town was now tainted— and perhaps in danger—due to the presence of two notorious gunmen. He turned, pulled his coat tighter around him, bowed his head against the wind and made his rounds. All was serene in Texarkana.

"Marshal Buck?" Jim's head jerked up as he opened the door to his office. The wind picked up, a gust whipped through the door, papers flew into the air and the lamp's already low flame was threatened with total extinction. "I'm Preacher."

Jeezus, Jim thought. I'm caught like a damn tenderfoot. He eyed the tall man in black. The man made no threatening moves. Jim thought: Hell! He doesn't have to. Fast as I've heard he is, he damned well don't need the drop. Jim closed the door. Preacher stepped to the desk and turned up the lamp. Jim watched him. Then, the big marshal removed his coat and hat.

"You here to turn yourself in?"

"Straighten out a few things, Marshal. Reasonably."

"I'm a lawman. Not a judge."

"But you know the judge. He'll see you privately."

Jim Buck began to relax a little, all the while being careful that it wasn't too much.

"Care for some coffee?"

"I'll drink some."

Jim began preparations to brew a pot, thinking, considering, pondering what gamble he might be taking.

"Why the hell should you get special treatment, Preacher?" The question was harsh. The tone was also harsh. Jim Buck backed both with a hard look straight into Preacher's face. He stopped what he was doing and it was obvious that he expected an answer immediately.

"Because I'm a special case." The answer somewhat caught the big lawman off guard, but he recovered quickly.

"Who says so? You?" Jim returned to fixing the coffee.

"I can ride into almost any town anywhere, Marshal, and the local peace officer will find reason to be gone. That was sometimes the case before I had posters on me and a price tag on my hat. Difference is, the lawman's little town wasn't in any danger then. It is now."

Jim shoved the big black coffee pot to the center of the old #10. He decided to gamble again. He reached down and unstrapped his rig. He swung it behind him, turned, eyed Preacher, buckled the belt together and hung it next to his hat.

"Bounty hunters, Preacher? That what you mean?"

"Some of the best."

"And the worst."

"Those kind too." Jim Buck moved behind his desk and sat down. He motioned for Preacher to sit. Preacher turned, grabbed a chair and put it opposite Jim Buck at the desk. "It'll take a Federal judge to lift the bounty on me. There may be two or three who'd do it under the right conditions. But they wouldn't draw the attention Judge Parker will get."

"I'll be damned! All you want is the attention."

"In a manner of speaking, Marshal, that's right."

"You're a real case, mister gunman. A real case. You sure don't lack moxie. I'll give you that." Jim wagged his head in astonishment. "Get the Federal Marshal to haul you in and the Federal Judge to get you publicity. By God! That's a good one."

"When Judge Parker has lifted the bounty and the dodgers are out of circulation, I can go back to my trade and the attention, as you call it, won't be on me anymore. Your town, and a lot of others like it, won't draw flies once you're rid of the dung heap." Jim Buck frowned. Had he heard right? Was the notorious J.D. Preacher referring to himself as a pile of shit?

"That the way you rate yourself, Preacher?"

"How I rate myself doesn't matter, does it, Marshal? Some fella said," Preacher frowned, remembering, "uh, if you've got the facts and the legend, print the legend."

"So ever'thing I've heard about the man they call Widow Maker is just legend. That right?"

"You help me separate the two, Marshal," Preacher said, half smiling, "and judge for yourself."

"I'll go back to my first question, gunman. You here to turn yourself in? You want me to arrest you? Ride you up to Fort Smith?"

"Telegraph the judge. Set up a meeting. You, him, me. Just let me know when. I'll be there."

"And I'm supposed to trust you?" Jim thought: How stupid! The man had come in on his own. "I could arrest you right now." Jim thought: Stupid again.

"I won't be pushed, Marshal." It was the first indication of any resistance by the gunman. Jim considered him.

"That a threat?"

"That's a fact."

"And if I don't agree?"

"Then I'll ride out. Try somewhere else." Preacher got to his feet. Jim tensed a little. "I can't promise you a trouble-free stay, but I'll be leaving Texarkana by noon tomorrow."

Jim Buck stood up. He was half a head taller than Preacher. Forty pounds heavier, he figured. They considered each other. Jim rubbed the tip of his nose. "You still want that coffee? Sounds like it's boilin'."

Preacher sat back down. "I'll join you, Marshal Buck."

There wasn't a hell of a lot left to say. Jim Buck had been offered a bargain from a wanted man. He wasn't sure if Preacher wanted to sell his gun to the court, like Poole had suggested, or he simply considered himself so infamous that lifting a bounty would result in widespread peace. The two men eyed each other through the steam. Jim thought: There could be another reason for a bargain to be struck. Maybe, just maybe, J.D. Preacher hadn't done what the law claimed. Maybe their claims were just a part of the legend.

"There's another gun in Texarkana," Jim said. "Name's Bill Longley." He didn't see a reaction. "Calls himself the Tall Texan. He doggin' your trail?"

"Not as I know of," Preacher replied, "but I've heard of him."

"He know you're in town?"

"Can't say, Marshal."

"He'd likely try you if he did. Just for the reputation."

"He got paper on him?" Jim nodded. "Maybe you ought to bring him in."

Jim Buck stood up. "Or sit tight 'til he wants to strike a bargain. Or let you and him kill each other and be done with all my troubles at once. He's got plenty doggin' him—like you. Hell, with both of you out of the way, there'd be no reason for any gunhand in Texarkana. Even less for 'em to stay."

"That's a possible, Marshal," Preacher said. He got up now and moved to the door. "But you don't strike me as a man who likes to deal in possibles. I'll be where you can get an answer to me 'til noon tomorrow. Good night, Marshal Buck."

Jim Buck leaned back in his chair and took a deep breath. J.D. Preacher didn't frighten him. Neither did Bill Longley. If he had to face men like them, he would make his decision at the time. If he was too far wrong—or too damned slow—they'd bury him. It went with the job. What did bother him was misjudging a man completely. Particularly too soon. Making a decision that was not only wrong but unnecessary in the first place. Trying to figure too many angles and missing the only one that really mattered. He'd done that once. He didn't want to do it again. He knew it would be very easily done with a man like J.D. Preacher.

2

Corabelle's girl spent the night with Bill Longley. She did manage to slip Corabelle another message. Longley was an early riser. He'd be down wanting a breakfast of steak and eggs and plenty of black coffee. Corabelle sought out the Reverend Poole and revealed what she knew. They agreed to meet for their own breakfasts by no later than five o'clock. They did.

"I didn't mention it last night," Poole said, after merely nodding a good morning, "but Mister Bill Longley is not our only famous guest." He sipped his coffee, studying Corabelle's face and rather enjoying the obvious suspense. "Ever hear of the gent they call the Widow Maker?"

" 'Course I have." Corabelle's answer was given before the question had made its full impact. Her mouth opened again, but no words came. Poole waited. "Gawd A'mighty. Is he the one Jim Buck was lookin' for?"

"He is." The fourth step from the top of the stairs squeaked with any weight at all upon it. It squeaked now. The Reverend and Corabelle both looked up. Bill Longley was coming down. He stopped about halfway down and carefully surveyed the casino. Satisfied, he walked on down, spotted a corner table, which put his back to the wall by the bar, and moved to it. He looked around again and then took his seat.

"I'll tend him, personal," Corabelle said. She got up. "Mebbe we oughta send for the marshal."

"I'm afraid," Poole said, gesturing toward the front door, "that your suggestion comes a tad too late. Unless I miss my guess, the gent about to come through the front door will be one, Mister J.D. Preacher."

Poole watched Longley. Corabelle looked at the door. It opened. The man was tall. Not, she thought, as tall as Jim Buck, but not far from it. He was slimmer though, rangy like Jim had said. Handsome, she thought. She noted that he closed the door with his left hand, never looking at what he was doing but, instead, following the same procedure Bill Longley had executed, only quicker. In a flash, his eyes were focused on Longley himself. Neither man moved. It was a study. A sizing up. No one but Preacher was aware of his advantage. Based on Jim Buck's information, Preacher had a pretty good idea who was seated at the corner table. Longley had never seen Preacher.

"Breakfast?" Poole finally asked. He didn't shout but the word came out that way, reverberating through the emptiness that was the Gilded Lily at five o'clock in the morning. Corabelle jumped. She felt foolish.

"Mornin'," she said, forcing a smile she didn't feel. As she spoke, she started toward Bill Longley. Longley, at once, got to his feet. She had come between the two. Preacher stood fast.

"Just coffee," Preacher said.

"I don't fancy takin' breakfast alone," Longley said. His voice was deep, commanding. He offered a winning smile. Corabelle got her first good look at him. He too was tall. Over six feet. Probably about the height of the man called Preacher. Longley wore a moustache and goatee, the latter showing streaks of premature gray. She wasn't certain to whom he'd spoken. "Care to join me, mister?" He left the word hanging. A blank spot behind it for its intended subject to fill.

"Preacher," came the reply. "I'll sit with you, Mister Longley." Reverend Poole eased his hand off the butt of his forty-four. No one noticed the faint smile which crossed his lips. He'd been ready. Inside, he was chuckling. He didn't know just what the hell he'd been ready for, but he'd been ready.

Corabelle took the orders and disappeared into the back. Neither of the men spoke another word until she'd returned, poured the coffee and both had consumed about half a cup.

"I heard a lot of talk about you up in the Dakotas, bounty man. Some of it was right down unpalatable."

"That a fact." Preacher sipped his coffee. Longley smiled. "Most of what I've heard about me is unpalatable."

"You dogging a trail?"

"No."

"Somebody dogging yours?"

"Likely."

"You long in Texarkana?"

" 'Til noon, Mister Longley." Preacher finished his coffee just as Corabelle returned with Bill Longley's breakfast. She set the heavy platter down and then started to pour more coffee into Preacher's cup. He put his hand over the top of it.

"You said you'd sit with me," Longley said. He straightened in his chair as he spoke. Corabelle tensed.

"The breakfast looks good," Preacher said. He smiled up at Corabelle. "Skip the coffee. Bring me what he's got."

"Sure thing, Mister Preacher," she said. Her relief was obvious.

"Drop the mister, please," Preacher said. "And I'll call you . . . ?"

"Cora . . . anyhow some do. Corabelle Dancer's the name." She gestured with a sweep of her hand. "The Lily's mine." She chuckled. " 'Cept on Sundays." She turned and pointed toward Reverend Poole. "That day belongs to our good Reverend there."

"*Him?*" Longley laughed. "He's a damn Bible thumper?"

"Sure is." Cora answered without looking back at Longley. She was still watching Reverend Poole. He, in turn, had stood up and was looking out of the window. The lower half of the glass was frosted but something, obviously, had prompted Poole to get to his feet.

"Billy shit!"

"Poole?"

"Four gunnies."

As big as he was, Josephus O.E.L. Poole could move quickly. He did so now, crossing the room in surprisingly long strides and managing a spot behind the bar before the doors opened. When it did, a rotund little man in an ill-fitted suit and clutching at a derby came through the opening, nudged from behind by an ugly entity who was brandishing a shotgun. A few feet inside and the ugly one was flanked by two companions. Both wore double rigs with tie downs.

Preacher and Longley had both gained their feet, moved a little away from the table and separated by ten or twelve feet. The ugly man poked the little man with the derby in the back.

"Which one is he?"

Caleb Fitzhugh Hornback was as white as a sheet. His right hand, now clutching a half crushed derby, shook uncontrollably. He cleared his throat, looked around, pausing for just a few seconds too long when he saw Preacher.

"I . . . I don't see him."

All that saved Hornback from losing his head was the entry of a fourth man, his back to the others, a rifle in his hand, his eyes on the street.

"We got a tin star comin'." Hornback took the stock of the shotgun over the back of his head and dropped like a poled steer. The ugly man leveled the scattergun right straight at Corabelle Dancer.

"First man that even thinks about makin' a move kills the little lady." He looked straight at Preacher and grinned. His teeth were a dark brown and Preacher could see the sparkle of spittle as the man shifted his quid from left to right. It took Preacher only a split second to consider his situation. even his best shot wasn't fast enough to stop ugly's reflex action. Corablle would end up all over the mahogany bar. The man to ugly's right was poised for action and staring right straight at the Reverend Mister Poole. On the left, the peach fuzz faced kid was grinning at the Tall Texan, Bill Longley.

"I'm Preacher. It's me you want."

"You said that right, bounty man." Ugly kept his eyes on Preacher, but cocked his head a little and twisted his mouth to the left. "Where's that law man?"

"Half a block."

"That's close enough, Vinnie. Hold 'im right there." The door went shut. Everyone heard Vinnie's voice.

"Marshal, we got a real touchy situation here, real touchy. But we're about to do the law a big favor. Clear the county of a real menace. I'd say might be best for you to wait in your office. We'll bring 'im along right shortly. No trouble neither, 'less'n somebody gets in the way—you know—kinda blunders in—accidental like."

Marshal Jim Buck knew his job and he knew most of the faces of the men who kept him doing it. This one, Jim knew, was Vincent Jasper Honeycutt. Texas born. Raised in hell. Wanted in both.

"Honeycutt, you son-of-a-bitch, lay the rifle down."

"Got a woman. A fat man. A drummer. A bounty hunter an' a man I'd guess to be the Tall Texan under a scattergun, Marshal. The woman—she'd be first. Why Jake'd blow both her tits off, Marshal," he laughed, a kind of staccatoed sound which seemed to originate in his throat, "just to watch 'em bounce." Big Jim stopped. The sheepskin coat was unbuttoned, the pistol butts appeared extra shiny in the early morning sun, just making its appearance at the far end of First Street.

Inside the Gilded Lily, Jake Kildare barked out two more orders. The first was directed at Corabelle. He licked his lips and said, "Girlie, I want you to walk right straight over here to me real slow an' easy like. Don't want you lookin' 'round or movin' one way or the other. Just nice and straight right

into ol' Jake's arms." He looked into Preacher's
eyes the whole time he spoke. He grinned again.
"You think you're good enough, bounty man, you
try."

"Tom," he barked, suddenly turning slowly, "take
the bounty man's purty pistol. Longley's too."

"The man that wants my gun will have to kill me
to get it," Longley said, "and that woman don't
mean a damned thing to me." Preacher knew what
was going to happen, but it didn't. It didn't because
Corabelle Dancer let out a little whine and dropped
to her knees and a voice from the top of the stairway
finally distracted the trio of gunmen.

"Mornin' gents, welcome to Texarkana." All three
heads turned. Perhaps Jake Kildare's age and
experience resulted in him being the first to register
the error he'd made. Whatever time it took was too
long. The error aside, Jake was also the target for
three of the four men he and his cronies faced.

The Reverend Mister Poole moved remarkably
fast with the long barreled ten gauge. The shot
pattern was tight. Between that blast and the two
shots he took from Preacher and the young gunman
on the stairway, Jake Kildare didn't have enough
brain left to send a signal to his trigger finger.

The fuzz-faced kid on his left was Tom Muncie.
He'd gotten drunk and screwed his first woman
just three months earlier when he turned 18. He
was fast, frightfully fast. He got off two shots even
half blinded by blood and brain matter, most of
what was left of Jake Kildaire's head.

One shot took off the bootheel of the left boot on
the young man firing from the stairway. His own
speed was not lacking, although the two were so
evenly matched that either's survival would have

been in doubt under other circumstances. In this case, Tom Muncie died with a bullet through the heart.

The third man was known to even his closest companions only as Faro. He had distanced himself far enough from Jake to have avoided being caught in the fire directed at Kildare. He was also a well practiced hand with a six-gun. The Reverend would have been his target had he lived that long. Poole had to relieve himself of the shotgun and then clear his own pistol. Bill Longley, his brain working as fast as his eyes could take in the action, switched targets when he realized Faro was already out of the fight. So did Preacher. Even faster.

The first sound—the shotgun blast—brought a smile to Vincent Honeycutt's thin, cracked, scaly lips. He winced a little when one of the cracks broke open. His chapped lips were the reason for the somewhat controlled laughter a few moments earlier. The almost deafening exchange of gunfire which immediately followed the shotgun blast pursed Vincent Honeycutt's lips, twisted his pocked face into a tight little knot of shock, which turned to pain, which turned to dead. He never cleared leather.

Jim Buck wasn't polite. He kicked the door in, pistols in both hands and then pivoted and flattened his huge frame against the wall.

"Corabelle! Reverend Poole!"

"We're both here. Both breathing," Poole answered. Jim Buck, pistols still at the ready, pivoted again and moved through the doorway. Instinctively, he looked to the stairway. Conchudo smiled. Jim then examined the three men on the floor. He holstered his guns and stood up. He eyed

Preacher and then Bill Longley.

"You in on this, Longley?" Jim pulled the lapel of his coat back and Longley's eyes darted down to the badge.

"The best side of it I'd say, Marshal Buck."

"He stood with us, Jim."

Jim glanced at Corabelle. He felt a twinge in his belly. A twinge that a man feels when a worry he's got is replaced with the fact that he doesn't have to worry anymore. The twinge bothered him.

"You come through clean?" he asked. He didn't know what else to ask, but he felt foolish not asking anything.

"I'm fine." Cora gestured toward Poole. "So's he."

"Only, I'm afraid, due to the almost perfect timing of that young man on the stairway. I'd wager the outcome would have been somewhat less pleasant but for his most timely appearance." Poole was looking right straight at Bill Longley as he spoke. Jim caught the look.

Longley frowned. "No man takes my gun." He was looking straight at Jim Buck.

Preacher sensed a possible he didn't like. "Your young friend there just happening by, was he, Marshal?"

"Not hardly. It was Conchudo who saw these buzzards ride in. He overheard enough of their questions at the livery to know there was big trouble ahead. He got to me in time. I told him where to go and how to get there."

"And when?"

"That was more luck than planning, Reverend."

"The Lord's Temple isn't standing because of blind luck, Marshal."

Jim glanced down at the bloody trio at his feet. "I'd say there was nothin' blind in this room, Reverend." He glanced up at Poole. "Don't quite see how you figure this is the Lord's work."

"Simple enough, Marshal. The Devil thrust those foul and evil men into His presence and He countered with the gentlemen who stood against them. I believe Messers Remington, Colt, and one or two others, no doubt, provided the means."

"And the men themselves did nothing. That right?"

"By no means, Marshal. All men face choices. These men made theirs. They stood fast. They provided the grit, Marshal Buck. The grit." Jim Buck, and at least one of the other onlookers, Preacher, grinned when the Reverend Mr. Poole made the sign of the cross on his chest, using the barrel of his fourty-four. "Ah men," he said.

Jim turned back to business. Business with the Tall Texan. Bill Longley. "I've got paper on you, Longley."

"You callin' it in, Marshal?"

"Ride on out of Texarkana. If you value your hide, Longley, you'll keep on riding right on out of Texas. If you don't, I'll get you. If I don't, some Ranger or one of Parker's deputies will. I've got right urgent business to attend, and I don't make offers lightly or often."

"I don't take well to bein' hurrrahed, Marshal."

"I don't hear the marshal pushing you, Mister Longley," Preacher said, turning to face the lanky Texas gunman.

Jim Buck took umbrage at the apparent defense. "I don't need a bounty killer speaking for me, Mister Preacher. I got paper on you, as well."

"Don't misunderstand me, Marshal. I'm not speaking for you. You and I have got some business to finish, and I'm just a mite impatient. I don't plan to wait around while you deal with Longley here or anybody else, for that matter." Preacher turned back to the Texan. "I've got priority with this gent, since I spoke with him last evening. Now if you're going to have a difference with him, I'd like to settle up first."

Bill Longley considered Preacher. Killing the notorious Widow Maker would most certainly enhance Longley's reputation. That aside, Longley was gut curious if he could beat the man, head to head.

"You're a damned sudden man with a gun, Preacher, 'bout one of the best I ever saw." Longley grinned. "Think you can take me?"

"I do," Preacher answered, cooly, "but I'm hoping you won't give me cause."

"More'n 20 have said them words to me, or ones like 'em, Preacher. Most just before I killed 'em."

"Those are right healthy odds, Longley, for you. Best if you don't press them."

"Longley," Jim Buck said, stepping between the two gunmen, "I'll ask you again—and only once again—ride on out. The gunplay in Texarkana for today is all done with unless I start it." He looked hard at Longley and then turned and looked equally hard at Preacher. "And I'm hopin' neither of you will give me cause."

Jim half smiled. "I'll promise you one thing. If you do any standoff between you two is going to come up one short."

Midway through Jim Buck's warning, Bill

Longley stepped back to the table, retrieved his hat, put it on and then looked straight at Jim. The marshal stopped talking. Longley smiled.

"Another day, gents. Another day." He touched his hat brim, pushed by them and walked outside. The group watched, silently, as one of Texas' more dubious native sons departed Texarkana.

Hornback moaned.

"Goddam," Jim said. Everyone had forgotten Hornback. He was a man easily forgotten. Corabelle and Poole got him to his feet and moved him to a nearby table. Jim looked down again at the pile of slaughter. "Conchudo . . . will you . . ." the half breed smiled, nodded and left to fetch Joe Ryman, the burying man. Jim then turned his attention to Preacher. "I'd be obliged if you'd spare me the time to finish this job. When I'm through, I'd like to come back and buy you a drink." Preacher considered the big marshal. "Teton Jack, isn't it?"

"It is."

"Mighty fine drinkin', Teton Jack. Real sippin' whiskey. I could never afford it." Preacher said nothing. "Be a birthday drink I'd be buying you, Preacher. Thirty-first birthday, if my records are straight."

"They are."

"I'd be giving you my answer then, too." Jim Buck carried a big, gold pocket watch. He slipped it into his hand, popped open the cover, looked at it and added, "You could still ride out by noon."

"I'll be here," Preacher said.

"It's all over, folks. Go open your businesses. There's nothin' to see inside that you'd want to gawk at before breakfast." Preacher stood inside the Gilded Lily and watched as Jim Buck dispersed the town's curious. He shook his head. Corabelle joined him.

"We don't have many gunfights in Texarkana, " she said. "They tend to bring out the worst in folks." She gestured toward the outside with a tilt of her head. "They're right nice people mostly."

"If you say so."

Corabelle frowned as she looked into Preacher's eyes. Then she felt a sudden tugging at her insides. It made her shiver. She couldn't define its origins.

"Hornback. The little fella. He'll be fine."

"Good for him."

Corabelle shivered again. "Coffee?" Preacher nodded.

Outside, Jim Buck found himself with only one stubborn citizen. A youthful looking sort decked out in a somewhat trail-worn, store bought suit.

"Somethin' I can do special for you?"

"I'm a newspaperman, sir. Breed's the name." He extended his hand. "Nate Breed." He looked toward the Gilded Lily and then back and up at big Jim Buck. "Is J.D. Preacher is there? I was told he would be."

"That right? An' who told you that, Mister Breed?"

"A gent named, uh . . . uh," Breed found a slip of paper, unfolded it, read, looked up, smiled and added, "Hornback. He said there would be a showdown." Breed tightened his mouth and sighed. "Looks like he told me right and I got here too late."

Jim Buck rubbed the end of his nose, considering Nate Breed. He thought back to the comments made by Caleb Hornback. Something, Jim recalled, about remuneration. Money for a story. His story? Preacher's story, Jim thought.

"You doggin', Mister Hornback?"

"I was supposed to meet him here. I mean, in Texarkana. He simply told me he'd have some information for me that he knew I'd be interested in."

"About the gunman."

"About J. D. Preacher."

"You come along with me, Mister Breed."

Nate Breed swallowed. "Am I under arrest?"

"Just come along." Breed eyed the Gilded Lily. Jim Buck eyed Breed. Breed eyed Jim Buck. Right then, the Gilded Lily looked smaller. Breed went along.

Nate Breed grew increasingly nervous as he watched Jim Buck make a fresh pot of coffee. Once it was fixed and had a good fire under it, Jim pulled out the two dodgers on Preacher, pointed Breed to a chair, handed him the posters and said, "Tell me about the Widow Maker. Or as much as you can anyhow."

"What exactly do you want to know?"

"You been doggin' Hornback. Hornback's doggin' Preacher. Why?" Nate smiled. He was beginning to relax a little.

"You've got it wrong, Marshal. Hornback is a rather recent addition to my sojourn."

"Your what?"

"My journey over the years, Marshal, to dig out the truth and tell it. The truth about J.D. Preacher."

Jim straightened in his chair. He leaned forward.

"Just how long have you been chasin' this story, Mister Breed?"

"Ten years."

"Jeezus! I heard tell about the Widow Maker before Hornback walked in here. I saw a pulp or two about him. Never read any of it. They did the same thing with Hickok. Now they're doin' it with those boys up Missouri way.''

"The James brothers.''

"Uh huh. Just what the hell is so special about J.D. Preacher that you'd chase him for ten years?''

Breed's eyebrows raised. "Why, Marshal, I'm surprised at that question. Given what he is, the very fact that he's stayed alive for ten years is quite a story.''

"It is if you believe ever'thing you read,'' Jim replied. "I don't!'' He got up and moved to the stove. "Coffee?''

"Uh . . . yes . . . please.''

Jim grabbed a tin cup, looked inside it, frowned, pulled out a corner of his shirt tail and wiped it, looked again and then filled it with hot coffee.

"Best let that cool a spell, Breed. It boiled.'' Breed nodded. Jim poured himself a cup, resumed his seat and then checked his watch. He looked up. "We've got some time, Breed. And across the way there is a fella we're both interested in, no matter that we got different reasons.'' Jim's eyes stayed on Breed's face. Jim tried to sip his coffee. It was too hot. He blew at it.

"That gunman has tried to strike a bargain with me. Now I'm going to strike one with you. He said somethin' to me. Sort of odd, I thought. Mebbe it wasn't.''

"What did he say?''

"Uh . . . somethin' like . . . if you've got a fact and a fairy tale . . . uh . . .''

"If you've got the facts and a legend, print the legend? Was that it?''

"Yes, sir. That was it. Then he said somethin'

about me helpin' him to separate the two and judging for myself which is which."

Breed smiled, looked down and shook his head. "Something wrong, Mister Breed?"

"No, no, Marshal. Nothing at all." Breed relaxed completely. He leaned back, keeping the hot tin cup rotating between his fingers. "I'll tell you about J.D. Preacher, at least as I know him to be. Maybe I can help you sort those facts out of the legends, and maybe you can help me keep them sorted."

"Talk, Mister Breed. I'm listenin'."

3

" . . . so," Breed concluded, sighing, "that's the story as I know it. Preacher?" Breed smiled, wistfully. "He won't tell me anymore and now there are more holes. Months, a lot of them when I don't know where he was or what he did. Oh, I've got rumors. Bits and pieces, but only J.D. Preacher can put them all together."

"It's a hell of a story," Jim Buck said, stretching his long legs out to their full length, leaning his head forward and massaging the back of his neck. He sat up straight and then turned to face young Nate Breed. "But he's still a cold-blooded killer."

Breed was shocked. His expression revealed it. "Weren't you listening, Marshal?"

"I listened. I heard." Jim leaned, reached the coffee pot and, without asking, refilled Breed's cup, then his own. He replaced the pot. "Parents murdered. Sister butchered and the killings of two women he loved. Jeezus! It's the stuff of a book all right, but hardly justification for his actions. The same thing must have happened to a lot of men during the war—and after. God. I know one right here in Texarkana. He's a bookkeeper with a wife and three younguns. No damned murderin' gunman."

"You listened, Marshal," Breed said, a definite change in his tone, "but you miss the point."

"The hell you say. Well, boy, you straighten me out. You tell me about killers. This I want to hear."

"Oh, I know what you're saying, Marshal. The law's the law. A man don't do right, then he's doing wrong."

"But you see it different. That right?"

"You're damned right I do," Nate Breed shot back. He could feel his face getting warm. It didn't stop him. He leaned forward. "It's a long, lonely and frightening ride between lawmen in the country, Marshal." Breed snorted out a smirk. "More often than not, when you do find a man with a star, he's not a whole lot better than what you're scared of. Either that or he's got the backbone of a rattler."

Breed seemed to be warming to his subject. He got up, turned and walked to the window. He stared out. He turned back. He lashed out. "Hell, yes, what happened to J.D. Preacher happened to a lot of other men, but we're not all cut out of the same bolt of cloth, mister lawman. Or hadn't you noticed? How many men answered your call to sign on as a deputy?"

Breed was staring at Jim Buck with what Jim thought was almost a look of pity. "Some of us, Marshal, well, we're just a little flawed. We just don't quite have the courage of our convictions." Nate Breed jammed a finger into the air, in the direction of the Gilded Lily. "That killer, as you call him, he doesn't just ride for J. D. Preacher. He rides for every one of those others you talk about. He's doing what any of them—hell—what all of us would do—if we had the courage."

Marshal Jim Buck got to his feet. He pulled out the gold watch again. It was just past eleven o'clock. He glanced back up and saw that young Nate Breed had moved over to the window again. He was staring down the street toward the Gilded Lily.

"That was quite a speech, Mister Breed. Ever think about going into politics?"

"Not real hard I haven't, Marshal. Seems to me I've got enough hard-headed folks to talk to now."

"Mebbe, but the pay's better in politics." Jim Buck grinned. Nate Breed wasn't grinning. "That killer down the street ought to supplement your income pretty well. Hell. You do about as good a job of campaigning for him as any I've ever heard for a politician."

"You're not much on a man's circumstance giving him cause, are you, Marshal?"

"Ever' man I've ever faced, or for that matter, ever' man that lives with a gun has a cause. Powerful reasons that they think the law ought to understand."

"And what about you? Hell, as I see it, the only difference between you and J. D. Preacher is that little tin star."

Jim Buck's brow wrinkled. He gave Breed a studied look. "I guess that's a fair comparison," he finally said. "And the only difference between a man being free or not is a little piece o' parchment they keep back in Washington. Thing is, I don't recollect it protecting a man like J.D. Preacher." Jim Buck had stood against the young, well educated newspaper man and he felt he'd won. He put on his coat and walked to the door.

"Marshal, that little piece of paper came to pass because of men like J.D. Preacher. So did your right to wear that tin star. They had no parchment. No star. Recollect them, Marshal?" Breed smiled. "Nathan Hale. Gentlemen farmers like one named Washington. Boone, Crockett, Bowie, Carson, Bridger . . ."

"I don't need a damn lesson in American History from a wet-nosed newspaperman, Breed. How in hell can you put the name Preacher in with the likes of the man you've just mentioned?"

"Oh, I'm not, Marshal, but I wonder what names will be added on one day. Hickok? Cody? Siringo? Isaac Parker, maybe?"

"And J. D. Preacher, maybe, Breed?"

"And James Charles Buck. Maybe, Marshal?"

"I was beginning to get edgy about you, Marshal. You're running mighty close."

"I was palaverin' with an old friend of yours, Preacher. Young fella named Breed." Jim Buck took his coat off and threw it over a nearby chair. "A couple o' whiskeys, Charlie," Jim said to the barkeep. "Teton Jack."

"Yes, sir, Marshal Buck."

Jim studied Preacher's reaction to the revelation about Breed. "You do know him, don't you?"

"We've cut trail a few times."

"You got yourself quite a wag tail there, Preacher. He could give quite a speech 'bout how nice a gent you are an' prob'ly convince most folks."

"But not you?"

"I don't count," Jim replied. He considered Preacher and then added, "And I don't think you'd give a damn anyway." He started to make a question out of postscript, to ask Preacher if he would care what a U.S. Marshal thought of him. He thought better of the idea.

"Do we have a meeting, Marshal?"

"Sunday afternoon in Parker's chambers. They're in the old headquarter barracks at Fort Smith. Two-thirty."

"Three of us."

"Three of us," Jim answered.

"Obliged for the drink, Marshal," Preacher said, "the next time, I'll buy. 'Til Sunday."

"None o' my affair," Jim said, "but that's five days away. I struck a bargain with you. I'll keep it. No need for you to ride out of Texarkana on my account."

"I wouldn't," Preacher said. "And you're right, Marshal, it's none of your affair."

Jim Buck treated himself to another Teton Jack. He watched Preacher's head and shoulders bobbing just above the frosted window glass as the bounty hunter rode away. He shoved his hat back on his head. Reverend Poole sauntered up. Just then too, Nate Breed walked in.

"The bounty man riding out is he, Marshal?"

"He is."

"I trust that you thanked him properly," Poole said.

"For what, Reverend? Standing against those men this morning? Hell, it was him that brought 'em to town."

"You haven't talked to the little drummer?"

"Hornback?" Jim smiled. "What for?" Nate Breed joined them. Poole nodded to him in greeting. The big marshal ignored the reporter.

"From what I gather, Hornback had some rather grandiose plans. Make himself a nice little poke and maybe a name at the same time." Poole looked around the marshal. "You were going to write the story for him, weren't you, Breed?"

The barkeep walked up. "A beer," Nate said. At the same time, he nodded an affirmation to Poole's question.

"Corabelle is upstairs with Hornback right now. I gather the gents we ridded ourselves of this morning were more by accident than design. Hornback didn't know about them. He hired somebody to stage a showdown."

Jim Buck straightened and frowned. He turned to Nate Breed. "That right, Breed?"

"Marshal, I have no idea. I assumed I simply arrived too late to see the action. My paper gave Hornback an advance based first on Preacher actually being in Texarkana. More would come if Hornback could produce a story. What he did with the money I have no knowledge."

"The bounty hunter wanted out of town by noon so that more trouble would be averted. Or so he told me, Marshal. He didn't know about those gents this morning either. Apparently he does know that someone is dogging him."

"But who?" Jim asked, softly. "And when?"

"Well," Poole said, off-handedly, "my guess would be sometime this afternoon as to the when."

"The two o'clock stage?"

"Perhaps. Mr. Preacher seemed unflagging in his determination to depart Texarkana by noon today. The who is another question."

"One I can answer. Oh Jesus! Hornback is scared to death." All three men looked toward the stairway. Corabelle was at its foot. She too was obviously frightened. Fear was something rarely displayed by Corabelle Dancer.

"Corabelle? He tell you somethin'? Who has he hired?"

"Holt Ferraday."

4

Preacher broke his camp along the Red River and cut to the east about five miles. Fort Smith was almost due north of Texarkana but he didn't intend to be bushwhacked. In fact, a piece in the Little Rock newspaper had caused Preacher considerable grief. In addition to the men he'd confronted in Texarkana, he knew, personally, of at least three more who wanted to collect that $3,000.

The death of his good friend, Jim Hickok, had capped a year of grief for Preacher and the lanky gunman had tried to vanish. He'd ridden out of Deadwood, D.T., and wintered in Denver. It was there he met Caleb Hornback. It was there he faced Pete Houchins in a gunfight and killed him. It was there he learned Hornback's true colors.

The brooding Tennessean recognized his position and knew he must free himself of the ever increasing price on his head. The killing of a Wells-Fargo station agent in Fort Pierre, D.T., had finally pushed Preacher on the wrong side of the ever narrowing trail he rode. The shadow line between the law and the gallows. Preacher had now amassed enough evidence to support his contention that he should not be a wanted man. Presenting that evidence however, could not be done just anywhere. The bounty hunger had made far more enemies than he had friends, and there were plenty of lawmen who choked on the words, bounty hunter.

Finally, of course, he had himself become the hunted. Men such as those he'd faced in Texarkana didn't present much of a problem. They were as plentiful as diamondbacks on the desert.

Such men were not professionals. They were merely gunmen seeking to collect bounty and build reputations which would assure them that their enemies would hightail it out of the country at the mere mention of their names.

Two other breeds were more troublesome. The first could be found among the elitist group to which Preacher himself belonged. Skilled shootists who feared no one, including others of their ilk. In the decade or so since the war, their numbers had slowly but steadily increased. As the flood of humankind continued to inundate the west, such men would appear in greater numbers. By the very nature of his skill and considerable reputation, J.D. Preacher was numbered among the best of this lot. That was a fact in spite of his personal motives.

Finally, of course, the most dangerous threat of all. Jim Hickok had died from that one. The rank amateur. The man, like Caleb Hornback, who got in over his head and tried to cash in on someone else's reputation. Failing in that, they one day would draw a gun, slip, unseen, into your life and, as Jack McCall had done to Hickok, murder you.

By the narrowest of margins, Preacher had accomplished in Texarkana what he had journeyed there to do. He had taken considerable risk to do it, however. He was very much aware that the most formidable foe ever to threaten him was closing the distance between them. His name was Holt Ferraday.

Preacher had been keeping to a narrow trail along a serrated ridge for more than three hours when he heard the screams.

"Easy, Prince," Preacher whispered to the big, black stallion. He dismounted, pulled the fifty-eight from its short boot and edged to where he could look.

The valley below was a drab beige color but showing signs of coming to life with the imminent advent of spring. A thin line of blue gray poked above a stand of cotton woods. Preacher reckoned them to be a mile to a mile and a half distant. Hidden among them was a cabin with a fire going. Also blocked from view were whatever events prompted a scream. A faint, shrill, feminine squeal of fear.

Preacher mounted up. Prince balked at the rocky slope below him but Preacher's urgings resulted in the big horse's effort. He pawed, picked and chose his footing carefully. Halfway down, the slope gentled and Preacher gave his mount some additional urging. Prince broke into an uneven trot, then a gallop. Horse and rider reached the bottom. The stallion took his head. Preacher, one handed, levered a shell into the chamber of the horse pistol.

They splashed through the bend in a shallow creek. Its flow was a series of switchbacks through the stand of trees. They splashed across it again. And once more. They broke into the open. Preacher counted four horses. No riders. No screams. He reined up, dismounted, dropped Prince's reins, tucked into a crouch and moved toward a small, log structure with a lean-to. It was out of the cabin that the smoke came.

Preacher might have reached the house unseen had it not been for the coonhound. A Blue Tick which had probably caught Prince's scent before Preacher had even dismounted. She let go a mournful bay and a pattern of yaps that passed for barking by a Blue Tick.

"Damn," Preacher mumbled to himself. He was right out in the open and the hound was yapping and running right straight to Preacher. The cabin door opened. One man, tall, shirtless, stepped out. He was holding a Winchester. He moved to his right. A second man, wearing only his long-johns, followed. He, too, carried a rifle. Both looked toward the dog's baying. Both saw Preacher.

"There he is," the tall one shouted. At the same time, he dropped to one knee, brought up the rifle and fired. He was close. Too damned close. Preacher felt a stick hit his boot top. Preacher fired the fifty-eight on the move, going down and rolling. The bullet hit the door hinge, tore it off, ripped a head-sized hole out of the wood to which the hinge had been attached, passed, harmlessly, through the cabin's interior and took out an apple-sized chunk of wood from the opposite wall.

The second man fired at Preacher from a standing position. He missed. All three men had levered their next shots into their respective weapons. Preacher saw a canvas window drape move.

"What the fuck is going on?" A third man. Preacher was prone. He aimed the fifty-eight's barrel at the center of the window opening. He fired.

He rolled. Dirt and grass struck his cheek from the tall man's second shot. He rolled again, working the lever action on the pistol-carbine. The man at the window disappeared. Blown backwards. Now, another scream.

The man who'd been standing fired again. Preacher grunted. The bullet struck the stock on the fifty-eight calibre. The impact jerked the weapon from his grasp and drove an inch long sliver of the stock deep into Preacher's palm.

A shotgun roared. The man standing by the door nearly doubled up backwards! His body then shot forward, faced down. Most of his back was torn away. The kneeling man's eyes got big. He turned toward the door. Preacher could not see into the dark hole that was the interior of the cabin. The man stood up and levered a shell into the rifle's chamber. Preacher stood up. The man fired into the cabin. Preacher winced as he pulled the sliver of wood from his palm, tearing the flesh. The man levered the Winchester again. Preacher drew his hip pistol, extended his arm, closed his left eye, aimed and fired. The man with the rifle pulled the trigger. The bullet slammed into the dirt just ahead of the man. The man fell dead.

The woman, more a girl than a woman Preacher reckoned, was probably 20. She had an Indian blanket wrapped around her otherwise naked body. Her lower lip was bleeding and swollen. Her hands and arms trembled. Preacher saw an old, single shell shotgun on the floor. An unfired shell was half jammed into the breech. Preacher stepped inside, his pistol still in his bleeding hand, the fifty-eight calibre in his left hand.

"Oh, please, mister. Please don't. Please . . ."

"It's over," he said, softly. "You're safe." She
was sitting on the edge of an old wooden bed. She let
her body tumble sideways and the tears came hard
and fast. Preacher let them run their course. The girl
slept.

"Good evening, ma'am." As soft as the voice was,
the girl still jumped, sucked in a mouthful of air and,
instinctively, pulled a cover up around her breasts.

"I . . . uh," she looked down at herself. She was
still wrapped in the Indian blanket. She looked up.
"You . . . you saved my life."

"You all right?" Preacher asked.

"I am now." She shivered. There was a dark spot,
three or four feet across the cabin floor. "You . . .
you cleaned up."

"They're in a shallow grave down by that
stream." Preacher noted that the girl was suddenly
quite uncomfortable about sitting there with
nothing on but a blanket. "I need to check the stock
before it comes full dark. There's coffee made." He
stood up. She saw a blood soaked rag around his
hand.

"You're hurt."

"Not bad."

"I'll dress." She emitted a kind of giggle, a
nervous little laugh of embarrassment. "I'm
hungry," she said. "Are you?"

Preacher smiled. "Matter of fact, ma'am, I am."

The stock Preacher checked amounted to Prince,
an old Hereford which needed milking, a mule with a
somewhat unpleasant disposition and the Blue Tick
hound. The hound had taken a shine to Preacher and
stayed on his heels as he checked the animals and
then made a wider swath to survey the surrounding

grounds. He wanted the best and fastest way out if the trio down by the stream ended up having saddle companions or kin.

"I was makin' flapjacks this mornin' when . . ." the girl looked at Preacher when he entered the cabin. She smiled. A pretty smile. She looked older suddenly. Her hair was pulled up on the back of her head and she looked clean, freshly scrubbed. Her lip was just a little puffy, but it didn't distract from the sparkling eyes or the pert, turned up nose.

"Flapjacks sound good," Preacher said.

"Eggs? They're fresh this mornin'."

"Three."

They ate most of the meal in silence. A few times, the breeze rustled some leaves. Once, the Blue Tick perked its ears. The girl's eyes grew big and she looked at Preacher. He smiled and she felt safe again.

"What's your name, mister?"

"I'm called Preacher."

"That what you do? Preacherin'?"

"No. It's my name. J. D. Preacher. I prefer just plain Preacher."

"Mine's Amelia. Amelia Lashtrow."

Preacher took a swallow of coffee to wash down the last bite of flapjack. "You live out here alone?"

"Me'n an' my brother, Jess." Preacher frowned. Amelia glanced down. "He went out huntin' two days back. He should have . . . I mean he was due . . ." Her voice trailed off and Preacher recognized the reaction. Fear. She looked up again. "I heard some shots a way off day before yesterday."

"You know, Amelia, that your brother may not be coming back?"

She looked up. The big, brown eyes were moist.

Sad looking. She nodded.

Preacher hauled enough water to the cabin so that Amelia could do the dishes and fill an iron kettle. He built a good big fire and put the kettle to heating for bath water. While Amelia washed dishes, Preacher found a file and set to work smoothing down the stock on the horse pistol.

While Amelia bathed, behind a hastily rigged, horse blanket partition, Preacher cleaned his weapons and his hand wound. It had been more painful than serious, but it was his right hand. He dared not risk infection and loss of use even temporarily.

The blanket slipped from the rope and Preacher looked. Amelia was naked. Even across the small room, Preacher could catch the mingling of scents he'd not experienced for too long. Talcum's sweet odor and that of a woman.

"They were going to hurt me. Those men. But they didn't. You came. I'm afraid there might not be another. If there isn't you first."

The only light was that which found its way between the hinge seams on the fire door of the potbelly. It cast thin, dancing shadows on the floor and the blanket where Preacher and Amelia lay together.

She closed her eyes and Preacher positioned her at his will. He began softly, gently, slowly. He let his finger tips trail along her shoulders and down her arms. He nibbled at her ear lobes and felt faint stirrings as she tensed her stomach muscles. Preacher's own desires, too long dormant, had to be controlled by considerable willpower on his part.

Preacher's long fingered and powerful hands moved to the girl's breasts. He kneaded the pliable flesh, arousing the nerves beneath its surface and bringing soft sighs from deep within the girl's body. He raised himself to his knees, straddling her and repositioning himself for better balance. Her eyes opened.

"Love me," she said. "No man has before you."

Preacher leaned down and let his tongue explore. Amelia's nipples hardened at once. He spent time with each, alternating until both were as taut and sensitive as he could make them. He slipped lower, replacing his tongue with finger tips. He kissed her naval. He went lower.

The line of hair was lower than on most women. Softer too. It was the down of youth, not the wiry bristles of maturity. He went still lower.

"What . . . what are you doing?" Preacher found the split with his tongue, applied more pressure, secreted more moisture and licked its full length. Buttocks tightened, hips arched, legs stiffened. He repeated the procedure from bottom to top. All the while, Preacher's fingers stroked, caressed and gently tweaked the pink summits of the twin mounds that were Amelia Honeycutt's tender breasts.

Almost instinctively, Amelia moved her legs apart and gave Preacher easier access. He continued to tantalize with his tongue, both for his own enjoyment of a woman's special scent and taste and in preparation for the ultimate joining of his body with hers. After nearly a quarter of an hour, Amelia was soaked with the juices of virgin passion. Her breathing was rapid and her head rolled back and forth on the blanket. Preacher, used to a woman alternating aggressive and submissive positions, had been too long celibate. He was additionally aroused by the youthful innocence of Amelia Honeycutt.

Preacher entered her with considerable caution. He was much better endowed than the average man, and as equally concerned for his sexual partner. Still, Amelia whimpered with his first attempts. She let out a little cry when, finally, the tissue burst and the very depths of her womanhood were invaded for the first time. She felt as though she was stretched to the limit as Preacher thrust deeper and deeper. Then, with equal suddenness, a new sensation swept over her. It increased with what was now the steady rhythm of Preacher's body.

"Oh . . . oooh Gawd . . . what is it? Yes . . . oh yes!" Amelia screamed. The entire experience flooded through her all at once, like the bursting of an earthen dam. Preacher's masterful control of himself now added to the pleasure of both. Passion too long pent up flowed into and mingled with passion never before released. The volatile combination drained the partners. They lay side by side in silence. Then, they slept.

Dawn brought reality back with a jolt. As Amelia continued to sleep, Preacher explored. No more than half a mile north of the cabin, he found the body of a young man. He didn't need to ask who the man was, and he didn't feel the urge to confirm to her what he believed Amelia already knew. He buried her brother and said nothing. Perhaps more than most, Preacher knew just how much pain could accompany the truth.

Preacher found no more tracks than there should have been. Still, he didn't want to linger. Living in that part of the country was a daily gamble. Wayfarers of all breeds rode west, often straying from the main roads and trails. Besides, Preacher knew who was behind him—somewhere.

It was after ten o'clock before Preacher, his new found charge and a well loaded pack mule, departed the cabin. On a nearby hillock, Amelia stopped and turned back. She looked, wistfully, on the little cabin, the clearing, the clean, crisp stream that ran nearby.

"I was born there," she said, turning back and looking at the lanky gunman. "It's hard to leave it. Have you ever had to leave something you cared about?"

Preacher felt the tug in his gut. "Once or twice," he said, looking at the ground, "a hundred years ago or so," he added, almost in a whisper.

"What?"

"Nothing. We'd best ride, Amelia."

"Preacher."

"Yeah."

"About last night . . . I . . . I don't want you to think that I would . . ."

"I think it was very nice," he said. "That's all I think." She nodded.

5

Ramon Tomas Esquival did not know his parents. He knew nothing of his place of birth. When he tried hard, he could remember a few faces from years ago. Women's faces. Different faces. He didn't try very often anymore.

What he did know was that he was approaching the summer of what was probably his twentieth year. He knew it could be the nineteenth or the twenty-first as well. He mostly knew how he felt. He'd had one woman. An old woman. Forty, he reckoned. Fat. That was five years ago.

He knew a few other things too. He knew that he had always struggled. Fought any way he could. He knew that kind of life had started when he was in the summer of his eighth year. Maybe it was the ninth. Maybe it was the seventh.

Ramon Esquival knew something else. He knew guns. He was very good with guns. Someone, he didn't remember who, had said that he was a natural. He stole a gun and a holster and a belt that was too big around for him. That was the summer of his twelfth year—maybe. It was the same year he'd killed the gringo in that dirty little cantina in

Sabinas down in Coahuila. He killed that man with a knife. It was a Bowie knife. He'd stolen it also.

He ran. He hid. He drifted north. Always north. He rode drag for three summers for trail herds headed to Kansas. Three bosses. Three more dead men. He broke horses, he worked in a dozen livery barns and an equal number of cantinas. Between jobs and with all his off time, Ramon practiced. The gun was no longer too heavy, the belt no longer too big around. He drifted north.

Ramon drifted into Texarkana in the high summer of 1873. He found employment at the livery. He found something else too. He found a friend. Harvey Willibrand had treated Ramon almost like his own son. Harvey, Ramon learned, once had a son for one week. The pox took both wife and son.

Harvey Willibrand's brother was a lawyer. Harry Willibrand took a liking to Ramon when he visited. The visits came more often and by the end of Ramon's third year in Texarkana, he had two new acquisitions. Both had come from Harry Willibrand. A stack of law books and a name by which the entire community would soon know him. The name was Conchudo, the wily or crafty one.

In the absense of U.S. Marshal Jim Buck in the fall of 1876, Conchudo had agreed to make nightly rounds in town. It meant checking door locks and keeping too many rawdies from congregating in one spot. The marshal felt confident. He'd be gone for only two days and only one night. Conchudo felt confident until just after dawn on the second day.

No one knew the names of the three men who rode, hell bent, into Texarkana that morning. They only knew that two of them shot up the mercantile store, broke in, stole guns and ammunition and then took three citizens hostage. Among them was a nine-year-old girl, Estelita Occaros. While two of the men watched the hostages, the third rousted out the bank president, forced him to turn over most of the bank's cash and then shot him.

Conchudo thought the men had freed all three hostages when they finally completed their orgy of horror. He was wrong. Conchudo was fast—very fast. He was not fast enough to prevent a single bullet from entering the back of Estelita Occaros.

The trio of nameless men were buried in unmarked graves in the Texarkana pauper's cemetery. Estelita Occaros could no longer walk to school. Or run. Or ride a horse. Or play. A doctor said she might, if a skilled surgeon could operate. It would take much money. Much more than the reward Conchudo received from a very grateful but very conservative bank.

Marshal Jim Buck did his best to raise the money to help Conchudo and Estelita. Together, Jim Buck and Conchudo didn't represent the kind of collateral a bank required for a loan. Neither did Harvey Willibrand's already mortgaged livery business. Harry Willibrand might have helped if he hadn't died suddenly.

Conchudo was bitter but determined. He would not wear a badge. He would do his law work not with a gun but with a gavel. He knew it was no principle but greed which served as his incentive. All of Jim Buck's advice and personal efforts failed until two days ago. It was then that Conchudo began to realize that between the gun and the gavel there was a much more lucrative profession, bounty hunting.

Conchudo didn't understand all he knew about

Jim Buck and Corabelle Dancer and a gunman named Holt Ferraday. He wanted to know and understand all of it. It was this motivation and Corabelle's fear which forged a bargain between them.

The bargain had its origins with the revelation by Caleb Hornback that he had, he believed, hired a man named Holt Ferraday to participate in a scheme, Hornback was playing both ends, and as many tops and bottoms as he could manage, against the middle. The middle, supposedly, was a bounty hunter named Preacher.

Hornback arranged appropriate, professional witnesses for the event he'd called the showdown of the century. He'd called it that in a letter to his most professional and reliable witness, Nathan Hale Breed. Breed, after all, had originally been assigned the job of tracking down and reporting the real story of the notorious shootist, J.D. Preacher from Tennessee. Hornback could see money there. Preacher had a bounty on his head. He could see money there. Jim Buck had a solid reputation as a lawman and Hornback had heard that if anyone could take Preacher, it would either be Jim Buck or Holt Ferraday.

The best laid plans of Caleb Hornback had gone awry almost from the beginning. Now, given Preacher's departure and what would surely be viewed as a trap, Holt Ferraday would find him and kill him. If the story he'd heard in Texarkana was also true, U.S. Marshal James Charles Buck would be of no use in preventing the incident.

Conchudo rapped lightly on Corabelle Dancer's door. As he'd been asked to do, he'd been careful not to be seen slipping upstairs. The door opened.

Conchudo sucked in his breath. Corabelle was clad in a dressing gown, its front only loosely held together.

"Come in quickly." Conchudo did. "No one saw you?" As she asked the question, she looked up and down the hallway and toward the stairs. There was no one about.

"No one saw me," Conchudo said, irritably. "No one knows I'm here." He was, at once, more irritated. Corabelle virtually ignored him. She walked the length of the room, her fingers and thumb acting as a vise against her temples. She stopped. She turned.

"He wasn't on the Dallas stage. He wasn't on the Shreveport stage. . . ."

"And he did not come in on the run from Fort Smith, as Mr. Hornback believed he would."

"Ferraday is coming in alone on horseback when he damned well pleases, and probably after he's certain that Hornback was no Pinkerton man."

"I've heard of Holt Ferraday," the young breed said, "but why is he so special, so frightening to you?"

"Conchudo, I want you to take this message to the marshal." She handed him a sealed envelope. There was writing on it that was obviously not hers. It didn't match the note he'd received from Corabelle. "Take it now."

"We have a bargain, senorita."

"Later, Conchudo. I'll tell you everything later."

Conchudo usually didn't balk. Usually, those with whom he dealt knew he didn't balk. Now, he balked. "What does it say?" he asked, holding out the envelope.

"Please Conchudo. Not now."

"Now, senorita Corabelle, or our bargain is forfeit."

"Damn you!"

"No, senorita Dancer, damn you! I'm no muchacho anymore. No livery boy to be ordered about. No half breed Mexican and Apache to be patronized." He moved toward her. She looked quizzical, even a little frightened. "You know why, senorita?" He smiled and his hand moved in a blur of speed to his right hip. "This! The pistola, senorita. This is why."

Corabelle smiled weakly and nodded. She backed up and sat down on the edge of the bed. Conchudo holstered the gun, pulled a wooden chair from the corner, reversed it and sat down.

"I'm listening," he said.

"Jim" she swallowed and looked down. "Marshal Buck, he's got a bullet in him inside close to his spine." She looked up. "The doctors can't take it out without great risk, yet each day is a risk. I don't understand all of it, only that if it is dislodged from the muscle it could kill him."

"So?"

"Holt Ferraday put it there seven years ago."

"He shot Jim Buck in the back?"

"No Conchudo, in a gunfight. Face to face. When Jim tried to arrest him. Ferraday had just killed a sheriff. Jim was his deputy."

"And this gunman let Jim Buck live?"

"He believed Jim was dead. Any other man would have been. Jim's size—his strength—it's what saved him. Then, two years later, Jim became a deputy marshal. He was riding the Indian territory working for Ev Nix. He was chasing two half breed . . ." she looked down.

"The term doesn't bother me," Conchudo said, "only those who use it and know it's spoken with hatred behind it."

Corabelle's head jerked up. Her eyes, for the first time, displayed their usual fire. "I don't hate you. I don't hate any man because of what he is. Only for what he does or doesn't do."

"Then don't be ashamed of what you call him. Please, go on."

"He rode into El Paso. He heard that Holt Ferraday was there. He spent three days drinking, searching his soul, trying to discover his fears or lack of them. He spent two of those days with me. Finally, I talked him into setting a trap for Ferraday."

"He agreed?"

"Yes."

"You were the bait?" Corabelle's mouth opened. No words came. She nodded.

"What happened?"

"Ferraday was taken. He was sentenced to five years in Yuma on the most recent charge the law could prove. I thought he'd hang. So did the marshal."

"When did Ferraday get out?"

"Eighteen months ago. He openly announced when he intended to do. He sent telegraphs all over the West using a false name, hoping for a response from Jim Buck. It was one of those telegraph cables, and a few other things that led Hornback to make his deal."

"And this envelope?"

"It's a phony message from a rancher east of here. It says that Holt Ferraday is holed up on this man's ranch waiting for his horse's leg to heal."

"It gets Jim Buck out of Texarkana to safety."
She nodded. "And you want me to face Ferraday?"

"Oh God . . . no . . . no Conchudo . . . oh God,"
Corabelle shook her head, got up, moved to the
chiffonneir and poured herself a healthy slug of
whiskey. She downed it and turned around. "You
must think me nothing more than an animal."

"Love can do very strange things to people. To
women. To men." He eyed her voluptuous body. His
look was not love, but lust. He knew that there had
been a time in his life that he would have simply
taken from her what he wanted. Corabelle saw the
familiar expression.

"I just want you to meet Ferraday as marshal.
Tell him Jim was killed by that man."

"The Widow Maker? Preacher?"

"Yes . . . yes. Tell him Preacher killed Jim and
rode out. Holt Ferraday won't bother with
Hornback. There's no paper on him. You've no
reason. I mean a marshal has no reason to hold him.
Get him out of town."

"Lie to Jim Buck, to my friend?"

"If he is your really your friend, you'll do it,
Conchudo. Because if you don't, Ferraday will kill
him and anybody who stands with him."

"You think I'm not good enough to stand against
Ferraday?"

"Yes, Conchudo, that is exactly what I think. I've
seen you both. You haven't."

"And Hornback? He could be trouble."

"Uh uhhn. Hornback knows that if he so much as
utters a word or shows his face I'll kill him
personally."

"And if I do this thing for you," Conchudo said,
standing and replacing the chair in the corner, "you

will do for me what I asked?"

"I will. You'll have your grubstake and the names of the men I know who will help you get started as a bounty hunter."

"Perhaps . . ." Conchudo began, once again letting his eyes roam over the soft undulations which were quite visible beneath the satin dressing gown. ". . . there should be . . . more." He smiled.

"Me? You want me, Conchudo?" Corabelle laughed, a forced laugh which belied the frown of her brow. In a deft movement, she freed the single button which held the gown closed. She shrugged out of it and stood before Conchudo naked. Naked, soft, scented, inviting. She clasped her hands together, interlocking her fingers and placed them atop her head. Her breasts grew taut under the strain of stretching. The nipples jutted out and somewhat upward. They hardened. So did Conchudo's penis.

"Not . . . not now. Not this way."

"When then?" she said, moving just enough to cause a swaying of her breasts, "and where, Conchudo? Where?"

"Bitch!"

"Whore, Conchudo, or have you forgotten?" She laughed again. The same stacatto as before. "I'm a whore, not someone's little wife or fiance."

"You love Jim Buck so much, you would do this?" He'd seen more than her nakedness. He'd seen inside. Corabelle grabbed up a blanket and covered herself. She was, for the first time in more years than she could remember, embarrassed. Perhaps, she thought, Ramon Tomas Esquival was more a man than she'd believed.

Big Jim Buck read the message. It was signed by

Jim Page. The marshal knew Page. The man maintained a good livery at his ranch to tend his own stock. Jim had not seen Page for sometime, but that didn't surprise him. Page was an infrequent visitor to town. Twice a year usually for supplies. The marshal was very wary.

"You say a boy gave you this?"

Conchudo nodded. "He was 12 or 13 years old maybe." The marshal knew that Jim Page had a son about that age. He eyed Conchudo again. The half breed forced a smile. "How many men will you badge, Jim Buck? I wish to be the first." Somehow, Conchudo felt the offer would lend credibility to the sham.

"None," came the reply. "Holt Ferraday would smell a posse a dozen miles before it got there. It's a one man job. I'll go in from the north, along the hogback. I should be able to get a look before I ride in."

"I still wish to go."

"No!" Jim winced at the sound of the word and his own voice. He could almost feel the bullet entering his belly and stopping near his spine. "I need you here, Conchudo. Make the rounds. Keep the peace. If I work this thing right, I'll be back this afternoon."

"And if you are not?"

"Send a telegraph and then ride like hell for Fort Smith. Get help."

"They would give it? This Ferraday has no 'wanted' on him."

"He'll be wanted if you have to send the telegraph." Conchudo swallowed. "For . . ."

"For murder. Mine. He's out to kill me, Conchudo, and mebbe Corabelle Dancer, too, if he knows she's here. Sometime," Jim Buck said, getting up, "I'll tell you all about it." The marshal opened a desk drawer and withdrew a small, leather covered box. He opened it. He handed it to Conchudo. The boy looked down. In the box reposed a shiny, silvered deputy marshal's badge. "It was mine. The first. I want you to wear it, Conchudo, to keep it untarnished."

"Jim Buck, I can't . . ." he stopped and shook his head. He wanted to tell the truth. He also wanted to keep his pledge to Corabelle Dancer because he believed her story. He knew Holt Ferraday would kill Jim Buck. At that moment Conchudo hated himself. He hated someone else even more. The bounty man, Preacher. Had he remained he could have commanded enough of Ferraday's attention to allow someone else a chance to kill the notorious gunman. Perhaps, Conchudo thought, they would have killed each other.

As they parted company, both knowing that it could be for the last time, Jim Buck and the half breed deputy, Conchudo, were thinking their seprate thoughts, keeping their own secrets, feeling their own fears. Unknowingly, they shared another bond. They were both ignorant of a series of events which had occured only a few weeks earlier in the Texas trail town of Nacodoches.

Two members of a California gang, both with healthy rewards on their heads, became involved in a shootout with a small posse. They were faced with capture—or death—when Holt Ferraday intervened. The additional firepower he provided drove off the surviving members of the posse. It also afforded the two men an opportunity to escape. They took it and fled to Nacodoches.

Recognized by the town sheriff, they were quickly threatened again. They proved too good for their would-be captors, killing two deputies and disarming the sheriff. J.D. Preacher confronted them. Both were buried the following day and Preacher rode away with a bounty which Holt Ferraday considered his property. One man in Nacodoches seemed very anxious to assist Ferraday in his effort. He had been a witness to the incident because he'd been dogging Preacher's trail since the gunman rode away from Deadwood in August of seventy-six. The man was Caleb Hornback and a deal was struck.

All of Hornback's fears, Corabelle Dancer's efforts and the half breed deputy Conchudo's lies were ludicrous. Holt Ferraday wanted J.D. Preacher. He knew nothing of Texarkana's Federal Marshal or who now owned the town's most infamous saloon and bawdy house.

Holt Ferraday was a Lousianan by birth, a Texan by adoption and a gunman by desire. He killed his first man in a head-on gun fight when he was only 17. He worked for another decade for a gunsmith, learning the trade, becoming an apprentice and a skilled practitioner. He avoided military service because of his occupation—one he stayed with until war's end. In his free time, Holt Ferraday honed his skills and developed a deadly mechanism to assist them in their execution.

The mechanism was a lightweight belt to which was affixed a metal attachment. It allowed a pistol to be locked onto a swivel by a special hookup and then slipped into a slot. The pistol did not have to be drawn from a holster, merely swiveled into position to be fired. Ferraday mastered the mechanics and, in witnessed fights, only one man who had ever faced

Holt Ferraday managed to clear leather. That man was big Jim Buck.

Ferraday was a man of slight stature, barely five feet, ten inches tal and weighting about 160 pounds. He sported a handlebar moustache and a closely cropped goatee. He had close set, dark brown eyes, an extremely slender, pointed noise and thin, perpetually snarling lips.

He dressed conservatively save for two articles of wear. His boots were custom made with exceptionally high heels. They added to his height and coupled with the high crowned, perfectly round hat, he managed to appear taller than he actually was. It was a physical characteristic about which he was most self conscious, and on which he would tolerate no comments.

Over the years, Holt Ferraday had earned his keep by gambling, conducting singular man hunts for considerable recompense and bounty hunting. That he was independently wealthy attested to his skills and success.

Ferraday, by virtue of the country in which he worked and his forced absence for more than three years, was unknown north of Texas. Where he was known, Holt Ferraday was ranked as second to no man when it came to gunplay and killing.

At the moment Marshal Jim Buck rode east, out of Texarkana, headed for the ranch of the Page family, Holt Ferraday was making camp for the night. He'd found a pleasant, sheltered spot along the Red River, five miles south and west of Jim Buck's town.

6

The scent of burning pine is exhilarating. It teases the sense of smell, offering a promise of both warmth and food. Preacher felt a fire was safe and built a good one even before nature had shed the shawl of night. After checking stock and rounding up more wood, Preacher returned to camp to find Amelia preparing breakfast.

"That smells mighty like hogback," he said. He sniffed. The bacon's odor was now mingling with that of boiled coffee. He smiled. "Seems you loaded that mule down with a few things I didn't know about."

"You just struck me as the cut of a man who eats a hearty breakfast." Now, Amelia smiled. "I didn't try to tote no eggs an' I didn't think you'd want me to take the time for sourdoughs." Preacher got himself some coffee and sat, Indian fashion, near the fire.

"Beans and bacon are more than I usually get on the trail." He sipped at his coffee and grinned. "I never have sourdoughs. Never got the hang of making them." Amelia dished up the food, poured herself some coffee and sat near Preacher. He was eyeing the hills to the north.

"They're easy enough," she said.

Preacher looked quizzical. "What?"

"Sourdough biscuits. Mebbe you don't tote the right makin's. Most men forget the 'tater."

"A potato?" Preacher grinned. "I carry a couple usually, but not for biscuit makin'." Amelia laughed. "That funny is it?"

"Your no chuck wrangler, that's sure. You use the 'tater fer makin' the sourdough starter."

"Starter?" Preacher looked down and snickered. "You mean, they need priming, like an old pump."

Amelia laughed. He liked to hear a woman's laugh. It was one of the things that pleasured a man in this hard country. Like the wind in the Aspens, the first bawling calf of the new spring herd, or the smell of burning pine.

"The starter makes the dough rise. Without it . . ."

"Without it," Preacher interrupted, holding up the horse pistol, "I've got more minie balls for this." She laughed again. They ate and drank coffee and talked of pleasant things. Then they broke camp. Amelia watched Preacher kill the last of the fire. The act seemed so final. The warmth was gone. The smell was gone. The chill was back in the air. Amelia shivered.

Some thirty miles to the south, Holt Ferraday, feeling nothing but a desire to get on with the day, doused the coals of his fire with the last of thick, black coffee. Minutes later, he was headed toward Texarkana at full gallop.

The sly one, Conchudo, stood before the piece of broken mirror in Jim Buck's office. He let his finger tips and thumb stroke his face. Their nerve endings searching out the first bristles of beard. He felt nothing and cursed under his breath. He splashed some water on the smooth skin, rinsed his mouth with a cheek full of mash, spit and got dressed.

Conchudo loaded the scattergun, the sixth chamber of his own revolver, slipped on his tattered, wool coat, exited the office and headed for the Gilded Lily and some morning eye opener. He was hoping Corabelle would be up and around. He wanted to apologize. It was something he had done very few times in his life, and then only at the threat of someone capable of whipping him if he didn't. Conchudo thought that his feeling of wanting to signalled a new achievement in his search for those things that make a man.

Corabelle wasn't around. He ordered whiskey but he got coffee instead. Reverend Poole was behind the bar.

"A man should start each day the way the Lord starts His. Clean. Take your constitutional of a morning too, son."

"My what?"

"Your bowel movement, boy. Clean out your gizzard. Settle your constitution and your nerves with some coffee. Hold off partaking of the Devil's brew 'til that time of the day when you're most likely to run into one of his disciples."

Conchudo drank coffee. He wrinkled up his nose. It was strong. Bitter.

"It's Loozy-ana coffee boy, half chickory and half swamp water. You'll have the gallops about ten thirty. After you're cleaned out, you'll have an appetite big as a 'gator's."

"If it don't kill me first."

"I've been drinking it for nearly thirty years

now," Poole said, smiling wryly, "an' I've only heard o' five men it ever killed."

"Jeezus!" Poole laughed.

Twenty miles east of Texarkana, big Jim Buck stood up in his stirrups and surveyed the pleasant looking little valley below him. A white frame house was located about at its center. It was surrounded by several outbuildings, a sizeable cattle pen, horse corral and big, well built barn. Blue smoke curled up from the big brick chimney, unmolested by the wind until it reached the height almost on a level with the hillock. It was a serene setting with nothing to indicate the presence of so violent a man as Holt Ferraday.

Jim dismounted and slipped the Winchester from the boot. He levered a shell into it, propped it against a nearby tree and tethered his mount. He turned back and two heads bobbed into view.

"Well, I'll be damned," Jim Page said. "G'mornin', Marshal. What on God's earth brings you out our way?"

"Your message," Jim Buck replied. Page frowned and looked at his companion, a boy of about 15.

"What message?"

"My deputy, you know him, the half breed, Conchudo. He said your boy here rode in with a message yesterday. Said the boy gave it to him to give to me." Jim Buck was already fishing for it. He found it and handed it to Jim Page. Page looked at it and then looked up.

"Not my message, Marshal. The boy here never left the place." He handed it back.

"That's your name there on the bottom, isn't it?"

"Sure 'pears to be alright, but it's not."

"You're sayin' this isn't your handwriting?"

"Marshal, they ain't but one in my clan what can write, an' I'm not them. Wife can—a little."

"God, oh God!" Jim Buck grabbed his rifle, freed his mount and leaped on her back in a single bound.

"Marshal?"

"Jim. You seen any strangers about? Got anybody stayin' with you? Seen anybody ridin' by?"

"Answer to all o' them questions is the same, Marshal. No!" Jim Buck wheeled his horse, dug spurs deep into her flanks and rode down the far side of the ridge. In less than two minutes, he was out of sight.

The morning barkeep came on duty. Conchudo dallied over a second cup of Poole's coffee all the while watching the stairs. By the time he'd finished with Corabelle Dancer still nowhere in sight, he shrugged.

"You makin' the marshal's rounds, are ya?" the barkeep asked. Conchudo nodded. "Got a letter here I was meanin' to drop at the stage stop yestiddy. You mind, Deputy?" Conchudo looked up. The barkeep of the morning was Bob Tope. He'd never much cared for Conchudo. He'd never called him anything nasty, but he'd never called him by name either. That he acknowledged Jim Buck's decision and Conchudo's tin star was quite a step for him.

"Be happy to, Mister Tope."

"Name's Bob, Deputy."

"Mine's Conchudo, Bob." The barkeep smiled pleasantly and nodded.

"You mind company?" This from Reverend Poole.

"C'mon then."

"Give me a minute to get my coat."

"We're runnin' short of a few things, Mister Poole," Bob Tope said. "You want me to roust out Miss Corabelle?"

Poole started putting on his coat, looking down, thinking. He looked up. "Make a list. We'll go over it when I get back." Tope nodded. The door opened. All three men looked toward it. Two of them, Poole and Conchudo, looked first at the man's face, and then down at his hip.

"Jeezus," Conchudo whispered to himself. Poole set his teeth together, steeling himself to the possibility of dying at any moment. Bob Tope's complete ignorance of anything suddenly served a purpose.

"G'mornin', mister. Welcome to the Gilded Lily. Got whiskey, coffee, breakfast, 'bout as quick as we can git the cook sobered up an' damn near anythin' else a man would ever want, sometime right after noon."

Holt Ferraday payed no mind to any of the men. He did not even acknowledge the shiny, tin star on Conchudo's coat lapel. His eyes scanned every corner and every half lighted recess in the room. Satisfied that he would not be back shot, he walked toward the bar. He changed direction about halfway to it and moved to its end, nearest him.

"What'll it be, mister," Bob Tope asked. His voice was more tentative now. He sensed something was wrong.

"You got law here?" The question was a barb. A delicate goad. Only a blind man could miss seeing Conchudo's badge.

Bob Tope was suddenly scared. Scared shitless. He felt the urge to answer but he was certain that anything he said would be wrong. He swallowed.

Reverend Poole moved to the bar, cautiously. He smiled.

"I'm the Reverend Poole, sir. The marshal is running an errand this morning. He should be back by noon or so. Is your business of an urgent nature?"

"I'm the law," Conchudo said, sharply. He took two short steps away from the bar, pushing his coat back, away from his gun. Ferraday didn't even glance at the boy. His eyes were on Poole.

"I'm looking for a man called the Widow Maker. A bounty hunter. His name is J.D. Preacher. He's tall. Rangy. Wears a moustache like mine. Dresses in black. Carries two pistols, one inside his coat, one on his hip. Sometimes he carries a short barreled piece, carbine. You ever see such a man?"

"I saw him yesterday. Like I said I'm the law so you do your talkin' to me."

"Easy, Deputy," Poole said, smiling.

"More than easy, Reverend," Ferraday warned, still ignoring Conchudo. "You tell the half breed to keep his mouth shut. I don't truck with his kind, and he's smelling up the place."

A door banged upstairs. Footsteps shuffled along the hallway. Ferraday shifted his position so quickly, no one had time to blink. Now he could cover all three men and the stairway. Poole knew it was Corabelle.

"The gent you're looking to find was here. He rode out. Headed North. Fort Smith, I believe." As Poole spoke, he eased his hand toward his pistol. Upstairs, a second door slammed. The footsteps could no longer be heard. Poole raised his hand to the top of the bar.

"Who is your law, Reverend?" Ferraday asked.

At the same time, he stepped away from the end of the bar, out toward the center of the room. Poole tensed.

"I told you," Conchudo said. "I'm the law. You got questions, you talk to me. You ask me and you say please and thank you." Conchudo raised the scattergun as he spoke. It was leveled at Holt Ferraday's middle. He wouldn't die fast enough to stop him from pulling the triggers. He was too close to miss.

An upstairs door opened and closed. Footsteps shuffled along the hallway. Poole looked up, Bob Tope looked up. Conchudo did not.

"You down there, Reverend," Corabelle shouted. Poole sucked in his breath, his eyes shifted to Ferraday's. Conchudo looked up. Ferraday's brow had just the slightest wrinkle in it. The kind a man displays when he has a faint recollection of something familiar.

"Conchudo," Tope shouted. Tope died. The shotgun's blast reverberated through the huge, nearly empty saloon. Its deadly shot ripped into the edge of the bar, tearing out a huge chunk of wood with such force that slivers from it were driven into the stairway bannister. None of the shot struck Holt Ferraday. He'd dropped to one knee, twisting slightly as he did so. It allowed his shot at Tope. The second killed Conchudo, passing through his head at an upward, 30 degree trajectory. It entered through his upper lip, driving all his front teeth into his gums and ripping away most of the roof of his mouth. The second blast from the shotgun smashed into the second floor baluster. Corabelle screamed. Poole raised both arms high above his head, stepped away from the bar and dropped to his knees.

"He knows you're dogging him," Poole said. "The man. Preacher. He told me you were after him but he is riding north. I swear to you."

The front door opened. Ferraday whirled, fired and the shot ripped off the inside doorknob. A man cried out, jerking backwards. The door slammed shut from the force of the shot. In that instant, Poole drew. He had not planned to try. He saw a woman's ankles as the woman started down the stairway. Other doors had opened. There were screams and some shooting. Poole could think only of Corabelle Dancer.

Poole's little forty-four Remington was a single action. It took even the most skilled gunman an extra split second to cock it. Poole also used that time to anticipate his opponent's next move. He assumed Ferraday would turn back to his left after firing at the door. Poole was wrong. Ferraday completed the turn and fired two warning shots at the second floor balcony. Poole fired. He no longer had a target.

"Ah-men," the obese, good-natured Reverend managed just before Ferraday's shot struck him in the belly. He groaned, his face contorted in pain, his pistol dangling from his trigger finger. He fell face down. He didn't see Ferraday's next move. He let go the pistol on the swivel rig and his right hand shot across in front of him, reappearing a fraction of a second later with a fully loaded, short barreled Smith and Wesson. He back to the door, pulled it open, stepped through it and glanced both ways. He'd scared off the earlier intruder. His eyes scanned the buildings across the street. Gun in hand, Holt Ferraday made the distance to his horse, lightly mounted, once more looked in both directions, backing the horse as he did so. A minute later, the street was deserted. Holt Ferraday was approaching the Texarkana city boundary at the north end of town.

The crowd gathered in front of the Gilded Lily was all the evidence Jim Buck needed to know that he was too late. He dismounted on the run, letting his horse continue another third of a block. He pushed his way through the crowd, giving them no chance to open a path. He heard shouts. Men calling his name. He heard Poole's name. He wasn't listening to anything.

Josephus Obidiah Ezekial Lounsdon Poole was laid out, in an unintentional but nonetheless macabre twist of irony, on the billiards table. Jim Buck's first sight inside the Gilded Lily brought a gasp of relief. Corabelle Dancer stood at the end of the table weeping softly. As he approached, he saw the two linen dusters, boots protruding from beneath both. One pair he recognized. They were Ramon Tomas Esquival's.

"Conchudo," Jim whispered, "damn you. Damn you all to hell." Jim approached the table. He looked down on Poole. Suddenly, the gunman-gambler turned man of God didn't look so big. He looked small. Frail and pitiful. "Doc?"

"I don't know. I've done my best." The doctor looked into Jim's face. "He's gut shot, Marshal, but that layer of tissue, that girth we've laughed about so many times, may be his salvation. I just don't know."

"Save him, Doc. Please." Jim looked toward the dusters. "Who . . ."

"Young Conchudo and Bob Tope." The doctor

turned and looked up. "You'd best keep an eye on Miss Dancer. I'm most concerned about what she might be thinking."

Jim frowned. "I don't follow."

"We've another victim upstairs. A drummer."

"Jeezus! Hornback?" The doc nodded. "Dead?"

"No. He lost his nerve. Jerked the gun from the look of it at the last possible second. Bullet grazed his jaw. Cracked it I think. He's out now and I put a man to watching him. Fortunately, he tried to do himself in with a Deringer. Anything bigger would have taken his whole jaw off. I gave him enough laudanum to put a horse to sleep."

"But Corabelle?"

"She blames herself. Mumbled something about a note and getting you out of town. Don't make much sense to me. Do you . . ." Jim Buck was no longer standing there or listening.

"Corabelle." She didn't move. Jim reached up and turned her head. Their faces were inches apart but Corabelle's eyes were fixed, staring through Jim Buck. He'd seen the look before. He stood up. One of the girls, Martha Ann Barkley, walked up.

"It was a man named Ferraday. I got that much out of her, Marshal. That and the fact he was lookin' for that gambler, the handsome one."

"Preacher?" She nodded. "You take care of Corabelle," he said, his tone stern. "I'm holding you responsible for her—personal. You take care of her. You understand me?" The girl nodded.

Jim Buck gathered up the shotgun, a second rifle, plenty of ammunition, trail supplies, switched mounts to his oldest and best trail horse and made a final stop on his way out of town. It was at the Western Union telegraph office.

"Marshal, I heard about what happened. I'm sure sorry." Big Jim didn't respond. He handed the agent a cable. "Send this right now." The agent read it and nodded.

"You want me to bring you the reply?"

"I'll get the reply," Jim said, "personally."

The agent watched Marshal Buck spur his horse and set a trail due north for Fort Smith. A few moments later, he was keying Jim's message. He'd sent the first half. It requested that Judge Parker issue an arrest warrant for J.D. Preacher. Preacher was to be held pending Big Jim's arrival. The agent started the second half. It warned of the danger of a man called Holt Ralston and ordered his arrest as well for murder. He was to be brought into custody dead or alive. Suddenly the telegrapher stopped sending. He'd been interrupted. He waited, listened and then wrote.

"First transmission completed. Second transmission delayed. Generator failure . . . this station."

"Damn," the agent mumbled.

7

Fort Smith, Arkansas was the nearest thing to civilization that Amelia Lashtrow had ever seen. Unlike the rowdiness of the Texas trail towns, even those the size of Texarkana, Fort Smith boasted brick buildings downtown and freshly painted, clean looking frame homes on its residential streets. There was a fancy brick church and a school house with more than one room. She was impressed. Actually, she was in awe.

"I'll find you room and board," Preacher told her. "One day you can repay me."

"I . . I thought we'd be . . . well . . . together."

"I don't ride double," he said, "just often." He didn't seem to possess the gentleness she'd first felt with him. He seemed suddenly hard, almost cold.

"Will I ever see you again?"

"Trails get cut very often in his country. You might."

She climbed down from her horse. They were in front of a two story house which boasted a yard sign.

Room and Board

By Day or Week

After the appropriate introductions and some
background on the girl, Preacher paid the landlady a
month's rent. The woman's son helped Amelia tote
in her meager possibles and then tended the stock.
It gave Preacher a moment or two alone with the
landlady.

"I'll leave you with an additional $100. If
the girl doesn't have a job by the end of the
month, use it. If she does, keep it for her. I'll
trust you to do the honest thing when the time
comes."

"What is she to you exactly?"

"Someone I'm putting in your care," Preacher
replied. "I'll take it personal if bad times befall her."

"They won't," the woman said. Amelia waited in
her room for some time before she finally ventured
downstairs and found the landlady.

"I'm Amelia Lashtrow."

"I know who you are, darlin' an' why you're here.
Your gentleman friend told me all I need to know."

Amelia smiled, nervously and nodded. "Where is
he?"

The landlady frowned and studied Amelia's face.
The girl didn't know. The woman wiped her hands
free of the flour she was using, walked to Amelia,
put her arms around the girl and hugged her.

"Honey, he rode out not five minutes after he got
here with you. I doubt you'll ever see him again."
She stepped back and looked into Amelia's eyes.
"You in trouble with him?" Amelia shrugged.

Preacher found lodging in Fort Smith too risky for

himself. It had been risky even to tend to Amelia's needs, but it was only Friday and he didn't want to be seen by anyone on either side of the law before Sunday afternoon. He ran one more risk, purchasing some supplies and then rode east. Along the Arkansas River, he found an appropriate and tenable camp site. There, he set up to stay until it was time for his meeting with Marshal Buck and the now famed Judge Isaac Parker.

"Good morning, Hec," Judge Parker said when Hec Thomas entered the judge's office. "Coffee?"

"No thanks, Judge. I come only because the boy from the telegraph office ran me down. Said this here was for you." He handed the judge the message. Parker opened it quickly, read it and then looked up.

"Who is here besides yourself, Hec?"

"Tom Kane, uh, Jed Thorpe's in town an' Hank Lacy, Judge. I think most o' the rest are doggin' one trail or another." Hec Thomas frowned. "That trouble," he asked, gesturing toward the telegraph cable.

"Could be the very worst kind. Jim Buck sent it. He asked me for a meeting Sunday, himself and another man. Now," Parker continued, leaning back and taking a deep breath, "he wants the man arrested."

"Well, sir, I don't go back into the field 'til Monday an' with three of us I can't imagine we won't be able to accomodate the marshal." Hec Thomas had a winning smile and a demeanor which was most disarming. Parker had never seen him angry, not even riled to the point of raising his voice. He was cool-headed, even-tempered and highly skilled. Too good a man, Parker was thinking, to lose.

"I'd prefer to wait until Marshal Buck himself arrived if it's at all possible. Besides, right now I don't know where this man is." Hec Thomas looked puzzled. He was not accustomed to Parker displaying caution. There were signs of a considerable amount of it in both Parker's action and his tone.

"Judge, just who is this fella Marshal Buck wants hauled in?"

"Preacher," Parker said, leaning forward. "J. D. Preacher."

Hec Thomas shoved his tongue into his left cheek and pursed his lips. "Whoo eee! The Widow Maker himself. Right down here in Fort Smith. An' he's got quite a price on his head as I recollect."

"He's a bad one, Hec. The worst ever to come into my jurisdiction. He's the man I was supposed to meet with on Sunday—me and Marshal Buck. Something has gone wrong. I don't want to lose good men to the likes of that bounty killer."

"Well, Judge, speakin' honest, I'd just as soon not have to try handlin' him alone. I hear he's greased lightnin'. I'll wait for Buck."

Hec Thomas's skills with a gun were by no means lacking. He was quick and accurate to a fault. He'd faced down more than his share of gunmen since assuming his duties in Parker's jurisdiction. If they were, in fact, his equals, even the likes of Chris Madsen and John Tolbert conceded that Hec was the most skillful all 'round of the Fort Smith gallows gang as they had become known.

Thus it was that Judge Isaac Parker, while wanting to protect Thomas, was himself surprised that Thomas had so readily agreed.

"What do you know of this man, Preacher?" Parker asked. "First hand, I mean?"

"Have I seen him work, you mean?" Parker nodded. "No sir, never have. But I'll tell you this. I know the man who taught him or so's I've heard. Name's Morgan Lake. Him I've seen."

"And could you take this Lake into custody? I mean if it came to facing him down with a gun. You and Lake alone?"

"No, Judge, I couldn't."

The door to Parker's chambers opened and Tom Kane came in. He looked stern. He shut the door behind him, turned around and merely nodded a greeting to both men.

"Sam Luckenbills' boy just ran me down over to the mercantile. We got ourselves a bonafide killer on our hands, gents. He just rode in."

"We know," Hec said, "we were just now talkin' about it.' Tom looked stunned. "We agree that the best way to bring him in is to wait 'til Marshal Buck gets here. 'Tween us . . . I'd guess we can corral him.''

"Hec . . . uh," Tom looked at Judge Parker, incredulous. "What charge will you bring ag'in him?"

Now it was Parker who assumed a look of surprise. "Why, Tom, we don't need a charge. We've got Marshal Buck's request right here." He handed Tom the telegraph cable. Tom read it and looked up. "Something wrong?"

"Sure is, Judge. This is not the fella I'm talkin' about. Damn! If this is true—an' what I just heard is true—we got ourselves a whole passle o' trouble. Man I'm talkin' about is Holt Ferraday."

Indeed, Holt Ferraday had ridden into Fort Smith less than half an hour before Tom's intrusion on Parker and Thomas's conversation. Even now, Ferraday was ensconced in the Gallows Saloon. It was, in spite of its name, Fort Smith's most popular gathering place. Judge Parker had, on more than one occasion, done his best to close it. He found the name and the surroundings in contempt of what Fort Smith hoped to achieve. Unfortunately, even his considerable powers found limits in their execution against otherwise law abiding citizens.

Neither Tom or Hec could recall Isaac Parker with quite the expression on his face that, at that moment, he displayed. Finally he got to his feet. "Gentlemen, it's my belief we're about to find Fort Smith the site of a very prominent gunfight. If it is allowed to take place, most of our achievements will become academic. I would further contend that the powers in Washington would replace me and any personnel now in the employ and jurisdiction of this court. Therefore, I am directing you to round up any and every man who has ever served my court, deputize them and take whatever action is necessary to maintain order."

There was no need for either man to ask a question. The edict, as was the case with most of Judge Parker's edicts, was simple. They just nodded and took their leave. Parker straightened himself to his full height, left his chambers and strolled across the open area which had once been the parade grounds. It now separated his barracks chambers from his private residence. He entered, said nothing and immediately changed his clothes. His wife, somewhat outspoken and never reluctant to question her husband, eyed him. He had on his Sunday best suit. It was the one he wore only on two occasions. Church and a hanging which involved more than one prisoner. He'd purchased it to wear for the event of hanging six men simultaneously.

"Isaac?"

"Mother, please. We have a most disturbing situation developing in Fort Smith and I feel that my personal intervention may be of some assistance."

"Very well," she replied. "But do try to be home by mid-afternoon. This is our evening to have dinner with Mayor Roberts and his wife."

"I'll make a special point of it," he said, kissing his wife on the cheek. Parker knew, as he left the house, that his wife would try to see where he went. He didn't want to concern her so he simply returned to his chambers. After a few minutes, certain that she would go back to her chores, he slipped out, around the building and headed for the Gallows saloon.

Marshal Jim Buck had stumbled onto a piece of the worst kind of luck. His horse found a gopher hole. He winced as he pulled the trigger. The animal had been with him for a very long time. He cursed his luck, aloud, then hefted his saddle and his possibles over his shoulder and began walking along the road north. He knew of two farms close enough to the main road to be of help. He'd have to use his authority to get a horse, for he had very little money. At that moment, however, he didn't care. He had to get to Fort Smith fast.

Hec Thomas, Tom Kane, Jed Thorpe and Hank Lacy all entered the Gallows Saloon at the same time. Then, as was their custom and training, they quickly spread out. Each carefully eyed the patrons, the darkened corners and satisfied themselves that there was no immediate danger. Most of the customers were residents of Fort Smith and knew the men very well. No one moved. No one spoke. Usually, these men did not travel together unless they were working. They socialized only at the old Fort Smith compound. To do so elsewhere brought the threat of ambush.

"You gentlemen looking for me?" The man behind the voice was slight of build, neatly groomed and had a harmless appearance. None of the lawmen needed confirmation of his identity. Hec Thomas was the senior man present.

"We are if you're Holt Ferraday."

"I am. I'd guess you to be Hec Thomas."

"You'd guess right. I'm askin' that you accompany us over to Judge Parker's office. We've no paper on you, but he'd like a visit in private."

"And it takes four of his best deputies to deliver that message?"

"We heard some rumors, Ferraday. The judge would like to straighten them out." The bat wing doors opened. Judge Isaac Parker walked in.

"Mister Ferraday, there's no reason for you to come to me. I'm here. I'll come right to the point. I won't allow gunmen in Fort Smith."

"I'm pursuing my trade, Judge, and collecting what is rightfully mine. I understand the man I'm looking for is here. I don't think you'll find paper on me. As to gunplay, that's his decision."

"No, sir. It isn't. Not in Fort Smith. Granted, I have nothing on which I can hold you. That is not the case with the man you're looking for however, and he is inside my jurisdiction. I will consider it interference with the court and with those charged in carrying out the court's orders if you should confront this man in here."

"Let's make certain we're talking about the same man, Your Honor. I'm looking for a man named Preacher."

"He's the same man and I have an order for his arrest from my Chief Marshal in Texarkana."

"Then we have a touchy situation, Judge Parker. One which could result in a most unpleasant conclusion."

"I will not be threatened, sir, nor will the court of the United States which I am charged to defend. I am, under such circumstances, authorized to remove from my jurisdiction any threat to its function. You, Mister Ferraday, seem to pose just such a threat."

"Judge Parker, as I've seen it for sometime now, you and I have the same goals." Ferraday smiled, slightly changing his stance and eyeing the positions of the deputies. "We even use the same tools."

"I'm sorry, Mister Ferraday, but I would take issue with that contention. The tool of my court is a law book and a gavel. Those who wish to avail themselves of it will receive the full benefits of both. Now at either end of that court, there is a decision making process. My deputies make one of them, use of a gun. I make the other, use of a gallows. And there, sir, is the extent of it, and of my effort to keep you from running afoul of it."

"Seems to me you went to a lot of trouble, Judge."

"I did. I usually do not. I won't again. Nor, sir, will I extend myself any further in your case."

"Is J. D. Preacher in Fort Smith?"

"I don't know," Parker answered.

"You know, Judge, you haven't a man in this room who can take me in."

"Perhaps not," Parker replied, icily, "which is why there are four of them and only one of you."

"Judge," Ferraday said, frowning now, "I'm tired of this conversation, same as you." He slipped his coat away from his gun. "Four isn't even enough."

"Are you certain about that, Mister Ferraday?"

"Are you, Judge? I guess that's the question, isn't it?"

"Needless killing violates everything this court stands for, to say nothing of my personal revulsion to it. You've done nothing. Very well, Ferraday. If that changes, we'll both have the question answered."

Judge Isaac Parker's presence at the Gallows saloon may or may not have made the difference. In any event, no one got shot, Ferraday had learned that Parker meant business, and Parker had saved face by the simple expedient of Ferraday's clean record. The deputies were once again at ease but Hec Thomas knew it wasn't finished.

"What happens come Sunday, Judge, if hell don't bust loose first?"

"I want all of you, if necessary, to escort J. D. Preacher through town."

"You figure Jim Buck'll be here by then?"

"I do. Even the famous Holt Ferraday won't go against odds like those."

"Anything else, Judge, for right now, I mean?"

"Only two. Keep the men away from Ferraday and find Preacher."

Jim Buck got a horse. It wasn't much of a horse

but it was better than walking. As he rode, a little better than a good gait, he couldn't help but remember his only other meeting with Holt Ralston Ferraday. He shuddered as he remembered. By every rule Jim Buck should be dead. In some ways, he'd have been better off had Ferraday killed him. The bullet he still carried could kill him just as quickly as the fastest gun he might ever face. A wrong movement, a sudden jar to his body, even the act of sex could kill him. He fingered the badge on his vest. He cursed under his breath. Jim Buck felt the fire in his belly again. It was the fire of revenge. He wanted Holt Ferraday.

Jim Buck was in conflict, deep conflict, with himself. He had guilt feelings about ordering Ferraday's arrest. He was sending other men to do what he'd failed to do. Maybe, he thought, some of them would die. On the other hand, even Ferraday wouldn't stand against too many of Parker's deputies. Once in custody and on trial, Jim would have his chance again. At some point, Holt Ferraday would try to escape. This time, Jim thought, he'd be ready and waiting.

Then, of course, there was the man called Widow Maker. Jim hadn't quite figured him out yet. He found, within himself, a liking for this man. He couldn't explain it. By every standard he understood and what evidence he had at hand, J. D. Preacher was no different than Holt Ferraday. Somehow, big Jim Buck knew better than that.

Jim's horse snorted. The marshal reined up. He was on a wooded ridge. He stood up in the stirrups and gazed down along the gentle slope ahead of him. Lights twinkled in the gathering darkness. Fort Smith looked bigger, he thought, than when he had

last been there. He also thought of Corabelle Dancer
and the Reverend Mister Poole and the breed,
Conchudo. He could feel the fire in his belly again.
Fear or hatred or determination? Jim Buck wasn't
sure. He was sure of only on thing. There, below
him, was his destiny.

Hank Lacy was feeling his oats which were
considerably more sensitive after having been plied
with near a fifth of Tennessee mash. He'd been
regaling the clientele of the Razorback Saloon with
his tale of the morning's confrontation with Holt
Ferraday. Twice, the barkeep had tried to settle him
down. Twice, Hank had threatened him. Now, not
only the barkeep but several nearby Fort Smith
citizens were genuinely concerned. Hank was new to
Judge Parker's force. He was young and fast with
guns and cocky and bent on becoming the most
famous lawman in the west.

"I'll tell you, by God, I never thought I'd see
ol' Hec Thomas back off o' nuthin', but I did. Well, I
wouldn't have backed off. That damn gunny don't
scare me none."

"I heard there's not a faster man in Texas than
Holt Ferraday. Hell, I even heard he backed down
Bill Longley."

"Nothin' to that," Hank said. "I'd do the same if
Longley was here right now." Hank finished the rest
of his whiskey, set his glass on the bar, wiped his
mouth and ordered another. Two men at a nearby
table grinned at each other and one of them nodded.

"That's big talk from such a little man, badge or
no. Pretty safe too, considerin' Longley's nowhere
near here. Course, I'd have to eat muh words if'n
this loudmouth deputy marshal stood down the man

what stood down Longley, wouldn't I?"

Hank whirled, gun in hand. "Loudmouth? Fetch him, mister. Right now. Walk on down to the Gallows an' fetch Mister Holt Ferraday."

"Hank," the barkeep implored, "Hank, boy, you been drinkin' a bit much. Why don't you . . ."

"Why don't you just keep shut, Will?" Hank cocked the revolver. A somewhat customized Colt's. He turned again to the men at the table. "Well, I'm waitin.' "

"I was just joshin', Deputy. You don't really want me to bring that gunman down here, do you?"

"What did I say, Mister? You got a hearin' problem?"

"He'll kill you, boy."

"Fetch 'im, mister, or it'll be you I shoot." The man looked at his table companion, smiled, shrugged, stood up and walked toward the door. Hank didn't see Will, the barkeep, slip a note to Tess Richards. She hurried out the back way and started running toward Fort Smith's City Marshal's Office.

Two blocks away, Hec Thomas had just left his hotel room and was also headed for the Marshal's Office. Marshal Luke Sorrel often used one or more of Parker's deputies to make rounds. Fort Smith was getting bigger. He needed help and the state had not yet provided the funds for him to hire more than one deputy. Tonight, Saturday, was always one of the most rowdy. Hec had agreed to take his turn.

Holt Ferraday sat in a corner at a table with four other men. The quartet was playing poker. Ferraday looked up when a stranger approached the table.

"I'm lookin' fer a Mister Ferraday," the man said,

nervously. "I got a message for him."

"I'm Ferraday."

"Deputy down to the Razorback Saloon says he wants you down there. Says you're a liar about facin' down Bill Longley. Says he'd have taken you this mornin' if it hadn't been fer Hec Thomas an' Judge Parker hisself bein' there."

"You tell the deputy if he wants to see me, I'll be right here."

"I don't think he'll take too kindly to that, Mister Ferraday. Uh . . . he said if'n you didn't come back with me, he'd badge a dozen men an' come get you."

"You're a liar," Ferraday said. "A liar and a man with a backbone like a cow rope. How much money have you got riding on this fight?" The man's face turned red. He shifted his weight. "Well . . . how much?"

"You got it all wrong," the man said. "This deputy . . . he did say what I tol' you an' he's waitin' right now."

"Get out of my sight," Ferraday said, returning to his cards. "You make me sick." The man backed away a few feet, turned slowly and then walked toward the front of the saloon. As he neared the door, he turned back. He looked around. No one was paying him any mind.

No one ever paid any mind to Frank Martin Winslow. That was a fact of his life. A life which had amounted to little more than a useless series of events, tenuously linked by an occasional moment of excitement.

Winslow reached the door. Slowly, he turned around again. Indeed, no one had deigned even to look upon him with contempt. He drew his pistol, an old Navy Colt's. He cocked it. A saloon girl glanced up. She saw his face. She saw the pistol. She saw his movement. She screamed.

The first shot was high—way high and to the left. Winslow was firing at a target some sixty-feet distant and he was no marksman. He adjusted slightly and fired again. The adjustment was made too fast. Two of the four men at the table had dived for cover with the first shot. The third simply stood up, frozen in awe and stared toward his would-be killer. Winslow fired a third shot. It was about head level on Holt Ferraday, now also standing. While the shot was at the right height, it was too far to the right.

Holt Ferraday released his revolver from the swivel mechanism on his belt, raised the weapon, extended it to arm's length and squeezed the trigger. Frank Martin Winslow died instantly.

The batwing doors banged open. Two men burst into the room and then moved right and left respectively. The one on the right wielded a shotgun. The one on the left, a pistol. The first was Hec Thomas. The second was Fort Smith's city marshal, Luke Sorrel.

"I think you're looking for me," Holt Ferraday returned his revolver to the swivel rig. "He pulled on me. Fired three shots."

"I'll need a full report," Luke Sorrel said, holstering his own gun. Hec Thomas wasn't so quick to back off.

"That's Holt Ferraday," he said.

"Damn!"

"You mind if I do some askin, Marshal?"

"Not at all," Sorrel replied. In fact, he was somewhat relieved by Thomas's request. He too, of course, had heard about that morning's confrontation. He needed no more convincing. He wanted as little to do with Holt Ferraday as possible.

Hec Thomas lowered the shotgun and walked toward the gunman. The crowd moved back in neat lines to make a path. Eyes belonging to the spectators told the story. No one moved. No one spoke.

"Ferraday. I'm ordering you to leave Fort Smith. Now!"

"Mebbe you didn't hear me Deputy. The man tried to kill me."

"I heard you. It doesn't change anything. You're presence in Fort Smith is a violation of the sanctity of the court's authority. That's all the reason Judge Parker needs to request you to leave."

"You've done your duty, Deputy. You've made the request."

"It's not a request anymore, Ferraday. It was a request this mornin'. Now, it's an order."

"You've got a lot of grit, Deputy," Ferraday said, smiling. "By sundown tomorrow. You have my word on it."

"By midnight tonight," Hec Thomas replied, calmly. "And you can spend part of that time down to the marshal's office giving him a report."

"I won't be pushed, Deputy. And you're pushing."

"Yes, sir. That's exactly what I'm doin'. Now you can gun me here an' now." Hec Thomas gestured over his shoulder back toward Luke Sorrel. "The marshal too. You're prob'ly good enough." Hec chewed tobacco. He'd taken a quid just before he and the marshal heard the shots at the saloon. He shifted it now, glanced down, found a spitoon and ridded himself of the excess saliva. "Do that, an' there'll be two dozen men on your trail before you clear the city limits. They'll get you. If they don't, someone else will. Ferraday, if you stay in Fort Smith, you're a dead man." Hec Thomas smiled that winning smile. "Look at it this way, I'm tryin' to save your life."

"Mine, Deputy, or your own?"

"That too," Thomas said, "but I don't put quite the same value on my hide as you do on yours." Hec spit again. "If I did I wouldn't have taken up a badge to earn my keep."

Holt Ferraday had ridden into Fort Smith looking for a man. A man he wanted to kill. That man wasn't Frank Winslow or Hec Thomas or Luke Sorrel. Ferraday picked up his winnings, smiled at Hec and walked out.

8

Hec Thomas got his satisfaction. Luke Sorrel got his report. The young deputy, Hank Lacy, got sobered up enough to be damned scared and Marshal Jim Buck got to town. He rode directly to Judge Issac Parker's home. It was near one o'clock in the morning.

Judge Parker was sleepy-eyed when he answered the knock at the door but he smiled when he saw Big Jim. He stepped back, Jim entered and followed Parker to the parlor. Jim waited while Parker roused his wife and instructed her to make some coffee. Then he threw some cold water on his face and joined Big Jim.

"It's good to see you again, Jim. Damned good."

"Forgive the lack of amenities on my part, Judge, but we've got some talking to do."

"Well, I did get your message, but we've not found the man." Jim frowned. "I've got Hec on it."

"Which man?"

Parker reared back and stared. "Why the gunman. Preacher."

"And Ferraday?"

Judge Parker smiled, looked down and then up

again. "Now there's one for you. Hec ran him out of town. Why, it hasn't been more than two hours ago." Judge Parker looked up. He looked strange. He suddenly realized that Jim Buck shouldn't have known Ferraday was even in town.

"Jim, how did you know about Holt Ferraday?" Jim told him everything. Parker showed the big marshal the telegraph cable he'd received.

"Well, it's easier to understand why Hec had no more trouble with Ferraday than he did."

"It doesn't take away from Hec's guts one little bit," Jim said. "If Ferraday had wanted to stay . . ."

"Hmmm . . ." Parker nodded. Parker's wife brought in coffee, welcomed Jim and dutifully returned to bed. They both drank nearly full cups before either spoke again. "This man Preacher? Will he be here tomorrow?"

"I think so."

"Do you know what he wants?"

"Yes. He wants the bounty off his head. He claims he's got evidence that will convince you to lift it. And," Jim added, with some disdain, "he wants the publicity that will accompany a judgment about him by a man as famous as you've become."

Parker had asked the question but he really didn't hear all of the answer. He was pondering the conditions which now existed in the very heart of his jurisdiction. He didn't like the possibilities.

"Jim. Do you have any idea what a meeting between this man Preacher and Holt Ferraday would mean to Fort Smith, to this judicial district and, speaking candidly, to me, personally?"

"Yes, Judge, I do," Jim replied, standing. "I won't let it happen."

"It's not just your message, but Ferraday is now as much a wanted man as J. D. Preacher. I'll order as many men deputized as it takes to bring both of them in. I'll be damned if Fort Smith is going to revert to its pre-Parker days." He smiled. Jim smiled back for the first time.

"I'm your chief deputy, Judge. Let me badge the necessary men."

"So ordered, Marshal."

Dawn brought sunny skies and unseasonable warmth even for Arkansas in March. Preacher was moving back toward Fort Smith before full daylight. He planned on skirting the main part of town and simply riding out to Parker's court at the old fort site. It was, he reckoned, the most security he would be able to find until their afternoon meeting.

As Preacher was breaking camp that morning so was Holt Ferraday. He was less than a mile south and west of Parker's residence. He'd reasoned that the bounty hunter, Preacher, would come to Fort Smith for only one reason. Either to hire his gun to the court or pick up the names of those men who were most wanted and therefore worth the most money. Holt Ferraday was not a man to be run out of someplace he wanted to be. Right now, he wanted to be in Fort Smith. He'd been run out once. It wouldn't happen a second time.

"Good morning, ma'am."

Mrs. Isaac Parker looked strangely at the visitor. A slight man with a handlebar moustache and a small goatee.

"Yes?"

"Is Judge Parker in?"

"No, I'm sorry, he isn't. I must say you've found a

most unusual situation. He usually is at this time of the day but he was up very late and had a very early meeting.''

"Then he would be in his chambers?" She nodded. "Then, ma'am, step back inside and stay very quiet." Mrs. Parker gasped as she looked down and saw the gun, a short-barreled pistol which the man had extracted from inside his coat. She complied. "Do you have a parlor?" She nodded. "Take me there." She did and the man ordered her to sit down. Again, she complied.

She and her husband had often discussed the possibility of either herself or their children becoming hostage to one of the Judge's enemies. He'd made many even in the short time since he'd assumed office.

"I have children upstairs, sir," she said, calmly. She thought that the revelation might have been a mistake after she did it. After all, she didn't really know the nature of the man now threatening her, and the judge had often said that such men were wholly unpredictable.

Mary Parker looked like a school teacher. She was, by her husband's own opinion, a bit too conservative. Her looks belied her personality however. She was a stern woman, almost stiff-necked at times. A disciplinarian where her children were concerned and very supportive, as well as protective, of her husband. She was barely 30 and had dreaded Fort Smith from the moment she first saw it.

Back in her home state, Missouri, Mary Parker was considered a first rate wife and mother and a strong candidate as a good First Lady. It is more than likely that, had the Parkers remained in the state, the judge would have become Governor Isaac

Parker.

"What is it you want of me, sir?" Mary tried to maintain a calm in both voice and action. Inside, she was far more frightened than she could ever remember being before.

"I want you to write a message to your husband. I will tell you what to put in it. Do you have a child old enough to deliver it?"

"Yes . . . but." She stopped.

"But what?"

"You can't possibly hope to get away with this."

"Let me worry over that, ma'am. I'm not here to harm you or the judge. If you do as I ask, and your husband does as well, I will be out of Fort Smith and your lives by noon today."

"Do you realize that my husband is a Federal Judge and that he cannot allow what you are doing to go unpunished?"

"Write, ma'am." Mary Parker nodded and readied herself. She looked at the man. "Bring me J.D. Preacher. I want him here this morning. I know you can comply with my request. The sooner you do the sooner your wife and children will be out of danger. Make no mistake, Judge, they are in danger. Send him to the house when he arrives. Also, write an order giving me passage out of Arkansas and your word that I will not be pursued by your deputies. Write a response. Done or not done."

The man said no more and Mary looked up. She waited. "Am I to affix a signature to it?"

"Sign it Ferraday, ma'am."

Isaac Junior toted the message. His father, sequestered with Jim Buck, Hec Thomas and four other deputies, read it. His face flushed with the anger he felt—and the hatred. He read it aloud. Then, he looked from face to face. "Now," he said, with a deliberate iciness, "you may get a better understanding of why I order men like this one hanged."

"You'll have to tell him the facts, Judge," Jim Buck offered. "I doubt that Preacher will show up here a minute sooner than we've arranged."

Just then, one of the court's security deputies opened the door.

"What is it, Ramsey?" Parker asked, irritably.

"A gent here to see you, Judge." The door opened wide. Parker strained to see the man. Jim Buck did.

"That's Preacher," Buck said.

Preacher was quickly appraised of the situation. He read Ferraday's message himself. He handed it back to Judge Parker.

"Will you comply with it?"

"I can't," Parker said. Every man present saw the moisture in Isaac Parker's eyes. The judge looked across the room at his oldest son. "He's here at least and here he'll stay."

"Judge . . . you can't let . . ."

"Marshal Buck. Please! If I negotiate with this man, I'll either have to resign my post or spend the entire district's budget in defense of my home. Either option is out of the question. If I step down, other judges will be put in untenable positions. The same is true if I deal with him."

"You missed one option," Preacher said.

"I hold you in little more esteem than I do that bastard across the way sir. You're a damned killer."

"But it's me Ferraday wants. Not you or your family. Seems to me I might have reason for some say in the matter."

"What's your proposal, gunman?"

"Deputize me."

"If this situation was not so serious, sir, that

would be laughable.''

"I haven't the time to argue the point, Judge. By the look of it, neither do you.'' Preacher's hand movement to the inside of his coat brought five six-guns to the ready. He smiled. "I'm right handed,'' he said. He handed Judge Parker a sheaf of papers. "Read them. They're why I came, and they're inclusive of my own story. I didn't come here to trade your good judgment for a badge. I'll throw that in because of the man now in your house.''

Parker had not yet even looked down at the papers. He was looking straight into Preacher's eyes. Parker's stare could be devastating. Nearly any practicing attorney in a half a dozen states and territories could attest to that fact. Preacher stared back.

"I will not compromise this court, sir. I don't give a damn how threatening the circumstances. You see, it isn't my wife, my family that is hostage across the way. It's the entire system, sir. The system upon which the civilized portion of this nation rests. The system which will finally civilize the rest of it if it is to be civilized.''

"Then you're refusing me, Judge?''

"I'll consider these papers—your story—but not in exchange for a favor—personal or otherwise. I'll deputize you and await the outcome of your confrontation with Ferraday.'' Parker smiled, sardonically. "If nothing else it will buy me some time.''

"And my request? My arrangement with Marshal Buck here?''

"I agreed to a meeting, sir. Nothing more. As to your request, I would have processed it through the usual procedure. Now on that, I am willing to take a short cut in exchange for your services rendered here this morning."

"What short cut?" Preacher asked.

"I'll appoint an attorney to represent you and present these papers in a formal court session. A private court session. I'll make my judgment at that time. With other considerations due."

"I've heard you were a stern man, sir, but fair."

"And now?"

"I'd have to say that what I heard was right."

"And I've heard that your gun skills are second to none." Isaac Parker's face contorted with the first expression of fear he'd displayed. "Are they good enough?"

"They're good enough, Judge."

Isaac Parker hastily wrote out the terms of the agreements he'd outlined. Both he and Preacher signed them. Jim Buck then stepped forward and issued the oath to formalize Preacher's appointment as a special deputy to the Western Arkansas Federal District Court.

"Preacher," Jim Buck said, as the gunman walked to the door, "Ferraday left a bullet in me. He's the only man who ever did. He wears a special rig on a swivel. He's fast. I've not seen faster."

"Thanks, Marshal."

Judge Parker exited the chambers. He said, "Let me walk with you to the outside door." Preacher nodded. Parker said nothing more until they reached it. He glanced toward his house. He swallowed. "You know, Preacher, your agreement still doesn't free me from bartering with this man. He expects to ride away after he kills you."

"He won't kill me, Judge."

"How can you be certain? I make judgments

about men every day of the week. I'll confess to you in more cases than not, I'm not sure."

"But you make the judgment, nonetheless, on the best evidence you've got. I've got all I can get on Holt Ferraday, but it's at that point the comparison ends."

"How's that?"

"In your case, only one side is judging, the law's. In my case, both men have to make a judgment. Holt Ferraday will hesitate in that fraction of a second before he acts. Every man who lives by a gun does that." Preacher smiled. "All but one. Me. I won't hesitate."

"In God's name I hope not. I will never, as I told you, compromise my professional office. Personally I will forever be in your debt."

The men, all of them highly skilled with weapons, gathered at the windows of the room in which so many men had already been sentenced. Within weeks of assuming the bench, Judge Isaac Parker had heard more than 90 cases. In one of them, six men were found guilty and sentenced to hang. The event, for which Judge Parker ordered a special gallows built, drew spectators from as far away as St. Louis and Nashville, Tennessee.

A frugal man as well as dedicated, Parker was told he could have twice the gallows for about one third more expense. He had already determined that hanging was the most effective deterrent to the commission of crimes within the Indian Territory and the remainder of the district for which he was responsible. The result was a specially built gallows which could, as Parker phrased it, accommodate a dozen of society's failures simultaneously. Using some of the funds he'd saved the court, Parker then employed, full-time, a professional executioner. He was one George Maledon.

Maledon was a crusty old curmudgeon of a man who, wherever he journeyed, could be seen wearing his two revolvers, cross-draw style. There had been occasions during which he was forced to use them. He bragged however, that his skill as a hangman was such that no man had ever returned to request that the job be done over.

"Ferraday!"

Mary Parker jumped at the sound of the voice. Holt Ferraday walked to the window and, very carefully, peered out. He saw one man approaching the house. The man was tall, dressed in black and there was a pistol on his right hip.

"Ma'am, let's go outside to the porch."

When the front door of the Parker house opened, Preacher stopped. He was some 75 feet from the house. Mary Parker emerged. Isaac Parker, from the window of his private office, saw her and took a deep breath. His mind was running rampant with those things which he had, albeit briefly, considered. Among them, posting his best rifle shot on the roof and cutting down Holt Ferraday from a distance. Ferraday's reputation and blinding speed with a gun quickly dispelled any such scheme. Parker looked down. His hopes and dreams for a fine family and a happy life rested at the moment with a 31-year-old shootist from the state of Tennessee.

"God be with you, J.D. Preacher," Parker whispered.

"You J. D. Preacher?"

"I am."

"Did you advise the good judge what would happen if he tried to post a man with a rifle somewhere?"

"I didn't have to, Ferraday. He knows about you."

"Then where is the written response I requested?"

"I'm a special deputy to his court, Ferraday. You have my word that if you survive, you can ride away." Ferraday laughed.

"And who speaks for you after our little meeting, Widow Maker?"

"I do," Parker yelled down from the now open window.

Holt Ferraday, for the first time, came into view. He glanced at Mary Parker. He eyed each of the windows in the old barrack court house and scanned each roof of each building.

"You're under arrest, Ferraday." Preacher's mind flashed back to the last time he'd spoken those words. He'd vowed never to speak them again. Now, here he was, in Arkansas. A deputy U. S. Marshal.

"Go on over to your husband, ma'am."

The request caught Mary Parker by surprise. She had steeled her nerves for the imminent death of one or both of the men in the courtyard. She only hoped that there would be time to dash into the house and get her other child away. "May I get my other son?"

"You may not. Walk. Right now, Mizz Parker."

Holt Ferraday had been in more than 30 gunfights. He knew the rules as well as any man and obviously had abided them rather successfully. Now, for a reason that was incomprehensible, he tried to buy himself an edge, an extra measure of

certainty at the last moment. He was certain
Preacher's eyes would shift to the woman when she
moved again.

Mary Parker stood up. Isaac Parker's mouth
opened and closed. Jim Buck whispered to himself.
"Watch him, Preacher. Jeezus, watch him." Mary
Parker took two steps toward the edge of the porch.
Holt Ferraday's right hand blurred, swiveled the
revolver and pulled the trigger. The movements
were so smooth and in such proximity to one
another, the human eye—even at close
range—would not have been able to separate them.

The range was 75 feet. It was not typical
of a gun fight but then, neither were the
antagonists. By the time Mary Parker had reached
the edge of the porch and Holt Ferraday had fired a
shot, J.D. Preacher had unholstered his hip pistol,
brought it to eye level and fired into Ferraday's blast.
It was the single incident the eye witnesses could
determine with certainty. Ferraday had fired first.
The swivel mechanism allowed a man that extra
fraction of a second to which Preacher had alluded in
his last minute conversation with Judge Parker.

While Holt Ferraday used his edge trying to buy a
second one, Mrs. Parker's movement, J. D. Preacher
used his to assure himself accuracy. Preacher's eyes
blinked as his hat flew from his head. He felt the
sting and heat of flesh sliced as though by a razor.
In that moment of darkness when his eyes were
closed, Preacher's bullet found its target.

Holt Ferraday didn't know he'd missed. He didn't
know he was hit. He died too quickly. Preacher's
shot, fired at a slightly upward angle because of the
elevation of the porch, struck Ferraday just above
the tip of his nose. His body wasn't quite certain in

which direction to fall. It hovered there on the Parker's front porch for a time long enough to allow Mary Parker to turn around. She had negotiated the first two steps and her back had been to Holt Ferraday. She watched as his brain, short circuited now, tried in vain to communicate with the rest of him.

His hand went first—the gun slipping from it. Then, almost as though he'd planned it, his body did a little twist to the left and then fell forward. The impact had been just slightly more to the left than the right of his face. He was dead by the time he landed.

Preacher holstered his gun, removed the badge and turned back to the courthouse. Judge Parker hurried by him to meet his wife, running by now. Hec Thomas even passed them by and, at the judge's orders, went to the house to fetch the Parkers' second son. Most of the other deputies simply stared at Preacher when he re-entered the building. The exception was Marshal Jim Buck.

"That was one hell of a fine shot," he said. "But you took a hit."

"He grazed me. Nothing more." Preacher was holding a damp towel to the upper right side of his scalp. There was a needle thin red line beneath it. He eyed his hat and smiled.

9

"O yez, O yez, the United States District Court for Western Arkansas is now is session, the Honorable Isaac Parker presiding."

Judge Parker in his customary black robe took the bench. Present at the proceedings were his wife, Mary, their two children, Chief Deputy to the District, Marshal James Buck, Chief Deputy to the Court, Hec Thomas, attorney for the defendent, Temple Houston and the defendent himself, Jeremy James David Preacher.

"Attorney Houston, I have completed a detailed study of the evidence presented to me by yourself on behalf of your client. At this time, I will hear any new evidence or a summation of your case as well as a recommendation as to disposition.

Temple Houston stood, strode toward the bench and presented an air about himself that would have been more in keeping with the presence of a jury. It was, for Temple Houston, in no way out of character. The son of the Texas hero Sam Houston, Temple, as young as he was, had built a reputation for both flamboyant courtroom antics and a high degree of success on behalf of those whose cases he took.

"Your Honor, at once, let me emphasize that the decision making process in this case is an outstanding example of what the court system should be—rather than what, in fact, it usually is."

"Mister Houston," Parker said, almost shouting, "I did not convene this session of court to afford you a pulpit from which to vent your wrath upon the American system of jurisdiction. Do I make myself perfectly clear?"

"You do, Your Honor. Would the court entertain a formal motion?" Parker's eyebrows raised. Houston never gave up easily. This seemed too easy.

"What is your motion, sir?"

"I move to request that this court set a date for just such a purpose, sir. Requests of a similar nature have, apparently, failed to reach Your Honor since I cannot possibly conclude that he would have summarily dismissed them, or worse, sir, simply ignored them."

"Mister Houston! That will do, sir!" Preacher grinned. So did Jim Buck. The marshal had sat through such sessions before. Preacher had been warned by Temple Houston himself, that would happen. "Either," Parker continued, "deliver such summation as you have prepared or take your seat and hear the findings of the court in this case. Any option you select besides those, sir, will result in a contempt citation."

Houston smiled and shrugged, casting a glance at Preacher. "I recommend to the court, sir, that it find my client Jeremy James David Preacher, free of the unfounded charges pending against him. Charges for which no prima facia evidence can be mounted."

"After careful consideration of both the information provided by the defendant and the official records provided through the efforts of court appointed attorney . . ." Parker cast a disparaging glance at Temple Houston, "the court has reached a decision in this case. It finds that Jeremy James David Preacher is not guilty of the charges leveled against him in the Dakota Territories. It further rules that all bounties placed upon him as a result of those charges are null and void."

"Thank you, Your Honor," Houston said, getting to his feet. Judge Parker rapped his gavel against the bench. Houston assumed a quizzical expression.

"I have not yet dismissed this proceeding, Mister Houston."

"No. Of course not, Your Honor." Preacher leaned forward slightly and Jim Buck shifted his position. They eyed one another and then both looked at Temple Houston. He shrugged his shoulders. Behind them, drawing everyone's attention, the door to the courtroom opened. Two men entered. The first was Nathan Hale Breed, reporter for the New York *Tribune*. Just behind him, nervous as ever, was Caleb Fitzhugh Hornback, gun drummer. The door closed. Both men stood silently. Parker eyed them, frowned, cleared his throat and turned back to face Preacher.

"Will the defendant please rise?" Preacher stood up. "Mister Preacher, will you and your attorney please approach the bench?"

"Your Honor," Houston said, "this is highly unusual."

"Approach the bench, Mister Houston, with your client."

Temple Houston was clearly puzzled by Parker's actions. Preacher was angry.

"What the hell is going on?"

"Believe me, Preacher," Houston said, quietly, "I haven't the slightest notion." They approached the bench.

"You are aware, are you not, Mister Houston, that your client served as a special deputy to this court on the occasion of attempting to arrest the fugitive gunman, Holt Ferraday."

"I am, Your Honor."

"And are you further aware of the court's policies with regard to the appointment of special deputies?" The question hit Temple Houston with little less impact that he would have felt had Judge Parker struck him with the gavel.

"Is Your Honor referring to the contract of servitude calling for a period of service not less than one year?"

"I am. The court further stipulates that such service may be terminated only by reason of the death of the individual or by extraordinary circumstances which could give the court reason to itself rule the contract terminated."

"Your Honor," Houston said, glowering up at Judge Parker, "is it the intent of this court to hold my client to that appointment?"

"It is, Mister Houston."

"Your Honor, I wish to enter a formal protest to your ruling in the strongest possible terms."

"I will entertain such a protest, sir," Parker said calmly. He opened the court's docket ledger, ran his index finger along the column of hearing dates, looked up and added, "on June the fifteenth."

"You sonuvabitch," Preacher said. Temple Houston grabbed his arm.

"I will tolerate no such profanity in this court,

sir," Parker said, "particularly when it is directed at the court's highest representative." Parker looked, for the first time, directly into Preacher's face. "I will, however, take into consideration the special services rendered to this court and its representative by the perpetrator of the contempt. I will overlook it and issue a warning this time."

Parker looked back at Houston. "Further, I will deduct from the one year special service period that time which has passed pending his hearing. By the court's calculation, Mister J. D. Preacher has a balance of service due which amounts to ten months and 13 days. The court orders that such service begin at the conclusion of this hearing."

Preacher looked at Parker—then at Houston. The Tennessean was as angry as he had ever been toward the law. It required every effort he could bring to bear to prevent him from acting. He knew what would result if he did. He almost didn't care. He turned and stalked back to his seat.

"Your Honor," Temple Houston said, glaring up at Isaac Parker, "this is as blatant an abuse of the law by one of its own as I have ever had the misfortune to witness."

"You have a legal recourse, Mister Houston. I suggest you take it."

"Oh, I intend to, Your Honor. Indeed I do and I do not intend to stop there."

"Are you threatening this court, sir?"

Temple Houston was mad. As mad as hell. He'd crossed swords with Isaac Parker on many occasions, but win or lose he'd always considered Parker to be a fair and reasonable man. Neither term could be applied here.

"You bet I am, Your Royal Potentate!"

"You are in contempt, Mister Houston. I fine you one hundred dollars." Temple Houston reached into his coat pocket, withdrew a sizeable roll of bills, peeled of three one hundred dollar bills and slapped them on the bench.

"You are a disgrace, Parker. Your desire to elevate this district of the U.S. Court to a level equal to that of the Supreme Court has tainted your sanity." Houston jabbed his finger at the money. "Two more insults. A hundred apiece and well worth it!"

"And 48 hours in jail, Mister Houston." Parker banged the gavel. "Court is adjourned."

Isaac Parker sat alone in his chambers. He stared out of the window at nothing in particular. He found his eyes focusing on the front porch of his house and he could see Holt Ferraday again. He could see Mary, frightened and doing Ferraday's bidding. His mind conjured up visions of her frail body crumpled into a heap on the ground. He could see his children's faces, eyes closed, staring up from the confines of a satin lined coffin.

More from habit than desire, he said, "Yes?" in response to the knocking on his door. The door opened. He turned in his chair, regretting his response and knowing it was too late to change it.

"Isaac," Mary Parker said, stepping in and closing the door behind her, "you're wrong. I've known you to torture yourself for days about a decision. I've not always agreed, but I've always kept silent. Isaac. In God's name, you're wrong."

"This is court business, Mary. Have you forgotten our agreement?"

"No, Isaac, I haven't forgotten. Have you forgotten how to be a judge? Worse, have you forgot-

ten how to be a man?'' Parker's wife turned away
and left the office. The judge swallowed. He shook his
head trying in vain to clear it of the images. The
door opened again, this time not preceded by a
knock. Isaac Parker had to look up—way up. Jim
Buck strode to the desk.

"You can pin this badge on any man you choose,
Parker,'' Jim said, "and by any means you choose,
but I'll have no more of it—or you.''

"Jim! Don't quit me.''

"Nothing would please me more,'' Jim said, "than
to ride with a man like J. D. Preacher.'' Jim tossed
the badge on Parker's desk. "But not this way.''

"Ferraday has two brothers. Nat and Quincy.
They were on their way to meet him in Little Rock.
The three of them were planning to hunt you
down.'' Parker opened his desk drawer, removed a
letter and handed it to Jim Buck. Jim studied the
judge's face. He'd come to know that stern
countenance which, it seemed, was never marred by
fear. Of late, Jim had seen the look of fear more
often than not. He unfolded the page and read.

> You'll live, Parker. Hopefully a very long
> time. Long enough to remember the last
> time you see Mary, Isaac and Tom alive.
> Pleasant dreams Judge.

> Quincy and Nat Ferraday

"Jeezus! Why in hell didn't you show this to me
before? Or to Preacher and Temple Houston?''

"Jim, I can't involve the court in this. What
happens publicly must appear to be official and
proper. Quincy Ferraday is nearly 50 years old. He

taught Holt everything he knew about guns. Those men are easily Holt Ferraday's equal. Probably better. I need Preacher."

"Judge. For Chrissakes, the court is involved. You've got Temple Houston in jail and a special deputy hired by the court's power only. Why didn't you just appeal to Preacher?"

"Because appealing to him was a risk, a gamble. The stakes are too damned high. I can't afford the loss."

"We can badge as many men as it takes to bring in the Ferraday boys. Hell. . . Hec Thomas . . . Madsen . . . me. We'll all ride for you."

"I know that. I knew it when I was sitting on the bench this morning. If I did that, I'd be taking every available deputy and turning his services over to my own personal needs. The territory would revert. Every damned cheap tinhorn gunman west of the Mississippi would test my mettle and I'd have no men to stop them."

"And you think one man alone and hating you and not even informed, is the answer?"

"It's the best one I could manage," Parker replied. He stood up and looked into Marshal Jim Buck's face. "Can you handle the Ferraday boys?" Jim Buck hedged his answer. "What makes you think J.D. Preacher can?"

"Men like J.D. Preacher," Parker said, icily, "are expendable. You and Thomas and Madsen and the others, you're not. Preacher has a skill far beyond that of most men of his ilk. I need the skill. Indirectly, so does this court. If it is acquired by less than proper methods, so be it."

"The end justifies the means?"

"In this case, Jim, yes it does."

"And has it occured to you that Temple Houston may get your action overturned?"

"It's not only occured to me, it's likely." The two men considered each other. Jim knew the rest of the answer to his query.

"But not in time?" Parker nodded. "And if Preacher simply ignores your ruling and rides out, then what?"

"A bounty on his head that will even halt the Ferraday boys in their tracks."

"You've got every angle figured, haven't you, Judge Parker?" Jim Buck's tone was scathing. Isaac Parker felt the cutting edge and it hurt. He liked big Jim a lot. Parker looked down.

"I pray to God that I have, Jim." Parker looked up. "Ever since I got that letter I pray to God that I have."

Jim considered Parker. He still didn't agree with the judge's methods but he understood them now and he felt a deep sympathy for the man. Men of Judge Isaac Parker's class were too few and far between in the West in 1877. If there was ever a time when there would be more, someone had to take drastic actions now. Actions which were needed whether or not they were popular or even right by existing standards. Jim stepped up to the desk, looked down at the tin star, picked it up and pinned it on. Neither man said anything. Their eyes met. Jim left.

10

Preacher got drunk. It was only the second time in his life he'd done it. Hell, until he was 20, he didn't even drink. Now, he restricted it to the best whiskey money could buy—Teton Jack.

He repaired to the Ozark Hotel, rented a room, bought up the entire bar's supply of Teton Jack and tried to quell his considerable anger. Near midnight, someone was knocking at his door. The .58 calibre carbine slipped easily from its boot and he levelled it at the door. Drunk or no, the Widow Maker's senses were keenly attuned to their priority. Keeping J.D. Preacher alive.

"Who in hell is it?" There was no answer but the doorknob turned. Preacher hadn't locked the door and when it opened, he levered a shell into the mare's leg's chamber.

"Will you offer a lady a drink?" He was looking at Corabelle Dancer.

"What the hell are you doing here?"

She closed the door behind her and turned back to face him. She was smiling. The satin dress had a low cut bodice and Preacher found his eyes shifting to what it revealed. Corabelle smiled.

"My place is mortgaged with the Fort Smith Mercantile bank. Now that I'll be running the place alone, I thought I'd better talk to them." Preacher set his glass aside and got to his feet. "Poole didn't make it?"

"We don't know yet. Doc says it's too soon to tell. He's afraid of gangrene or some such settin' in. The Reverend's been delirious mostly."

"It's not a good time for company," he said, refilling his glass. Corabelle ignored him. "How about that drink?" He looked at her as though she should have left after his comment. She didn't appear to him as having any intention of leaving. He poured her a drink.

"How'd you find me?"

"Jim told me. He told me what Parker did to you as well." She sipped her drink and they studied each other in silence for a few minutes. "He ran off that newspaper fella an' Hornback, too."

"Am I supposed to be grateful?"

"Would it hurt anything if you were—just a little?"

"Jeezus!"

"He's a better friend than you deserve," Corabelle said.

"I didn't come to Texarkana or Fort Smith looking for friends."

"Why not? From all I've heard, you don't have any."

"I don't want any," Preacher said. He drank. "I don't need any. I left the only friend I ever had under six feet of Dakota territory sod."

"Oh I see. Anybody who doesn't measure up to your dead friend is a bastard. That it, mister fancy gunman?"

Preacher considered her. He drank. He said, "That's about right, lady. Yeah."

"Aren't you feeling just a little sorry for yourself?"

"If I am, what the hell business is it of yours?"

"It's mine because you ended up facing Holt Ferraday and killing him." She finished the rest of her drink, got up, walked to the nightstand and refilled her glass. She took a sip and then turned around. "If you'd waited in Texarkana—if you'd faced him down there—Conchudo and my barkeep would still be alive and Poole wouldn't be laying on what might be his deathbed."

Preacher drank. He smiled. "Now who's feeling sorry for themselves?"

"Hell, yes, Preacher. And with damned good reason. I've got friends. And I'd like to keep them. I care about somebody besides myself. Holt Ferraday came looking for you—not me—not Jim Buck—not Conchudo or Poole. He was your responsibility."

"He was a half-assed gunman who thought I'd cheated him. 'Til he did something to get a price on his hat, lady. Holt Ferraday wasn't worth the bullet it took to kill him. At least to me."

"Then why did you face him down here?"

"Because I was a goddam fool. I trusted a lawman's word and a judge's reputation." Preacher poured himself another glass of whiskey. He drank. "I was wrong on both counts."

"Then why don't you ride out?"

"I may." Corabelle swallowed. She knew what that meant. It was likely that Jim Buck would be assigned to bring Preacher back to face Judge Parker. She had a sick feeling that Jim wouldn't come back. She knew this lanky Tennessee shootist could kill Jim in a standup fight. She drank.

When Corabelle Dancer got up again to refill her glass, she found Preacher's hands slipping beneath her arms and fondling her breasts. She sucked in her breath. It had been a very long time since a man had wanted her as a woman. Her first impulse was to resist. She didn't.

Preacher unbuttoned her dress. She made no effort to stop him. He helped her remove her petticoats and then stepped back, picking up his drink and smiling. She could feel his eyes roaming over her body . . . piercing the thin veil of what few garments remained. She stripped.

Preacher dropped to his knees in front of her and Corabelle took a wider stance. He kissed her stomach and let his hands gently roam upwards until they found the pliable flesh of her breasts. The nipples had hardened now and he tweaked them between thumbs and forefingers.

Preacher's lips and tongue began their ministrations on her abdomen and below. Corabelle stiffened and steadied herself with her hands behind her and resting on the edge of the nightstand. He found her love bud and teased it with the tip of his tongue. Corabelle moaned. Preacher continued. The combination of his breast play and his tongue was volatile when mixed with the desire which had risen within her. She reached a shuddering climax, forcing Preacher's head more tightly between her thighs. She breathed out, relaxed and Preacher stood up. Corabelle stepped toward him, put her arms around his neck and kissed him hard.

"Get comfortable," she whispered to him when she pulled away. He did. Corabelle now undressed him, straddling his body just below his waist.

Corabelle rubbed Preacher's bare chest, tugging at the hairs and let her hands work downward. Her fingers circled his navel. She scooted backwards, spreading her own legs and leaning down. When her head was resting on his crotch, she looked up. Preacher's eyes were closed. She thought: How vulnerable he is at this moment. She had harbored the thought many times before—once with Jim Buck. These men—so skilled with their guns, so feared by their enemies, fell into a state of infantile helplessness under her touch. It was, she concluded, a feeling of power she was enjoying.

She kissed his stomach, licked at it and then took his hardened tool into her mouth. Even in her profession she had encountered few men so well endowed. As she sucked, stroked and caressed him, she could not help but make a comparison with Jim Buck. She even found an internal chuckle about it. Jim was a good four to five inches taller than J. D. Preacher. Preacher, she thought, had the additional inches where it mattered—at least to a woman.

She found him highly sensitive to her touch, particularly in one or two crucial spots. She concentrated on them. He reacted. She brought him to a state of near completion and then, with the sense that only a woman of her experience could judge, stopped. Preacher knew what to do. They switched positions and Preacher entered her. He was surprised to find a youthful tightness. Too, there was the unspoken, instinctive cooperation found only between consenting adults. Corabelle was not Amelia.

The rhythm between the two increased in both speed and intensity. It was natural, smooth and each enjoyed the other. They were not simply performing the act merely to reach a conclusion. Several times, both stopped or slowed the movement so that they could kiss or touch. In their final act, the rhythm was slow—deliberate—pleasure filled. They climaxed almost simultaneously and without deliberate effort.

"Thank you," Corabelle whispered, "I guess I was hoping it would happen when I came up here tonight."

"Were you sent?" The question brought immediate resentment but it vanished just as quickly.

"No."

"Why then?"

"I'm not really sure. Is it important?"

"Not if you weren't sent."

"You're bitter." Corabelle propped herself up against the headboard of the bed. Instinctively, she pulled the covers up until they hid her breasts. "I mean," she continued, "more bitter than just what happened to you here in Fort Smith. Why?"

"It's my affair," Preacher replied, looking at her. "If it's true."

"Are you saying it isn't?"

"I'm not saying anything." He got up and began to dress.

"Will you stay? Will you do what Judge Parker assigned you to do?"

"I don't know, Corabelle." He tucked in his shirt. "Should I stay?"

"I can't answer that for you, but I'd like you to stay."

"Why?"

"You're needed. You have a lot of things that are needed and wanted."

"And what about Marshal Buck?"

"We . . ." she looked down and then up again, "we're friends."

"That's it?"

"That's the way it is. Does it matter?"

"It does if he riles easy. I get pushed by him about you and I'm in a tight. Somebody always has to come out of the bad end of a tight."

"Have you ever?"

"No."

"It won't happen."

"And where would you be if it did?"

"If it was the way you just described it—right in the middle. I don't like to think about that so I won't let it happen." She got up and began to dress. Preacher followed her movements, the sway of her breasts, the ripple of flesh molded over soft muscle. She slipped into her dress. She turned and looked Preacher straight in the eye. "Seems to me you're in kind of a spot either way you decide, but staying is the less threatening. It could also be the most rewarding." She walked to him, put her arms around his neck, pulled her face down and kissed him.

Corabelle Dancer was gone from Preacher's room before dawn. He knew when she left but he didn't acknowledge it. She thought he was asleep and decided not to disturb him. Preacher had some pondering to do and he wanted to do it alone. It was not to be. Shortly after sunrise, he had another visitor. The court's chief deputy, Hec Thomas.

"I don't hold with how you make your way, gunman, but I think the judge done wrong by you." Preacher was getting dressed. He didn't stop.

"That what brought you here, Deputy?"

"Not altogether. We seem to have a connection

somewhere back down the trail. Or so's I heard. I come, mostly to find out."

Preacher did stop now. He looked up. He was curious. He didn't know Hec Thomas. He'd heard of him only a few short days before he arrived in Texarkana.

"What might that be?"

"More a who than a what, Preacher. My contact goes back about five year ago. Just a little before I took on my first badge. I was over on the Red River. Little town in Louisiana. Nachitoches. Ever hear of it?" Preacher shook his head. "Well, no matter. Anyways, I got into a kind of a corner with a couple o' gents with mean streaks clean through. All happened durin' a friendly little card game on a packet boat. I guess mebbe it could o' ended for me right there, 'cept for this fella what stepped in. I'd taken out one o' these gents. But there was a third. I was purty green, I guess. This fella saved my hide."

"Are you saying this gent knew me?"

"Little more'n that. So's he claimed. Claimed he gave you what you needed, to do what you had to do. Never was quite sure what he was talkin' about," Hec Thomas said, scratching at the back of his head, "but he said if'n I ever cut your trail I was s'posed to be sure to give you his best."

Preacher felt his nerves tingle. His blood was pumping faster. Only one man could make such a claim and he'd been dying of a cancer.

"What did this gent call himself?"

"Morgan Lake." Preacher's expression froze in place. He considered Hec Thomas carefully. Certainly Thomas had no reason to lie to Preacher. On the other hand, no one knew about Preacher and Morgan Lake but the two of them. No one, unless

Lake had spread the story.

"I knew a man named Morgan Lake," Preacher said, "but he was a dying man even then. Ten, eleven years back. Right after the war."

"Well, sir, I don't know nothin' about that. This fella, mebbe he looked a little peaked but he sure wasn't dead."

"I think somebody was handing you an empty poke, Deputy."

"Mebbe. But why?" Preacher had already asked himself the question. It made no sense. Thomas was unknown then. So if it was a bounty man or gunny trying to find Preacher, Hec Thomas wouldn't be a likely candidate to help them.

"What brought me—that is, my name—into your conversation?"

"Piece in the N'Orleans newspaper. Quite a story as I recollect. Anyways, that's when he tol' me he'd presented you with a pair o' pistols an' some fair to middlin' advice. I recollect he grinned an' said it looked to him like you'd followed it."

"Deputy. Let's just say that what you're telling me is what happened and that the man you met was actually Morgan Lake. Seems like you've made quite a point to carry out his request. Why?"

"Well, sir, one of 'em is pure selfish I'll admit it. I wanted to meet you. See that horse pistol I've heard stories about. Even if most o' what they write about you is horse dung, you're still a mighty sudden man with a handgun."

"And the other reason?"

"This here fella Morgan Lake is lookin' to kill you, bounty man."

"What the hell are you talking about, Deputy?"

"Six months ago over to Baton Rouge totin' back

a prisoner, I heard his name mentioned. Two lawyer fellas talkin'. I inquired of one of them. Seems some wealthy gent, a sportin' man, had hired a top gunhand to put you under. The fella tried an' failed. Anyways, this sportin' gent put up ten thousand in cash to any man that could gun you, squared off—stand up—face to face. Seems he got took up by this here Morgan Lake."

"Six months ago?" Preacher pondered the story, considered again the man who'd told it to him and then said, "I don't think it's Morgan Lake."

"Mebbe not, bounty man. Mebbe not." Hec Thomas rubbed his forehead and then snapped his fingers. "There was sumthin' else. He tol' me he gave you another piece of advice. One, he said, that would come in mighty handy if you took to playin' cards for your keep."

Preacher's eyebrows raised. A lot of men could learn a lot of things about Preacher from reading the newspaper accounts, particular those written by Nate Breed. No one, he thought, would know about Morgan Lake's little advice to him about poker.

Preacher's mind drifted back over the years. Back to the riverboat and Cairo, Illinois, and the little gambler named Morgan Lake. Preacher had been holding a winning hand and he knew it. Twice, he licked his lips. Lake warned him about the idiosyncracy. A professional, Lake told him, could spot it in a minute. Preacher looked up. "What deputy? And be exact if you can. What advice?"

"Well, sir, as best I could recollect it, he said, don't lick your lips."

Preacher got one more bit of information from Hec Thomas. He learned that Nathan Breed and

Caleb Hornback had taken up lodging in a private rooming house on "F" street. He found them taking their breakfast. Hornback was certain that the Widow Maker was about to add one more widow to his dossier. Breed calmed the little gun drummer but, admittedly, he was surprised to see the mustachioed gunman in the mourning clothes.

"I've got a bargain to strike with you, Breed," Preacher said.

"Well," Breed said, smiling nervously, "I'll have to say that this is quite a switch." He cleared his throat. The landlady approached the table, eyeing Preacher with some suspicion. "A guest of mine," Breed said. "Coffee, mister . . . uh . . . Preacher?"

"Preacher? Well, sir, a man of God is always welcome under my roof." Breed grinned. Preacher looked up at the woman. Hornback coughed.

"Coffee is fine, ma'am."

"What's your bargain?" Breed asked.

"Simple enough. You've been wanting a story about me for as many years as I can recollect. You do me a service and you'll have it." Breed considered the wily gunman. A service? Coming from J. D. Preacher, the man known far and wide as the Widow Maker, a service could be a hell of a dangerous bit of business.

"What do I have to do, Preacher," Breed asked, grinning, "kill somebody?" Breed smirked at his own humor. It was the single service which Preacher didn't need done by anyone else.

"As I recall it," Preacher said, "you did get yourself involved with me one time where that was necessary. But no, not this time."

"One thing, Preacher." The landlady returned with the coffee. She poured it, her eyes never leaving

Preacher's rugged face. She nearly over-filled the cup.

"You know, sir, I don't mean to be disrespectful, but you sure don't strike me as bein' a man who'd be doin' the Lord's work."

Breed was grinning again. Preacher looked the woman straight in the eye. "Ma'am," he said, "looks can be mighty deceiving. Why I doubt that any other man of God in Fort Smith, maybe in all of Arkansas, has seen to so many men meeting their maker as have I." The woman's mouth opened as Preacher spoke, his voice deep and commanding. She shook her head in agreement with him.

"The coffee's free, Preacher man."

"God bless you, ma'am." Hornback coughed. Nate Breed laughed.

"All right, Mister saver of men's souls, what's your bargain?"

"Hold it, Breed. You started to say something. I'd like to hear it first."

"Oh, yes, I almost forgot. My friend Hornback here. He made a kind of bad mistake back a few weeks ago. Damn near cost him his hide—and mine too."

"And mine. Hornback!" Hornback swallowed. His Adam's apple bobbed and he coughed again.

"Yes, sir. Mister Preacher."

"You ever try to set me up again, Hornback, for anybody, for any reason and I'll kill you. No matter what else happens, I'll kill you."

"Oh, yes, sir . . . I mean . . . no, sir. I mean . . . I've taken a new job with Mister Breed's newspaper. You see, I do know my guns."

"That's what I wanted to tell you, Preacher," Breed said, "Hornback is in any deal we make. Any deal I make with anyone. He's an expert."

"I don't give a damn who you take in as a partner, Breed. Just so long as you keep them off my trail. Now, I want you to find Morgan Lake."

Breed frowned. "Morgan Lake? The name . . ."

"He's the man who put me on the trail I rode . . . mostly anyway."

"The riverboat gambler? A shootist first class? But—"

"He was supposed to be dying. According to Hec Thomas, he's very much alive and out to kill me for money. A lot of it. Find him, Breed, or find the truth."

"Where is he?"

"You talk to Thomas." Preacher finished his coffee and stood up. "Find Morgan Lake or the truth. Or both. Do that and you've got your story. You've got my word on it."

Nate Breed stood up. He smiled. He thought about the decade of work. The roads he'd ridden. The treachery he'd seen. The violence which had so often touched this tall Tennessean. "It's a bargain, Preacher." They shook hands. "Will you answer me a question now?"

"I won't stop you from asking it."

"What do you plan to do about Judge Parker's actions? For what it's worth I think he was wrong."

"Seems most do. And it's not worth a heap of buffalo dung but I've decided to wear his damned tin star."

"I have to write about it, Preacher, and about what happened here."

"Yeah," Preacher said, "I know you do. So you write it. Do it well, Breed, and see to it that it gets widely reported. Do whatever you have to, but find me Morgan Lake."

"Or the truth?" Preacher nodded, cast a parting and none too pleasant glance at Celeb Hornback and took his leave.

The morning was not a pleasant one. A steady rain was falling and many of Fort Smith's less traveled thoroughfares were already transformed into muddy quagmires. Preacher's big stallion made sucking noises with each step he took. At the end of the main street, nearing the entryway to the old Fort, Preacher reined up.

"Hold. Easy Prince. Hold boy." Astride his own horse, directly in Preacher's path, sat Marshal Jim Buck.

"I've been waiting for you, Preacher. I reckoned that eventually you'd ride out here. I know why. I need to know what you plan to do."

"I don't plan to kill anybody, Marshal, if that's what you're worried about."

"The thought had entered my mind," Jim Buck said. He glanced down. "There was even a moment or two when it would have been damned difficult to blame you."

"But no more?"

"No more, Preacher. It's wet and miserable out here, and before you talk to the judge, I'd like to talk to you. There's nobody in the deputies bunkhouse right now. Will you join me?"

"Lead the way."

Both men removed the oilcloth slickers, poured themselves coffee and, albeit silently, once again sized each other up. Preacher finally took a seat at one of the long dining tables. It was, he decided, Jim Buck's move.

"I've known Judge Parker for quite a spell, Preacher. I haven't always agreed with him, but I've never seen him do anything I considered totally wrong until now." Preacher smiled, shook his head and looked down. "That strike you funny?"

Preacher looked up. "Only that your vote makes it damned near unanimous."

"Well my vote isn't a solid as it was, and what I think he's wrong about is not the same as ever'body else's. He needs your guns, Preacher, and I happen to think the best way to get a man's help is to ask him for it straight out and truthful."

"That's real admirable, Marshal."

Jim ignored Preacher's comment and said, "I'd planned on askin' you to pin on a badge if the Judge didn't. I'd like to know what answer you'd have given me."

"No."

"What have you got against the law, Preacher?"

"You ask me in here to talk. So talk, Marshal. I'm listening."

"I asked you a question. I'd like an answer."

"It's none of your business."

"You make it damn tough for a man to like you, gun hawk."

"I don't give a damn if you like me or not, Marshal. I didn't come looking for you. Or asking you to do what you did to win favor with you."

"All take. No give. That the way you live, Preacher?"

"What I ask of you, I asked because I heard you were a professional. As a lawman, you had direct access to another man who I also believed was a professional. I didn't ask you to like me—before or after. The law owed me, and I was trying to get the debt squared without anybody else having to die."

"Then you do give a damn whether people live or die."

"Only to the extent that their life or death interferes with me."

"And to hell with law?"

"That's Preacher's law, Marshal."

"Every man can't live just by his own rules, mister, not if he lives in society."

"When I take up social living, Marshal, I'll consider your opinion. Until then, I'll thank you to leave me be."

"Most bounty men I've cut tail with do what they do for the money. I don't believe that's your reason. At least not all of it."

Jim Buck wasn't through, Preacher was. He stood up. "Marshal, what you believe is up to you. I'll respect it as long as you respect what I believe, and we keep the two separated."

"And anybody that breaks Preacher's law gets himself killed. That right?"

"I've never killed a man that didn't have it coming," Preacher said.

"Judged by Preacher's law again?"

"Judged by the man's actions. Talk is cheap. Bullets are cheaper."

"We'll see, bounty man. I brought you here to tell you why Judge Parker did what he did. His actions. You said you didn't come out here to kill anybody. Mebbe you'll feel different after you've listened."

"Why doesn't he tell me?"

"He's got a handicap, Preacher. One you don't seem to have or to know anything about. He cares about somebody else. Has a way of clouding a man's judgement at times."

Preacher smiled and nodded his head. "To quote your young attorney friend, Houston, I rest my case, Marshal."

Jim Buck considered the gunman. He thought how Preacher appeared so confident all of the time. How the shootist had said, without hesitation, and he could take Holt Ferraday. And he did. He couldn't help but wonder if Preacher was ever lonely or confused or hurting, deep inside his gut. Jim concluded that he would probably never know the answers. Almost ignoring all of those thoughts, Jim said, "I feel sorry for you, gunfighter. You must be one lonely son of a bitch."

Jim Buck told Preacher everythng he knew about Judge Parker's actions and motivations for the decision he'd made in court. Preacher listened.

"That's it," Jim Buck said. "Personally I don't think the judge did right by you, but I sure as hell can't find fault with his motives."

"I came to tell him I'd wear his badge. Your story hasn't changed that."

"Why?" Jim held up a hand. "Not why hasn't the story affected your decision. Why did you decide to wear the badge without argument?"

"Let's just say I've got a need, Marshal, and leave it at that."

"All right, Widow Maker," Jim said, harshly, "I'll leave it at that for now. But let me tell you something. I put a lot of stock in what this little tin star stands for. I won't sit idle while some self serving bastard uses it to safisfy his own personal grudges or problems. I couldn't do that even for Judge Parker. That's why I told you the facts. If you step out of line with it, Preacher, I'll find you. I'll take the badge off of you and I'll see you eat it."

Preacher, sitting on the edge of one of the tables, got to his feet. Jim tensed, reflexively. "Marshal," he said, "I don't doubt your word for one damned minute. Now let me tell you something. You've called me a gunman—gunfighter—bastard and a son of a bitch. I figured all of them just fit in with your frame of mind at the moment. I took no offense. Still don't. I do take offense at being called the Widow Maker. Don't call me that again." Jim expected something entirely different. Still, as small as it seemed, he knew Preacher meant it. He nodded.

11

Preacher picked up a copy of the New Orleans newspaper . . . the *Times-Picayune*. What he sought he found, this time, on page three.

The Gavel and the Gun

J. D. Preacher's Story

by

Nathan Hale Breed

Preacher rarely read the body of the stories, but he wanted to be sure that Breed was still writing. Still working and searching. April and May had come and gone. Preacher had heard nothing from Breed. He found himself more edgy, tentative and, he concluded, even bored.

Corabelle had returned to Texarkana with Jim Buck. Most of the court's deputies were in the field. Preacher had located an abandoned cabin just north of the fort and moved in with Amelia Lashtrow. Daily court sessions were now the rule and Preacher did little more than stand guard. He was, he reckoned, little more than Judge Isaac Parker's personal bodyguard. It was beginning to rub a raw spot.

Preacher had asked Parker to release Temple Houston from his contempt charge and lockup. The judge did. However, Houston would not promise that he would leave the judge's actions alone.

On a warm afternoon in late June, Preacher quit the court early. Deputy Jed Thorpe assumed the security duty and Preacher rode out to his cabin. He saw the usual smoke from the chimney, but there was a strange mount tethered out front. He dismounted, slipped the horse pistol from its boot and approached, cautiously.

Preacher's eyes scrutinized the surrounding terrain. He could see nothing to indicate anyone's presence. There was only one window in the front of the cabin. No one was at it. When he got closer, he could see that the horse was rigged with an English riding saddle. Nothing a man would use. Too, it was absent of trail trappings. No bedroll, saddlebags or rifle boot.

"Amelia!" As he shouted the name, Preacher levered a shell into the carbine's chamber. The door opened and a woman stepped outside.

"J. D. Preacher," she said, smiling. "I was beginning to think you found me out."

"Who the hell are you," he asked, "and where's Amelia?"

"The girl is fine. She has the best in the house at the hotel—at my expense." The woman stepped aside and gestured for Preacher to enter. He approached carefully, stopping at the window and peering in. The woman was alone. He entered, still holding the .58 calibre.

"Do you sleep with that thing?" Preacher didn't answer. She shrugged. "Well, then, if you'll put it down and relax, I'll explain."

Preacher sat down. A moment later, she handed him a glass of whiskey. She'd poured it from a small, silver flask. She smiled. "It's Teton Jack," she said.

"Talk, lady." Preacher's tone was firm but he could not hide the fact that his eyes had taken in everything he could possibly see. He was already imagining the rest. The woman, he thought, was about five and a half feet tall. Her manner of dress revealed a wasp-sized waist and breasts which overflowed the top of her black, satin dress. Each breath she took swelled them even more and each movement caused their exposed portions to sway or bounce gently and invitingly.

"I'm Millicent Larchmont," she said, "and I need your help, Preacher. I need it desperately. I haven't a great deal of money, but I assure you that you will be well satisfied with my offer."

"Why me?"

"Because you're the best gunman in the country. And I need the best."

"Why?"

"Have you ever heard of a man named Hence Lowman?" Preacher nodded. He had. Lowman was wanted by Parker's court—dead or alive. Even then, Deputy Chris Madsen was hunting for Lowman, among a half a dozen others.

"Lowman wants to kill me. I'm afraid he may be getting very close to me now. You see," she continued, "I was engaged to a sheriff up in Missouri. Lowman's younger brother came to town to look over the bank. He had three men with him.

He was recognized. My fiance used me to distract Lowman."

"You set Lowman's brother up?" She nodded. "What happened?"

"My fiance killed him and one of the other two gang members."

"The third man got back to Hence?" She nodded. "He rode in?"

"No . . . my, uh . . . fiance rode out." Preacher could see the moisture in the woman's eyes. She looked down, sniffling. "He took a great deal of money when he did. The town's people . . . well, they thought I'd taken part of that too." She wiped her nose and looked up again straight into Preacher's eyes. "I didn't and they couldn't prove anything."

"They just asked you to leave."

"A little stronger than that," she said. "They stripped me . . . covered me with sorghum and sand burrs and . . ."

"Yeah. All right, Miss Larchmont, what makes you think Lowman wants you?"

"He caught up with my fiance."

"Money and all?"

"He tried to buy his life. First with money. Then with information. Finally with both. None of them worked. Lowman has the money now. He's vowed to get me and turn me over to his men and when they're finished, kill me."

"Lowman is a wanted man. Judge Parker has a deputy looking for him now. Unless you know where he is . . ."

"I do. That's why I came to see you finally. I mean I've been reading about you for sometime. I've been hiding in New Orleans with friends. They didn't even want me to risk the trip here. But I had to."

"Then tell me," Preacher said. "We can badge enough men to bring him in? You can simply stay here at the Parker's home until we get him."

"No. He'll be alerted to a posse. No. There's only one way to get him for certain. He wants me alive. I'm the bait again."

"Where is he?" Preacher asked.

"I won't tell you that until you've promised to help me. My way."

"I can't do that. Not just yet."

The woman stood up, her body stiffened. Her lips curled. "Then don't plan on seeing Miss Lashtrow again. She's not at the hotel. I lied. I had to be certain you'd help, and I'm not. After you have, she'll be sent back to you. I'll pay you $5,000."

"Out of what? The town's money?"

"The money is mine. That town owes me."

"Where's Amelia?" Preacher stood up.

"You don't frighten me. I've known too much fight to be frightened of you. I won't tell you."

Preacher was mad as hell. He'd had weeks of inactivity and nothing about Morgan Lake from Breed. Nothing either about the Ferraday boys. He was still seething over Judge Parker's entrapment. Now, it seemed, it was all happening to him again. He thought about Jim Buck's words. Not caring about anybody. What, he thought to himself, about Amelia?

Preacher finished the whiskey, broke out the last of his own supply, poured himself another shot, downed it and then walked to the door. The woman said nothing. He stood, looking out, itching to be free again. He'd come to dislike organized society and its myriad problems. Once, his life had been simple. A friendly poker game, a gunny with a price on his head. Bring him in—dead or alive, rid the country of one more rattlesnake, collect and move on. Now he was caught up in Judge Parker's personal troubles and this woman's personal troubles. Plus Amelia Lashtrow's sudden dilemma and the ghost of his past. Jim Hickok once told him that he'd get to that point. Jim had said, "When it happens, make trail for the high lonesome."

Preacher had been deep in thought. Too deep. He'd turned his back on a stranger. A stranger and an amateur. He realized he hadn't even heard a noise. A movement of any kind. Such distractions were due to his involvements. Another damned good reason to avoid society and its laws. He turned around. Millicent Larchmont was naked. Preacher sucked in his breath. He'd never seen so large a pair of breasts on a woman. Not, at least, a woman whose other proportions were near normal for her height and weight.

They stood out almost straight. There was none of the sagging one might expect with such size. The aurioles were as big around as a coffee cup. And the nipples, hardened by their exposure to the air, were the size of minie balls. There was almost no sign of pubic hair. Just flesh.

"I told you, Preacher. I have very little money. Now, consider it," she smiled, "consider me as advance payment."

Preacher had bedded Amelia Lasthrow several times during their weeks together. She served his purely biological need. He hadn't bedded with a woman since the night with Corabelle. He hated himself for having the need under these circumstances. He eyed the woman again. The hate vanished.

Millicent positioned herself at the head of the bed up on her knees. There was a single wooden shelf just above the headboard a few feet. She stretched her arms upward and grasped its edge. The breasts seemed even bigger.

"They're very sensitive," she said. "I enjoy . . . I love to have them tickled. Sometimes, I can't stand it. If that happens, tie my arms."

"Jeezus," Preacher mumbled. He doused the light, stripped and moved to the bed. He assumed a position similar to Millicent's and began kneading the soft flesh. Millicent groaned. He tweaked her nipples and her body stiffened. He repeated the process. He knew he wasn't getting everything out of it that he wanted. Or that Millicent wanted.

He could feel her struggling to hold still. "Use the ends of your fingers," she whispered. "Just run them over my nipples back and forth." Preacher complied. The effect was incredible.

Preacher had made love to a few women who were not too ashamed or embarrassed to tell him what they liked. Most were whores. Millicent was no whore, but she knew what she liked, and how to get it.

"I can't stand it," she squealed, "but I don't want you to stop. Tie my arms. For God's sake, tie them. Use my corset ties."

Preacher took it a step further. If Millicent was enjoying it, he was finding a new outlet for his own pent-up lust.

Preacher stretched Millicent's arms high above her head and secured them so that it was impossible

for her to move. That done, he found a length of
rope, cut it in half and secured each of her ankles to
the headboard. Her legs were widely spread.

"Oh, Preacher. My God! What are you doing? Oh
. . . oh Jesus." He found a neckerchief and forced it
over her mouth, trying it tightly at the back of her
head. He re-lighted the lamp and turned the flame
on low.

Millicent's eyes were huge and wide open as she
saw Preacher's hardened tool and began anticipat-
ing events yet to happen. She tried to squirm. She
couldn't. Her head rolled back and forth. Preacher
climbed on the bed in front of her. His face was next
to hers. Their eyes met. His hands came up slowly
and his index fingers began wiggling to and fro
across her nipples. He was smiling and Millicent's
gaze was transfixed on him.

Every nerve ending in her body was ablaze with
the sensations which began at the tips of her breasts
and flooded her entire being, culminating finally in
the tender pink recesses hidden between her thighs.

Millicent moaned through the gag, straining
against the bonds which she herself had requested.
Preacher became almost merciless in his passion. He
continued tickling her for several minutes. When he
finally did stop, the respite for her was short lived.
Preacher made himself comfortable on the bed,
positioning himself until his head was between her
legs. He blew gently on her privates. She moaned.
He moved closer. At last, he made contact with lips
and tongue. Simultaneously, he reached up and once
again toyed with her nipples.

Millicent climaxed almost immediately. She
pulled and strained to free herself. All in vain. After
a few minutes, she realized that Preacher had no

intention of freeing her. Soon, he was again positioned in front of her. Again, he began stroking her breasts. Seconds later, Millicent was reacting as though he had never touched her before.

Lou Ingalls was the Western Union telegraph officer at the railroad station in Texarkana. He was filling out some company forms when the receiving unit began to click. He sat down at the desk, tapped out the code indicating he was ready to receive a message and then began to write. He confirmed reception, rewrote the message on a company customer form and read the priority status at the message's beginning. It was for Special Deputy J. D. Preacher. Lou had been instructed to deliver any such messages to the office of the City Marshal. He did so now. Marshal Sorrel was out of his office making his early evening rounds. Lou wrote him a note.

Marshal Sorrel delivered Preacher's message to Judge Parker less than two hours after it had come into the train depot. The delivery was already too late.

Preacher did not release Millicent from her bondage until he had satisfied her several times and himself twice. Neither spoke to the other until they were dressed.

"He's less than a two hour ride from here," the woman said. Preacher looked up. Millicent was smiling. "The girl is perfectly safe. I told her I was your sister and wanted to pay you a surprise visit. She's in town. I won't tell you exactly where. Not just yet."

"Lowman. Is he alone?" She nodded. "How do

you know?"

"I sent him a message and told him I wanted to deal with him. I told him that more money had been stolen than what he'd gotten and that I knew where it was."

"And you think he believes you?"

"I don't know about that, but I was hiding in the woods near the cabin where he was supposed to meet me. He came alone. I waited for about half an hour to make sure no one else came in behind him. After that, I came straight here."

"He could still have men nearby. I'll help you," Preacher said, "but you'll do it my way."

Millicent smiled. "So far," she said, throatily, "your way is just fine."

"When were you supposed to meet him?"

"Tomorrow morning. Just before sunup."

"We change that. We go in tonight."

"Tonight?"

"Right now. It will lend some credibility to the story if you show up early and scared."

"Scared of what? Besides him?"

"Scared of getting caught. I assume you must have enticed him down here with a story that this money is pretty close to that cabin." She nodded. "Then we go in tonight. About ten minutes out, we split up. You go in alone and you tell him there are deputies from Fort Smith gathering up a posse. Tell him you don't know why for sure, but you don't want to take any chances."

"What if he doesn't believe me?"

"You made him believe you once. Do it again."

"Then what?" Millicent asked. Preacher noted a sudden change in the woman's demeanor. Her eyes seemed more full of life. Sparkling. Her voice less strained and her words less tentative.

"Then, you lead him back to me. We'll find something when we split up. A tree. Something for a landmark. That's where you bring him. Once you do, as soon as he dismounts, ride like hell."

"It sounds risky. Dangerous for you."

"You just do it, Millicent, and let me worry about me."

Less than ten minutes later, Millicent Larchmont and J.D. Preacher were headed west. Almost at the same moment, Marshal Jim Buck was pounding on the front door of Judge Parker's home. Mary Parker responded.

"Why Jim, what a pleasant surprise." Atypical for Jim Buck, he pushed his way by her and then turned. "I've got to see the judge," he said, "immediately." She considered him for a moment and then nodded.

"Wait in the parlor, Jim. He'll be right down." Jim helped himself to a whiskey and was about to pour a second when Judge Parker entered the room.

"Jim?" The judge looked puzzled. "Mary seemed to think there was something wrong."

"There is, Judge. Where's Preacher?"

"I assume he's at his cabin. Why?"

"It's too long a story to tell you right now, but in a nutshell, Preacher's life is in considerable danger. Where is his cabin?"

"Just north of here. Not too far. I wanted him to stay here but he declined. He said he wanted some privacy. I couldn't deny him that."

"How's he seemed lately?"

"Fine, I guess. A little distant, maybe, but that seems to be the man's nature. Are you riding out there?"

"I am. Right now."

"Then, Jim, I'll ask you to deliver the telegraph he got. I'd planned on giving it to him in the morning, but as long as you're going . . ."

"Telegraph? from who?"

"Why, I don't know. It was sent from New Orleans."

"Breed! Get it," Jim said, "quickly, Judge. Please." The judge complied and Jim ripped it open, ignoring Judge Parker's protests. He read it and then looked up. "Is Preacher still living with that girl . . . uh . . . ?"

"Amelia Lashtrow," Parker said, scathingly. He nodded.

"Not anymore he isn't." The revelation came from Mary Parker. Both men looked at her. "I saw her being moved into Grant's boarding house by a woman. An older woman . . . that is. . . nearer Preacher's age."

"Damn, Judge. Preacher is being set up. That woman is working for the man hired to kill him. Round up some men. I know there aren't many here, but get what you can. I'll be needing them."

Judge Isaac Parker had all but run out of patience. "Marshal Buck, just what in God's name is going on here?"

"Not now, Judge, I'm sorry. But there just isn't time." Jim moved to the door, opened it and then turned back. "Send the posse after me. I'll mark the trail with seed corn. Trust me, Judge." Jim smiled and looked at Mary Parker. "You might even throw in a little prayer that I'm not too late already."

Nate Breed's message had been short and sweet. The sporting man from New Orleans was one "Gamblin' Jack"—John W. Bainbridge. He had hired Morgan Lake to face Preacher down and Lake had employed the best ruse in the world to entice Preacher. A beautiful woman. The trap was set.

Judge Isaac Parker denuded the security force around his home save for one man. Deputy Jed Thorpe would lead the posse and he chose young Hank Lacy to stay behind. Lacy had undergone a considerable change since the day he'd been drunk and threatening Bill Longley. He'd been subjected to a stern tongue lashing from Judge Parker and a warning. If he wished to remain a deputy marshal, he'd have to do some fast growing up. The youth was skilled but immature. He'd taken Parker's advice to heart and now felt rewarded with the considerable responsibility he'd been given.

The posse was little more than 30 minutes on the trail when Jilly O'Hara showed up on the Parker's doorstep. She was a saloon girl at the Cattleman's Hotel. Hank knew her and ushered her inside and then summoned the Parkers. Jilly was visibly nervous and uncomfortable in the presence of Judge and Mrs. Parker. Finally, however, she blurted out the reason for her visit.

"The Ferraday boys rode in about two hours ago. They run ever'body out o' the saloon 'cept fer two o' the girls, me an' the barkeep." Mary Parker moved next to her husband and gripped his arm tightly. "They said to tell you they'd be makin' a personal call on you real soon."

"How many men with them?" Hank asked. He tried to control his words and force a deeper tone.

"All I saw was four. The Ferradays. A mean lookin' gent they called Ryker an' a boy called Jayhawk."

Judge Parker looked at Hank Lacy. He thought

that Hank did not appear at all intimidated. "Deputy," Parker said, using the title for the first time ever in Hank's case, "what is your recommendation?"

"Miss O'Hara," Hank said, "is Marshal Sorrel aware of the presence of these men?"

"I don't think so. He was out o' town last I heard. Fetchin' a prisoner. Think I heard he was due back tomorrow or the next day, mebbe."

Hank turned to the Parkers. "The Ferradays won't bother you until they've had a chance to check out the security around you. I'm sure they're tryin' to figure if somebody'll come after 'em. Or wait for them to make a move."

"Your plan?"

"Too many of 'em to handle alone, particularly with Sorrel gone. I'll catch up with Jed and the posse and turn 'em back. Then I'll try to find Marshal Buck."

"And Preacher?" The question from Mary Parker. Hank's eyes shifted from hers to those of her husband and back again.

"Ma'am. You an' the Judge are a heap more important than that bounty hunter."

"He's not a bounty hunter now, Hank," she said, eyeing her husband, "he's a special deputy to his court."

"Yes'm," Hank Lacy said, setting his jaw, "but no differ'nt than the rest of us. He's expendable, ma'am. You an' the Judge here ain't."

12

Preacher reined up, dismounted, slipped the mare's legs from its boot, knelt down and began studying the ground. The lengthening shadows of late afternoon hampered his tracking. Millicent Larchmont steadied her mount as its head pitched back and its nostrils flared, sniffing the air. Preacher's own horse snorted and the gunman looked up.

"Yeah, Prince. I sense them too." Preacher straightened up and considered his female companion. He jabbed a finger toward the ground. "There are tracks here of probably half a dozen riders. Maybe more. They're no more than a few hours old. Where is this shack you told me about?"

"Uh . . . well," she began, stammering, "I . . . I can't be positive." She jerked her head toward him and looked into his eyes. "I mean . . . from right here. It's not far. Not much more."

The Widow Maker studied her. The cockiness was gone. The air of confidence, prompted supposedly by fear or hatred—or both—seemed suddenly absent. "What's your game?"

"Game?" She laughed. A forced laugh. Her horse jerked. Prince snorted. "Look. I told you why I'm here." She swallowed and pointed to the ground. "Anybody could have made those tracks." She looked up. Preacher thought she had recovered rather well. "We have a deal. Or are you reneging?"

Preacher didn't respond immediately. Instead, he eyed the surrounding terrain. Off to their left was a gentle slope and at its foot was a stand of cotton-woods. "Fetch Lowman," he said, "tell him the money is down there."

"And where will you be?" Preacher looked around again. He spotted to a small outcropping of rocks. They were about 150 yards to the left and a little above the stand of trees. He pointed. "There," he said, looking back into Millicent's face, "waiting and ready." She smiled. A weak smile. She nodded. A weak nod. She turned and spurred her horse to a gallop. Preacher waited nearly ten minutes. He lead Prince, finally, down among the trees, across a rivulet of water which passed for a stream, climbed the slope on the opposite side of it and found a solitary old cottonwood. It was an exceptionally large tree. Its girth would easily hide a man's presence. Preacher dropped Prince's reins, slapped the big stallion on the rump and watched him trot off toward an open meadow. He knew Prince would not wander too far. Preacher waited.

Hank Lacy caught up with the posse when they were less than two miles beyond Preacher's cabin. Jed Thorpe was stunned to see the young deputy. He was also angry. The Parkers had no protection whatsoever. He waited. Hank talked. Thorpe listened.

"You've done right, boy," Jed said when Hank finished. "Get on with it." Almost before Hank

could turn his horse, Thorpe and the small posse
were on their way back to Fort Smith. Hank quickly
found the seed corn trail being left by Marshal
Buck. He trailed it, at a walk, for almost a mile. He
knew he wasn't moving fast enough. He stopped,
studied the ground ahead and put his brain to work.
He'd been raised in that country. He knew it.

The youth dug spurs into his mount's flanks,
leaned forward low in the saddle and rode, hell bent,
to the west, ignoring the seed corn trail. Ahead of
him a few miles, another man had been forced to
almost the same procedure. Jim Buck was cursing
his ill fortune. He stared at the ground beneath his
horse and the mound of seed corn. He kicked it in
disgust. The cotton sack had worn through where it
touched the saddle. He knew there was no time to
salvage the corn. He looked back toward the east.
He cursed again. Even with the corn as a trail, he
knew the posse would not have an easy time
tracking him. Without it? He didn't ponder too long.
He remounted and looked west. Neither would he
find it easy. But he had tried and without the trail
marking to slow him down, Jim saw no reason to
move at a trot.

Preacher had been behind the cottonwood for
nearly half an hour when he heard the horses. He got
to his feet, pressed his back to the tree trunk and
eased to his left. Two riders were coming from the
west. They were too far away for him to distinguish
identity. They were moving slowly. They halted and
one of them stood up in the stirrups and pointed
toward the stand of trees. The second said something and then both dismounted. The gunman
squinted. The first rider had to be Millicent Larch-

mont. Was the second Lowman? Preacher didn't think so. There was something vaguely familiar here. The two figures moved toward the cottonwoods but Preacher noted the second rider's head was turned more toward the outcropping of rocks.

The two figures were very close to the cottonwoods now. Preacher could clearly recognize Millicent Larchmont. He still had not gotten a clean look at the second rider, but his thoughts trailed back to the dodger he'd seen on Hence Lowman. This rider didn't fit. Both now stopped. The one he didn't know was partially hidden from his view.

"Preacher, come into the open." The voice was raspy. Still there was an air of familiarity. "Talk, Preacher. For right now, just talk." J. D. Preacher's mind was disgorging subconscious information, digging into its memories, trying to remember, to put a face and a name with the tone. "We've got no riverboat deck under us, my friend. This will have to do."

"Jesus Christ," Preacher said to himself. "Morgan Lake!" Preacher stepped from behind the huge cottonwood, fired the mare's leg into the air, levered another shot into the chamber and dropped the barrel until it was pointed at the second rider. The shot had brought him into full view. Preacher could see the pistol in his right hand, drawn and ready by the time Preacher had taken his action. "Hello Morgan."

The man was smiling but Preacher could see the gaunt, pale features more clearly now.

"Preacher." The man holstered the handgun inside his coat. "You plan to use that thing on me?" Preacher's belly was crawling. The little gambler with the lightning hands was obviously not well, but he was not a split second slower.

Preacher whistled. Prince came to him. Preacher booted the .58 calibre and then walked down the slope toward the trees. If he knew little else about the events unfolding at the moment, he was sure of one thing. Morgan Lake would never kill him in cold blood.

"Hello, Preacher." Lake's right arm was extended. Preacher dropped Prince's reins but he declined the offer of the handshake. Lake smiled. "You learned damned well, didn't you? Maybe too well. Too well honed an edge gets brittle. Easy to break."

"I heard you were looking to kill me, Lake. Why?"

"First things first, my friend." Morgan Lake stepped back, motioned for the woman to move up and then he turned back to Preacher. "There's someone I want you to meet."

"We've met . . . thanks."

"No, Preacher, you haven't. By profession the lady is an actress, a very good actress I think." Lake smiled again and looked at her. "Of course, I'm somewhat biased." He stepped forward and looked into Preacher's eyes. "I want you to meet Morgana. Morgana Lake, my daughter, Preacher man."

The bark of the .58 reverberated through the rocks and trees and was not lost in the country's vastness nearly so quickly as would have been a pistol shot. Even Jim Buck knew its sound, having never before heard it. It was his assurance that J.D. Preacher was alive and well. Still far behind the man he sought, Hank Lacy also heard the shot. Spurs dug deeper.

Jim Buck's big chestnut mare was one of the

fastest horses in all of Texas. He'd bought her when he returned to Texarkana after the loss of his first horse. Judge Parker had allowed additional expense money for the purpose and Jim took more than full advantage of it. The animal had thoroughbred blood in her veins, a Kentucky sire, the wind for a mother. The distance between Marshal Buck and J. D. Preacher was halved in a few minutes.

"You managed to bluff me again," Preacher said, "just like that night in Cairo." He eyed Millicent-Morgana. He turned back to her father. "My question stands. Why?"

"Fetch the others," Morgan Lake said to his daughter. She turned away at once. Preacher's right hand filled with revolver. Lake's eyes rounded and his brow wrinkled. "You did master the speed. I'm impressed. Very impressed." Morgan Lake gestured toward his daughter. "She has to do it. There's still the girl, Preacher. Amelia I think it is."

"You bastard."

"I had nothing to do with that. I didn't want any of this kind of thing. I'm sorry, Preacher, but it isn't all my show. I'm merely one of feature players." Preacher holstered his gun and Morgana Lake mounted up and rode back to the west. "Come sit with me," Lake said. He with drew a small flask from his coat pocket. He held it out. "Teton Jack," he said.

The two men sat down. Both took a drink. Lake took a second, then a third. He replaced the cap on the flask when Preacher declined another.

Lake eyed the gunman. "You look like you should have that moustache now." Lake had once told Preacher that the moustache didn't impress him. It was, Lake had said, for the ladies. Preacher got riled. It was another of Morgan Lake's lessons. Preacher remembered, too, that this frail little gambling man had made him, Preacher, look the fool when it came to gunplay.

"You were dying Morgan. Or was that a lie?"

"You know better. I'm still dying, but the doctors were wrong, weren't they?" Lake smiled and shrugged. "Even they don't know why I'm alive. One of them called it, uh, remission. My cancer is in remission."

"Under other circumstances, Morgan, that would be cause for us to get drunk together. Now, sorry but I can't draw a happy face for you."

"Another doctor said I'm a carrier. Maybe I'll never die of it. Maybe I'll live to be a hundred." Lake smiled. Preacher didn't. Lake turned sullen. He gestured over his right shoulder with an extended thumb. "She won't unless she gets a very special kind of operation. One they do only in Germany. It's very expensive, Preacher."

"What am I worth to you, Morgan?"

"Ten thousand dollars. Dead by my gun in a stand up fight."

"There are half a dozen ways for you to raise ten thousand dollars, Morgan. Why'd you pick this one?"

"It's a personal matter, Preacher man, but I've got my reasons."

"I won't face you."

"Yes you will."

"What makes you so damned sure? You knew me once. That was ten years back. A lot has happened. A lot has changed."

"Survival, Preacher," Lake said, coolly. "The

animal instinct that directs the lives of men like you and me. You'll fight back because you've been fighting back for all those ten years. A little longer even than that. Ever since you rode back to Tennessee after the war."

"And if you're wrong?"

"I'll kill you anyway," Morgan Lake said. "Because I made a bargain and I won't break it, not even for you."

"And you'd still collect your fee?"

"Oh, no. The bet would be off if you didn't fight back." Lake got to his feet. He was still talking to Preacher, but he was aware of something else. Someone else. Approaching from the wrong direction. So was Preacher. He too stood up.

The voice was deep. "Preacher?"

"Down here, Marshal." He expected Morgan Lake to act quickly. Instead, Lake just turned to face Preacher. "It wasn't my idea," Preacher said.

Jim Buck rode into view, stopped, eyed both men and then dismounted. "I came to bring you a warning," Jim said. "I'm glad I'm not too late." He walked up, never taking his eyes off Morgan Lake. He handed Preacher the telegraph message. He read. He smiled.

"This is Morgan Lake, the woman's father, my one time mentor." Preacher stepped back. "Morgan, meet U.S. Marshal Jim Buck." The two shook hands. "We'll have some additional company in a bit. Maybe you'd like to tell us who, Morgan."

"John Bainbridge. He's the man who hired me. He's got two gun hands with him. The man he's betting with, Jacque Ducas, and a pair of his best and, of course, my daughter." Morgan Lake eyed the big marshal, eyed his guns and the way he wore them and then looked at Preacher. "I'm a little surprised you've got friends on both sides. Most lawmen of Marshal Buck's ilk don't truck too well with bounty killers."

"We've got something in common," Preacher said, bending out the lapel of his frock coat. Lake then saw the badge.

"I read where you'd ridden for the law. I didn't believe it."

"It wasn't my idea either," Preacher said.

"Seems you don't do much of anything that is your idea." Preacher looked down at the ground, smiled a little and then looked back up at Morgan Lake. "Gent told me once to play the hand I was dealt. I am, Morgan, and you won't see me licking my lips."

"Marshal!" All three men whirled, guns drawn, at the sound of the voices. In fact, had he been inclined, Hank Lacy could have dropped any one of them. He'd managed complete surprise. He would have only gotten one. That was certain, but the carelessness which had allowed his approach had to be shared by all three.

"Another lawman? By God, Preacher, you came well prepared." Lake smiled. "Or wasn't this your idea either?" Hank Lacy considered Morgan Lake and then simply ignored him and addressed himself to Marshal Jim Buck. He told Jim everything. When he'd finished, he turned to Preacher.

"Ridin' out with some woman and leavin' the Parkers to fend alone don't set well with me, bounty man."

"Seems to me," Preacher replied, coolly, "they were in pretty good hands, Deputy."

"That'll do," Jim said. "We ride out. Right now. I

hope to God Jed stays put and the Ferradays don't make their move 'til tomorrow.''

All four men turned to the sound of more horses. Morgana Lake and the men her father had recently described rode into view. The four gun hands in the group spread out. Three of the four were wanted men in the territory. Only Gamblin' Jack's upraised arm stopped them from pulling down on the trio of unknowns. All of them, of course, assumed Morgan Lake would have sided with them, and he was worth all four when it came to gunplay.

John Bainbridge was a big man. Not big like Jim Buck. Big in the sense of a medicine show's fat man. A 300 pounder, with a bull neck, heavy jowls, a girth even larger than Reverend Poole's and legs which seemed almost inadequate to their task.

He rode out front of the others, seemingly uncaring about the presence of two lawmen. He stopped and looked down at Morgan Lake.

"I heard a shot." He eyed the others. "Seems our little outing has drawn more interest than we expected." He looked straight at Preacher. "If I was betting on it, I'd wager you're the famous Widow Maker."

"And if I were betting," Preacher shot back, "I'd wager that you find it very unhealthy to address me by that sobriquet. The name is Preacher. See to it you use it, if you have reason to speak to me at all."

"You taught him well so I've heard, Lake. Perhaps you should have taught him some manners." Bainbridge's girth shook when he laughed. "Anyway, no matter." He looked back down at Preacher. "I will remember to tell the buryin' man to put Preacher on the board, and not Widow Maker." He looked at the sky. The first real evidence of another night was visible as the sun began its final drop to the horizon. "We're running low on daylight, gents. Shall we get on with it?"

Nearly everyone present was surprised by the next words spoken. They came from the lips of Morgan Lake. "Our agreement will have to wait, Bainbridge." Lake smiled. "These gentlemen have a little party of their own to attend and they've been kind enough to invite me along."

Bainbridge turned red-faced. "We have a deal, Lake. You're not welshing on me."

"I don't break my word, Bainbridge, but I didn't set a deadline. You did. Anyway, you might manage a few dollars more for your trouble." Lake knew Bainbridge's flaws as he had known Preacher's.

"How so, Lake?"

"Seems the young deputy here said something about some gunnies in Fort Smith. Among them, the Ferraday brothers." Morgan looked at Hank Lacy. "Four all told, didn't you say?" Hank wasn't sure just how to reply. He looked at Jim Buck, than at Preacher. Finally, he nodded. "Well, then, there are four of us. Ride on in, Bainbridge. Make your wagers. Get word to the gents that we're coming in at sun-up."

Bainbridge didn't need much encouragement. He was well aware of the potential for making good money in Fort Smith. Judge Parker's famous verdicts, and often plenty of hangings, had sweetened the pots and lined the pockets of more than one betting man.

"This is law business," Jim Buck said, stepping forward. "Lake, you weren't invited. You're not a lawman, and nobody is going to make bets on the outcome of any confrontation with the Ferraday boys."

Bainbridge laughed. "And just how do you propose to stop us, lawman?" He gestured behind him. "It seems to me you're a little outgunned."

"That's right, Bainbridge, so I'll make certain of one thing. You'll be the first to go I promise you that." Every man there shifted his position slightly —save one. A gunny named Tilson, then in the employ of Jacque Ducan. He drew a Bowie and held it to Morgana Lake's back.

"You got it wrong, lawman. The first to go will be the lady with the nice bit titties." No one who knew Tilson ever knew his first name. It was too bad because he didn't live long enough for anyone to find out. Whatever arrangements Morgan Lake ever made were not meant to include his daughter unless he did it. Lake whirled, Preacher anticipated him. Tilson died first. The man to his immediate right was next in line. Between them, Lake and Preacher dropped three of the four gunmen present. Jim Buck took out the fourth and Hank Lacy covered the two gamblers. It was over before the first smoke had cleared.

"Marshal, if you can round up one more tin star I'd be most happy to back your play in Fort Smith." Jim Buck eyed Morgan Lake and then J. D. Preacher. He thought: It would be worth it just to keep those two from killing one another. He'd drawn the conclusion that such would be the result of any standup shootout.

"Our deal," Bainbridge said to Lake, "it still stands. I did nothing."

Lake looked up. His eyes were dark, his lips curled back in a display of pure hatred. "That's exactly right, Bainbridge, you did nothing. You'd have let that man kill my daughter. We've got no deal and, if you're as smart as I've always heard, you'll ride out of here back to New Orleans." Morgan Lake walked over to the gambler's horse. "And I wouldn't advise that you even plan on staying there too long. I will be coming back and I don't want to run into you again."

The small party watched as Ducan and Bainbridge rode off. It was near dark. Lake mounted up. "Gents," he said, easily, "shall we go pay a call on the Ferraday boys?"

13

The twenty fifth day of June, 1877, dawned beneath clear skies in Fort Smith, Arkansas. Judge Isaac Parker and his wife were both up and dressed even before daylight. Just after six o'clock they made their way, accompanied by several deputies, to the Judge's chambers. Mary Parker sat in a corner chair and watched her husband swear in another special deputy. Morgan Lake was assigned temporary duty to be set by the authority and discretion of J.D. Preacher.

Upon the completion of his formal task, Judge Parker got to his feet, looked upon the four men standing before him and said, "Anyone of you who does not return to this court by five o'clock this afternoon to join my wife and me for a small celebration is subject to a contempt citation." He was smiling. It was the nearest thing Judge Parker ever did to wishing a man God Speed and Good Luck.

At seven twenty-five the four men who had been present in Parker's court that morning were walking, abreast, toward the Cattleman's Hotel. Marshal James Charles Buck was on the far left flank. Young Hank Lacy had earned himself a spot

next to the territory's Chief Marshal. Next was the
little man who looked, for all the world, like a
drummer of women's undergarments, Morgan Lake.
On the right flank, walked J. D. Preacher.

Marshal Buck had sent word to the hotel and
ordered the Ferradays and their saddle companions
to step into the street and throw down their
weapons. They were ordered to comply no later than
seven-thirty.

Birth right and a fast gun had elevated Quincy
Ferraday to the dubious post of clan leader. By 1877
there wasn't much left to lead. Quincy had killed
his first man when he was barely 14. It was an
important event, however, because it gave him the
status he'd been seeking—that of gang leader. The
man was his own father and the gang was made up
of five boys. Himself and brothers Nathaniel, Holt,
Josiah and Tate.

Tate went first. He was the victim of the irate
father of a girl he'd bedded, impregnated and
deserted. Josh was cut down at 19 in the blood
soaked streets of Abilene, Kansas. Had he lived
another month or so, he might have achieved at
least the fame of being a victim of James Hickok's.
As it was no one knew who shot him. They did it
from behind. Holt Ferraday's fortunes ran out when
he stepped in front of the guns of J.D. Preacher.
And now there were two.

On either side of the Ferraday boys, one could
almost always find the sinister looking man called
Ryker. He carried a customized Colt's in a
weatherbeaten holster on his waist belt. He drew in
cross draw style and was known to carry a second
pistol, out of sight but very near his left hand.
Thomas Hayden Ryker was no cheap, whiskey

swilling, loudmouthed braggart. He was, in his own circles, a skilled and deadly gunman.

About the fourth member of the Ferraday gang, the kid called Jayhawk, little could be said that could not also be said about a pile of fresh dung.

When the four U.S. Marshals drew abreast of the Continental Saloon, the Ferraday brothers exited the hotel. They were preceded by Ryker with the kid Jayhawk behind them. They moved quickly into the street. Marshal Jim Buck held up his right hand, his companions halted and he stepped out ahead of them.

"Throw down the guns, boys. Our buryin' ground is about full up. You are all under arrest by order of the Judge of the Western District Court of the Soverign State of Arkansas." The gunmen eyed each other, drew line abreast, ignored Marshal Buck and began walking. Jim Buck stepped back into his own line and hollered, "this is your last warning, gents." Still, the gunmen advanced. Jim cocked the hammers on his shotgun. It signaled movement for the quartet of lawmen.

About half a block had separated the two lines. The distance vanished quickly. When it had been reduced to about twenty-five feet, both lines stopped. Now, the antagonists studied one another. Ryker, like Jim Buck, toted a shotgun. Nat Ferraday was wielding a Henry rifle. A sudden and warm gust of wind found its way to the street and swirled along in the form of a dust devil, picking up a scrap of paper here and there and darting between horse trough and hitching rail. There was no other sound.

Out of sight were two dozen or more townsfolk, held in the frozen awe of their own morbid curiosity.

They peered through smoke glazed windows, through knot holes in rotting boards or squinted between the louvered slats of batwing doors. The dust devil scurried away.

The kid from Kansas, Jayhawk, moved first. He'd eyed the four men he was facing and sneered at young Hank Lacy. Jayhawk and Lacy could have been brothers or just saddle compadres, drinking and carousing together. The west was filling up with such zealous, adventure filled youths. They weren't. Instead, they were testing each others skills.

Jayhawk was very good. He died knowing he'd been very good, but die he did. He left his mark behind him however, for his own shot tore through Hank Lacy's right boot and ripped away his big toe. Lacy staggered and dropped to one knee. His bullet entered Jayhawk's forehead.

Jim Buck winced at the pain of buckshot scraping across his scalp. It began on his forehead, about at the hairline, and went back to about the middle of his head. It tore a few strands of hair away, but it wasn't fatal. Jim had lunged forward, diving toward the dusty street and firing the shotgun at the same time. Ryker fired too. Jim's blast caught Ryker full in the chest and catapulted his body a dozen feet to the rear. He landed flat on his back dead.

Nat Ferraday never cleared leather. His mouth opened and closed with no sound emitted, when Morgan Lake's bullet struck him. He staggered, managed to steady himself for a split second and then fell, face down, with his hands clawing at the ever growing red spot on his chest.

Quincy Ferraday had taught young Holt everything he knew about guns. If Holt had done anything, he'd improved on what he'd learned. The fancy swivel mechanism he'd developed was clever, workable, and deadly. Quincy however was never impressed with it. He was simply a natural hand with a six-gun and 18 or more men—he didn't even know for sure—had stood before him and felt the fatal sting of that skill.

He drew against J. D. Preacher on that June morning in 1877. He drew and he fired. His shot cleared Preacher's left shoulder by no more than two inches. Preacher used his cross draw. His right hand blurred with what had become instinctive movement, disappearing inside his frock coat and reappearing almost at the ready. He fired only once with uncanny accuracy and speed. Quincy Ferraday's face assumed a quizzical expression. He probably felt a split second's worth of pain when the bullet entered his forehead and before it tore through his brain and exited the rear of his skull just a little above dead center.

The gunfight was done. It was a confrontation between good and evil which had come to pass by the law of the gavel, carried out by the justice of the gun. Marshal Jim Buck ordered the streets cleared, the bodies displayed for an appropriate period and a doctor to treat Hank Lacy. Then he, Preacher and Morgan Lake returned to Judge Parker's chambers.

"Judge," Morgan Lake said, after devouring a home cooked breakfast, "I'll admit that the cooking is better in your profession than it is in mine. Nonetheless," he continued, handing Judge Parker the Special Deputy's badge, "I'll have to decline your flattering offer."

"You did tell me you're a dying man, Lake. For that I'm sorry, but if one is faced with the inevitable, why not make it count for something?"

"I told Preacher here that I had a good, but very personal reason for having chosen so disgusting a way to raise ten thousand dollars." Lake eyed his young mentor and then looked back at the judge. "You see gentlemen, there is nothing wrong with my daughter. Morgana is the picture of good health."

"No operation in Europe?"

"No operation, Preacher man. No disease."

"What then?"

"Morgana is not my only child," Lake said. "I have a son. He'll soon be 25. The money is for him."

"He has need of the operation?"

"He's in the Yuma territorial prison," Lake said, "for something he didn't do. The ten thousand dollars is to get him out, and that has to happen soon. Very soon. Right now, no one knows he's Morgan Lake's son, but when they find out, he's as good as dead."

"You said he wasn't guilty of anything. Can you prove that, Mister Lake?"

"I can Judge, I won't."

"You're not making much sense," Preacher said.

"Probably not to you I'm not." Lake gestured toward Judge Parker, "or to him either. No matter. The simple fact of it is this. If I went to the court with the facts, John Morgan Lake would be dead and buried long before they took action."

"Well, then, Lake, just what do you plan? After yesterday the ten thousand is sure not possible." Preacher considered the little gambler. "Was the money to pay somebody off?"

"I'd sooner not say." Lake answered Preacher but

he was looking at Parker. The Judge looked grim. Lake now turned to Preacher. "There is one possibility."

"Which is?"

"Hence Lowman."

"Lowman is wanted all over this territory, Mister Lake. I have no less than two deputy marshals assigned to bringing him in. Most of the crimes he's committed are against those within my jurisdiction. Respectfully, Lake, the gunman, Hence Lowman, is mine, and I'll see him hang."

"Don't count on it, Judge. He's wanted in Missouri too, and he's got one hell of a big price on his hat." Lake smiled at Preacher. "Isn't that a fact, Preacher?"

"It's fact. At last count, $20,000 from all sources."

"A man alone can't take Lowman alive. Hell I'm not sure two can, but they've got a better chance than one." Preacher knew what Lake was talking about, and he knew that Lake couldn't bring himself to ask for Preacher's help outright. Lake didn't do such things. It was just his cut.

"Are you planning to hold me to this tin any longer, Judge?"

"You know what ruling the court issued on the matter, Preacher."

"You are the court, Parker, and I'm asking you. Do you plan to hold me to it?" Parker looked down. He knew he'd used Preacher. He'd even been able to reasonably justify his act. He couldn't now and he knew that too. He looked up.

"Keep the badges. Both of you. I'll pull the other boys off of Lowman and let you two go after him together."

"And then take him to Missouri so we can collect?" Parker didn't answer. He couldn't. Preacher pulled out his lapel, removed the badge and placed it on the table in front of Judge Parker. "You've got some damned fine men wearing these things, Judge, and if I'm ever of a mind to pin one on, I'd take it kindly if you'd let it be one of yours."

Parker smirked. "You know damned well I'd agree, Preacher. And you know just as well that you'll never wear a badge unless you've got no choices." Preacher got to his feet. Morgan Lake did the same. The two shootists shook hands with the judge. "I'd stop you," Parker said, "if I could."

"You could have stopped me, Judge," Preacher said, "but you didn't."

Preacher smiled. "Be honest with yourself, Preacher, could I have stopped you?" Preacher was honest with himself. He didn't say it aloud, but he knew the answer was no. Parker couldn't have stopped him. Not this time.

Preacher and Lake found Jim Buck and Luke Sorrel in Sorrel's office doing the paperwork on the shootout. "That's the part of your job I find the toughest," Preacher said when they walked in.

"In ten more years there'll be more of this than anything else." Jim got to his feet. Morgan Lake shook his head as he looked up. "I think you gents are makin' a mistake in what you're about to do." Lake and Preacher looked at each other and then back at the marshal. They were stunned. Big Jim grinned. "While you were goodbying over at the barracks, Jed Thorpe stopped by. He'd just talked to Judge Parker."

The four men said their farewells and Lake and Preacher were all but ready to ride out. Jim Buck came out of Sorrel's office, shut the door and glanced back to be certain that Sorrel was properly distracted.

"Hence Lowman is somewhere in Kansas, headed back to Missouri." Jim was speaking in low tones. "I got a telegraph from my office in Texarkana this morning. Field report from Chris Madsen. Lowman was near the Colorado border two weeks back, movin' east. Madsen's latest report came from a Pinkerton field man. Told Chris that Lowman was Missouri bound. Mebbe to join up with those two young James boys."

"Thanks, Marshal," Preacher said. Jim knew it wasn't a word the Tennessee gunman used very often. "And tell Corabelle Dancer that I'll drop in on her one day."

"I'll tell her, Preacher." Jim turned to Morgan Lake. "Pleasure to stand with you, Mister Lake." Lake nodded but said nothing. Jim Buck watched the two men ride out of Fort Smith, and perhaps out of his life.

Three days out of Judge Parker's town, Morgan Lake and Preacher rode into the Missouri bootheel. They followed the river up through New Madrid and then cut north and west into Sikeston. Lake wanted to stay the night but Preacher did not. Here too, there were memories. He'd lived in Sikeston, honed his gun skills near there, shortly after he'd met Morgan Lake the first time. He'd met a girl there. They moved on.

At a campsite deep in the Ozark country one evening in mid July, Lake got a little drunk. He said. "You know, Preacher man, you didn't really ask me too much about this business with Lowman.

After all, that's the man whose name I told Morgana to tempt you with. Aren't you curious?"

"Not too. I've learned to keep free of things folks don't outright volunteer. Asking questions prompts having to answer them. I don't take well to answering questions."

"You've learned a lot, Preacher, a hell of a lot since that night on a riverboat at Cairo, Illinois." Lake frowned. "I'm not sure it's all good."

"Maybe it's not," Preacher said, sipping luke warm coffee, "I don't ponder on it much."

"Maybe you should. You've done a lot more in ten years than most do in a lifetime, but it wasn't ever supposed to leave an empty shell."

"Is that what you see, Lake? An empty shell?"

"Two thirds. You are not a whole man, Preacher."

"Why? Because I don't have a wife and kids?"

"That's a good start. I've lived by the turn of a card or the draw of a gun most of my life, but I took some time to tend my needs. A man's needs run deeper than poker and gunpowder."

"Yours, Lake. Not mine." Preacher sloshed the last swallow of cold coffee around in the bottom of the tin cup, eyeing it. He finally threw it into the fire. It hissed and a puff of steam belched out of the center of the flames. "Your daughter was temptation enough to draw me to you. Lowman was a bonus. Both of you took one hell of a risk. I'm a little surprised that you'd have run it, gambler that you are. It could have gone all sour on you."

"You mean like ending up having to face you?"

"It could have happened."

"You can't take me, Preacher, not even after all these years. I'm older, a little sick and tired. Scared for my kids."

"But no slower."

"Not one damned tenth of a second, Preacher." Lake pulled on the bottle.

"I'll admit to being a little curious about one thing," Preacher said, getting to his feet. "I didn't see or hear anything more about your daughter after we faced the Ferradays." Preacher packed away his tin cup and pulled the bed roll off his saddle. "Why not?"

"She left for Yuma the same day. She should have her brother out of jail by next week at this time." Preacher was spreading his bedroll out and he stopped, straightened and gave Lake a studied look.

"And how's she going to manage that?"

"A payoff." Lake sat up and then got to his feet. Only the fire separated the two men. "I borrowed a little money out of the good judge's town, Preacher. Morgana," Lake unbuttoned his coat, "and Bainbridge."

"You son-of-a-bitch! That whole setup was rotten from the beginning."

"Sorry friend. It's the hand I was dealt, so I played it." Lake held up his hand. He shook his head. "Don't mistake on it. The money goes back, every penny of it just as soon as you and I bring in Hence Lowman."

"You used everybody in Fort Smith, Lake, and you've got the gall to tell me I'm not a whole man? Lake, we've got no deal."

"I hope that's not the case, Preacher. I didn't like it. I liked even less keeping it from you. I couldn't keep it anymore. That's why I told you tonight." Lake's hands dropped to his sides and he shifted his weight so that it was more evenly distributed on both feet. "But I won't let you pull out on me."

Preacher grinned. "Lake, if you killed me I'd be pulled out on you. If you didn't—if I killed you—same result. You know what I think? I think you're curious again. I think it eats at you that I'm not. I think you'd really like to know if your student learned his lessons well enough to whip his teacher."

"And you're telling me you're not curious? Lake held up his left hand and used his thumb and forefinger to illustrate. "Not even this much?"

"Not even that much," Preacher replied. "I already know the answer."

"You really think you can take me, don't you?" Preacher ignored the question, repacked his bedroll and hefted his saddle over his shoulder. "Just what in hell do you think you're doing, Preacher?"

"I'm riding to the nearest telegraph office and I'm sending a message back to Fort Smith." Preacher put the saddle up on Prince's back and tightened the cinch. Then he turned to face Lake. "Then, I'm going after Lowman, alone."

"Like hell you are."

"Morgan, ride the hell away from here right now. Tonight. Get down to Arizona. Get your son and daughter and go off someplace together." Preacher wasn't wearing his frock coat and he'd removed his hip rig. Morgan eyed the vest pistol. "I won't stop you. I won't turn you in. But the slate will be rubbed clean between us."

"You're a damned poor liar, Preacher, or a poor actor. Christ! You like those people back at Fort Smith. And you don't want them thinking ill of you. Isn't that a fact?"

"Fact? I'll give you a fact, Lake. The fact is they're law. I don't truck much with the law. I leave it alone and I expect it to do the same with me."

"Then let me give you a fact. I left a letter in Judge Parker's office desk. He should have found it by now. I told him everything. The money. How much. Why. And that you weren't in on it. You got no worries about Fort Smith, Preacher. Or the law. Now I need Lowman. I need him alive, and you're the second handiest man I ever saw with a handgun. Ride with me, Preacher. Help me get Lowman. Take the goddam money back to Fort Smith and I won't cut your trail again."

Preacher noted a sudden strained look on Lake's face. A look of pain. The little gambler sucked in a short breath and then forced a smile. He continued. "Then, Preacher, after all that, then the slate will clean."

"And just why in the hell should I believe you now, Lake? You've been lying to me since the minute your daughter rode you in." Preacher stepped closer to Lake. He was stern. "For all I know, gambler, you've been lying since that night in Cairo, Illinois."

Morgan Lake smiled. "I think you know better, Preacher." Lake pointed, carefully, toward his pistols. "You know about these. They're not lies."

Preacher considered the little gambler. He knew Morgan Lake was ill. Fatally ill. Remission? Preacher wasn't sure exactly what that meant. It seemed certain what it didn't mean. Lake was, now or later, a dead man. He had a daughter he loved, a son he'd steal for right from under the nose of the toughest man to wield a gavel in the whole damned country. Finally, of course, there was Preacher's personal connection with Lake. Angry, cocky, bitter Jeremy James David Preacher of Tennessee who would no doubt have long since been gunned down in some God-forsaken, nameless crossroads had it not been for the guns and the advice of Morgan Lake.

"All right, Lake," Preacher said, "tomorrow we ride against Hence Lowman. The day we get the bounty on his head we split trail."

"Agreed, Preacher."

"One more thing," Preacher said, continuing to talk as he once again unsaddled his horse, "I've got the name to fit a pulpit, but you seem to have the words." Preacher swung the heavy saddle easily over his left shoulder. He turned. Lake was looking straight at him. "I'll thank you to keep them to yourself."

"You've turned colder than a week-dead cat."

"And you're preaching again, Lake." The two men said nothing more to each other although both lay awake far into the night, each considering the other's changed life.

14

Missourians adopted an altruistic attitude about one of their own. Never mind a native son's occupation. That he was a native son gave him a status in Missouri which made finding him akin to the search for the proverbial needle. Hence Lowman was a James family friend and confidant.

Making matters even more difficult for those seeking out the James's or anyone riding with them, was the fiasco in Minnesota in the fall of 1876. On the eighth day of October, Jesse, Frank, the Younger brothers and one or two other gunhands, tried their luck against the First National Bank of Northfield. The James's irresistible force had finally come upon an immovable object. Only Jesse and Frank got back to Missouri, and both quickly faded into obscurity.

After a disappointing summer of chasing empty leads, dogging trails which always ended up in box canyons and trying to sift Missourians' tall tales from the truth, Preacher and Morgan Lake decided to part company. They did so after spending much of the fall and winter in or around Joplin, Sedalia and Springfield. They also agreed to use a common mailing address near the center of the state. Each would check it once a month. Neither man would move against Hence Lowman without the other.

The spring of 1878 was as disappointing a time for the two bounty men as well but in late May, Preacher got a fresh and promising lead. Hence Lowman, it seemed, had repaired to Kansas once again. Dodge City.

The Dodge House had no vacancies. Preacher wasn't surprised. The first of the Texas trail herds had just hit town and Dodge itself had thrown out the welcome mat. Adding to the melee was the date, July the third.

"Help you, Mister?"

"If you have a room you can," Preacher said.

"Got one you can share. It's the best I can do. The gent said he'd rent out his other bed to any man desperate enough to pay the week's cost."

"Which is?"

"Thirty-five dollars." Preacher wasn't surprised at that either. In winter a man could rent a room at the best in town for two dollars a night. Preacher payed and was given the room key. "Gent's name is Holliday." The clerk ran his finger along the register page. "Yeah. J. Holliday." The clerk looked up, half smiling. "He said if he had any fool takers, and they wanted to meet him, he'd be playin' poker."

"I'm grateful," Preacher said. He gathered up his gear and went directly to the room. The unmade bed told him which was his and he made himself comfortable. Preacher napped for more than an hour. After that he bathed, shaved and broke out his second set of clothes. Even they were pretty roady but there wasn't much he could do about it. He cleaned his pistols, stashed the mare's leg out of sight and made his way to the casino. Few paid him any mind but a man, obviously the floor manager, approached.

"My name is Eubanks, sir. Lyle Eubanks. I'm the night manager here and I'd like to welcome you to the Jubilee casino. What's your pleasure?"

"For right now, some information. I'm looking to find two gents. They're not together as I know of. One's name is Holliday. Got an initial for a first man. J."

"Yes, sir. Mister Holliday is with us." Eubanks turned a half turn and pointed to a corner table. Six men sat around it. "The gent in far seat next to the wall is Mister Holliday." Eubanks turned back. "I believe his name is John and I've heard several at his table call him Doc. Now, sir, the second man?"

"Hence Lowman." Eubanks frowned and looked down. He shook his head. "Sorry, sir, the name is not familiar. I've been here near a year now. I feel certain if he was a regular at the Jubilee I'd know him."

"Uh huh. Seems likely, Mister Eubanks," Preacher said. "I'm grateful." Preacher walked away, threading his way through the crowd. He reached the corner table just as the winning hand was played. It belonged to the man called Doc. Somewhere, Preacher couldn't recollect exactly, he'd heard the name before. Perhaps he'd even met the man. He gave the dark haired, dark eyed man a studied look. In fact, Holliday and Preacher could have passed for kin. Holliday raked in his winnings and then looked up. He smiled an easy going smile. "We look to be full up, mister, but I'd guess there'll be an empty after one more hand."

"I'm not interested in your game," Preacher said, "I've just stopped by to inform you that I'm the fool taker." Preacher paused long enough for Holliday to digest both the phrase and the revelation. When Holliday leaned back in his chair and grinned, Preacher spoke again. "I took the bed that was made, the closest that was empty and the bottom drawer of the chiffonneir, Mister Holliday."

"I'll be damned." Holliday swallowed a shot glass full of whiskey, wiped the corners of his mouth with a motion which revealed a background of good breeding and got to his feet. "Deal me out of a few hands, gentlemen, I've some other business to attend." Only one man at the table protested.

"I don't fancy a man that quits on a winning hand."

Holliday's pleasant demeanor suddenly vanished. It was replaced with a piercing stare and square jawed, tight lipped countenance and words which tripped out of mouth like bullets from a repeating rifle.

"I don't give a damn what you fancy. I leave a table when I'm ready, winning or losing and I do it with no explanations and no apologies. If you have any further quarrel with me, I'd suggest you take it outside and I'll be happy to oblige you." Holliday stepped back and gestured, with a wide sweep of his arm, toward the front door. The man's eyes scanned the faces of the others at the table. He was looking for support. It wasn't there. He looked back at Holliday, swallowed and shook his head.

"I didn't come to sit in, and I didn't come to disrupt," Preacher said.

"I'd like to know a little about a man who's going to sleep in the same room with me. Particularly when he was fool enough to pay $35 for the privilege." Preacher couldn't help but grin. He nodded. The two worked their way back to the bar and this time. Both drew attention. The incident at the table had drawn some curiosity. Now, patrons were eyeing the duo's similar looks. Preacher was taller. Two or three inches maybe. He was darker of complexion as well and less hollow of cheek. Still, the resemblance was uncanny.

"What'll it be, gents?"

"Tennessee green," Holliday answered. He turned to Preacher.

"Teton Jack." The barkeep shook his head.

"Well, my new bunk mate at least displays good taste. You won't find the likes of Teton Jack in here. The Dodge House will serve it and likely the Long Branch. What's your second choice?"

"I try to avoid second choices," Preacher said, "and when it comes to what I drink, there is none."

"Barkeep," Holliday shouted, "forget the Tennessee green." As he spoke, Holliday's eyes never left Preacher's face. "My new bunk mate and myself are about to introduce some refinement into Dodge City's drinking habits."

Chalk Beeson owned the Long Branch. It was Dodge City's most renowned saloon if not also its most plush. Holliday had already carved himself a corner for his personal use. He paid to keep it that way. High stakes poker games with herd owners, trail bosses and buyers, were Holliday's specialties when he was flush. Right now, he wasn't.

The two men got their liquor and Holliday downed two quick shots. He stifled a cough and then looked up and smiled. "Holliday. Formally, John Holliday. Most call me Doc. I'm not, strictly speaking. I was a dentist."

"Preacher," came the reply, "that's good enough."

"Not quite," Doc replied, "unless you happen to be J. D. Preacher."

"I am."

"I'll be damned." Doc downed another drink. "I've got a gent I'd like you to meet." Holliday pulled out a fancy pocket watch, looked at it and nodded, replacing it in his vest pocket. "He'll be around shortly. He's a deputy." Doc emphasized the last revelation, obviously looking for a reaction. He didn't get one. "That little flaw in his makeup aside, he's a likeable sort." Again, there was no reaction. "What brings you to Dodge? Or maybe I should ask who?"

"Hence Lowman. You happen to know him?"

"I've heard the name and a little about the reputation which goes with it. Enough not to want anymore."

"I can appreciate that," Preacher said, sipping his whiskey and smiling a little. "I've about had all of him I can stand as well."

"Lose him, did you?"

"Never found him—yet."

"He must be worth one helluva poke for the great J.D. Preacher to dog his trail."

"If that's a question, he is."

"It wasn't, but how much?" Doc asked, smiling and adding, "That's a question."

"Ten thousand. If he's still breathing and an old due bill cleared off the books."

"Are you in need of a partner in this little venture?"

"Sorry, Doc, no. I've got one already, and that's one too many." Doc Holliday laughed. Suddenly his face twisted into contortions of pain and the laugh, a hearty, carefree laugh, turned into a wracking, gut-wrenching cough. Holliday covered his mouth with a kerchief until the spell had ceased. He folded the kerchief and tucked it inside his coat pocket. The seizure was the first thing about Doc Holliday which brought a reaction from Preacher. He frowned and studied the man's face.

"Sorry," Doc said, weakly. "I've got the consumption. It's supposed to have killed me by now. It hasn't. Like a bad woman, it's always there and never a pleasure."

Doc looked toward the saloon's front entrance and smiled. "Be right back," he said. Preacher watched him as he made his way to the bar. A mustachioed man with a face which looked like it had been hewn from granite stood there. At Doc's arrival, the man spoke, listened as Doc spoke and then nodded. Preacher also noticed several men eyeing the pair. A moment later, both came back to the table.

"This the gent I want you to meet." Preacher wasn't sure to which man Doc was addressing himself but he stood up. "Wyatt. Meet the man they call the Widow Maker. J. D. Preacher of Tennessee." Doc turned. "Preacher. This is Deputy City Marshal Wyatt Earp."

"You look like a preacher," Earp said, "and I've heard that your sermons are pretty final."

"Depends on the audience," Preacher replied. The men shook hands and Doc pulled out a chair. Wyatt Earp sat down. "I've heard some about you too, Marshal, and a brother or two."

"The Easterners seem to fancy gunplay, strong whiskey and loose women. The writers don't seem too interested in the truth. Between the two I've done enough to kill a human being."

Preacher grinned and nodded, "Uh huh. Me too."

Wyatt considered the lanky gunman however and then shook his head. "On the other hand, I've been told by professionals that you're the fastest man with a gun that they've ever seen. Up there with Hickok and Frank Leslie."

"I do what I have to do to stay alive, Marshal. I don't much care about how I'm ranked."

"What brings you to Dodge."

"Hence Lowman."

Marshal Earp considered Preacher. Lowman was wanted by the law in a half a dozen Kansas cow towns. Earp didn't think it likely that Lowman would come back into Kansas. "What makes you think Hence Lowman is here?"

"I got it on pretty good authority. He was in Missouri to join up with the James boys. I guess after what happened to them up in Minnesota, they're making themselves pretty scarce. I'd stake a bet on my information. Lowman is here or has been within the past day or so."

"The law has first call on him," Earp said, "and it won't look kindly on a bounty man doing his work in Dodge City." Earp leaned back in his chair and took a long swallow of cold beer. "I can tell you, too, the county sheriff won't like it one bit better. You are hunting him for the money aren't you? And not for the law?"

"A little of both, Marshal, but if I take your meaning, I'm not wearing a badge. I also don't want him dead. By anybody's gun. The money is payable only if he's breathing. I intend to see to it that he is."

"You sound damned set on it, Preacher. Man ought not get too set. Things happen. Now I could arrange to get you deputized. Maybe save some, uh, problems."

"If I'm badged, Marshal, I can't collect on the man."

"Well," Earp said, standing up, "I was pleasured to meet you, Preacher. Hope we can again, and I hope Hence Lowman doesn't put a gun between us. I don't much fancy being ranked either."

Wyatt Earp drained the beer mug and set the glass on the table. Preacher studied the young lawman. He reckoned that Earp was about 25 or so. Not much younger than himself. Preacher also glanced at Doc Holliday. Holliday was grinning. He was enjoying the peaceful confrontation. Still, Preacher knew he was the outsider here. In any real face-off, Doc Holliday would be on Wyatt Earp's side of the line. Neither Holliday or Earp had the widespread reputation that Preacher found so much of a burden, but he decided that they, in fact, had the skill.

"I don't want trouble," Preacher said, standing up, "just Lowman, alive." He looked straight into Earp's eyes. "It's damned important to me, Marshal, or I wouldn't be so hard about it, but I'll do what I need to do to get him."

Earp nodded his head once. "I believe you, Preacher. I just hope you don't do it in Dodge." Earp walked away. Preacher sat back down.

"He's not a man who backs off," Holliday said, "even sometimes when maybe he should." Preacher looked back at the consumptive dentist. "And he's good enough to stand for what he says."

"And where does Doc Holliday stand?"

"Wherever is best for Doc Holliday," came the reply.

"I've kept you long enough from your poker game, Doc," Preacher said, "besides which I'm ready to call it a day." Both men stood up. Just as they did, there was a woman's scream, a sudden rush of men away from the bar and a high-pitched, somewhat squeaky voiced shout.

"You called me a liar, mister. No man calls me a liar and stays breathin'." Doc and Preacher saw a short, wiry haired youngster with a peach fuzz growth above his upper lip and several pustules on his chin. He was dressed in denim, a plaid shirt and leather vest and was carrying a double rig which looked cumbersome. It was black, hand-tooled leather with matching holsters in which reposed twin Colt's.

The man he was accusing stood ten feet away. His hands were shaking. He wore no gun and had the look of a chuck cook or aging drover. He was sure no gunman.

"I got no gun, mister. Don't never wear no gun an' I didn't mean no offense. It's just that I saw that gunplay . . . an' . . . well, sir . . . you're just wrong that's all. No liar. Just wrong."

It was a none too uncommon occurance in the Dodge House—indeed in Dodge City itself—of an evening. It became more so when the trail herds were in and the next day was the Fourth of July. Usually, one or the other of the antagonists would back down and walk away. In this case, the pock-faced youth saw a chance to show off.

"Hickok was a murderin' back shootin' blowhard," the kid said, "just like I said he was, an' you got about one minute to get yourself a gun."

"Excuse me, Doc," Preacher said.

"Hold up, Preacher," Doc Holliday replied, gently taking a hold on Preacher's arm. "You figuring to mix in their affairs?"

"I don't make it a habit, Doc, but Jim Hickok was a friend of mine." Preacher eyed Doc's hand, looked back up and added, "So like I said, excuse me." Doc Holliday nodded his understanding and stepped away.

Preacher moved through the aisle. He stopped about 20 feet away from the kid.

"I'm wearing a gun," Preacher said, "and I'm telling you the same thing he did, boy. You're wrong. Hickok was a personal friend of mine and he was no blowhard or backshooter." The kid was surprised by the appearance of the intruder but he stood his ground, grinning. Preacher continued. "If he'd ever wanted to be either one, I'd wager he could have taken lessons from you. Now, boy, if I were you, I'd walk on out of here, sober up and cool down."

The pock-faced kid turned red and his cheeks puffed out. "Are you standin' for this old mule ass?"

"I'm standing for Jim Hickok, since somebody about like yourself put a bullet in the back of his head and he can't stand for himself."

"Mister, I'm about to kill you for what you just said. And when I'm done I'm gonna take your gun, give it to old mule ass here and then kill him."

Preacher ignored the words and, intead, directed his attention to the old man. "What's your name?" Preacher asked.

"Benton," came the reply, "Elias Benton."

Preacher turned his attention back to the kid as he spoke. "Mine is Preacher," he said, a little louder than he'd been speaking before, "J.D. Preacher. I'm pleased to make your acquaintance, Mister Benton."

"An' I'm mighty proud to make yours, Mister

Preacher."

The kid swallowed, his mouth went as dry as an alkali bed. His skin was crawling and his eyes shifted to some of the other faces in the crowd. Preacher knew that anyone—even a wet nosed gunny like this one—could be pushed too hard and too far. He decided to give the kid an out.

"You know, I've seen many a man in my time that looked a whole hell of a lot like somebody else. Mebbe the man you saw just looked like Wild Bill. You suppose that's a possible?"

The kid's fingers were opening and closing just inches from the butts of the twin Colt's. He swallowed again. Preacher gave him one last out.

"Anybody can make a mistake. Takes a damn good man to admit it." The kid swallowed. "That's likely what happened, Mister Preacher. Yeah. That's real likely what happened." The kid looked down and then pushed his way through the crowd and out of the Long Branch.

"I want to thank you, Mister. Me'n mine I sure do." Preacher just nodded and then turned around. "I'll say goodnight, Doc."

Doc Holliday, a broad grin on his face, nodded at Preacher and moved toward the bar.

Preacher found the room door unlocked. He opened the door hard and then stepped back. A moment later, a woman stepped into view. She smiled.

"Doc Holliday is not here," Preacher said, "and you couldn't know he had inherited a roommate. Sorry."

"I'm not here to see Doc Holliday," she said. "I'm looking for the bounty hunter called Preacher."

"You've found him." Preacher stepped inside, glanced around the room and then back at the woman. She was tall, willowy, very attractive. A blonde haired, blue eyed woman who, by Preacher's reckoning, was about twenty-five. "Now who are you?"

"Ellen Caldwell." Preacher looked even closer. She was expensively dressed and coiffed and it was obvious she was well bred. She didn't fit into Dodge City society. Mostly because Dodge City had no society. Not at her level. "My maiden name was Lowman."

Preacher consider her. "As in Hence Lowman?"

"As in Hence Lowman. He's my brother." Preacher motioned for her to sit down. She declined.

"What do you want from me?"

"Nothing." She removed an envelope from her purse and handed it to him. It was thick. "There's ten thousand dollars in there. In cash. It is, I believe, the same amount being offered for my brother's capture."

"If he can be taken alive. Yes."

"I want him alive also, but there is a bounty on his head in his state. Five thousand. Dead or alive. I'm offering that as as addition incentive to assure that he will be taken alive, and that the man who earns it will allow nothing . . . uh . . no one . . . to stand in his way. I have been given to believe that you are the best bounty hunter alive."

Preacher didn't need a picture drawn for him. He tossed the envelope on the bed. "You'd best sit, ma'am, and tell me everything you know."

"Is that absolutely necessary?"

"If you want me to pick up that envelope it is."

"And if you don't like what you hear?"

"Then it leaves with you."

Ellen Lowman Caldwell sat down. "You've got competition. I guess it's pretty good competition."

"Good is not as important as how much?"

"Only two that I know of. Already in Dodge City. A man named Payson and another I believe they call Tatro."

"Harry Payson is the first one." Preacher smiled. "We've cut trail before, but never after anything this big. Tatro? He must be a local."

Preacher considered the woman. He felt a stirring in his groin. He forced it out of his mind. "Does your husband know you're here with ten thousand dollars and talking to a bounty hunter?"

"I don't have a husband," she said. "He was in the army. He died at Apache Wells, if you've heard of that."

"I heard." Preacher felt the stirring again. Again, he forced it out of his mind. "And the one man who counts in all of this. Hence Lowman. Where is he?"

"At my ranch." Preacher frowned. "I hate him," she added. Her tone was calm and even. "I hate him with every fibre of my body, every ounce of my soul." She looked down and then up again. "But I am an actress, Mister Preacher. A very good actress. Not by profession. By necessity. Hence believed me when I told him I'd help. He only came back after he'd heard about my husband. He thinks me bitter and vengeful now."

"But you don't hate him enough to want him dead?"

"Oh yes. But gunning him down is much too fast. I want him to have sometime to ponder his fate. I want the swaggering little bastard to cower before his executioner. And he will. Oh God! He will when the time comes. I want to make sure it does."

"You may not find revenge tasting as sweet as you think it will, Mrs. Caldwell."

"Perhaps I won't, but I've earned the right to judge that for myself, sir."

Preacher couldn't help but wonder if every facet of this woman had turned as cold as her heart. He thought how much a waste that would be if it was true. "Payson? And this Tatro? Are they riding together?"

"No but Payson is very close to finding my brother. He was inquiring this morning as to the location of my ranch. He knows there is a connection between us, even if he is not yet sure where Hence actually is."

"And Tatro?"

"I've told you all I know about him."

"And me? How did you find out about me and this room?"

"From my foreman. In winter he works as a deputy to the county sheriff. He recognized you from an old wanted poster. I think he told the sheriff."

"Who is?"

"Bat Masterson."

"And the room?"

"There aren't many places in Dodge for a man like you, and I have many contacts. Many friends. It wasn't difficult."

Preacher eyed the envelope. "And you're willing to give me that money right now before I do anything? How do you know I won't just take it and ride out?"

"I don't. Not for certain. But I'm satisfied that you won't."

"Why?"

"Because you're the only other person in the world that I know about who wants Hence Lowman alive. I don't care about your reasons. That you do gives us a common goal. And you possess the skill. I'm willing to pay for that skill."

"Your brother? Is he alone?"

"Hence is never alone. He rides with two men. A half breed Ute who is mute and a scar faced gunman he calls Blinky. I don't know the man's name. I've never heard it. He has an affliction in his left eye and takes his name from that."

"And your sometimes lawman . . . foreman? Why doesn't he go after Hence? He surely knows the man is out there."

"No he doesn't. Only my maid knows and she's trustworthy."

"Would he try something if he did know?"

"Of course. But he'd die and Hence and his hired guns would ride out again. This is the first time I've had a chance at him for two years. The last try I made cost the man I hired his life and me my money. I don't want to miss again. Hence suspects me about the first time but he couldn't prove it and right now he needs me."

"So if somebody tries and misses, you're dead."

"Yes."

"And you're not scared of that?"

"I'm scared, Mister Preacher, but hate is a much stronger emotion than fear."

"And what's happened to blood being thicker than water, ma'am?"

"When I was 16 years old, Hence and two of his filthy friends raped me. They were drunk. I . . ." for the first time, the woman's voice wavered and she could not maintain eye contact with Preacher. She paused, coughed to clear her throat and regained her composure. "There was a child. My mother took her own life. My father ran Hence off the place and sent me away when it was time. The baby was given to adoption."

"Is there a barn on your place with a loft?" Ellen Caldwell was caught short by the seemingly disconnected question. She looked up, considered Preacher and then nodded. "On whatever pretense you can manage get your brother and his two friends into that barn tomorrow just after daylight. I'll be in the loft. I'll take it from there."

Preacher got to his feet, retrieved the envelope from the bed and slipped into his coat pocket. "That's all you want to know then?" she asked.

"If it wasn't you'd be the first to know."

"I'm . . ." she sighed, "relieved. I didn't know if you'd help me or not." She pointed at his coat. "Not even for ten thousand dollars. I'm . . . thankful that you believed me."

"Believing you has nothing to do with it," Preacher said, "except about Hence Lowman. He had to have somewhere to hide out. If not he wouldn't have come back here. I don't want to miss my chance at him and I won't. Even if you're lying about everything else."

"Then . . . then you don't believe me?"

"Let's just say that none of the rest of what you told me matters."

"It matters to me. Like your asking mattered to you. I told you the truth. Every word."

"You also told me you were a damned good actress, Mizz Caldwell." They locked wills and eyes in silent combat. Preacher won. Little could stand against his icy stare. Many a dead gunman was mute testimony to that fact.

"All right then, bounty killer. 'Til sun up." She strode to the door, jerked it open, passed half through it and then turned back. The woman in her sensed the timing was right for Preacher to soften. She smiled a hard, cold smile. "Five miles north. Two east," she said.

" 'Til sun up, Mizz Caldwell." The door slammed.

15

If Preacher had planned his moves against Hence Lowman they could not have been better than those fate had dropped in his lap. Lowman, supposedly set up and unsuspecting. And the Fourth of July to occupy the time and talents of the local lawmen. Preacher also reckoned that the two bounty hunters would be too preoccupied with the Dodge City crowds to be watching for Lowman.

Armed with the mare's leg, Preacher hoofed it the last mile to the Caldwell ranch. He had no trouble gaining the loft and he got comfortable to await sunup. He'd been there about an hour and the sky was light enough now to create silhouette visions of objects. The door at the front of the Caldwell home opened, a dog barked, a rooster decided that daylight had come at last. Ellen emerged, attired in riding clothes. Behind her, the Ute breed, followed by her brother. The door closed.

"Damn!" Preacher whispered the word and eyed the second floor windows. Where was the gunny called Blinky? The trio was fast approaching the barn. By the time they reached the entry door, Ellen Caldwell gave final proof of her sincerity.

"Isn't it a little risky? Sending Blinky to town that way?"

"I need eyes in town. Anybody shows up lookin' for me? Today's likely."

"I suppose," she said. She opened the door. The trio entered. Ellen found a coal oil lamp, lighted it, handed it to the breed and repeated the process on a second lamp which she kept. "The horse is in the end stall. Have your man bring him down to this one. You can examine him then."

Hence Lowman nudged the Ute, pointed and the Ute trotted away. As far as Preacher could discern, the Ute was unarmed save for Bowie knife. Hence Lowman wore a shoulder rig. Double straps with a pistol under each arm. Morgan Lake's style. Lowman was good. So Preacher had heard. As good as Lake? He doubted it, but he'd move accordingly if it came to that.

He'd picked a spot just over the entryway. He could see below through a gap in the boards. Ellen Caldwell set the lamp on the floor and said, "If all goes well at the bank tomorrow, big brother, you'll have your grubstake." As she spoke she eased her foot foward and kicked over the lamp. "Oh. Damn!"

"Smart lady," Preacher whispered to himself. "She's a smart lady." Lowman looked down, stepped one step forward and bent over. Preacher dropped quickly and quietly atop him, the butt of the .58 calibre landing first. Lowman grunted and went on down. Out cold. The Ute had just backed the big stallion out of its stall. He was mute but his ears were more than an equalizer. He swung the horse, slapped it, hung to its neck and the two of them were outside the barn in a flash.'

"Damn it!" Preacher couldn't get off a shot because the Indian stayed on the opposite side of

the big horse. "Tie him and gag him," Preacher
shouted. "Tight, ma'am." Preacher made the other
end of the barn and saw the horse galloping off to
the north—with no half breed.

The two by four caught the barrel of the carbine
and drove the butt into Preacher's gut. He grunted
and dropped the weapon. The breed swung again.
Preacher rolled to his left and avoided the blow.

The Indian tried again and the board struck the
ground. Preacher kicked out and the Ute was bare
handed for just a second. He was very fast with the
Bowie. Preacher cleared his own. He didn't want a
shot that would rouse anyone else, and most of the
hands were on roundup.

Sparks flew the first time that cold steel met cold
steel. The two men circled, warily—waiting—studying—nerve endings tingling in anticipation of the
opponent's next move. The Ute stepped in swinging
Preacher parried and thrust. The Ute dodged and
circled. They repeated the steps and the actions
several more times with no results.

Suddenly, the Ute drew his right arm down
straight and back and then forward. The Bowie left
his hand. Bowie knives were not made for throwing,
but at that proximity, they could be fatal. This one
wasn't, but it was deadly. The razor sharp edge
slashed a deep wound into the Tennessee gunman's
left arm just above the elbow. He winced and jerked
to his right reflexively. The big breed was all over
him. Preacher's own knife flew from his right hand
and he felt the air gushing from his lungs as he
landed on the middle of his back with the weight of
the breed atop him.

Preacher brought his right leg up, bent it and put
the knee into the groin of the Indian. The breed
groaned, Preacher struck with his right elbow on the

Indian's jaw and the man rolled off. Preacher rolled in the opposite direction. The Indian was fast. Damned fast. He recovered quickly and actually got to his feet before Preacher did. The fight mustn't go on. Preacher knew it. The Ute breed lunged. Preacher drew from the hip, fired and flew backwards when the big man's body hit him full in the chest.

Preacher lost the gun but the Ute had lost much of his fight. He'd been gun shot. He was big, muscular and still a threat. He was on his hands and knees, getting back to his feet, groaning and coughing blood. Preacher kicked him square in the face. The nose broke. The breed struggled. Preacher kicked him again and he went over onto his back. Preacher retrieved the .58 calibre. The breed was sitting up. Preacher turned the weapon end for end. The breed was in a crouch. Preacher stepped toward him, swinging the carbine like an axe. The breed lunged. The butt missed its mark.

The shotgun's first barrel nearly tore the breed's arm off. His body went down. He gritted his teeth. Spat out blood and started pushing himself up again. The second blast struck him full in the face. Preacher had the carbine end for end again and a shell in the chamber. Standing in the barn door's opening was a man he'd not seen before.

"Pete! Pete! Don't shoot again." Ellen had screamed the order without stopping to think that the shotgun was empty. The man was Pete Autry, her foreman. Ellen knelt down and double checked the tying job she'd done on her brother. Satisfied that he was secure, she jumped up and started running for the other end of the bar. Pete and Preacher eyed each other and then Pete's eyes shifted to the wound on Preacher's arm.

Ellen was about half the distance to the two men

when there was a shot. Pete Autry's eyes grew huge. His jaw dropped. The shotgun dropped and then Pete dropped. He was dead with a bullet through the back of his head. Ellen stumbled. Preacher couldn't discern the shot's origin. He dived for the cover of a stall shouting, "Get down woman. And stay down."

"Step into the open, bounty man. You an' the woman both. Do it now or I put a hole in the back of Lowman's head."

Preacher peered between the boards toward the other end of the barn. He could see nothing. No one. The shot had come from behind the foreman. Two of them. Who?"

"You can't see me, Preacher, but I'll give you to the count of three. Arms up to move where I can see you or Lowman dies. Makes no never mind to me I get paid either way."

Preacher stood up. So did Ellen Caldwell. Still, no one was visible. Preacher heard footsteps behind him. "They're up."

"Get his guns. Two pistols and that mare's leg he totes. Now Preacher, don't figure on your speed, not if you want Lowman to stay breathin'."

The man had talked enough to give the Widow Maker a chance to place the voice by location. The speaker was just to the right of the small entry door. There was, Preacher recalled, a piece of the wall's board missing. A man with a rifle could shove the barrel through it and level it on Hence Lowman's head. The thickness of wood between Preacher and the speaker was the outside wall of the barn and the opened door. Too, there was the distance, perhaps seventy-five yards. If he missed, Lowman was dead, and likely himself and Ellen Caldwell.

The .58 barked, Preacher dived, rolled, drew from

the vest and killed the man approaching from behind with a single shot between the eyes. A rifle discharged at the other end of the barn, but the bullet tore through the loft floor and straw was floating down from above. The .58 tore through the man's chest ripping out both lungs.

The intruder inside the barn proved to be Hence Lowman's own henchman, Blinky. Ten thousand dollars has turned the head of many a man. Preacher knelt by the body of the second man.

"Do you know him?" Ellen asked.

"I know who he isn't. He's not Harry Payson." Preacher got up. "I figure Tatro."

"My God! Hence's own man. And it nearly did us all in."

Some of the hands had gathered. Ellen spoke to them and most went back to their chores. She returned to Preacher. He'd gagged Hence and trussed him up on the back of a horse.

"I'm borrowing a horse," he said. "I'll leave her in town at the livery. I'll buy one there to transport Lowman back to Missouri."

"Take this one," Ellen said. "Don't ride back into Dodge. You've got Hence. You've got what we both wanted. Just get out. Ride out while you can. Promise you'll let me know where and when they're going to hang him. That's all. Just promise me that."

"You've got my word on it. I will feel a little easier if I don't have to visit Dodge City again for a spell."

"What if Tatro had friends?"

"Uhn uhn. Men like him ride alone."

"You mean mean like you. All of you. Don't you?"

Preacher glared at her. "Now it's done. I'm just another Tatro. With a little higher price. Jeezus! I've got a horse to fetch," he said.

Preacher rode Prince back through the barn, but as he emerged, his senses alerted him to something awry.

"Leave the man killer in the boot or the lady here will lose all that pretty, blonde hair."

"Hello, Payson." Preacher dismounted on the wrong side of the horse. He kept his hands well in front of him. "You slowed up that much so's you need a skirt for an edge?"

Payson shoved Ellen Caldwell out in front of him and then he stepped into the sunlight.

"I've always wondered if I could take you, Preacher. And I finally decided that I could, if the stakes were high enough."

"And they're high enough now?"

"Oh yeah. $20,000. So's I've heard." He chuckled. "That goddam Tatro ended up amountin' to somethin' after all. Hadn't been for him an' Lowman's own man I'd likely have ridden out here too late. I'd have to dog your trail all the way back to Missouri."

"Riding out here at all was the biggest mistake of your life, Payson. And worse."

Payson frowned. "Worse?"

"It was also your last mistake."

Harry Payson's skills with guns was nothing to be belittled. He'd faced down more than 18 men, three of them all at one time. None had cleared leather and Harry Payson had never been shot. He toted a short-barreled, customized Smith and Wesson. He wore it on his waist belt just to the right of his navel. The butt was cocked at an angle toward his right hand.

Harry's draw was clean and fast. The bullet from it ripped a quarter inch deep trough in J.D. Preacher's gunbelt on the right side. Preacher would think later that Payson was, perhaps, going for Preacher's hand, hoping finally to put the Tennessee shootist out of commission.

Such were the flaws of many gunmen. Overestimating their own skills or underestimating the skill of their opponent. The fact that Payson cleared leather and got off a shot at all attested to his speed. Preacher, his left arm paining him, hanging limp at his side, and his senses somewhat dulled by the loss of blood from the knife wound, perhaps was a fraction slower than usual. He was no less accurate.

At 40 feet, Preacher's shot struck Harry in the forehead, passed through his brain and ripped out a chunk of skull just behind his right ear. Four ranch hands, Ellen Caldwell's maid, and Ellen herself witnessed the shootout. None would ever forget the movements, intensity or accuracy displayed in that fraction of a second by the man in black from Tennessee. Upon holstering his gun in the vest holster, Preacher staggered. Only Ellen's intervention kept him from falling. She believed that he had been shot. In fact, the loss of blood was finally taking its toll.

Things might have gone a great deal differently had not Ellen Caldwell personally brought an evening meal to Preacher on his fourth night of recuperation. She had given strict orders to her hands to keep quiet about what had developed and the results. Preacher was going to leave the Caldwell spread on the fifth morning. Two events transpired. The first at the ranch itself. Ellen sat and visited while Preacher ate. When she leaned down in front of him to pick up the tray, he pulled her to him.

"All you have to do is tell me no," he said. His big, long-fingered hands closed around the resilient flesh of her breasts. She sucked in her breath. Their eyes met. This time there was no silent combat. Rather, desire and quiet approval. They kissed.

Preacher's arm was not fully healed, but it was sufficiently improved so that it did not prove to be a hindrance. Ellen disrobed. The body was all—and more—that Preacher had fantasized. She straddled him first, rubbing herself against his nakedness until she felt the hardness between her legs. She leaned forward and twisted a little from side to side so that Preacher might savor the taste of her nipples.

She threw back the sheet and slid her lithe body along his, remaining atop him. His hands found her breasts now, and their mouths locked in the growing passion each felt. Ellen raised slightly and moaned as Preacher moved and twisted until their bodies could be locked in place by his tool. She frowned in an instant of pain as Preacher's size probed deeper than any man had gone before him. Then, the pain gave way to the pleasure. A tightness, a fulfilled feeling of having a man inside her. A real man. A complete man.

Their initial gyrations gave way to a slower and more rhythmic movement, and they extracted maximum sensations from each other's efforts. Soon, the initial desire had passed through the tender, passionate stage and erupted into raw lust. They pumped, heaved, groaned and squealed as nerve endings tingled and body sweat lubricated flesh against the increasing friction.

The climax was the ultimate release of both outward passion and deeply hidden needs. Preacher's buttocks leaped from the bed, his long legs stiffened in an attempt to brace his body against the pulsating release of his semen. Ellen Caldwell's own body responded, reacting to a celibate state which had been in excess even of Preacher's. They moaned. Their bodies were so tightly pressed to each other, pain might have been felt under other circumstances.

The end came with a rush of air from lungs, a flood of body fluids, a total elimination of muscle tension. They collapsed. Sated. Sleepy.

In Dodge City Jack Richards was drunk. When the wrangler drank too much he became loud and swelled up on his own self worth. In this case, Richards had just related to a half interested crowd, details of a gunfight he'd witnessed. Or so he claimed. He told them he'd seen the fastest man with a six-gun he'd likely ever see. The man's name was Preacher. J. D. Preacher. The showdown, he said, had been on the Caldwell ranch.

Among the more interested individuals who listened to his tale was a dapper young gent who carried a cane, an ivory gripped Colt's, and wore a derby hat and a brass badge. His name was Bartholomew Masterson. He was the sheriff of Ford County, Kansas Territory. He was known to the locals simply as Bat.

Preacher's body alarm always served him well. It functioned no matter the state of his exhaustion during the previous night. On this morning, Preacher was up and ready to ride a full hour before sunup. He left Ellen Caldwell a note. He rode east and a little south. The sky turned gray as the sun shed its first light, even before it was visible above the horizon. Preacher was about five miles from the Caldwell spread. The riders appeared in the road ahead of him. One carried a shotgun.

"You'd be J. D. Preacher?"

"Who's asking?" Preacher reined up and quickly loosened the button on his coat.

"I'm Bat Masterson. Sheriff of Ford County. I believe you are holding a man wanted in my jurisdiction. I've come to pick him up." Masterson smiled, reached over and pushed the barrel of the shotgun the other man held, so that it was pointing downward. He looked back at Preacher. "No questions asked."

"If you're referring to Hence Lowman, Sheriff, you're wasting your own time. And mine. Lowman is no longer in your jurisdiction." Masterson frowned. He looked around. Preacher was trailing another mount behind him, but it was set up for a rider, not as a pack animal.

"Where is he?" Masterson's tone was less pleasant, the words a little louder. Preacher pointed beyond the two lawmen.

"Four miles due east in a line shack. Half of that distance is in Kiowa county, Sheriff. The last half, Kiowa county has no sheriff."

"I'm not as much in opposition to bounty hunters as some of my colleagues, Preacher, so under other circumstances, with another prisoner, I'd just ride off and wish you well. In Hence Lowman's case, I can't," Masterson rubbed his chin and looked down a moment. "Uh. . . let me restate that, sir, I won't do that."

"And I came to Kansas looking for Lowman. Not trouble with the law. Mebbe under other circumstances with another prisoner I'd do the riding off, Sheriff. Not this time."

"Well then," Masterson said, dismounting quickly, "I've a bargain to strike. The young gent there with the shotgun is my brother, Jim. Now I propose to disarm you, Mister J.D. Preacher, one way or another. If I fail, young Jim here will ride hell bent right back to Dodge City." Masterson turned to the youth. "That understood? Is it, Jim?"

"Yes, sir."

Masterson, spreading his feet apart, turned back. He was a little surprised to see the lanky bounty hunter had also dismounted and stepped several feet away from his horse. "Uh . . . now then . . . if I should do what I've come to do, Jim there will ride to the line shack and fetch the prisoner." Masterson smiled and tossed his cane away. "I'll promise also to see to it there are at least three mourners at your funeral and the appropriate words are spoken over your pine box. Now, then, do you wish to reconsider?"

Preacher said nothing. Masterson reached for the Colt and was already staring down the barrel of Preacher's vest pistol. "I stood against a man once," Preacher said, "when I felt the need to place my shot. It cost me a bullet in the shoulder. I said I'd never do it again, Sheriff. I meant it." Preacher eyed the younger Masterson who had moved his arm about three inches. "If you move that shotgun so much as the length of a gnat's leg one way or the other again, I'll kill you."

Jim Masterson let the weapon slip from his grip to the ground. Preacher turned back to the sheriff. "I've never pulled on a man I didn't kill 'til now. I want you to know two things Sheriff. I did it because I made a friend back in Dodge, a man who spoke well of you, John Holliday."

"Seems I owe Doc more than I'll likely be able to repay." Masterson released the grip of his Colt's. "You said you wanted me to know two things. I'd take a guess that the second one is the fact that you won't pull on another man and not kill him. Friend or no?"

"You'd guess right, Sheriff."

"You must have a mighty powerful reason for wanting Hence Lowman bad enough to stand against the law. I hope we break trail again sometime, Preacher. You're the most sudden man with a gun I've ever seen. Just like young Jack Richards told it."

Preacher mounted up, careful not to become too careless at the tone and seeming sincerity in Masterson's voice. "If we cut trail again, Sheriff, I'd find nothing sour about it, and I appreciate how you feel about your duty. If we were on opposite sides in this thing I might have done the same." Preacher holstered his gun, touched the brim of his hat, spurred Prince and rode away. The two Mastersons watched.

"God A'mighty, Bat, I never thought I'd see the man that could beat you to the draw."

Bat was still looking in the direction Preacher rode, thinking about the tall man in black and the speed with which he could handle his guns. Jim's voice broke the spell. Bat looked up at his younger brother.

"Doc Holliday could best me Jim. Wyatt Earp and I? Well, that might be a tossup. I'd have been pushed to outgun Harry Payson, but not a one of 'em would have kept me from clearing leather." Bat removed his derby and wiped the sweat from his forehead. He looked up at the sky. "It's going to be one hot son-of-a-bitch today. And I'm grateful to be around to complain about it. Goddam! Is that man fast!"

16

Hence Lowman died almost exactly as Ellen Caldwell had said he would. Screaming and begging until the hood stifled some of it. He dropped through the trap door of gallows number three on the 7th day of October, 1878. Judge Parker's hangman, George Maledon, pronounced him dead and Lowman's body was placed in a pine box and lowered into a six by six hole in an unmarked plot.

Ellen Caldwell was present. So was Amelia Lashtrow. Marshal James Buck rode up from Texarkana to be there. Morgan Lake—once again suffering the pain of his affliction—bundled up against a raw north wind and stood with his daughter to watch the event. The Reverend Mr. Poole was there—fully recovered from his near fatal gunshot wound. The little gun drummer turned newspaperman, Caleb Hornback looked on standing alongside Nathan Hale Breed. Most conspicuous by his absence was the Widow Maker, Jeremy James David Preacher.

The Parkers hosted a gathering of the principal characters who had, each for different reasons, wanted to see and end to Hence Lowman. They had, for better or worse, intimate or casual, become involved with one another over the preceding weeks. Now, the command bonds which had lured them were both gone. Lowman was dead, the victim of both the gun and the gavel. Preacher had vanished.

"I never thought he'd lie to me," Nate Breed said to the group. "He gave me his word that I'd have his story and I never doubted him."

"Did he say exactly when?" The question came from Jim Buck. Breed looked up.

"That's a damned sneaky thing to do. I assumed he meant . . ." Breed suddenly realized that no man could assume anything about J.D. Preacher. "Shit!"

"What does this do to my job?" Hornback asked. Several people in the room grinned. Breed did not.

"Shut up, Hornback. Goddam it. Just shut up!" Hornback did. "Anyone got even a hint where he might have gone?" Breed's eyes scanned the faces. None showed reaction until he reached Judge Isaac Parker's. The judge unfolded a paper and handed it to the newspaperman. It was a dodger.

"The biggest bounty in the Indian territory—after Lowman—was on that man. The Tall Texan. Bill Longley."

"You think Preacher went after him?"

"I did. But Longley was taken in by two Texas Rangers less than two weeks ago. He'll be here in my courtroom within a fortnight. He'll hang. Like Lowman."

"Why give me this then?"

"Because Longley was captured in company with a woman. Her name is Ashley Langehorne." Breed's eyes lit up.

"He was going to marry. You . . . you know about

his past, Judge?"

"More than I need. The woman is near ten years older than Preacher. She is the last of the ties to his youth. Rosamonde Langehorne's sister. She'd left Tennessee even before the war broke out. He didn't tell me for certain that finding her was his intent. But I'd wager it is."

"By God! So would I."

"Thompson was captured in Texas, and the woman, so I was told, immediately departed for the Indian territory. If I'm right, J. D. Preacher is either there or back up in Kansas. Ashley Lange-horne apparently has a lot of friends in both places and on both sides of the law."

Much of the discussion at that gathering centered on Preacher. Most gave their opinions and impressions of him freely. Breed wrote voraciously. Ellen Caldwell related Preacher's shootout with Harry Payson. And in those few months since Preacher's departure, Bat Masterson, Holliday and the Earp brothers had suddenly gained national attention. Masterson's own words about his single meeting with the Tennessee shootist only added spice to Breed's growing story. Most frustrating of all, however, was Breed's position. It was unchanged in ten years. The object of his story—of his seemingly obsessive sojourn—had vanished again.

It was, finally, Morgan Lake who offered perhaps the best advice to Nate Breed.

"You can dog that man's trail on information from the good judge. Or anyone else in this room. Or anyone else that has now met or ever will meet Preacher." Lake smiled and shook his head. "But your best chance of finding him doesn't come from such information."

"Sorry, Lake, but I don't understand. Without the information, just where in the hell do I start?"

"Preacher is past 30. He's killed more men than you know about and he hates notoriety. He's not looking for fame or bounty. Mebbe not even his past. He's looking or something far more important to him than anything else, and he's learned that he'll only find it when he can have solitude, be left alone, given time to ponder his life."

"For Christ's sake what is it, Lake? What is so damned important to J. D. Preacher that he cuts himself off from humanity to find it?"

Lake looked at each face, smiling. He ended on Nate Breed's face. "He's looking for J.D. Preacher, son."

Preacher drifted throughout the balance of the decade. In even those places where society and humanity were still rudimentary his presence was quickly harrahed. When that happened, Preacher moved on. By official count, he was forced to kill four men in 1879, and at least two others rumored. Throughout the last half of 1879, Nate Breed was certain Preacher had either left the country completely or been gunned down and buried in the countryside.

August of 1879 took Breed and Caleb Hornback from Denver back to the southwest. Preacher was reported to have faced down a trio of brothers in the mountain settlement of Raton, New Mexico Territory. By then, Breed was not alone in his interest or pursuit of stories of the life and times of the legendary shootist from Tennessee. A new pen appeared and under each story it signed:

Ned Buntline

In fact, Preacher had become more and more a man within himself. He found that he was less and less interested in hiring out his guns. He was far less tolerant of men who pushed him, either unknowingly or believing that he had softened, who hoped to gain a reputation by burying him. During this period, Preacher's legendary reputation stood him well.

On the evening of September 1, 1879, Preacher entered the Trail Dust Saloon in Selma, Texas. It was a Saturday. He knew it would be difficult to remain alone. Nonetheless, he finally found an isolated table, played some friendly poker with several changing faces and by nightfall sat alone, sipping Teton Jack and bothering no one.

"You. Dude." Preacher glanced up. "You got the only table left in the house. You're alone. I got two friends with me. I'll take the table." Preacher saw a trim man with a full beard, handsome, sharp features, thin, tight lips, curly, thick brown hair and pale blue eyes which seemed to pierce everything they observed. The man wore a single gun rig—cross draw on a hand tooled belt. The two men with him were both young, cocky and seemed anxious for Preacher to argue with their friend.

"You can ask me if I mind moving, friend," Preacher said, "and then be courteous enough to honor my answer. As to taking the table, you can't." Silence came upon the crowd almost as though they had suddenly been frozen. The only movement was that of the man. He was wearing a Prince Albert, single breasted frock coat. He pulled the left side of it back and tucked it into his belt.

"I said I'm taking the table. I'm not askin' anything, dude." Preacher didn't move. "Haven't seen you here before, so you're due some information. My name is Allison. Clay Allison. Tennessean by birth, Texan by choice. Best man in Texas with a gun. By proof."

"And the biggest loudmouth in this saloon by action," Preacher said. As he did so, he got to his feet. "I'm a fellow Tennessean by birth and by choice and this is my table. I don't choose to give it to you and your friends under any circumstances, and my name is Preacher."

"Preacher?" Allison's expression changed. "You be J. D. Preacher? The bounty hunter?"

"I am. And you're Clay Allison. The Texas gunny."

"Don't press me. I'm as good as you've ever seen."

"Not even close, Allison."

At a front table, near the door, a trio of men had heard every word. They were Tate, Reese, and Matt Poulen. They were the sons of Jeeter Poulen, one of the biggest ranch owners in the area. He had more than 50 men riding for him during the high summer. And few in Selma ever argued with his sons.

"Goddam," Tate said, "we could writ down our names fer good tonight. Right now. Hell. They're so wrapped up in one t'other, they'd never know what hit 'em."

"Count me out," Reese said. "I ain't tryin' to face down neither one o' them gents. Let alone both."

"Shut up," Matt ordered. He was the oldest. He'd also been the only man in Selma ever to wear a badge. That was a year back when there was a town council and somebody who had guts enough to stand up for law. Under Matt's badge—and a few crooked townsfolk—the plan was short-lived and the town was wide open again. Thing was, Matt still had the badge. He was as proud as any 27-year-old ever gets about anything. And he saw a great chance for the Poulen name, his own in particular to be ranked with the likes of Austin and Houston in Texas history.

"When I say," Matt told his brothers, "you get your guns out. When I say again, we stand and we shoot and if we have to we take out them other two with Allison. It'll be over before they know it happened." The brothers looked at one another. The temptation was too great—the opportunity too infrequent in Salem, Texas. It was now or never. "Get 'em out boys." They slipped pistols into their sweaty hands. Matt saw that the confrontation between Allison and Preacher had been reduced to a stare down. "Cock 'em," he whispered. They did. "When I say now, I mean now."

If there was any man in the place who'd not heard of Preacher, it might have been understood. Not a one had missed hearing about Clay Allison, and the young gunman was in a tight. He knew every man's eyes were upon him, the loud-mouthed, Texas gunfighter.

"Don't believe I care to shoot down a fellow Tennessean," Allison finally said, smiling. He stepped back, relaxed his stance, shrugged and added, "You mind if me'n muh friends sit a spell with you. Like to visit. Buy you a drink?"

"Now," Matt Poulen whispered. Three chairs scooted, three men leaped up, turned and fired. All three were firing into gray-blue gunsmoke. The man to Allison's left took a Poulen shot through the head. Allison killed Matt Poulen with a single shot and took a slug in the shoulder from Reese Poulen's gun. Both Reese and Tate managed only one shot. Preacher killed them both—standing sideways—making a narrower target—and firing from waist level with his hip pistol. Allison stumbled backwards and into a chair. Preacher waved his pistol and made a path toward the back of the saloon, backed through it to the rear door and said, "The table is yours, Allison. So is this town. The people in it and the state of Texas." Allison swung around, wincing and frowning at Preacher. "And if I ever cut trail with you again, I will kill you, Allison, on sight."

Nate Breed, this time leaving Hornback behind, arrived in Selma just two days after the confrontation. Ned Buntline was already there. They wrote their stories. They filed them. The headline blared out the facts as well as the legends. Preacher had faced down four men, including the notorious Texan gunfighter Clay Allison and left—for the first time— one victim only wounded. He did so, Buntline wrote, because of the unwritten code of honor among shootists.

Preacher read the account, cursed it and headed for the isolation of the southwest territories. He lingered nowhere for very long. He grew a full beard for the first time in his life. He hunted down a few small time criminals to supplement a meager income from small stakes gambling. He drifted for six long and lonely months.

On the fifteenth day of February, just 21 days shy of Preacher's thirty-fourth birthday, he rode out of the Dragon Mountains and into the nearly founded mining settlement of Tombstone, Arizona Territory. He believed it to be, at last, a town and a country which might swallow up the legends of J.D. Preacher.

He found the town to his liking, his beard hiding his identity and his gambling skills a needed trade. Just two days after his arrival, Preacher was hired to deal high stakes poker at Tombstone's newest and finest nitery—the Alhambra.

Tombstone had been little more than a mining camp only a year before. Now, it was growing by leaps and bounds with a town council, a newspaper and an honest to God courthouse. Preacher heard that there was soon to be a gavel and the town council had approved money for gun—legal—with an accompanying badge.

Law and order—early on before the drifters and hotheads came in—and J.D. Preacher would not find it necessary to ride with one or face the other. Many of the most notorious gunmen were gone. What could happen in the isolation of Tombstone, Arizona Territory that would attract the likes of Nate Breed or Ned Buntline? Preacher decided, contentedly, that nothing could.

Preacher became a peaceful gambler, putting aside at least his involvement with the gavel and the gun.

THE LAST GUNFIGHT

Dedicated with Love to
Mr. B. R. McElwain
of
St. Regis, Montana

My Dad

Prologue

J. D. Preacher blinked once and then opened his eyes. It was daylight. He took a deep breath and swung his legs from beneath the covers. He crimped his toes and dug them into the deep shag carpet. He stood up and walked to the window. It was a fine, blue sky day. The kind a man should appreciate. Preacher didn't.

He shaved himself . . . a close shave . . . carefully trimming handlebar moustache and the sideburns. He doused his face and neck with toilet water. He walked to the closet and took out the black suit, a new, white linen shirt and black string tie. He dressed.

Preacher packed the rest of his personal belongings. He wanted no delay after his job was done. He'd made meticulous and very discreet arrangements for transport once his task was accomplished.

He made a final check of his weaponry. The customized, matching pistols gleamed as he holstered them. One in a vest holster just below his left armpit, the other on his right hip. He'd even cleaned the big Bowie knife he carried in a special sheath which reposed just below his right armpit.

Preacher took a last look around the room. Then he put on the black Prince Albert coat. He topped everything with a brand new, flat crowned, black hat. He eyed himself in the mirror and grimaced at the thought of his mission. He'd faced none in his entire life for whom he held more dread.

Preacher checked out of the hotel and stepped into the street. He looked both ways and then turned to his right. As he walked, he remembered. He remembered back to his home, to the big house at Bradburn Hill in Tennessee. He remembered what he'd found there when he returned from the war . . . and that what he'd found had changed the course of his life.

He stopped. Ahead just one more block was the building. In a few minutes, he would enter it and, for the first time in his life, violate the law by which he'd lived. Preacher's law!

Preacher found Nathan Hale Breed in the restaurant of the Mark Hopkins Hotel. Breed didn't look that much older. Preacher wondered if he did. After all, when the two men had first cut trail, Preacher was barely into his twenties. Though he'd never known, he'd reckoned Breed to be no more than a year or two younger than himself.

Now, here in San Francisco, Preacher was just past sixty. Few would have guessed it. He'd put on a little weight and there were streaks of gray in the chestnut hair. As he'd eyed Breed, the reporter now eyed him. Breed gestured to the gunman and Preacher sat. Neither had spoken a word. Both were remembering.

Preacher had once promised Breed an exclusive story. The real story, Breed liked to call it, of the most famous shootist in the West, the Widow Maker . . . Jeremy James David Preacher. The promise had not been kept because Preacher had chosen not to commit to a time and a place. Now he had, and Breed would finally get the story.

"What brings you to San Francisco, Preacher?" Nate Breed asked.

Preacher considered Breed and then motioned toward the notebook Breed was holding. "You think that'll be big enough?"

Nate smiled. "I've got a case of them in my room."

Preacher's own smile faded. "San Francisco is now, today, the present. I was given to understand you wanted the past."

"I want your story, Preacher, all of it." Breed leaned back. "But I'll leave it to you where you want to begin."

"When did I last promise you a story? "

Nate Breed pondered the question and then said, "Eight-one. It was the Fall of Eighteen and Eighty-one and we were stitting in the dining room of the Oriental Saloon in Tombstone, Arizona."

"Yeah," Preacher said. "I recollect it now."

Preacher looked at the bottle of Teton Jack Breed had ordered. He poured a healthy shot and downed it. "Eighteen Eighty-one." Preacher leaned back. "That seems a likely place to start," he said.

1

Tombstone, Arizona territory was in its infancy when J. D. Preacher first saw it in the Fall of 1879. Like any infant, it was growing like a weed. Gold and silver finds in the nearby Dragoon mountain range had planted the seed of life in the desert's womb and now all make and manner of humanity came to nurture the infant. Preacher, however, was seeking something of far more value to him than riches. He wanted anonymity.

Jeremy Preacher was thirty-three years old and the most renowned shootist on the frontier. Some said he'd killed a man for every year of his life, but then they said that about damned near every man who made his way with a gun. Preacher considered the question academic in any event. He was a bounty hunter and he was sick of the dime novel fame. Each new story produced one or two more young gunmen who wanted to test their mettle and their skill against the tall Tennessean in the mourning clothes, the man the eastern press had dubbed the Widow Maker.

Preacher had let his handlebar moustache grow into a full beard. Behind that beard, using the name Jeremy David, Preacher turned to his second trade, gambling. In Tombstone, he would be considered a tinhorn but if he ran an honest game and kept to himself, he might find some of the isolation he sought.

There was ample justification for enterprising newspaper reporters to hound Preacher. He'd ridden twice with the legendary General Custer, he had been one of only three or four men who were on a first name basis with the late James Butler Hickok and his story had surfaced when he'd hunted down and killed the carpet baggers who had taken from him his fiance, his family and his home. Among the lot was his own brother.

Such stories were eagerly sought in the east and one of the most prolific seekers was a young man named Nathan Hale Breed.

Young Breed had been assigned to get Preacher's story back in Sixty-six and what started as just another assignment had now become an obsession. Breed had cut trail with Preacher on more than one occasion but the last time, so Breed believed, would bring him the success he sought. Preacher struck a deal. The gunman needed information to which Breed had access. In short, Preacher needed Breed's help and Preacher promised his exclusive story to the young reporter in exchange for that help. Preacher got the help but took advantage of a minor point in their bargain. Preacher didn't say *when* Breed would get the story.

Preacher set up housekeeping in a sleeping room over the Alhambra Saloon, the most lavish of more than a score of such establishments which dotted Allen Street. The Alhambra's staff was complete however, and so Preacher took employment just across the street at the Eagle Brewery.

The bounty man had become somewhat of a fixture in the town's nightlife and had gained no small measure of respect as Jeremy David. He felt, at last, somewhat free of the shackles of his past. The first event to disturb his serenity showed up in Tombstone just three months after his own arrival. The event was the arrival of a man named John Clum and the subsequent opening of Clum's business . . . Tombstone's first newspaper, *The Epitaph.*

John Clum was an intellectual, possessed of a dry wit and a talent for turning a phrase. While Clum did seek out the most likely sources of local news, including the morose appearing poker dealer at the Eagle Brewery, Preacher was relieved to find that Clum had no additional interest in him. Mostly, Clum wanted Preacher and others like him to keep Clum informed about the arrival in Tombstone of anyone of prominence.

Tombstone, like most boom towns, attracted both the good and the bad elements of society. Preacher had seen it before and he knew trouble rode with many of the new arrivals. Making matters worse at the outset was the fact that Tombstone had no law. By the end of Seventy-nine, it was obvious some would be needed and the town council made their appointment.

The new city marshal was a stocky, balding man

with a better than average skill with his weapons. His name was Joseph O'Rourke and his Irish heritage was as obvious as his bulbous nose and pudgy, red cheeks. They were the marks of O'Rourke's love of Irish whiskey.

No one could fault O'Rourke, however, for the dedication he displayed for his job. He added to his popularity when, just two days after his own appointment, he named a deputy. He selected a young apprentice blacksmith named Billy Meeker. Meeker had won two shooting contests in Tombstone and everyone knew and liked him.

"Mornin', Mister David."

Preacher nodded at the Eagle's day barkeep, Ben Koop.

"You're in a mite early today, aren't you?"

"A little," Preacher said, "got a package to go out on the stage."

"Care for some coffee while you're waitin'?"

"I do Ben, thanks."

Ben Koop had never known a gambling man who drank nothing but coffee, day and night. In fact, the Tennesse gunman Koop knew as poker dealer Jeremy David, really didn't drink much else. What he did drink, however, had become almost as much a trademark for him as his gun skills. It was a fine New Orleans liquor known as Teton Jack. Preacher kept a flask of it in his room but never drank it openly for fear of someone connecting him to it.

"I heard the stage was running late," Preacher said.

Ben Koop was wiping glasses. He stopped, leaned over the bar to get closer to Preacher and spoke in a hushed tone, as though he was sharing some critical confidence. "I heard tell it took a detour to pick up some fine lady." Koop grinned. "I hope the boss has hired us a dancin' girl or a singer mebbe, like Lily Langtry."

Preacher grinned and then glanced up at the big clock. He finished his coffee in a single swallow, picked up his package and walked out. It was the tenth day of December and a cold, biting north wind was whipping down from the Dragoons. Preacher hurried along.

Preacher had bowed his head against the bite of the wind and he didn't look up until he heard the stage pulling in. When he did hear it, he picked up his pace. He was about half a block away when the first passengers stepped out of the Concord coach. Preacher stopped dead in his tracks.

Three men had exited the coach, all dressed similarly to Preacher . . . black, broadcloth suits, white shirts and string ties. They had both the appearance and the actions of gentlemen. The tallest of the trio stood by the coach door and helped a lady out, then a second. These would prove to be the wives of two of the men. The third lady was obviously the one to whom Ben Koop had made reference.

Preacher was almost certain he knew at least one of the men but this was neither the time nor the place to confirm it. He beat a hasty retreat to his room and there, out of the window, did indeed confirm his suspicions. The first of the men he'd seen was a man he'd met up Kansas way. A sometimes lawman named Wyatt Earp.

Preacher tried to slip out the back way but he was too late. The Earps were in the lobby. Wyatt spotted Preacher and gave him the studied look one man gives another when he senses something familiar. Wyatt asked the desk clerk, "Do you know that gent?"

"Yessir. That was Mister David, poker dealer at the Eagle."

Wyatt frowned in a moment of recollection. "David?"

"You know 'im, Wyatt?" Jim Earp asked his brother.

"Not certain. Seems more'n a little familiar to me." Wyatt Earp looked again, shook his head and added, "Guess not. Can't recollect where I might have cut his trail."

"Prob'ly worth watchin'," Jim said. "You left more'n one back in Kansas who'd like as not back-shoot you if they got the chance."

"I'll just wander over and sit a spell with him this evening," Wyatt said. "If I know him, it'll come to me then."

Nothing as honorable as keeping the peace had motivated the Earp boys to come some 750 miles to settle in Tombstone. They smelled money. Silver could be found in abundance along the two mountain ranges which bounded the plateau upon which Tombstone rested. The Dragoon range had already been assaulted by half a thousand prospectors. Those finding nothing were now violating the previous sanctity of the Whetstone range. In the case of the Earps, however, no such back breaking pursuits were planned. There was a better and much easier way to separate silver from its source. In the Earp's case, the source would be the miners who'd already dug it from the ground.

The trio planned a saloon of their own, or at worst,

gainful employment in an already established money maker. Gambling, liquor and women were their inventory. They were their own security.

2

"Evenin', Mister David."

Preacher looked up and nodded at one of his regulars, Justin Hildebrand. He was, at least for the moment, Tombstone's only banker.

"Take a chair," Preacher said, "couple of our Tuesday night regulars will be a little late, and Hendricks won't be in at all. I was about to round up a substitute."

Hildebrand nodded and sat down.

Preacher excused himself but he'd gone only a few steps when a voice stopped him. "You there, dealer."

Preacher turned.

"Heard you had an empty chair at your table this evening. Mind if I take it?" Preacher was looking square into the face of Wyatt Earp.

"Word travels fast. I only found out I'd have an empty a few minutes ago."

"I knew it a little ahead of you, dealer. I arranged it."

"Why? There's plenty of poker in Tombstone."

"I was told you run an honest game. I'm a gambler, not a damned fool."

"You're welcome, Mister—"

"Earp. Wyatt Earp."

"Mister Earp," Preacher said, gesturing toward the table. Wyatt approached the tall gunman, eyeing each and every wrinkle in Preacher's clothing. He extended his hand. Preacher gripped it.

"I've got a feeling I know you," Wyatt said.

"David . . . Jeremy David." Preacher stepped back, motioning again toward the table, "Now you do," he said.

By the end of the evening, Wyatt Earp had accomplished what it had taken Preacher near a week to do when he'd first arrived. Wyatt had talked the saloon's owner into a Faro game which he, Wyatt, would run. He also left Preacher's table some three-hundred dollars better off than when he'd taken his seat.

"I'd like to buy you a drink, Mister David," Wyatt said.

Preacher's first thought was to reject the offer. Instinct, however, warned Preacher not to treat Wyatt as he might treat others. Wyatt ordered a whiskey and looked at Preacher. "He knows what I drink," Preacher said. When the barkeep returned, Wyatt frowned.

"Coffee, Mister David? After all that you drank earlier?"

"It's all I ever drink."

"To your good health then sir," Wyatt said. He downed his drink and declined the barkeep's offer of a refill. A few minutes later, Jim and Virgil Earp joined their brother. Wyatt introduced them to

Preacher . . . Mister David . . . and bought another round. This time, Preacher did decline. "You mind if we all repair to your table, Mister David?"

"Please do," Preacher answered, "but you'll have to excuse me, gentlemen. It's been a long day."

The trio of brothers watched Mister David take his leave. Jim Earp said, "Well, did you remember 'im, Wyatt?"

"No," Wyatt replied, still pondering the tall man in the Prince Albert coat. "But I did find out who he isn't."

Virgil Earp looked quizzical. "What?"

"He's no damned poker dealer. There's more to the man than that and it's still familiar."

"Then we'd best keep an eye on him."

Wyatt nodded.

Virgin went on. "Got a cable from Morgan."

Wyatt looked up and smiled. "He comin' down?"

Virgin nodded.

"Good! It'll be the first time all four of us been together in a brand new town. By God I've got a hunch we're going to make our mark here. Yes sir. Tombstone, Arizona won't likely forget the Earp brothers."

The trio drank to Wyatt's pronouncement.

Preacher was drinking again too and this time it wasn't Ben Koop's coffee. He had downed a generous portion of Teton Jack when a knock sounded at his door. Preacher's vest pistol was at the ready before the echo died. "Yeah?"

"It's Allie," came the reply.

Preacher holstered his gun and opened the door. Allie often frequented Preacher's room. She too worked at the Eagle and Preacher had more or less let it be known that she was his company. She'd come to Tombstone with a young and ambitious man whose grubstake soon ran out. So did he.

"I just didn't want to be alone tonight," she said.

Allie was Alexander Howard. She was barely twenty, physically endowed beyond her years and very naive. Once, only briefly, Preacher had felt some remorse about bedding her. It passed.

Preacher hadn't realized his own feelings until Allie showed up. He stepped back. "I don't either," he said.

Braced with some Teton Jack, which loosened both Allie's tongue and her corset ties, she related her reason for the late night visit. "Josh Hazelton came in tonight. He got drunk and he," she paused and looked down. Preacher had learned to wait her out. She took a deep breath, "He made threats. You know, like before." Preacher nodded.

Josh Hazelton had been in partnership with Allie's man. They hit a small strike but when it petered out, Allie's husband, Clete Howard, knew he was in trouble. He'd borrowed and gambled heavily and one of the men to whom he owed the most was Josh. Clete ran and Josh vowed to collect his pound of flesh, literally, from Clete's leavings; namely, Allie.

"If he bothers you tomorrow," Preacher said, "let me know."

Allie's visits were rarely marked by changes in pattern. She was fearful of something or someone, sought out Preacher, told her story, got her reassurance and then paid her debt. She stripped as methodically as she spoke. Preacher, however, had no complaints.

Allie Howard's breasts were almost perfectly round and as firm as human flesh could ever be.

Preacher thought often of a set of pliant cannon balls. They were tipped with perpetually firm buds. Preacher always gave them plenty of his attention.

He began this meeting by licking at one and then the other until Allie's breath was coming in short gasps. She had a very limited staying capacity but Preacher's expertise prevailed. He knew precisely how far to go and for how long. The result was a prolonged enhancement of the act.

Preacher finally shifted his position, lowering himself until he could circle her navel with his tongue. His hands were still busying themselves with Allie's breasts and she was rolling her head back and forth, moaning and lost in her pleasure.

As he lowered himself still further, Allie shifted her limbs in accordance with what she knew was coming. It somewhat dulled the edge for Preacher. Too predictible, he thought. Still, Tombstone's female offerings were, at best, questionable and he didn't intend to starve himself in town as he was forced to do on the trail.

Allie moaned still louder when Preacher's tongue struck home. The little pink bud between her legs hardened, grew moist and caused sensations to spread through Allie's body which she had never known with Clete.

Allie climaxed. It was a sudden convulsion of pleasure which caught even Preacher off guard. Admittedly, he didn't have his mind totally on his work. It had never happened before and Allie seemed to take it as a sign of something very special.

She squealed with delight and locked her legs around his neck. "Oh my God . . . that was . . . it was," she sucked in her breath, "fantastic!"

Preacher freed himself from her unintended grip and assumed their love making was at an end. Allie Howard, besides having reduced staying power, also lacked the repetitive powers of her contemporaries at the Eagle Brewery. On this night, J.D. Preacher was in for more than one surprise.

He rolled off of her and onto his back. Allie was already up but she turned suddenly and literally leaped atop him. He grunted at the unexpected assault. Allie's hands went to work and she massaged his aching muscles and stroked at the most sensitive spots on Preacher's bare flesh. She seemed different, and she seemed bent on giving as much as she had received.

Allie had never used her mouth on Preacher. He had never pushed her to and had even given up hinting at it. Now, she crouched over him in a tight little ball and lowered herself until she could take him into her mouth. Preacher had known only a handful of women who could accommodate him in the missionary sex act, and even fewer who could give him oral pleasure. He was a man of considerable size.

Preacher was shocked. He could feel her mouth, her tongue, even her lips. Her teeth scraped along the base of his shaft and the moisture from her actions wet his pubic hair. Allie had taken him completely into her mouth. Others, he recalled, had tried. He usually heard them gagging and then their efforts ceased. Allie did not cease. Twice she seemed to sense that Preacher's staying limit had been reached and she stopped. He moaned and she smiled to herself, knowing the teasing pleasure she was administering. Little Allie Baines Howard had suddenly found herself with a very special talent and a very special power. A power over men.

Preacher could not recall, when the night was finally over, if he had ever reached so complete a release from a strictly oral encounter. He looked at Allie and he shook his head in disbelief. Asleep, she appeared completely innocent and barely more than a school girl. He found himself still perspiring with the mere memory of what she'd done. He promised himself it wouldn't be the last time.

3

John Holliday cursed as he wiped the sputum from his chin. The coughing spell had driven invisible, hot knife blades into his lungs and chest. His face was pale and emaciated. Now he stood by the window of his room and stared out at the big fluffy snowflakes. He shook his head, turned around and resumed his packing. The door opened and John Holliday looked up.

"Goddam Doc, I heard you we're pullin' out but I didn't believe it." Bat Masterson came in and shut the door behind him. "Christ Doc, you look like hell."

Doc Holliday gestured toward the outside by jabbing his thumb into the air, just over his right shoulder. "It's these goddamn Kansas winters."

Bat Masterson turned a chair around and sat down. He shoved the ever present bowler hat back on his head. "First Wyatt and the boys, now you. Won't be the same in Dodge without you."

"Take off that damned tin star and ride with me,"

Doc said.

"I'd like nothin' more, Doc, but I can't."

"Bull! You think these damn sod busters care about you? You'll get no fancier hole up on boot hill than them that you send up there."

"I've got an offer to take on a U.S. Marshal's job."

Doc shook his head and grinned.

"It could lead to other things, Doc."

Doc jammed his fist into the contents of the carpetbag to condense them still further. He pulled the top together, buckled it and then he looked at Bat Masterson. "Sure it could," he said. "Like mebbe gettin' shot out there on the street by a professional instead o' by some drunk citizen hero with a shotgun."

"You're a cynical s.o.b.," Masterson said.

"Just keep an eye on your backside," Doc said, "and hope you don't have to face many gents like that bounty hunter from Tennessee."

Bat winced. "Preacher?"

Doc nodded.

"You don't allow a man much forgetting, do you Doc?"

"It's just hard for me to picture a man so fast that he keeps you from clearin' leather." Doc shook his head. "I know you wouldn't lie about a thing like that but I could never figure out why you said anything at all."

"Better I tell it than some deputy that would make it worse than it was."

"Hell Bat, how much worse could it get?" Doc frowned. "He really beat you that bad?"

Bat nodded. "Clean, Doc. I never saw a man draw a gun that fast in my life. Not Frank Leslie, not you, not even Hickok."

"Well, I don't think you'll have to reckon with him again. Seems Mister J. D. Preacher just vanished. Prob'ly bushwhacked."

"I don't think so, Doc," Bat said, thoughtfully. "That gent kind of put me in mind of Hickok. Heard a hundred times how he'd been tucked under but never believed a damned one of 'em 'til they came up with a body."

"Yeah, well mebbe so. Anyway, I wouldn't mind cuttin' trail with Preacher again. Got to where I kind of liked him. Seemed a man who knew where he was goin' and didn't hold much with how to get there except his own way."

Bat Masterson walked to the window, looked out and shook his head. It was snowing even harder. "I'll have to admit that where you're going looks pretty inviting right about now but you sure picked lousy weather for traveling."

"Who the hell wants to leave when the sun is shining?"

Bat Masterson laughed.

The two men spent a final evening together, drinking, talking of times past and pondering on the maybes of tomorrow. The next day, Dr. John Holliday quit Dodge City, Kansas, for the warm climes of Cochise county, Arizona territory.

1880 began in Tombstone with a false promise. No one died on New Year's Day. The respite was brief and John Clum so noted it.

Tombstone! The town that serves up dead men for breakfast.

Irish Joe O'Rourke and Billy Meeker did their best. Most of the time, however, they were nowhere near a shooting. Even when there were witnesses most were terrified to speak up. While some of the shootings were simply the result of the sad foolishness of some drunken drover, there was a new breed of men infiltrating the town. Men who did not take kindly to orders or law or other men who stood for such things.

The peaceful citizens of Tombstone were growing more and more fearful and the town council was both disgusted and frustrated. They wanted O'Rourke out but there was no one to replace him. Billy Meeker simply could not stand up to the real troublemakers in town.

Along with the less desirable elements, culture was also making its appearance right about then. Billy and Lottie Hutchinson opened the Bird Cage Theatre. The opening night ceremonies verified Tombstone's growing reputation as the rowdiest, bawdiest and roughest newcomer to the expansion of the west. The night also revealed to all the answer to a perplexing mystery. The identity of the beautiful woman who'd arrived on the same day as the Earp brothers.

They came from as far away as Phoenix and Flagstaff to see her. She was Shentara Yazibel Muhasrana, Queen of the Nile, and soon to gain national fame as Fatima. Her specialty? The belly dance. On the opening night, the town council tried first to ban Fatima. When that failed, they tried to keep men from toting guns. Futile!

Inside the Bird Cage, when Fatima refused to do a sixth encore, the plush, red velvet imported and very expensive stage curtain became quickly dappled. The next day, through her tears, Lottie Hutchinson counted more than one hundred bullet holes.

In a shrewd business move, another establishment also opened its doors for the first time that night. No longer would the Eagle Brewery and the Alhambra dominate Tombstone's night life. The Oriental opened its batwing doors and advertised nothing more plush, elegant, expensive or entertaining anywhere west of New Orleans. Many men made the change at once, among them James Earp who became the night barkeep and Wyatt who took the job as the Oriental's floor manager and week night faro shill.

It was an exceptionally warm evening in February when Preacher closed down his poker game for the night and decided to visit the Oriental.

He was about midway between the two saloons when he heard the guttural brogue of Marshal O'Rourke. "You boys hold fast or I cut loose with this scattergun. Mind you now, no foolishness."

Preacher could see O'Rourke in the middle of the street and he was facing three men on horseback. A moment later, Deputy Billy Meeker emerged from the Oriental and looked over the situation. At the same moment, a fourth man on a horse appeared in the alleyway just behind Marshal O'Rourke.

Luke Tybold ran up beside Preacher, shouting, "Them fellas robbed us, took money, guns, ammunition. They robbed us." Preacher whirled. He'd already anticipated what was going to take place.

"Get down, Luke."

The man behind the marshal drew, fired and killed Irish Joe O'Rourke with a single shot to the back of the head. Billy Meeker now spotted the fourth man and drew and fired at him but the discharge of O'Rourke's shotgun had spooked the man's horse and it reared, Billy's bullet tore into the animal's neck and the rider was thrown to the street.

Behind Billy, even as the young Deputy moved toward the shadows of the building's corner, Wyatt and Virgil Earp emerged. The other three men now had their horses under control and simply opted to ride over anyone in their path. Firing toward the Oriental, they spurred their horses and charged toward Luke Tybold and Preacher. The fourth man, hidden from Preacher's view, now stepped into it and fired at Billy Meeker. He didn't miss. Preacher, having dropped to his knees in order to pull Luke Tybold down, now got to his feet.

"Watch yourself," Wyatt Earp shouted. He didn't know to whom he'd shouted and there was no time to find out. Wyatt and Virgil drew and fired two shots each at the galloping horsemen. All three were killed. The fourth man had a bead on Preacher as Wyatt turned again. Preacher's right arm moved in a shadowy blur and the man died.

Silence fell again over Allen Street and Virgil Earp was still staring toward the tall man in the black suit who stood in the middle of the street, his eyes scanning the buildings on both sides.

"Jesus Christ," Virgil said to Wyatt, "did you see that?"

Wyatt nodded. "I saw it Virg, and it jarred my recollection."

Luke Tybold got to his feet with Preacher's help and Preacher told him to fetch both the doctor and the head of the town council. As Luke hurried away, Wyatt approached. Preacher turned to face him.

"Evening, Mister Preacher," Wyatt said, calmly.

"No mister to it," Preacher replied, "and now that you know, I'd appreciate it if you'd keep it to yourself."

"Be glad to," Wyatt said, "but I don't hardly figure it'll make much difference." He gestured with a nod of his head toward the Oriental. "Must have been twenty or more men at the windows."

Preacher looked up. Wyatt Earp was right. "To hell with it," he said, rubbing his face, "this damned beard will be too hot this summer anyway."

"Then," Wyatt Earp said, pausing just a moment, "Preacher, I'd like to buy you a drink at the new Oriental saloon. I think we've got fresh coffee brewing."

Preacher eyed Earp and then shook his head. "No thanks, Earp."

Wyatt frowned.

"I'm sick of coffee. You got any Teton Jack?"

Wyatt laughed.

Inside the Oriental, Wyatt took Preacher back to the office and they were joined by Virgil. Wyatt made the formal introduction.

"You're the most sudden gambler with a gun I've ever seen," Virgin said. "And if I recollect, you're the fella Bat Masterson talked about."

Preacher glanced up at Virgil and said, "The town council is going to want somebody out of that fracas to put on a badge. I'm telling you boys, I'm not their man, and I won't wear one for you if you take the job."

"What makes you think we'd want it?"

"Call it opportunity," Preacher said.

Virgil Earp eyed his brother and then looked back at Preacher. "You got a quarrel with the law? Sure as hell didn't look like it out there on Allen Street a few minutes ago but I'll ask anyway."

"You wearing a badge now, are you?"

The question surprised Virgil and he shook his head.

"Then it's none of your business."

"I'll tell you something, Preacher, I may very well put on that badge. Then it *would* be my business, wouldn't it?"

"It would and you could get your answer by going through your dodgers. You find me in any of them, let me know."

Virgil had a short temper and he could see Wyatt wanted to talk to Preacher to he just turned and stalked out.

"Virg is not a man to make an enemy out of," Wyatt said.

"I appreciate the warning," Preacher replied.

James Earp entered the office with a bottle of Teton Jack and two glasses.

"Jim," Wyatt said, "this gent is J.D. Preacher."

"Glad to meet you, Preacher. Heard stories about you." James Earp was considerably different from Virgil. Really different from all three of the others. He'd inherited more of his mother's traits. He poured three drinks. "If they're all true," he said, smiling, "I figure you're about the best preserved gent I've ever met. I'd make you about a hundred years old now." He held up the whiskey and eyed it. "This the stuff that does it for you?"

Preacher couldn't help but smile. "What does it for me are several over active imaginations back east somewhere."

Jim Earp feigned a look of disappointment. "Damn," he said, "I was hoping it was the whiskey."

The three of them had one drink and James excused himself. Wyatt poured himself and Preacher another.

"I like your brother," Preacher said.

Wyatt grinned. "I won't ask you which one you mean?"

Preacher grinned. "I was a little hard on Virgil but I sensed what might happen and I don't want any part of it. I had to stop it before it began. Tell 'im that for me, will you?"

"No," Wyatt said. "You're no lawman, I'm no messenger."

Indeed, Preacher's predictions proved valid. The town council questioned numerous witnesses to the affair and then voted, unanimously, to appoint Virgil Earp as City Marshal. Virg wasted no time in appointing a deputy, brother Wyatt. A complaint was filed almost at once by John Clum. He charged nepotism and voiced his concerns over Wyatt's demand to be allowed to continue his dealing job at the Oriental while wearing a badge. The town council overruled Clum, yielding instead to the pressures of the citizen's committee.

In mid March, the Earl family's strengths in Tombstone were further enhanced with the arrival of the fourth brother. He was hot tempered, fast gunned and totally devoted to Wyatt. Morgan Earp pinned on a badge the very morning following his arrival.

Shortly after Morgan's arrival, Wyatt held a meeting with his brothers.

"It won't be long before this town has to grow up. We could be out when that happens, unless we do something now."

"You got a plan, big brother?"

"I have. The territorial governor will be here on the Fourth of July. I know him and he knows about us and Dodge. I've already sent a letter to Bat to put in a good word for us, too. John Fremont has nothin' but the highest regard for Bat Masterson."

"Yeah Wyatt, so all that happens. What's it do for us?"

"I'm going to ask Fremont to appoint me the U.S. territorial Marshal for a new district, this one." Wyatt was smiling. "I'll ask him to allow me one deputy and to grant me authority over all other law officers within the district."

"Hell Wyatt, that'd be a perfect set up but I've heard talk around town about local elections to name a sheriff."

"So have I, Virg," Wyatt smiled again. "How about little brother Morgan running for the office?"

The Earp plan went well on the whole but fell short of Wyatt's most ambitious goal, an Earp wearing every tin star in the southern half of Arizona territory. Indeed, Fremont jumped at the chance to make Wyatt a U.S. Marshal and Wyatt promptly named Virgil his deputy. Morgan's role proved more difficult.

John Clum was all the more dubious about the Earps' ambitions and the town council finally set a date for an election. Clum all but ran his own candidate, a young, ambitious, Christian family man by the name of Johnny Behan. The Earps had no newspaper, indeed, not even a press on which to print posters, unless they wanted to do business with Clum. They didn't. They worked the town personally and spent no small sum on liquor. In the final count, Johnny Behan was elected by a two to one margin.

"Sorry," Morgan said to Wyatt, "the people liked Behan."

"They can have him, but not without another Earp."

On that note of anger, Wyatt counseled with his family members and decided they would pool enough funds between them to pay Morgan a salary. So it was that Marshal Wyatt Earp ended up with two deputies and further ingratiated himself with the Territorial Governor.

4

Throughout the spring and well into summer, Preacher had managed to distance himself frrom the local fame of the Earps and certain factions which were rearing up in opposition to them. He had also elicited a promise from Wyatt that Preacher's real name would be kept quiet. Once or twice, John Clum nosed around about Preacher, who had shaved his beard but kept his *nom de plume*. Clum then got too busy to pursue any theories he might have held.

All of those things were shattered in mid July with the arrival in Tombstone of the tubercular little dentist called Doc Holliday. His exit from Dodge City had been quick enough but Doc could never resist a good poker game and a friendly woman. He ran into both in northern Texas and took root until late spring. When he did show up, he was in company with a raw boned, sometimes foul mouthed woman named Kate Elder.

Doc wasted no time in contacting the Earps. It happened that Wyatt was in Phoenix but while Doc was closest to Wyatt, he was welcome under any

Earp roof. He also learned of J.D. Preacher's presence and none of the Earp boys saw Doc's eyes light up. While in Texas, Doc had spent an evening with a young newspaperman named Breed. Nate Breed had made Holliday quite an offer. If he, Holliday, ever ran across Preacher and would get a story in print about it, Breed would see to it he was well paid.

Preacher learned of Doc's arrival that evening and he fully expected Doc at his table at anytime. It didn't happen. Preacher decided that Doc had just spent too much time with the Earp boys and was deadass tired afterwards. He'd see Doc in the morning, he reckoned. Preacher didn't see Doc at all, even when he went calling at the small house Doc had rented. Preacher met Kate Elder but she said she hadn't seen Doc for two days.

On Saturday night, Preacher got one of the other dealers to stand in for him and he went looking for Doc Holliday. He talked to all of the Earps and finally went to the sheriff's office. He knew full well that Johnny Behan would want to know the whereabouts of Dr. John Holliday. Behan didn't, and neither did his deputy. It was well past two o'clock on Saturday morning when Preacher showed up once again on Kate Elder's doorstep.

"How long you known Doc?" she asked.

"You mean how well do I know the man?"

She nodded.

"Not that well. Why?"

"He does strange things, Mister Preacher."

Preacher was surprised. He had decided not to reveal who he was to Kate Elder until he'd talked to Doc.

"I hope you don't judge him too harsh." Kate

handed Preacher a proof sheet from the Tombstone *Epitaph.*

He looked up at Kate Elder, his eyes fiery. "The little bastard!"

Doc was nursing a five day hangover, holed up in a back room at one of Tombstone's most infamous houses of ill repute when the knock sounded at the door. Clad in his longjohns and six gun, the little dentist jerked open the door and looked up with a scowl on his face. It tempered very little when he saw Preacher. "You got any idea what the hell time it is?"

Preacher ignored the question and jammed the Sunday edition of the *Epitaph* in Doc's face. "Look at this, you little son-of-a-bitch."

Doc opened it and sat down. There was a picture of J.D. Preacher and a double headline below it.

J. D. Preacher . . . Bounty Hunter
The Man Who Outdrew Bat Masterson
Infamous Widow Maker Living in Tombstone

"What's the matter?" Doc asked offhandedly as he tossed the paper aside, "they print somethin' that wasn't true?"

"Doc, goddam it, I came here to get away from dime novels and nosy newspapermen. I even worked out a deal with Wyatt. I don't appreciate you shooting off your mouth."

Doc virtually ignored Preacher and began searching for a bottle.

"You sober enough to understand me, Doc?"

Doc found the bottle he was looking for, uncorked it and took a long pull. He coughed, sat down and drained the rest of the bottle's contents.

"I heard you, bounty man," Doc finally said. He got up, found his pants and slipped them on, hefting his gun belt up far enough to accommodate the effort. He put the rig in place and tied it down, then he looked at Preacher again. "I heard you say you had a deal with Wyatt. Well, I ain't Wyatt and I don't make deals."

Preacher had never met Doc's ugly side. Obviously it was this kind of thing Katie Elder had asked him about, knowing the man. Liquor only made him worse. Doc wasn't yet thirty and he'd been told he wouldn't see thirty five. Preacher considered some of that but his own anger was still his priority.

"You want to tell tall tales to your drunken friends, tell them on somebody else." Preacher opted to let it go at that and turned to leave.

"Bounty man!"

Preacher turned back.

Doc's face was red and his eyes were like two black buttons. "You don't tell me what I talk about or with who or when. You don't tell Doc Holliday a goddam thing. No man does! You got an itch with me, you'd best scratch it, right now."

"You're drunk," Preacher said. He turned around again.

"That's the only goddamn edge you'll ever have on my, bounty man, so you'd best take advantage of it."

Preacher felt a tug in his gut. He liked Doc Holliday. He liked him well enough to want to get to know him better. The tug went away. If Doc pulled on him, Preacher would kill him.

"If you want me, Doc, it'll have to be in the back." The lanky Tennessean turned on his heel and had gained the hallway before Doc's brain registered the movement. Doc drew and fired. The shot took Preacher's hat off but the shootist didn't break stride. The second shot went between Preacher's boots and by then Doc was outside his room. Wyatt Earp bounded up the stairs and stepped around Preacher.

"You hit?"

"No."

"I'll take it from here." Virgil came up, nodded and the two Earps moved toward Doc, slowly.

"You're called out, Preacher," Doc screamed. "Now or later bounty man, you're called out."

Wyatt reached Doc just as the inevitable happened. The combination of liquor, anger and shouting was too much. Doc's gun dropped to the floor and the little dentist's frail body was wracked with a coughing spell which brought beads of perspiration to his forehead, excruciating pain to his chest and unconsciousness.

A quarter of an hour later, Wyatt came into the Eagle Brewery. He found Preacher at a corner table with a bottle of Teton Jack. "Mind if I join you?"

Preacher nodded toward the other empty chair. Wyatt accepted a drink and Preacher downed another.

"Somebody ought to stop him, Wyatt," Preacher said, "the man is killing off what little time he has left."

Wyatt smiled. "What the hell do you think he wanted?"

Preacher's head jerked up and he studied Wyatt's face. "Jeezus! You mean the little bastard wanted me to take him out?"

"He pulled on me," Wyatt said. "And let's see,

Morg and Virg, too. I think brother Jim is the only one of us he's missed. Tried Bat Masterson one time."

"What the hell for?"

Wyatt's hands came from beneath the table and he extended them outward, palms up. "I guess he'd rather a friend took him out than some two bit gunny."

Preacher snorted. "You seen the two bit gunny that could take Doc?"

"Yeah," Wyatt said, "if Doc gets one of his spells. That's what scares him. He don't want some no account building a reputation off of him. That scares him worse than dyin' in bed."

Preacher shook his head in despair and then said, "I'm sorry Wyatt, real sorry." He looked up. "But I won't be pushed, not even by Doc."

"I know that Preacher, but don't let Doc find it out."

Preacher sat back in his chair and considered Wyatt for a moment. "And just what the hell am I supposed to do about it?"

"Mebbe tell him something like I did." Wyatt grinned. "I told him if he ever pulled on me again, I'd blow off both his knees. Hell, Virg told him he'd get off one blast with that sawed off he totes and take off an arm or a leg."

"Jeezus! That's what you told him? And it worked?"

"He's never pulled on us again. I guess he figures we're good enough to do it and not being able to get around scares Doc a whole lot worse than dying. My guess is that Doc likes you a whole hell of a lot. I've never known him to act like that with somebody he doesn't like. Mostly Preacher, when Doc pulls a gun, somebody dies."

"And if you're wrong?"

"I'll likely have to say words over one of you."

Preacher poured them each another drink and pondered Wyatt's story about Doc Holliday. "Do you figure that's the reason Doc went to John Clum with that damned story?"

"Part of it, likely," Wyatt said, nodding. "But I'd be lyin' to tell you that's the only reason. Doc needed some money and you looked like a saleable, local commodity."

"Damn!" Preacher shook his head. "You know what kind of trouble that story will bring, don't you?"

Wyatt nodded.

"And you know I won't pin on a damned badge."

"Yeah, I know Preacher. Neither will Doc." Wyatt pushed away from the table and got to his feet.

Preacher corked up his bottle and the two men headed for the door.

"I'll be down tomorrow and go through your wanteds. I can't sit behind a damned table dealing poker anymore. If I'm going to be a target, at least I'm going to make it as tough as I can to hit me." The two pushed through the bat wings and Wyatt glanced in both directions. Tombstone looked peaceful enough at that moment. He turned back to face Preacher.

"You got any feelings about bounty men, Wyatt?"

"Yeah. There are more men that need huntin' than there are men to hunt 'em. You bring in a man to me, you've saved me the trouble. I got only one rule, Preacher. If we come up on a man at the same time," Wyatt poked his badge, "this gives me the first shot."

Preacher went back to his room and sat in the dark just pondering recent events in his life. He'd tried to become someone else. A different man with a different job. Granted, he'd grown tired of the publicity but he knew that changing faces and jobs didn't change him. He lived not by cards but by guns. So be it.

Preacher didn't like loose ends but he had some. He spent the following morning going through dodgers. He found three that he considered worth his time. The combined bounties totalled seventy five hundred. That would grubstake him for most of the rest of the year.

He wasn't ready to leave Tombstone just yet. He liked it there and he could not think of another place where, if push came to shove, he'd have some back up. He quit the Eagle Brewery, collected his final wages and then made a stop at the office of the Tombstone *Epitaph*.

"Sit down," John Clum said, smiling. He closed his office door and scowled at the two copy boys who stood just outside, gaping at Preacher. Clum went around behind his own desk, picked up a copy of the previous day's paper and held it up. "I assume you're here about this. Am I right?"

"Only to the extent that I wanted you to know what it would do."

Clum frowned.

"I know," Preacher continued, "that you pride yourself on being a good solid citizen. The story you

printed is going to bring some gents to town that
you call undesirables. Some of them are going to die.
I don't see much pride in that."

John Clum found himself surprised at Preacher's
intellect. He hadn't talked to Preacher that much
and simply thought of him as another tin horn, gun
slinging drifter. The two men considered one
another.

Clum opted to chance the offensive. He smiled.
"You know I can't very well hold back a story
because I fear the possible consequences of reporting it." Now Clum jabbed a finger right at Preacher.
"And you sir are news, whether you think so or
not." The gunman smiled and got to his feet. The
move surprised Clum.

Preacher said, "If I wasn't, I soon will be, and I'm
wondering just how you'll handle it then."

"Anytime," Clum said, somewhat irritated, "that
you are unhappy with what I report, you have the
right to talk to me. If the story is wrong and you
know it, correct it."

"You mean do your job for you, Mister Clum? No
thanks. You're the reporter, you make sure it's
right. I'm the gunman, remember? If I do my job
wrong, I'll end up in your obituary column."

"I have to rely on sources, sir. You are a source.
You tell me your story and that's what I'll print."
Clum stood up looking satisfied that he'd put
Preacher in his place.

Preacher had turned and walked to the door. He
stopped now and turned back. "That's fair, Clum,"
he said. He made the comment as he was turning
around. Now he looked straight into the publisher's
eyes. "And if your so called source doesn't tell you

anything at all, you don't print anything at all. Is that right?"

Clum said nothing.

Preacher smiled and added, "Yeah Clum, that's my point."

There was one more loose end and Preacher opted to take care of it that very morning. He found Doc Holliday sitting in a poker game with three other men. Doc was dealing when Preacher walked up and he didn't stop.

"You owe me a new hat, Holliday." Two chairs scooted back and their occupants jumped up and moved quickly away from the table. The fourth man was too frightened even to do that. Still dealing, Doc said, "They've got a new shipment over to the mercantile. I could use one myself. Come 'round in the morning and we'll both go over. You can pick one out.' Doc finished the deal and looked up, grinning. "On me."

"Ten o'clock alright?"

Doc nodded.

"One more thing," Preacher said, "you ever pull on me again Doc, and you'll regret it."

Doc was still grinning. "You talk to Wyatt, did you? You going to blow off my knee caps are you, or is it my fingers?"

Wyatt had been right but Preacher didn't want to make too light of it either.

"I'm not going to tell you anything Doc, except what I already did. Don't pull on me again, ever."

Doc shrugged. "Hell, I hate surprises worse than anything else."

Preacher had to stifle a grin. He knew what Doc meant and that was an end to it, between them, privately. Preacher walked away.

Preacher decided to look up Allie Howard again but he stopped at the Alhambra first to talk to Wyatt. Wyatt wasn't there and the barkeep hadn't seen him. The barkeep did offer Preacher a drink and the gunman accepted.

There were half a dozen men at one end of the bar and one of them had been eyeing Preacher almost from the instant he'd arrived. His name was Hank Getty and one of the other men was his older brother, Lyman. Hank was about nineteen and he'd just gunned down two claim jumpers up in the Dragoons. He wore a pair of matched Colt revolvers in a cross draw rig. Now he was a little drunk and too cocky and itching to use the Colts again.

"I'm buyin' a round o' drinks for ever'body at the bar," he said in a loud voice. The barkeep walked up. "Tennessee Mash all 'round." There were only four others at the bar, including Preacher. The barkeep knew Preacher. He knew what Preacher drank. When he served, he didn't serve Preacher.

"The gent in the black suit only drinks Teton Jack. Didn't figure you'd want to spend that much," the barkeep said to Hank. Hank grabbed the barkeep by the collar and pulled hard.

"I said a round for ever'body at the bar. That's what I meant. I said Tennessee Mash, and that's what I meant." He let go and looked down the bar at Preacher. He was sneering. "Serve 'im."

The barkeep complied. He eyed Preacher as he set the glass in front of him and he shrugged. Preacher nodded.

"You too damned high and mighty to drink a workin' man's liquor, mister?"

Preacher sighed. He suspected the boy knew who he was but either way, Hank had spotted Preacher as someone he thought he could goad.

"I'll be glad to drink with you," Preacher said, "I've just got too tender a pallet for your whiskey."

"Not right," Hank said, nudging one of the other men. "Seems to me a man offers up a friendly drink, another fella ought to take it."

Preacher was through arguing the point. He pushed the Tennessee Mash away and picked up his Teton Jack, with his left hand. He stepped away from the bar. "My name's Preacher," he said, "and here's to your good health." He downed the drink and set the glass on the bar.

Hank Getty wasn't satisfied but his brother had turned pale. "Goddamn Hank," he whispered, "that there is the Widda Maker. He's a gunfighter, Hank. Shit! Back off."

Hank Getty jerked loose from his brother, turned, shoved him away and then stepped still further from the bar. A silence fell over the room.

"I know who the hell he is and I'm wonderin' if that purty black coat is coverin' up a yella streak." Hank downed his own drink.

Three years earlier, when the Getty boys rode away from their family's run down Missouri dirt farm, Lyman promised their mama that he'd look out for young Hank. Thing was, Lyman was no gun hand. More often than not, the taking care had been the other way around. So it had been with the two claim jumpers. Now however, Lyman knew that Hank was in over his head.

Lyman jumped between Hank and Preacher and then walked toward Preacher slowly. When that happened, Preacher tensed. He'd seen this kind of set up before. Doc Holiday now got to his feet. Lyman wasn't trying to set up anything. He stopped about ten feet from Preacher.

"He didn't mean nothin' by that, mister. Hank's a little drunk."

"The best thing Hank can do is keep his mouth shut. He can't seem to handle liquor going in or words coming out."

"Yeah, sure mister, sure, I'll tell 'im."

Preacher turned and started for the door.

Lyman turned around just in time to see Hank's fist coming at him. It was too late to duck. Lyman went down with a bloodied nose. Hank moved to the spot where Preacher had been standing, picked up the Tennessee Mash and hurled it in the gunman's direction. It hit the floor and spattered the back of Preacher's britches.

"Now Mister Fancy Dan gunman, you gonna drink with me?"

"I drank to you," Preacher said, "I pick who I drink with. Now why don't you help your brother back to his feet and have another round, on me?"

"I'm callin' you out, gunfighter. Whatta say to that?"

"I don't want to kill you boy, but if you force my hand, I won't go for a leg or an arm."

Lyman Getty got to his feet. "For Chrissake Hank, please, please back off."

Hank Getty's palms were sweaty and his throat was dry. Both were sensations he had never experienced before. The first man he'd ever killed was an old sod buster armed with Colt's Paterson. Hank had swelled up on himself after that and never faced anyone who was even close to being a match for him. Now he began to sober up enough to realize he was facing a man whose reputation would fill more pages than Hank's whole life.

"Shut up, Lyman," Hank barked. A drop of sweat bubbled up beneath the band on Hank's hat, popped out onto his forehead and trickled down his nose to its end. There, it hung suspended and glistening in the lamplight for all to see.

"How about that drink Hank," one of the other men shouted. "Hell, the dude's all talk. He's not gonna pull on you."

Preacher didn't move his eyes off Hank Getty but he was grateful for the man's attempt. He had given Hank a way out without losing face.

Hank swallowed but it didn't help. He had no spit. He snorted, a gesture of contempt for the man he faced. "Fuck you, gunfighter. You ain't worth killin'." He turned around, forced a little laugh and walked back to the bar.

Preacher turned, pausing midway in his turn to eye Doc Holliday, and walked to the door.

At the bar, Hank Getty downed a quick drink and all was well with the world, until Hank's brother slapped him on the shoulder.

"Smart thing to do, Hank." Lyman's intentions were well founded, his remark was devastating.

Hank sneered at Lyman, spit on him and stepped away from the bar, making a half turn as he did so. "I'll show you smart, big brother. Gunfighter!" Hank's palms were still damp but fear had been replaced with artificial courage. There was much of it in the world and it took many forms. Hank's had come from a bottle of Tennessee Mash.

Hank's draw was good and he proved to be ambidextrous. Left and right, Hank was both fast and accurate. Both Colts went off and heavy calibre discharges in the confines of the room were ear shattering. At the sound of Hank's shout, Preacher began his own move. It was no contest. Hank died with a bullet in his heart. Hank's bullets buried themselves in the door jamb.

The instant Hank hit the floor, one of the men with him drew his own gun and fired at Preacher. Preacher killed him too. The bounty hunter raised his right leg and kicked away a table and two chairs. He moved to where they had been, at the same time holstering his hip pistol he'd used.

"Any more candidates for the burying man?" Doc Holliday had his own gun in hand, a reflex action. He holstered it and eyed Preacher. At that moment, Doctor John Holliday knew that he could never beat this quiet Tennessean to the draw. The man's actions defied description and a split second later, Doc got another demonstration.

"Goddam you," Lyman shouted. Another of the group, a youngster named Lou King, also drew simultaneously with Lyman. Doc was staring right straight at Preacher. Preacher's right hand appeared to vanish completely and all Doc could see was a puff of blue gray smoke when a pistol discharged. Doc wasn't even sure of the weapon's origin and the two shots fired from it were in such proximity as to sound as one. Both Lyman and Lou King were dead. Neither had managed even to get their guns to waist level.

"Bury them," Preacher said, "along with a bottle each of Teton Jack. They wanted to drink with me, let them." He'd already holstered his gun and he tossed a gold piece on the floor.

5

Tombstone's outward appearance suffered a serious internal flaw in the late summer of 1880. Its populace was divided over the law and order methods of the Earp brothers and those of their elected law officer, Sheriff John Behan. Preacher, whose reputation was now on a par with the Earps and Doc Holliday, did his best to distance himself from the feud. His efforts were weakened by his occasional fraternization with Doc Holliday and Preacher had about decided to go back on the trail in September.

On a steamy night in August the fissure widened to chasm. Tombstone had visitors.

"Wyatt," Virgil Earp shouted as he burst through the door of Wyatt's office, "we got troubles."

Wyatt shoved a stack of papers away and looked up.

"Seven of 'em," Virg said, "over to the Alhambra."

"Anybody we know?"

"Al Tracy, Obie Wheeler, Lackey Brokaw, Frank

53

Keene, a kid they call Ringo, and two I don't know."

Wyatt wheeled around, pulled a shotgun off the rack and tossed it to Virg, then took another down for himself. "Where's Morgan?"

"Out to the Hillman place. Pete Hillman said somebody rustled about twenty-five or thirty head from him."

"These boys at the Alhambra?"

"Likely," Virg said, "but we don't have to prove it tonight."

"Why not, you figuring they'll shoot it out?"

"That's likely too Wyatt, but we got paper on four of 'em either way it goes."

Wyatt loaded a sixth shell into his .45 and then strapped on the long holster for the Buntline Special. Virg shook his head when he got another look at the long barreled weapon. Wyatt smiled as he thought of the little reporter. Buntline had quit Tombstone and ridden back to Texas. Wyatt suspected he would return one day soon with Preacher's nemesis in tow, Nate Breed.

"Where's our illustrious Sheriff?" Wyatt asked.

"Over to the Bird Cage. Town council wanted him protecting that singer, uh, Petrilli or somethin' like that."

"Deputies?"

"Same as always, makin' rounds up and down Allen Street."

"Virg, warn Jim to keep a sharp eye. They find out his name is Earp and they're liable to kill 'im just out o' pure meanness." Wyatt looked down, thinking. He jabbed a finger at his brother. "See if you can find Preacher, too. I don't expect him to help but he needs to be warned. One or two o' those boys are likely to try him. I'll roust Doc."

"I think Doc's over at the Oriental Wyatt, but Preacher's right in the middle. He's in a poker game at the Alhambra."

"Damn! I'm going there first. Virg, you roust Doc."

Wyatt had gone barely half a block when he was confronted by John Clum. Clum was then head of the citizen's committee and the clear leader of the Behan faction.

"Marshal."

"Clum, I'm in a bit of a hurry."

"I know you are Marshal, and I know why. I've just come from the Bird Cage. I've informed the Sheriff of the situation. These men are killers and I'd hoped to catch you before there was a confrontation. I'm urging you to use restraint. Let the Sheriff handle this until we've had a chance to call a meeting of the town council. I think—"

Wyatt Earp was a model of self restraint given his attitude toward Clum generally and the pressure of the moment. "John," he said, "I know you don't hold much stock in my way of doing things, but the law is with me and I will not wait for the by God town council to meet. Good evening, sir."

"Earp, damn you. Innocent people can get killed in this thing. I'm not without contacts in the Governor's office you know. You'll lose that badge if I have my way." Wyatt simply kept walking and Clum finally yelled at him. "Earp! Earp! Did you hear me?"

"Go to hell, Mister Clum."

John Clum had never felt quite so frustrated as he did right at that moment. He clenched his teeth and swore he'd wreak vengeance.

Inside the Alhambra, the bar had been cleared of

patrons and the two barkeeps had been ordered to set up free drinks. The order came from one of two leaders of the seven man gang, Al Tracy. The seven, clad in linen dusters and smelling roady, were all armed to the teeth. Both Tracy and Frank Keene toted shotguns and another carried a short barreled rifle not unlike Preacher's .58 calibre.

Two of the gang, Lackey Brokaw and Obie Wheeler, had taken up positions on either side of the batwings. The two men Virgil Earp had said he didn't know were near the back of the room. They were a half breed Apache known as Indian Charlie Packer and a fast gun known only as Rio.

There were five girls working the floor that night and Frank Keene had corraled them at one end of the bar. A third barkeep named Tim Kelly had blundered in at the wrong time and tried to make a run for the back door. Now, he was lying on the floor with a sizeable knot on the back of his head.

"The next sonuvabitch that tries to be a hero will get Mister Kelly blowed all to hell," Frank Keene said.

There were also girls and patrons on the second floor of the Alhambra and the man assigned the task of getting them all down to the main floor was the seventh man, Johnny Ringo. Ringo had completed the task save for one room. That door was locked.

"Unlock the fuckin' door," Ringo yelled.

"Who's givin' you trouble up there, Ringo?"

"Don't know, but I'm about to find out." Johnny Ringo backed off, raised his right leg and kicked hard on the door just to the left of the knob. The lock gave way and the door flew open. In the same motion, Ringo shifted his weight and spun his body to the left. A shotgun blast echoed through the hallway and the shot smashed into the room door opposite Ringo's position.

"Ringo!"

"I'm fine." Ringo whirled, drew and fired into the room. A girl screamed and it drowned out the muffled grunt of big Mike Reese. The 250 pound Welshman was a former coal miner and he could have torn Johnny Ringo's head off with his bare hands, but he was no match for a .45 slug in the belly. He doubled up and lay on the floor groaning. The girl, Ellie Mae Jackson, was still screaming. Ringo slapped her twice and knocked her to the floor.

"What the hell is going on up there, Ringo?"

"Big fella decided to protect his whore, I guess." Ringo laughed. "He's got a belly ache now." The girl was whimpering and Ringo put a boot toe in her belly and then grabbed her by the hair and hauled her downstairs.

Big Mike Reese had been the security man at the Alhambra ever since it opened. Few men even tried to stand against him.

"Ringo!" The voice was booming, the shock paralyzing. Mike Reese was toting a bullet that would have killed a norman man instantly. Somehow, the big Welshman had gained his feet and the hallway. Now he stood poised at the banister and staring down at Johnny Ringo. Reese, with an ear splitting bellow and a mighty heave, threw himself over the banister. He took another bullet from Ringo, some shot from Frank Keene's shotgun and a bullet through the brain from the fast gun of the boy named Rio. None of it helped John Ringo. He suffered three broken ribs and a fractured clavicle and was out of the fight.

Throughout the opening act of the tragedy, J.D. Preacher sat in a semi-darkened corner near a rear window. He fooled with a deck of cards most of the time under the occasional scrutiny of the half breed, Indian Charlie. The breed didn't know Preacher and it was Preacher's only edge. He could have easily taken both the breed and Rio but not without someone up front dying. He opted instead to wait until he could get out through the window. Mike Reese did not die in vain. Not only had he taken Ringo out of the fight, but he gave Preacher his chance. Amid the screams of the women, Reese's bellowing voice and the firing of at least three guns, Preacher made his move

"You there." Indian Charlie whirled, his gun already out. Preacher drew and put a bullet between his legs. Rio spun around.

"Shit!" Rio made the mistake all wound-be gunnies make. They often assume that speed and accuracy are the only tools the trade requires. Rio was distracted by what had gone on around him. It was a distraction which most men would have ignored as too trivial to alter circumstances but most men don't live by the gun. The distraction gave Preacher time enough to fire a second shot and Rio's error was fatal.

Preacher doubled himself into a ball, tucked his head against his chest and went through the window. He landed just right to avoid injury, rolled and came up on his feet, facing the window. No one was at it and he moved down the alley to the street.

Out on Allen Street, Wyatt Earp had been joined by Virgil and Doc Holliday. They had sequestered themselves in the shadows across from Alhambra. Preacher found them there.

"What the hell went on," Wyatt asked.

Preacher told him.

"Only four left?"

"Yeah," Preacher said, "but it won't be easy. They've got people in there. The girls, two or three barkeeps, the kitchen help and half a dozen citizens."

Wyatt reached into his vest pocket and withdrew a deputy's badge. He held it out.

"We already talked about that, Wyatt. The answer is still no."

"Put it on," Doc said. He pulled the lapel of his coat back and flashed the badge Wyatt had given him. "If I can do it, you can too."

Preacher ignored Doc Holliday and addressed himself to Wyatt. "You need my gun, not me."

"Behan will have a field day unless every man with me is deputized," Wyatt said, firmly. "And yes Preacher, I do need your guns."

"I took two of them out as a citizen defending himself. Anymore I might get will be for the bounty on their heads. I won't put on a badge Wyatt, not again."

The arrival of Sheriff John Behan and a deputy put an end to the conversation. Behan, armed with a shotgun and strutting along the street like a Bantam cock, spotted Earp. He stopped, directed his deputy to take up a position at the corner of the saloon where it was paralleled by the alley way, and then he walked to the middle of the street.

"You men inside, this is Sheriff Behan. Come out one at a time. Throw your weapons out the doors ahead of yourselves and keep your hands where I can see them. If you choose to make a fight of it, you don't have a chance. I can badge as many men as it will take to get you."

Virgil Earp started for the street. "Stupid little sonuvabitch!"

No one present knew what Virgil might have had in mind. It proved academic in any event. Lackey Brokaw stepped to a window just to the right of the doors and fired two shots into the street. He couldn't see anyone or anything but one of the shots took off John Behan's hat. It was hurled into the shadows behind him, along with his courage. He dived for the dubious shelter offered by a nearby watering trough, dropping his gun as he dived.

"This is Frank Keene," came a voice from inside. "You got some mighty scared folks in here, Sheriff. They'll git over that. They won't git over bein' dead," he continued, "an' that's what they're gonna be unless you bring us the bankin' man. You got just about ten minutes to git 'im here an' shove 'im through the front door an' you got about ten seconds to give me an answer."

Wyatt Earp crouched down and made his way to Behan. "You killed our chances of mebbe makin' this safer and sure as hell a lot easier. Until he had a lawman or someone with some authority out here, he had nothing." Wyatt found his urge to jerk Behan to his feet and shove him through the front door.

Behan was embarrassed but he was also adamant. "He has those people in there, Earp, but I wouldn't expect you to care about them."

Wyatt snorted and made a threatening gesture. "Yeah," he said, "he's got 'em but they don't do him much good unless he can use them for barter, and they're no good dead."

Johnny Behan sat up and then got to his knees

and finally his feet. He was considerably shorter than Wyatt, which irked him all the more. Nonetheless, he was a sincere man who could not be faulted for his beliefs. He simply lacked the understanding and skills to carry them out. "I was foolish to make such an arrogant approach," he said, "but I am the primary law enforcement officer in Tombstone." Behan swallowed and extended his hand. "I'd like your assistance in this matter, Mister Earp."

Wyatt was stunned but he understood. Behan wanted to ask for help, not have it thrust upon him. In Wyatt's own mind, the job that had to be done called for the use of every asset at his disposal and he considered John Behan a liability.

"Behan," Frank Keene shouted, "your time is up. What's your answer?"

Behan and Earp stared at one another and then the little sheriff saw an almost imperceptible nod of Earp's head.

"I'll get the banker here," Behan shouted.

"Ten minutes Sheriff, that's all you got, ten minutes."

Wyatt and John Behan walked back to the others. Behan motioned for his deputy to stay put. He took a deep breath and said, "Is there a chance we might substitute someone else? Is it possible they don't know what Mister Hildebrand looks like?"

"Ringo is in there," Virgil Earp said, "and he knows the banker."

John Behan sighed. "Then it seems we have no choice."

"When they get the banker, they get the money they want. When they've got that, you've got dead citizens. They'll take as many with them out of town as they figure they need to make it. They'll kill them all when they're through." This from Preacher.

"Yeah," Wyatt said, "that's just what will happen."

"It seems to me," Behan said, "that we'll have to risk that. After all, they're here for money. Let them have it and they may ride out."

John Clum arrived along with two members of the town council. One of them was Justin Hildebrand. Clum considered the men with a studied look of disdain. He particularly abhorred Doc Holliday and of course he couldn't see Holliday's badge. "What is the status of this situation, Sheriff?" He had deliberately ignored Wyatt Earp but the marshal was grateful and a little amused.

John Behan gave Clum the report. He was about to explain what Frank Keene had requested when Keene shouted again.

"You're down to five minutes out there."

Clum wanted an immediate explanation about that. He got it and Virgil Earp added a footnote. He told Clum how it had come about. John Clum was a man of few words, very direct usually. Now, he had no words at all.

Sheriff Behan turned to Justin Hildebrand. Behan licked his lips and swallowed. He'd never had to ask a man to simply volunteer to die. The possibility of any circumstance which would require him to do so had never even entered his mind when he ran for office. Yet, there it was and John Behan would have rather stepped back into the street and faced all four gunmen.

Preacher didn't mind Behan's discomfort but the job wasn't getting done and that did make him uneasy. "Tell them the banker had to go to

Phoenix."

"They'll only want someone else," Behan countered. Like a Judas Iscariot, Behan wanted to do what he must do, quickly.

"It will buy us some time," Preacher said. He addressed himself to Justin Hildebrand. "If you were gone, who would have access to the safe?"

Hildebrand was still somewhat in shock over the revelations. He had been one of John Behan's most ardent supporters and he couldn't rationalize how he'd made such a rotten judgment. He blinked and looked at Preacher.

"Uh, uh," he felt embarrassed. He couldn't think. "Jack Kinsey can open it and Martin Walsh. No one else."

"It's awful damned thin," Wyatt said, "but it's better than our alternative." He turned to the sheriff. "Tell 'em Behan, and make it firm. If you don't, somebody in there is going to die."

John Behan's eyes went from face to face in the little group of men. At that moment, he seemed to find a hidden resolve. He was, he thought, as good as any of them in his own way and he owed them no proof of it. His debt was to the citizens who had elected him. He walked a few feet away, drew his gun and fired a single shot into the night sky.

"Keene, this is Sheriff Behan. Banker Hildebrand had to go to Phoenix and he won't be back until morning. There are two others who can open the safe. I'm assuming that's why you wanted Hildebrand. I have my deputies looking for them right now but it will take more time."

"You're a liar, Sheriff."

"If you believe that," Behan said, "there is no more reason to talk. Carry out your threats and kill

those people or as many of them as you can before
we get you." Behan paused. It was a timely pause, a
pause for effect, a political ploy. "And rest
assured," he added, "we will get you."

Behan stepped back into the shadows and waited.
There was no reply, no shots, nothing but silence.
He looked at the others.

"Helluva nice job, Sheriff," Doc Holliday said.
"Keene will ponder that one for a spell."

"Yeah," Preacher agreed, "and maybe we can put
the spell to good use. Doc, let's you and I take the
back."

Doc nodded.

Inside the Alhambra, Al Tracy was getting
nervous. He prodded one of the barkeeps in the back
with his shotgun and pushed him along toward the
back. They reached the spot where Frank Keene
stood.

"Earp is out there. Prob'ly his brothers too an'
now that goddamn bounty man."

Frank looked at Al and considered what he'd just
heard. He then looked down at Ringo. The young
gunny was half out, full of rye and pain.

"Shit!"

"Let's get the fuck out o' here. There's banks in
Mexico an' no lawmen, just *Federales*. Can't spend
nothin' when you're in a box."

"An' how the hell do we do that?"

"These women. They won't fuck with us if we got
these women. We'll tell 'em to give us 'til daylight.
We don't see no posse at daylight, we turn 'em loose.
Hell Frank, if we go now, we can be to the border by
daylight."

"Shit!"

"We got them cows hid too. They'll grubstake us

for a spell. We can git 'em after we turn the women loose. Hell, the law will be wantin' the women back. They won't worry none about us or them cows."

Preacher went through the alleyway a second time, ducking as he went by the window. Doc Holliday went around the opposite side of the building along the street. Both had clear shots at the Alhambra's back door.

Out on the street, Wyatt and Virgil had discussed their plan of action. They knew at least two men were covering the front door and that they would pose the most immediate problem. They hoped that their effort would distract the two men in back long enough to give Doc and Preacher a chance to move in.

John Behan approached Wyatt. "I'm no fast gun Earp, but I'm better than most with a rifle." Behan gestured toward his deputy. "So's he. We can lay down some pretty heavy fire through those front windows. I figure those men will be more anxious to save themselves than to kill anyboy inside."

Wyatt smiled, put his hand on Behan's shoulder and said, "You're right, Sheriff, shall we have at it?"

Behan asked for a moment to inform his deputy and he worked his way down the block until he could cross the street unseen by those inside the saloon. Wyatt and Virgil Earp waited, ready to move when Behan returned. Wyatt didn't need to insist that the citizens, John Clum among them, move out of the area. They did so as his first request.

Another shout broke the silence. "You got thirty minutes, Sheriff."

Doc Holliday was surprised to see the back door open. He looked toward Preacher's position but he couldn't see the gun man. What he did see were two of the women being pushed outside. Behind them, Frank Keene came along with his shotgun at the ready. Inside, Al Tracy was prodding two more of the girls toward the door. He'd locked the rest of the help in the kitchen pantry. He and Frank had conspired not only to get out of the mess, but to sacrifice Lackey Brokaw and Obie Wheeler in the process.

The two gunnies up front were totally engrossed in what might be taking place on Allen Street. After all, if there was to be trouble, that was the likely quarter from which it would come. They neither heard nor saw what their saddle compadres had hatched up and were now in the process of carrying out.

Franke Keene stayed on the steps to the Alhambra's back door for a moment. He let his eyes adjust to the dark after he ordered the women to stand still. He levelled his shotgun squarely on their backs. Frank was no amateur. He thought it likely that there would be at least a deputy out back. When he heard Al coming, he stepped down.

"On your feet, girlies," he said softly, and then in a little louder tone. "Don't see nothin' stoppin' us back here, Al."

Doc Holliday still couldn't see Preacher. All he could do was hope that the Tennessean was in position and ready. Doc made his move.

Doc Holliday drew his gun, stepped out of the shadows and said, "Evenin." Frank Keene's reaction had been predictable. He moved the scatter gun's barrel toward the sound and fired. Doc Holliday had spoken his words and then darted about twenty feet to the right. Now Doc fired.

"Shit," Frank Keene said, weakly. He dropped the shotgun, looked down at his chest with ever widening eyes and then fell dead of a bullet in the heart.

Doc's move had been a few seconds premature for Preacher's liking but the deficit was made up by the actions of one of the girls Al Tracy was behind. She pushed the girl in front of her out the door and the girl missed the step and fell. The other one simply threw herself face down on the floor. The result was Al Tracy's form silhouetted by the faint lamplight behind him. Preacher was ready and fired at the silhouette's center. Al Tracy never pulled the triggers of his shotgun. He took Preacher's shot in the breastbone, his body tumbled backward and he was dead when he hit the floor.

The gunfire served as the cue for the men out front. Behan wasn't yet back in position but he stopped where he was, did a half turn and raised his rifle. He fired three fast shots with the Henry. They served to keep Obie Wheeler occupied. The Earps had to make an even more sudden change in plans. They eyed one another and moved.

Wyatt went through the window on the right side of the door. There was an explosion of glass and the shards showered Obie Wheeler. In spite of that he started firing, four shots in the general direction of the window. Wyatt ended up on all fours behind a nearby table. He had filled his hand with the Buntline before he made the unorthodox entry and now he used it to end Obie's life.

Virgil timed his moves exactly with those of his brother. When Wyatt's big frame hit the window, Virgil calmly walked through the front door. Lackey Brokaw had backed up several feet and became enthralled by Wyatt's entry and Obie's death. A second later he saw Virgil and he reached for his handgun. Virg let go with both barrels of the shotgun, from the hip. He winced. He'd fired a little high. Lackey's head was gone.

6

Preacher's funds were on the ebb. He'd kept his room above the Alhambra, too expensive for a man without an income. He'd collected a small bounty fee on Al Tracy. Most of the last pay he'd received from dealing poker at the Eagle Brewery had gone down the street to the Faro concession at the Oriental. On top of everything else, he had a gut feeling that Ned Buntline would be back in town soon, with Nate Breed at his heels. If Doc Holliday's story hadn't done it, John Clum's lengthy reports on the Oriental shootout certainly would.

Preacher was pondering these things and alternatives to them on another hot night in Tombstone. It was late September. He was shirtless, sitting up on his bed and sipping iced down Teton Jack.

"Mister Preacher." The voice was barely more than a whisper. Still, he could tell it was feminine, throaty and just outside his door. He slipped his pistol into his hand.

"Yeah?"

"May I come in?"

"It's open."

As he spoke, the bounty hunter slipped from his bed, moved quickly across the room and waited. The door opened and a woman's head poked inside the room. She squinted in the half light and then walked in. She closed the door behind her.

"Mister Preacher?"

Preacher tucked the gun in his waistband. "Here," he said. He'd expected her to jump. She didn't. He walked toward her and he was giving her the once over as he did so. He liked what he saw. He turned up the lamp and considered her in more detail.

She was raven haired, dark eyed and possessed of an almond hued skin. Cajun, Preacher thought. She wore a frilly hat and dark green, satin dress with a revealing bodice. He imagined her breasts were pendulous.

"I came to say thank you."

"For what, Miss—" he stopped.

"Barrett. Janelle Barrett, and the reason is because of my sister."

"And who's your sister?"

"Margaret. Maggie to you. She worked at the Alhambra. She was the first one out the door that night. You loaned her your coat."

"She looked chilled." Preacher said. There was a pause. Janelle hadn't really said her thank you yet but there was no need to wait her out. "You're welcome."

Janelle Barrett did not seem ill at ease in the room of a strange, half naked man. She remained stationary but pivoted so that she might see his weapons and his few other trappings.

Preacher watched her for a moment and she

seemed very much interested in his belongings. He cleared his throat and she turned toward him "You're welcome," he repeated.

Janelle Barrett smiled. She reached up, stretching her breasts to their maximum, and undid the combs in her hair. She shook her head and let the black silk mass fall down around her shoulders. She started unbuttoning her dress.

"You put a lot into your thank yous," he said.

"Do you want me to stop?"

"I didn't say that."

She smiled again, stepped out of her dress and began undoing her corset. Preacher walked back to the corner table and turned down the lamp.

When she was naked, Janelle moved to the side of the bed. She put her hands on her thighs, sliding them sensuously across her pubic hair, up along her hips, waist and finally to her breasts. They are pendulous, Preacher thought.

She reached down and unfastened Preacher's belt, laying his pistol to one side. He pulled off his underwear. Janelle climbed onto the bed and got up on her knees. She wet her fingertips with saliva and stroked her nipples until they glistened in the dim light. Preacher's throat went dry watching her and Janelle licked her lips when she looked down and saw his shaft. It was at full attention and her eyebrows raised as she began to gauge its size.

"Move over on top of me," Preacher said, "straddling me, just as you are now." She didn't acknowledge him except by obeying. He reached down, put his long, slim fingers around the cheeks of her derriere and pulled. She scooted forward, looking into his face until she could see it no more.

Preacher moaned as his nostrils picked up the

first musky scent. His tongue darted from between his lips and disappeared into the black slit above him. He dug his fingertips into Janelle's bottom as he warmed, literally, to his task. Her body stiffened and her head lolled back and forth. Her own hands were busy caressing her breasts.

Preacher made her hold the position until her body was soaked with sweat. The self imposed discipline promised to draw the maximum enjoyment from the act. Twice Janelle climaxed but Preacher didn't stop. He'd learned long ago that some women merely considered such events as preliminary. So it was with Janelle Barrett.

When at last he moved her, she seemed to know exactly what to do. She simply lay down on her back and welcomed him with open arms and spread thighs. They ignored rhythm. They ignored minor moments of getting in one another's way. They weren't making love, they were fornicating. They both wanted it, they both needed it. They both enjoyed it and they ended it in a moaning, sweating, writhing, physical explosion.

Preacher was dressing. So was Janelle. He stopped and took a shot of Teton Jack. He held out the flask. She declined.

"If there's ever anything else I can do for you . . . or your sister . . . just ask."

"Would you do it?"

"Mebbe."

"There is."

"Then this wasn't all just a thank you . . . was it?"

"Would it make a difference?"

"Not right now."

Janelle finished dressing and then opened her handbag. She pulled out a somewhat yellowed wanted poster and handed it to Preacher.

He read.

> *Wanted for Murder and Robbery*
> *Coleman Hungerford Langston*
> *alias*
> *Cole Langston . . . Cole Langford*
> *Coley Lang . . . Langston Coleman*

$5,000 $5,000

> *Dead or Alive*
> *Contact: Wells-Fargo Co. Ltd.*
> *San Francisco, Calif.*

"You heard of him?" she asked.

He handed the poster back. "Cole Langston?" He smirked. "Who the hell hasn't? Last I recollect, he was responsible for about two-thirds of Wells Fargo's losses during the past three years."

"Why haven't you ever gone after him? I mean, isn't that what you are . . . or were . . . once? A bounty hunter?"

"That's none of your business, Janelle . . . no matter what we did, or will do."

"Then you'll help me?"

"I didn't say that either."

"Will you?"

"Why should I?"

"Five-thousand dollars doesn't interest you?"

"Sure it does," Preacher said, slipping on his vest and holstering the pistol. He noticed Janelle eyeing it. "But I could bring in ten men with five hundred dollar price tags on their hats and make the same money." He strapped on his hip rig. "And I could do it in half the time with half the risk . . . so I've heard."

"Maybe you've heard wrong?"

Preacher considered her and smiled. "I doubt it. I've known some damned good men who went chasing after Cole Langston." He put on his coat. "I've never heard of any of 'em since."

"You're scared of him?"

Preacher eyed her, smiled and shook his head. "You sure have a way with putting words in a man's mouth . . . or thoughts into his head. I didn't say that either."

"Are you?"

"No. But I'm not interested in getting backshot, bushwhacked or having to fight every two bit, would-be bounty hunter just for five thousand dollars. Hell lady, there must be a dozen men or more doggin' his trail right now."

"Would twice the amount change your mind?"

"Ten thousand's no more use to a dead man than five."

"Maybe you're not the man I've heard you were. It sounds like you want all of the money and none of the risk. Wells Fargo wouldn't put that much on him if he was that easy to catch, would they?"

"Likely not . . . but then easy or no . . . they've got the biggest stake in him. Sixty, mebbe seventy-thousand dollars over the last five years or so?"

"Nearly a hundred thousand," Janelle said, "and four Wells Fargo agents, three drivers and two shotgun riders." She opened her handbag again and removed a small leather case. She handed it to Preacher. He opened it.

"Well I'll be goddamned. A female Wells Fargo agent." He shook his head. "They are desperate."

"Not desperate enough to suit me," she said. " And not nearly so angry as I am."

Preacher considered her.

"You see, one of those agents was my father. One of the shotgun riders was my brother."

"And the little story you told me when you came up here tonight?"

"Partially true. The girl is my sister, and she's bound to find Langston too . . . with or without help . . . mine or anyone's."

"She looks mighty young."

"She is, but not young enough to keep her corraled. I've been near a year finding her and I almost lost her again . . . permanent. I would have if it hadn't been for you. Now I'm faced with the same possibility again."

"How's that?"

"She's as afraid for me as I am for her, Preacher. I've been close to Cole Langston several times. My being a woman . . . and the company feeling obligated to me . . . is how I got this job in the first place. I convinced them that a woman might have a chance to get close to him."

"And your sister?"

"She struck out on her own. I had to give up my own hunt for Langston to hunt for her. Now she knows where he is."

"For sure?"

Janelle nodded.

"But she won't tell you."

"Under the right conditions she will."

"Such as?"

"Such as, I find a gunfighter who will do the job when the time comes. At best, so she tells me, it won't be easy. My God, she'd slept with four or five men in an effort to hire somebody. Even—" Janelle cut herself short and looked down.

"Even what?" Preacher waited. No response. "Or is it 'even who?' "

Janelle looked up. "Doc Holliday."

"And after he slept with her, he told her no?"

"He told her no in the first place. She thought she could change his mind."

Preacher smiled a little. No one changed Doc's mind except Doc.

"You said ten thousand?"

Janelle winced. "Is that all you're interested in. The money?"

"No. I'm also interested in staying alive."

"Goddam! You are just as cold as I'd heard."

"In some things," Preacher replied, "probably."

"You bastard!" Janelle turned. She sniffled.

She was being a woman right then and Preacher wasn't sure if it was an act or the real thing. In fact, it didn't matter to him one way or the other.

Janelle turned back. "I have the other five thousand. Money that the company paid us for the deaths of our father and brother."

"Any other conditions?"

"Yes . . .the most important one."

Preacher looked quizzical.

"She won't tell me . . . or you . . . or anyone, until she is convinced that whoever it is will take us along."

"Bull shit!"

"That's what some others have said."

"Hell, that's what any man in his right mind would say."

"That's her condition . . . her main one. She claims she has to go, to lead whoever."

"Up to a point, mebbe. That's all."

"If that isn't part of the deal she'll go alone.

Sometime, somewhere, she'll lose me . . . and go alone."

"The man that agrees to go after Cole Langston with two females in tow is one of two things. Crazy now or dead later." Preacher reached for his hat. "If you'll pardon me, I'm late for a poker game."

"Then you're turning me down."

"I am."

"What if I could get another man and was willing to doublecross my sister . . . at the right time?"

"I ride alone, all the way."

"You wouldn't be alone in any event, Preacher. You said it yourself. There must be a dozen after him."

"They all know what your sister knows?"

"Three of them do, but one of those three has a motive similar to my own and my sister's. Cole raped and killed his wife."

"Who is he?"

"He is called Yanupi. He's a full breed Mescalero but an outcast from his people because he trusted a white man."

"Coleman Langston?"

Janelle nodded. "Yanupi's wife was the daughter of an Apache chief. The child she carried would have been his grandbaby, a kind of prince . . . a future leader."

"And how in the hell did your sister get involved with a Mescalero Apache?"

"She worked at the cantina at Medicine Forks over in New Mexico Territory. He tended stock."

"She bed down with him too?"

Janelle slapped Preacher's face . . . hard. Few women had mustered the courage to do that and, thought Preacher, even fewer had the justification he'd just given Janelle Barrett.

"Your sister must approve of this Apache."

"She almost insists on him, and not without good reason."

"What reason?"

"How good are you at tracking over rocks?"

Preacher considered the question. Rocks? New Mexico territory? An Apache? "Not worth a damn," he said. "What's in it for the Indian?"

"None of the money," Janelle shot back, "if that's what you're worried about. He wants Cole Langston."

"Or part of him anyway," Preacher said.

"Have you—"

"Changed my mind?"

Janelle bit her lower lip.

"Not yet."

"What else, Preacher? What will it take?"

"You said you'd doublecross your sister. How?"

"By keeping her out of it when the showdown comes. She may never forgive me, but she'll be alive at least."

"And you mentioned there were three men who knew what your sister knows. Who, besides the Apache?"

Janelle shrugged. "That I don't know. I'm not even sure she knows. Maybe only the Apache knows."

"And why not just hire the Apache? You've got a man, you can still doublecross your sister when the time comes, and you've five thousand ahead."

Janelle gave Preacher a look of contempt. "The money. The damned money. It's all you seem to talk about. Didn't you ever do anything for someone else just because it was the right thing to do? Even something for yourself! Was it always just for money . . . money . . . money?"

"I have . . . and I promised myself I wouldn't do it again."

"Doesn't it bother you that my main interest in you was your skill with a gun? That anything else was just a ruse?"

"You offering five-thousand for anything else I've got?"

Janelle launched another right hand.

This time Preacher caught her wrist. "One entitlement," he said, "and you've used your limit."

"Maybe your gun is as over-rated as the rest of you."

Preacher turned loose of Janelle's arm, stepped back and smiled. "If it turns out that way, you're five thousand ahead again."

"Bastard!"

"You bring little sister to me tonight. We'll talk some more."

"And if you're satisfied?"

"Tonight," Preacher said.

The girl seemed younger than Preacher remembered. Perhaps, he thought, it was because she'd been naked and he was paying attention to the wrong things.

"This is my sister . . . Margaret. Maggie is what I call her. Maggie, I guess you remember Mister Preacher."

"Preacher," he said, "just plain Preacher."

"I won't tell you anything until you write down what you promise."

"So I was told. It wouldn't make a damned bit of difference you know . . . written down or not."

"It makes a difference to me," Maggie said.

Preacher shrugged.

"You'll do it then?"

"If my conditions are met . . . yes."

Maggie frowned, looked at her sister and then back at Preacher. "Your conditions? But I thought—"

"Whatever you thought, little lady . . . you thought all by yourself. You've got your conditions, I've got mine."

"Such as," Janelle asked, scathingly.

"Such as, we ride out and meet the Apache. I get some answers from him and if I'm still satisfied, I get five thousand . . . cash. I'll collect the rest myself."

"That's damned big of you," Janelle said.

"The answer is no anyway. No one meets Yanupi until we're on the trail." This from Maggie.

Preacher got to his feet and shrugged again. "Have it your way," he said. He walked to the door, opened it, turned back, smiled and said, "Ladies."

"Damn you!" It was Maggie and she was addressing her sister, not Preacher.

"Why didn't you tell me what you wanted this afternoon?" Janelle asked Preacher.

"Because it wasn't you who could do anything about it."

Maggie spoke. "I've got more money, I'll pay you more . . . myself."

"If I don't meet the Apache, and if I don't get the right answers from him when I do, I don't ride with you . . . not for twenty thousand."

Maggie studied Preacher's face. She swallowed. She stepped backwards, feeling for a chair. She found one. She sat down. She looked from Preacher's face to Janelle's and then back again. She looked pitiful. Like a little girl who'd just lost her favorite doll. She sighed.

Preacher had seen all the symptoms before. Maggie needed Preacher's gun. Preacher considered her carefully. He suspected that Maggie had a stronger and probably even more personal motivation in the matter of Cole Langston than did Janelle. In any event, he knew she was whipped.

"Alright then. When can you leave?"

Preacher closed the door. "Where's the Indian?"

Maggie looked up. She was still dubious. She had no choice. "At a camp in the Dragoons . . . waiting. Half a day's ride maybe. If we ride out at sun up tomorrow, we could be there by noon or so."

"Uh uhn. You two buy tickets on the Saturday morning run to Phoenix, round trip. Five miles out I'll be waiting with your horses and everything else we need. I'll be pulling out Friday evening. No need to roust out the camp followers just yet."

Janelle put her arms around her sister's shoulders. Maggie got to her feet. They both looked at Preacher and nodded.

7

Preacher whiled away the rest of the evening in a poker game. About midnight he called it quits and stopped at the bar for a final drink.

Doc Holliday shouldered up next to him a few minutes later. "When are you going after Cole Langston?" Doc asked.

Preacher couldn't believe his ears. He considered Doc and the possibility that he'd been taken in by a woman he'd just bedded. The idea raised his hackles.

Doc held his hands out in front of him in mock defense. "I won't breathe a word of it," he said, "so help me." Doc was finding some humor in Preacher's discomfort. He chuckled.

"How in the hell did you find out about Cole Langston?"

"No surprises there, Preacher. The lady tried me first."

"Janelle?"

Doc nodded.

"How hard did she try?"

Doc Holliday knew Preacher's meaning and this time he didn't grin. "If she'd have tried that hard Preacher, Katie would have hung two scalps over her door."

"I'm not sure I am going after him, Doc." Preacher eyed his glass and found a swallow remaining. He drained it. "I'm a damned sight more doubtful than I was."

Doc straightened up. "She didn't say anything to me, Preacher. I happened to see her going into your room. It didn't take much figuring to know why."

Preacher was some relieved with that news.

"Doc, I'm going to call it a day."

"Me too, Preacher, but I didn't really stop in here to goad you. There is a gent in town who will go after Cole Langston and anybody else who might consider it."

Preacher frowned. "Do I know him?"

"You know 'im," Doc said, "by reputation anyway. Layne Payson."

Preacher's jaw went rigid and he clenched his teeth. "Damn!"

Layne Payson's history paralleled Preacher's own. The similarities were so striking as to cause some to believe they were kin. Payson was the scion of a wealthy tobacco magnate. He served with distinction during the war as a member of the raiders led by John Hunt-Morgan. At war's end, Payson found nothing to which he could return. He too found those who had ravaged his home and avenged his family. By then he knew little else but the law of the gun.

Preacher walked Doc back to Kate's place and they talked along the way. Doc had a proposition.

"Layne Payson," Doc said, "has one weakness. High stakes poker. I've heard he won't sit a game where the cards are worth under a hundred each."

"What are you saying, Doc, exactly?"

Doc rubbed his chin. "Janelle will have to stake you up front. You stake me and I'll get you a two day head start over Payson."

The duo reached Kate's place and Preacher stepped out so that he would be between Doc and the door. He turned and said, "You want me to stake your suicide, Doc. You tried to goad me and that didn't work so now you want to goad Payson. I won't do it, Doc."

Doc Holliday was about four feet from Preacher. He closed the distance to a foot. "Ya know somethin', bounty killer," Doc said, spitting the words out, "you've come to take your family name too serious. If I want preachin', I'll go to church. As to dyin', that's my business."

"Not if you try to get me to set it up for you."

"You scared o' dying, Preacher?"

"No, but I'm not ready yet."

Doc smiled. "Neither am I. Up Colorado way, the sawbones tells me I might buy a few more years. If that's true, I don't want to spend them all in some goddamn saloon. I'd like to take Layne Payson's money and I'd like to give you time to decide about helping that gal. You'd have time to talk to the Apache without Payson on your trail." Doc looked down and then up again. "And if things worked out right, I'd have a good partner up in Colorado."

Preacher was still dubious. "Pretty speech, Doc, but you did try to get me to pull on you and Layne Payson is greased lightning. You sure that what you just told me is all there is to it?"

Kate Elder opened the door just then and she didn't like what she heard. "You calling me a liar, Preacher?"

"I'm asking, Doc."

"No need to ask, Preacher, I just told you."

Preacher considered Doc, nodded at Kate and said, "I'll think on it Doc."

"Don't moralize with me, bounty killer. It doesn't suit you."

"I said, I'll think on it." Preacher turned to Kate. "Good night, Kate." Preacher stepped around Doc and started walking away. He turned back when Doc called his name.

"Couple of other things you ought to consider, Preacher."

"Like what?"

"Like your guns. Don't get too puffed up on yourself. You know there's never a horse that couldn't be rode," Doc paused, "and never a rider that couldn't be throwed."

"Good advise, Doc, but I don't need it."

"Then think on this Preacher, think on it about Layne Payson and think on it about Doc Holliday. Tying a man in a gunfight ain't a goddamn bit better than losing." Doc turned on his heel and pushed past Kate Elder. Kate and Preacher stared at one another for a moment and then Preacher walked away.

Preacher respected Doc Holliday and more important than that, he liked Doc. Before he dropped off to sleep, he'd decided.

Doc Holliday got his grubstake and Preacher got out of Tombstone with Janelle and Maggie Barrett unseen. The trail into the Dragoons was tough and Preacher was reminded again on the resourcefulness of the red man. Yanupi could have stood off an entire cavalry troop had it been necessary.

The Indian stood on flat rock, watching the trio. Janelle took the lead and held up a hand in greeting. Yanupi ignored her. He was cradling a Henry in his arms, he wore a silver studded hip rig and crossed bandolier. He also toted twin Bowie knives.

The trio rode to a spot below him and then climbed the rest of the way on foot. Yanupi leveled the Henry at Preacher's belly.

"He's a friend, Yanupi," Janelle said.

"Quiet, woman! Let the white eyes tell his own lies."

Preacher pushed past Janelle and moved to within a few feet of the Apache. He was not a big man, but Preacher could see the sinew in the arms and legs and abdomen. Preacher thought to himself that the best way to kill this man would be from a distance of sixty feet or so.

"We have a common enemy," Preacher said, "Cole Langston."

The Henry barked and laid a deep crease in Preacher's left boot. Preacher's Indian experience came into play. He didn't move.

Yanupi smiled and fired a second time. Janelle stepped forward and Preacher grabbed her arm and pulled her aside.

"If you want play boy's game Yanupi, then you do it by yourself. I didn't ride out here to see an Apache go through the ritual of manhood." Preacher shifted his weight. "One more thing. If you fire that rifle in my direction again, I'll kill you."

Preacher could see the barrel of the Henry move slightly but he wasn't worried. Yanupi would have to work the lever again. By the time he finished, he'd be dead.

"You have lied," Yanupi said. "You have no hate for the white eyes Langston. You do what you do for money." Yanupi spit on the rock between Preacher's feet.

"And you do what you do so your people will see you as God and welcome you back to their fires. Vanity and pride are riding with the Apache brave, not hatred."

"You know not of what you speak, white eyes. Of a wife, a child . . ."

"And a home, Yanupi. A home to return to and a people to welcome you. I know about loss, and I know about hate, and I know about revenge, and I know the emptiness of having no place to go back to. I was told you were a man." Preacher smirked. "You are a boy."

Janelle and Maggie moved away, certain that the hunt for Langston would end before it began.

Yanupi looked up just above Preacher's head and behind the gunman. He shifted the Henry to his left hand and pointed with his right. "The hawk flies above you white eyes, the sign of your death if your tongue speaks lies."

Preacher knew less of the Apache than of other Indians, but he knew enough to realize such exchanges could go on between them for several hours. He opted to put a quick end to Yanupi's doubts.

"The hawk is sent by Langston to make us enemies," Preacher said, "and it is the hawk which will die." Preacher went into a crouch, whirled, drew his hip pistol, sighted the hawk and fired. It was one hell of a shot and an even bigger gamble if he missed. He didn't. He holstered the pistol and turned around. Yanupi was duly impressed. "My gun speaks no lies, Yanupi."

The Apache's doubt vanished with the hawk.

According to Yanupi, Coleman Langston was holed up in the most rugged country in all of Arizona territory. The Mogollon Rim. The Rim was accessible by only two known trails. One from the north and the other from the south, the one Yanupi would use. Over the years, the Rim had become a place of legends. Spanish gold in great abundance was believed to be buried there and the infamous Cochise's stronghold was supposedly hidden by the Rim's natural fortifications. The trip to the Rim, Preacher learned, would include two stops.

The first was the Kohl ranch where Yanupi had a twofold mission. The first was to see his young friend, Ely Kohl. Yanupi and Ely had been friends since their boyhood days. Days when the owner and founder of the ranch, Elijah Kohl, was at peace with the Apache. Kohl's ranch was a horse breeding ranch and the fine stock Kohl had brought from the east mixed well with the toughness and stamina of the Indian ponies. The result was one of the finest range animals in the west.

Yanupi's second mission at the ranch he revealed to Preacher only after they had arrived. The women were bathing in the house, young Eli was still out on the range for the day's work. Yanupi caught Preacher tending his horse.

"The women will remain behind here. They will be safe and we can move faster." Preacher stopped what he was doing and looked up. Yanupi pointed south, the direction from which they had just come. "Others follow. Three or four. Before the sun of another day, I will go with young Kohl and we will run horses north. We leave a trail so that those who follow will not stop here.''

Preacher stood up. ''I think it's a damned good idea, Yanupi, but I wouldn't give even money on Janelle Barrett sitting still for it.''

''Then she must not know until it is too late.''

Preacher shook his head. ''God help you when she catches you.''

Yanupi showed his first sign of humor a moment later. He said to Preacher, ''It is not I but you she will catch, white eyes. I will be in the Rim facing possible death at the hands of Cole Langston.''

''How come you get the easy part, Yanupi?'' Preacher asked, drily. Yanupi blinked and then put his head back and laughed.

Ely Kohl returned to the ranch near sundown and he and Yanupi greeted each other as would two, long lost brothers. They hugged, danced around and generally made fools of themselves for a spell. At dinner, Preacher met the rest of the Kohl family.

Ely was young, nineteen or twenty, Preacher guessed. He had the calloused hands of a horseman and the obvious strength of a hard worker. He also carried a matched set of Colt pistols. They were, by Preacher's guess, the latest models of the already famed Peacemaker. Ely was friendly but also obviously in awe of Preacher. He dug out a dozen dime novels depicting the wildest of adventures in which the Widow Maker was supposed to have participated and he elicited a promise that Preacher would show Ely his guns.

The elder Kohl was near fifty but as hard as nails. He was short, stocky and barrel chested. His thick forearms stood out from his body when he walked, too muscular to come close to his sides. He had an unruly shock of gray hair and piercing eyes.

There was no Mrs. Kohl. A fever had struck the valley only a few years after the Kohl family arrived. Elsie Kohl tended her own offspring, some of those belonging to neighbors and many infant Apaches. The effort took her life. There was one more Kohl, however, and Preacher discovered she was the eldest of the children. Louisa Kohl was twenty-five, blonde, buxom and, Preacher thought, probably a virgin.

"You're the second most famous man we've ever had here," she said, during a lull in the dinner conversation.

Preacher smiled. "Who was the first?"

"Why, General Miles. He came and bought some of our stock. It was nearing winter and he was wearing a bearskin coat. It was then I learned why the Indians call him Bearcoat Miles." She put her hand to her mouth and giggled. "You know what he told me?" Preacher shook his head. His eyes met Janelle's and he could see her look of disdain. "He told me that Kit Carson told him once that he should wear the coat with the fur side next to his body. He said Kit Carson told him it would be warmer." She giggled again. "Then he said, he told Kit Carson it was funny that the bears didn't know that." She giggled. She was the only one who did. Preacher smiled but he found it difficult to keep his eyes above her bosom.

"Care for a good cigar?" the elder Kohl asked Preacher.

"No thanks," Preacher said. "I don't smoke but could I get you to join me in an after dinner drink?" Preacher produced his flask, "Excellent New Orleans bourbon, Teton Jack."

"Please," Kohl said.

After the drinks, Preacher wandered into the yard alone. He walked for awhile, admiring the surrounding country. It was rough, desolate, isolated, but there was, he thought, an attraction to it and he could understand Kohl's love of it.

Preacher found a spot on a corral fence and just sat. The faintest of sounds caught his ear and he turned suddenly. Yanupi was approaching. "You have the ears of the deer," Yanupi said. "See the purple shadows there. The Rim."

"It looks harmless enough from here."

"So does the snake asleep on the rock or the grizzly in its den."

"Yeah," Preacher said. He turned to Yanupi. "You said we were being dogged, trailed. Three or four. What's the confusion?"

"One could be a pack animal. They still come but tomorrow we will lose them."

"Any ideas who they are?"

"Some," Yanupi said, looking into Preacher's face, "but I thought you would have more ideas than I do. Men like you, perhaps?"

"That's possible," Preacher said. "Cole Langston is worth a lot of money." Preacher looked at Yanupi. "You an' me gonna have trouble over him?"

Yanupi shook his head. "I do not seek to kill Langston."

"What then?"

"I will cut off his tool so that he might not again know a woman. He must live long enough to know what has happened."

"I can't promise he'll live long if I meet up with him. The choice would be his."

"I will meet him before you," Yanupi said,

jumping down. "After that you may kill him."

Preacher jumped. "What's Maggie Barrett's interest in him and what's the connection between you two?"

Yanupi considered the Tennessee gunman and his question. "Langston raped her. She carries his child. I will avenge this thing and my own family's and then I will take the white woman as my squaw and save the breed boy by raising him as an Apache."

Preacher shook his head. The situation grew more complex with each passing day and he still suspected Janelle Barrett was into it for more reason than just her sister. Yanupi trotted off toward the stable and a good night's sleep. Preacher watched him and thought of the injustice of it. Yanupi had been half raised with Elijah Kohl's son, but was unable to sleep in the house because he was an Apache.

8

Janelle Barrett found no one in the kitchen of the Kohl ranch. She also noted there were no breakfast dishes and only one dirty coffee cup. Maggie was still dressing and Janelle walked to the front door and looked out. Louisa Kohl was coming from the barn, carrying a basket of eggs. Janelle returned to the kitchen and poured herself some coffee.

Louise smiled pleasantly when she saw Janelle. "Good morning, Miss Barrett."

"Where are the men?" Janelle asked.

"Why, daddy and most o' the hands rode—"

"I don't mean your men, I mean Preacher and the Indian."

Louisa turned and cast a puzzled glance at Janelle.

"Well, there are they?"

"You mean you didn't know they rode out this morning?"

Janelle lurched forward and grabbed Louisa's arms. Louisa was startled by the move and jumped back. Janelle felt silly.

"I'm," she paused and tried to compose herself, "I'm sorry but, no, I," she sighed, "I didn't know. Please, tell me what you can. It's really very important to me."

"I can't tell you anything Miss Barrett, except that long before daylight the gunfighter, the Indian and my brother Ely rode out. They rode east. That's all I know. Perhaps my father—"

Louisa Kohl was left standing open mouthed. Janelle skipped stairs hurrying to the bedroom. Maggie was just slipping into a dress.

"Get out of that and get your trail clothes back on."

Maggie looked up but never had a chance to say anything.

"Preacher, Ely Kohl and Yanupi rode out this morning. They're gone!"

Maggie stood up. "Where, for God's sake?"

"Does it make any difference? They double crossed us, both of them, your trustworthy Apache and that damned tin horn gunman."

"But what can we do now? We don't know where they went."

"That's where you're wrong, Maggie. Get dressed, I'll tell you about it while we ride. We've got no time to lose."

Snow had already fallen in the mountains to the north and was visible on the higher peaks as the trio of men closed the distance to the Mogollon Rim. The trail Yanupi was leaving was a devious one which would challenge the most experienced tracker. About midday, Yanupi called a halt.

"I will ride back to the south and determine if our

bait has been taken."

"And if it hasn't?" Ely asked.

"Then we must find in which direction they did ride."

Preacher had dismounted and he walked to Yanupi's horse. "Janelle Barrett told me there were three other men who could know as much as you do about Cole Langston's whereabouts. We got at least three trailing us according to you. Would they be the same three?"

"No," Yanupi said. "The ones the girl talks about would not ride together. That is why we must lead these three away until we can find out who they are."

"Okay Yanupi, but you tell me about the first three. Who are they?"

"The one who kills bear. He is called Teague."

"Big Mike Teague?"

Yanupi nodded.

Preacher looked puzzled. "He's not a bounty man. He's a trapper."

"It is said that Langston and those who ride with him killed Teague's partner and took their winter's work, skins and furs."

Preacher nodded. "Who else?"

"One like you. A white eyes who hunts other men for money. He is called Koop."

"Rollie Koop," Preacher said, shaking his head. Koop was a much over-rated gunslinger with a reputation for back shooting both the men he was hunting and his competition. He was usually in company with two or three other men just like himself.

"And the third man?"

Yanupi looked down as though he thought the

question unnecessary. "The gunman, Payson."

Preacher said nothing but stepped back. He glanced at the ground. He'd known about Payson from Doc Holliday but it was strange that the information was confirmed by an Apache. Preacher looked up again. "Watch yourself, Yanupi. We'll be waiting right here."

The Apache rode off.

Preacher picketed the stock and then tossed Ely a tin of beans. "Sorry, no fire yet."

Ely nodded. While he ate hungrily, he noted that Preacher was picking at his food. He wondered why. "You look like a man with somethin' gnawin' at him."

"Considering our circumstance and what we're out here for, I wouldn't think that would come as much of a surprise."

"Does when a man like you is involved. You want to talk on it?"

"Layne Payson," Preacher said. "You heard of him?"

"Sure I've heard of him," Ely said. He was a little stunned at Preacher's forthrightness. "You're not scared of 'im, are you?" Preacher smiled. That was always the way of a young man. Good sense was synonymous with fear.

"Aren't you?"

Ely Kohl frowned at Preacher. It wasn't the reply he'd expected.

"No sir, I'm not. I'm better'n most with my guns." Ely reached down and fingered the butt of his pistol. "Better'n you'd guess. Men like Payson get careless. Put too much stock in their reputation and tend to underestimate anybody they never heard of." Ely considered Preacher a moment and then added, "You're like Payson in one way, I mean a real professional. I could learn from a man like you." Ely stood up. "I'd like to show you what I can do."

"Don't bother," Preacher said. "I'm no teacher and if I was, you wouldn't be my choice for a student."

Ely Kohl took immediate offense. "Why the hell not?"

"Because you've got everybody figured out ahead of time except the one man who really matters."

"You mean Payson, don't you? Yeah, because o' what I said. You are scared of 'im an' it riles you some 'cause I'm not."

"No, I don't mean Payson," Preacher said, "I mean you. You think carrying a gun and being good with it is a game. A contest which, if you happen to win, makes you the better man."

"Losin' sure as hell don't."

"And winning only makes you worth one thing, Kohl. It makes you worth trying for the next fellow who rides by."

"What the hell are you? A professional gun fighter. A man who's killed, God, who knows how many men. Why are you so special?"

"Special?" Preacher smiled. "That's just the point Kohl, I'm not special and I recognize that fact. It's part of living by the gun. It's not a religion like Payson makes it, and it's not a simplistic belief like yours. It's a law."

Ely snorted. "Law? What the hell law do you live by?"

"Preacher's law." Preacher slipped the Mare's leg from its boot and tucked it beneath his saddle. Then, he stretched out.

"Preacher's law? Just what the hell is Preacher's law?"

Preacher reached up and pulled his hat down over his eyes. He said, "It's a lot of things Kohl, but in this particular application, it's the difference between living and dying. Now, if you'll take a little friendly advice, you'll get some sleep."

Ely Kohl didn't take the advice. Instead, he paced and concerned himself with Preacher's low regard for his, Ely's, gun skills. Several times he looked toward the dozing gunman with anger and contempt. He thought, one day soon, I'll show him how wrong he is. Preacher's law indeed! I'll show him Kohl's skill.

The Apache was back within three hours and his report was a mixed blessing. None of the trio of men had been baited by the new trail but neither had they ridden to Kohl's ranch.

"They are lawmen," Yanupi said. "When I realized I knew none of them, I simply approached them in friendship."

"That was damned risky, wasn't it?" Ely asked.

"More so if he hadn't," Preacher replied.

Yanupi nodded. "I knew they were not any of the men about whom I told you. They would not be together. The only risk was the possibility they might be riding to join Langston. If that was the case, I'd hoped we'd be able to pick up their track."

"But they was neither?"

"One says he is the chief, the leader of the Arizona Rangers. The others are his deputies. He said a third man already went ahead of them to the way station at Red Creek. They are going to the way station at Jake's Corners."

Preacher frowned. "This chief Ranger got a

name?"

"He said he was Troutman."

Preacher grinned. "That would be Bill Troutman. He's a good man and if he's as dogged as he used to be, you and I neither one may get near Cole Langston."

"I do not believe he seeks Langston," Yanupi said, "but perhaps I am wrong."

"Well anyways, we know who ain't followin'. I say we get on with it. Let's ride on into the Rim."

Yanupi looked at his friend and shook his head. He said, "No. We too will ride to Jake's Corners. It is there that Langston's men come for supplies. We must know when they come and how many."

Jake's Corners had been a way station since the beginning of stage service in the Arizona territory. One of the first runs served came from the west and up through Phoenix to Flagstaff. Now, two stages a week came through the Corners.

The place was operated by only four people. Jake Highland was the owner and employed two wranglers. They tended stock and handled maintenance. Jake's daughter, Evelyn, took care of the paperwork, interior cleaning and cooking chores. They did maintain three rooms for overnight stays during inclement weather.

The way station also served a widespread area populace with a small inventory of trail supplies. An occasional drifter or trapper was also a customer. Even the Apaches ventured into Jake's Corners once in a while. Jake had an agreement with them which, while self serving, also served the stage lines. He asked that they conduct no raids between his place and the station on either side. In exchange for that, he arranged to supply them with what they wanted. He drew the line at selling them guns but he would sell them ammunition if they already owned weapons.

The station was in a lush valley with three entrance trails. The most rugged was the trail heading west and north toward the Rim. The most narrow, and therefore the spot for the easiest ambush of an incoming stage, was to the east, toward Red Creek. The incoming trail from the south was the most visible and easiest to defend.

The station itself was a two story structure which served as the residence for the Highlands, housed the three guest rooms, a kitchen, dining area and a small saloon. There were two large out-buildings. One for stock and feed during inclement weather and the other for the blacksmith and maintenance work. Between the main building and the out-buildings was a large open yard where the teams could be changed and freight, if any, loaded, unloaded or transferred.

Jake Highland was an amibitious man who had tried to upgrade the station and, of course, his own station in life. He wanted a government contract in the worst way but so far he'd been unable to impress the army enough to acquire one. Most of the government business therefore, was kept to Phoenix or Flagstaff.

Jake also liked adventure in his life and found it exciting when the Apaches visited. Occasionally, the station was frequented by someone of notorious repute and Jake enjoyed recounting the events around the pot belly in the winter time. All his desires aside however, Jake Highland was an honest, hard working man who would not trade his principles for profit.

Little did he know that his station and those to whom he was closest were all about to become the focal point of the volatile development to come to Arizona since its recognition as a territory.

9

Yanupi led the trio away from the northbound stage road and into the rugged, heavily wooded country due north of the way station. He did not want to risk being seen too soon and perhaps by the wrong people. His precaution proved valuable but it fell to Ely Kohl to recognize it.

Yanupi pointed. "Jake's Corners. We have beaten out the white lawmen."

Ely Kohl stood up in his stirrups, eyed the scene below and said, "Mebbe so but we come second to somebody."

Preacher considered the boy, frowned, stood up in his own stirrups and eyed the area carefully. Yanupi had already dismounted and moved to a nearby rock where he could get a wider sweep of the terrain below.

"What's wrong?" Preacher finally asked. Just the question made Ely feel more important. He looked at Preacher and then turned and pointed toward the station.

"No smoke from the chimney. This is a stage run day. Stage comes up from the south. Passengers eat their breakfast at Red Creek station and their suppers here. Evie ought to be cookin' down there right now."

"Evie?"

"Evelyn Highland, Jake's daughter."

Yanupi returned and looked up. "There is no one in the corral, no one tending stock or making a team ready for a change."

Preacher dismounted. "Then either there is nobody down there, or there is somebody who shouldn't be. Let's find out which."

Ely stepped forward and touched Preacher's arm. "That'll be my job."

"You don't know what you're riding into."

"Wrong, Preacher. I'm the only one here who does. I know who should be down there and I ride in here regular. Nobody will pay much attention to me. I come to see Evie 'bout once a month." Ely looked hard into Preacher's face. "You look just like what you are Preacher, a gunfighter." Ely pointed to Yanupi. "Or do you think we oughta send him in?"

Preacher knew Ely was right. He considered the boy for a moment and then nodded.

"It will take time my friend," Yanupi said, "to get back to the south road from here."

"I won't come in from the south. I'll go back to the north trail. I'll tell 'em I was up to Pheonix buyin' supplies. Nobody down there'll know differ'nt."

"When you find out how many, make an excuse to get back outside," Preacher looked down toward the station and pointed, "there, just to the right of the well. Take your hat off and knock the dust off your britches. One hit for each man down there."

The door to the way station flew open and Rollie Koop jerked his gun from its holster and then cussed. "Goddam it Lyle, you come through that door like you got an Apache' on your ass. Less'n you actual do, it's a good way to git your goddam head blowed off." Rollie holstered his gun.

Lyle Reese looked foolish but he said, "We got comp'ny. Lone rider comin' in from the north."

"Git out an' tell Charlie," Koop said and then eyed the kitchen, "an' then git back in here an' hide in there 'til we find out who it is?" Lyle Reese nodded and went back outside. A second later, the door opened and he stuck his head back inside.

"Remember," he said, "you promised me that there gal." Koop made a threatening gesture toward Reese with an empty glass and Reese withdrew again.

"Goddamn horny sonuvabitch. Don't know he kin have some o' them fine N'Orleans wimmin when we git the goddam money. Stupid, horny sonuvabitch."

Less than a minute later, Lyle Reese was back inside. He was grinning. "Charlie says he'll keep a real close eye on 'em. That there rider, he ought to be comin' in 'bout a minute from now."

Rollie Koop mimicked Reese's squeaky voice. "Charlie says he'll keep a real close eye on 'em." Koop eyed Reese with disdain.

"O' course he's gonna keep an eye on 'em, goddamn it, that there is why I put 'im out there. Now git in the goddamn kitchen." Reese's smile faded and he nodded. Koop shook his head. "Stupid, horny sonuvabitch." Rollie Koop took a bottle from behind the bar and then moved to a table near the front door.

Koop was, as Preacher had reflected, a highly over-rated gunny with a record of accomplishment in his life which could have easily been written on a postage stamp. He'd robbed two banks and been caught both times. He mimicked a train robbery after reading about the exploits of the James brothers over in Missouri. That too had gone awry. His bady planned exploits had cost the lives of more men than he'd ever been able to entice into riding with him all at one time. Half a dozen or more. Koop wanted to be a leader. In fact, he needed leading.

The door opened and Koop tightened his grip on his hand gun. He had it in his lap, cocked and ready. His left hand was in plain sight, curled around the whisky bottle.

"Mornin'," Ely said, smiling. Koop nodded but made no other response. Ely looked around and then moved to the bar, looked behind it, glanced toward the kitchen door and then did a half turn and said, "Looks like I come too early even for breakfast. Damn, where is ever'body?"

Kook took a long pull on the bottle, then cleared his throat, but said nothing.

Rollie Koop only ran with men he was certain he could best. He put on no airs around such men. Confronted with anyone else, he puffed up, did his best to stand taller and straighter and lower his voice. Finally, he answered, "I figger Apache'," Rollie said, "prob'ly scared off them what run the place. I come in before daylight an' they was nobody here. You plannin' on catchin' the stage?"

"Nope," Ely said, "just on my way home from Phoenix. Live south o' here about half a day." He looked around again. "I could sure do with a cup o' hot coffee." He looked at Koop. "How 'bout you, mister? You like to trade that whisky for some hot coffee? I make a fair to middlin' pot."

"You ridin' alone?"

"Yeah. You?"

Rollie eased his gun off of his lap and slipped it into the holster. He assumed Ely hadn't caught the action but the assumption was wrong. Ely knew now he'd sold his bill of goods and he might find out what he wanted to know.

"No. I got another man with me. Matter o' fact, he's in the kitchen there, lookin' to fix some coffee." Koop grinned. "But his coffee's the worst I ever drank. If you can brew some, we'd all be better off." Koop banged the whisky bottle. "Reese, bring out a bucket an' fetch some water." Reese appeared in the doorway.

"Mornin'," Ely said, smiling, as Lyle Reese approached him. Lyle appreciated anyone who said a kind word to him and returned the smile.

"Mornin'."

He looked at Rollie and saw the frown on Koop's face. He looked down and then headed for the door. Ely wanted to make a move but he knew Rollie Koop had already lied to him. Ely knew the riding stock at Jake's Corners and there were three horses he'd seen in the corral that didn't belong. There was a third man here and Ely figured he was watching the Highlands.

"If you don't mind, I'll walk my horse to the corral. She could use some feed."

Rollie Koop did mind. He had the intruder in his sight and under his gun. He didn't want to lose that edge. "I'll have muh man handle it," Rollie said, getting to his feet, "while you fix that there coffee." Rollie had taken a stance as though he expected some argument. Ely recognized it and simply shrugged.

"Fine with me," he said. It was't, but until he could find the third man, he'd have to play along. He moved toward the kitchen as Lyle Reese came back through the front door. Unknown to any of them was the fact that the third man, Charlie Little, had been found by someone else. Yanupi.

The Apache had worked his way to the south of the station, having moved out almost at the same time Ely did. Preacher stayed on the ridge to the north, ready to move to help either man.

A dilapidated old shack, once a smokehouse, stood about a hundred yards from the rest of the station's complex. It was there that Charlie stood watch over Jake and Evie Highland and one of Jake's men, Jess Painter. The second man had blundered into Koop and his men at the time of their arrival. He'd made a run for it and Koop had sent Lyle Reese after him. According to Reese, he got the man. While Koop was doubtful, Reese was telling the truth. Yanupi found the man's body and back-tracked the double set of footprints to the smokehouse.

Charlie Little heard a noise in front of the shack. He'd forced his prisoners to lie face down on the floor. They were bound and gagged and grateful to be alive. The only reason they were was Koop's need for them when the stage arrived. Charlie eyed the trio on the floor and then moved to the door. He assumed what he'd heard was Lyle Reese again.

Charlie opened the door and saw nothing. He stepped out and saw nothing. He looked toward the station and saw Lyle Reese just entering it, carrying a bucket of water. He frowned, looked around, saw nothing unusual and turned around to go back inside. He got some unexpected help and lived just long enough to find out who'd given it. The knife in his back inflicted a fatal wound and the last thing he saw was Yanupi's face.

"My God," Jake Highland said, "Yanupi! Where did you—"

Yanupi put his finger to his lips and Jake Highland said nothing more. Instead, he freed his daughter while Yanupi untied Jess Painter.

"How many," Yanupi whispered. Jake held up two fingers. "Stay here." Jake nodded. Yanupi slipped out the front door and immediately to the rear of the smoke house. He eyed the north ridge in search of Preacher but he could not see the gunman. He went back inside. "Ely is in there." Yanupi looked at Jess and said, "You. Call out. Perhaps we can lure one of the others out here."

Jess Painter was unaccustomed to taking orders from anyone but Jake, let alone an Apache. He frowned, eyed Jake and Jake nodded. Jess moved to the door and shouted. "Hey in there, I need some help."

Inside, the sound of the voice brought Rollie Koop's gun out of its holster. He levelled it at Ely's belly. Both were still in the dining room. Lyle had taken the water to the kitchen and now returned.

"Fuckin' Charlie tipped our hand," Rollie said, eyeing Ely. He barked at Lyle Reese. "Git on out an' find out what he wants an' shut 'im the hell up."

Lyle nodded, drew his own gun and headed for the shack.

"You got no call to throw down on me mister," Ely said.

"Got all I need, mister. If they's anything wrong out there, if you was lyin' to me 'bout bein' alone or who ya are or anything at all, I'll kill ya."

Outside, Lyle got about half way to the old shack and hollered. It was one of the smarter moves he'd ever made. Yanupi could see him but at that distance, nothing would take him out but a gun and a shot then might mean Ely's death.

"I need some help," Jess hollered again, but he was not visible an Lyle didn't like it.

"What's wrong?"

No reply.

"Charlie?"

Yanupi clenched his teeth together. He'd come down from the ridge with only his handgun and knife. No rifle. He'd have to show himself in order to kill Lyle Reese. He nodded once more to Jess Painter. Jess tried, hard. "I said I need some help in here." Yanupi watched. Lyle Reese was backing up, slowly, his gun levelled toward the shack.

"Lyle," came a shout from the station. It was Rollie Koop.

Lyle stopped. "Somethin's wrong," he shouted back.

Rollie's eyes shifted for just a split second. Ely Kohl made his move. He drew and fired. At the sound of the shot, Lyle Reese whirled around. Yanupi now made his move. He stepped through the door, ran about twenty five feet and let out an Apache war whoop at the same time. Yanupi went down to his knees, his gun already drawn. There was a second shot from inside the station. Lyle turned, Yanupi fired.

Rollie Koop had managed a shot and it put a crease in Ely Kohl's left arm, just below his shoulder. Ely gritted his teeth in pain but the satisfaction of his accomplishment far outweighed the wound. A man had a drop on him, did little more than blink and Ely's lightning speed prevailed. Rollie Koop was dead. Outside, so was Lyle Reese. Yanupi put a bullet in his belly and Lyle died screaming and firing wildly toward the shack.

Yanupi broke the news of the death of Jake's other man while Evie Highland tended Ely's wound. Ely was busy himself, relating how he'd taken out Rollie Koop when Koop had the drop.

Preacher walked through the front door at about the same moment. "Save your story," he said, "our problem is far from over."

Ely looked hurt and angry. Jake Highland and Jess Painter both tensed at the sight of the tall man in black, armed with the vicious looking Mare's Leg. Evie Highland's eyes sparkled and she let them roam over Preacher's frame.

Yanupi got up from his examination of Rollie Koop. He turned. "He is a friend. He is called Preacher. He is a hunter of other white men. He hunts them for money."

Preacher didn't appreciate the introduction or the restriction on his prey. "Or red men," he said, "or black, or any other kind if I have the calling and a reason."

"I heard about you. I heard you killed more'n a hunnert men. Married men. They call you Widow Maker." It was Jess Painter who'd spoken. Preacher ignored him.

"Those Rangers are coming up on the south road. I'd guess they'll be here in half an hour or so."

"That is the trouble you speak about?"

"Nope. We got more company, somewhere up there." Preacher gestured toward the north, toward the ridge. "Two animals, one tracking close to the other and the second one somewhat smaller.''

"'A rider and a pack mule?''

Preacher nodded. "I'm guessing big Mike Teague.'' Preacher looked around. "This way station seems to have more attraction right now than fresh cow dung has for flies. I think we'd best find out why, and damned quick.''

Yanupi nodded and turned to Jake Highland. "You have had men you do not know, men you had not seen before a few suns ago, coming to buy supplies. Is that so?''

Jake nodded.

"How many come and when?''

"Two. Always two and they come on stage days. They'll be comin' today. Mebbe a little after noon or so.''

"It is as I thought,'' Yanupi said.

Ely, his arm wrapped now, got up and smiled at Evie Highland. She smiled back but he also caught her quick glance toward Preacher.

"I say one of us oughta take out Mike Teague.''

"You volunteering for the job?'' Preacher asked.

Ely frowned. "Well, I sure as hell ain't scared of it, if that's what you mean?''

"There was no meaning at all,'' Preacher said, "but it's not our top priority.'' He turned to Jake Highland. "What's coming in on a stage? Today's or any future one? I mean something extra special. Army payroll mebbe or a bank's money transfer. Something like that?''

Jake Highland frowned and eyed Preacher. Finally, he shook his head. "Sorry but I don't know of nothin'.''

"You'd best think on it Highland, real hard.''

Jake got irate. "I told you mister, I don't know.

I've tried to get army contracts and the like but I haven't an' if Wells-Fargo is doin' anythin' else, they sure as hell didn't bother to tell me about it."

Jake didn't like Preacher. The gunman made him nervous. "How's come you want to know anyway?"

"Because this way station is getting mighty damned popular. Now I know why most of the rest of the men who have come here, or will shortly, have done so. They want Cole Langston."

Suddenly, Preacher's revelation also hit Yanupi. "Yes," the Apache said, "they do want Langston but why does Langston wait here? What is so important to him that he risks capture or perhaps death to have it? What, besides money?"

Jess Painter had walked over to the window. He came back now and said, " 'Scuse me gents, but we got visitors."

Preacher stepped out of the front door. Yanupi covered the window and Ely Kohl slipped through the back door. A moment later they were all out front. The trio of Arizona Rangers rode into the yard.

Bill Troutman was first off his horse, eyeing Preacher most of the time. Finally he walked toward him, stopped and said, "Well I'll be damned, it *is* Preacher! J.D. Preacher. Hell, I should have figured you'd be in this somewhere if you was still kickin'."

"I'm still kicking," Preacher said. "How are you, Bill?"

"Same as you, still kickin'."

Introductions were made all the way 'round. Troutman's two men were Pete Hastings and a young buck named Keno Harris. Harris and Ely Kohl eyed each other warily, both somewhat interested in the other's rigs and possible speed.

Preacher was considerably more interested in Bill Troutman's pursuit of Cole Langston. Too, since Troutman was now an Arizona Ranger, his presence seemed to lend credence to the idea of something big passing through Jake's Corners.

"I won't figure you don't know why I'm up in this country Bill, and I've got a pretty fair idea about you, but it still needs an answer or two."

"If I stumble in to Cole Langston, Preacher, I'll take him in but it ain't Cole I'm after if that's what you figure."

"That's what I figured, Bill," Preacher said. "Who is it then, if you don't mind?"

"Mose Murdock. Busted out o' Yuma prison. Had plenty o' help doin' it. Most, so far as I know, come from his brother."

Preacher was surprised. Mose Murdock was supposed to have been hanged and Preacher never knew he had a brother. "When was all this, Bill?"

"Four, mebbe five weeks now. Cale, that is Mose's brother, he set it up. Most all done on the inside. When the break come, posse was onto 'em quick. Five or six men ambushed the posse about two days ride out o' Yuma. Shot 'em up bad. I think you knew one or two of 'em. Luke Poston. Marshaled for a spell up in New Meixco?"

Preacher nodded.

"Tom King, too. They killed him."

"Damn! Tom was one of the best lawmen I ever knew." The lanky Tennesseean leaned forward, gazing at the floor and thinking. He looked up and said, "You said something about the break being set up on the inside. Tell me about that."

"Can't tell you too much. Don't know fer sure. I do know that Cale Murdock got hisself some help from a female. Young, pretty gal they said she was. As to him gettin' in, that was not much of problem. See, ol' Cale, he worked for Wells-Fargo."

"Wells-Fargo?"

Bill nodded and looked a little anxious at the tone of Preacher's voice.

"This female, did she work for them?"

"Not as I know of," Bill replied, frowning. "You know somethin' I ought to be knowin'?"

"Maybe Bill, just maybe, but I'll ask you not to push me for it right now and answer me another question instead."

Bill Troutman didn't hold much stock in bounty hunters but he also didn't classify Preacher in that breed of men. It was a purely personal choice on his part, he just happened to like the gunman. "I'll sit on it a spell but I'll expect somethin' from you when the time comes."

"You'll have it, Bill. Meantime, do you know of any special shipments, money, guns, anything that would make Cole Langston hole up in the Mogollon Rim country and wait out a stage coach?"

"Sure do." Bill leaned back, took off his hat and scratched his head. "Hell, I shoulda figgered that it was Langston's bunch what bushwhacked the posse." He replaced his hat. "If Langston is up there and waitin' then it ain't money he's waitin' on. It's a man."

"Murdock?"

"Murdock'll be along right enough but he's doin' as much waitin' as Cole Langston. Nope, the man they're both waitin' on is a fella who worked for Wells Fargo too. They caught 'im stealin' an' fired 'im. He told 'em they'd be sorry for it. He was givin' information to Murdock an' Cale was passin' it on.

Mebbe to Langston.''

Preacher was now getting a picture which he didn't like. He considered what he'd heard and then Bill Troutman began to pick up the scent too.

"What do you think would prompt a man like Cole Langston to risk a good set up by helping to bust Mose Murdock out of Yuma prison?"

Bill Troutman leaned back in his chair, shoved his hat back on his head, looked for a spot to relieve himself of his quid, found one, spit, scratched his head and said, "Now that one has been causin' me a little grief too Preacher, an' right now I got no answer for it but I'll wager whatever it is, they needed Mose to git it done."

"I'm grateful for your help, Bill. I won't forget it."

"I'll count on you, Preacher."

Both men got up. Preacher was already planning what needed to be done next. It was nearing eight o'clock and the riders from Langston's camp would be on their way by now. Preacher was figuring what edge he might gain by knowing who was on that stage before it ever got to Jake's place.

Bill Troutman's voice jerked him away from his thoughts. "I got a fella ridin' fer me that you knew back down in Texas."

Preacher frowned.

"Name Siringo cause you any rememberin'?"

"Siringo? Damn! Is Toby Siringo riding for you? I heard he got it trying to stand off a lynch mob."

Bill frowned. "Toby did. Them years git on, Preacher. I'm talking 'bout his boy, Charlie. I got him over to Red Crik to check out who's on that incomin' stage."

"Jeezus Bill, that could be a bad mistake."

Bill Troutman reared back. "Preacher, little Charlie is no kid anymore. He's quick as a snake. Oh hell, he's no match fer the likes o' you but I think he could handle most. Anyway, I tol' 'im just to take a look-see, no gun play."

"Bill, there's one more man involved in this little affair that I will tell you about and if I recollect right, he had no love for anybody named Siringo."

"An' who might that be?"

"Layne Payson."

"I heard tell he was in Tombstone," Bill said.

Preacher now thought the old Ranger looked worried.

"I heard tell he tried to face down a gambler name o' Holliday. Doc Holliday."

Preacher tensed. "You say he tried?"

"Seems this here Holliday's got the consumption. Had a spell an' was coughin' blood. Only thing kept Payson from killin' 'im I guess, an' Holliday didn't want to stop it anyways. Took Marshal Earp an' his brother to git Holliday simmered down. Payson rode out but said he'd see Holliday ag'in."

"Bill, I'm riding with an Apache Indian who has a stake in this thing too. He's got the best chance of finding Cole Langston and we both need to know who's on that stage. Will you and your men sit tight here?"

"Figured to," Bill said. "I tol' young Charlie that once he knowed who was on that stage he should ride like hell fer right here. But now I'm wonderin' if—"

"Don't wonder Bill, I'm leaving for Red Creek station right now."

Preacher found Yanupi getting ready to ride north. He intended to know exactly how many of

Langston's men might be riding in today and to be prepared if it was more than two. If not, he'd follow them back into the Rim country.

"You watch yourself, Yanupi."

The Apache shook his head.

"I have nothing to fear," Yanupi said. He looked up at the sky and smiled. "It is a good day to die."

"That makes it even better for staying alive."

Preacher watched Yanupi ride off, then he saddled Cap'n. He also noted that Ely's horse was no longer in the corral. He finished saddling his mount and then returned to the station. Keno Harris' horse was also gone. Inside, Preacher found Bill Troutman angry and taking it out on Pete Hastings.

"Bill?"

The old Ranger ignored Preacher and stomped out.

Jake Highland walked up. "Young Ely an' that two gun Ranger slipped out and rode off together."

Preacher had a gut feeling about the news but he asked anyway. "Where to?"

"Red Creek station."

"Damned fools!"

Preacher was about to go after Bill Troutman when he heard two horses galloping into the yard. He went through the front door fully expecting trouble, perhaps Langston's men arriving early. He found the trouble but it was in the forms of Janelle and Maggie Barrett.

"You son-of-a-bitch," Janelle screamed. She was off of her horse almost before the animal had stopped running. She had a six gun strapped to her hip and was reaching for it.

Pete Hastings came around the corner of the station and took Janelle from behind. Maggie

Barrett came off her horse to aid her sister but was thwarted by Jess Painter. Evie Highland came out and with her father's help, got the two girls calmed down and inside.

"Bounty Hunter, git on over to Red Creek. Take care o' Bill for us. He's madder'n a hornet an' I think they's more trouble afoot than he figured on an' he won't bend where it comes to gettin' the job done. He lives by the law o' the badge. I don't know you mister, except by reputation, an' that's a poor thing sometimes to judge a man by. I just hope you got what it takes to ride with the likes o' Bill Troutman."

Preacher tugged at his hat brim in a silent goodbye and rode off.

Jake Highland had heard the conversation and now walked over and stood by Pete.

"I don't know the bountyman either," he said, "but I recollect some stories I heard about him down in Tombstone. He rode for a spell for the old Hangin' Judge, Isaac Parker, up in Arkansas but he lives only one way."

Pete looked at Jake.

"He calls it Preacher's law."

10

Preacher had never pushed the big stallion so hard. Cap'n's sides were heaving and frothy sweat seeped from around each and every bit of gear on the animal. Nonetheless, Preacher reached Red Creek station in a time that would have been the envy of any of the old Pony Express riders. What bothered him was the fact that he'd not caught up with anyone. Not Ely Kohl, or Keno Harris, or even old Bill Troutman.

The way station at Red Creek was a far different operation than Jake's Corners. It was barely more than a two room shack. Food was served out of tins and there was never more than one standby team in the corral. Preacher didn't like any of what he saw, which consisted of several vultures circling high. He placed them about a mile past the station. There was no sign of life.

"Cap'n," he said, softly, to his horse, "we part trails here but don't wander too far." Preacher didn't bother tethering the animal. Cap'n would be

close and Preacher's special whistle would bring him
quickly if he was needed, and if Preacher could still
whistle. He thought about his old army commander,
Colonel John Mosby. Never, Mosby had often said,
ride into any situation which shows no sign of an
enemy, until it has been reconnoitered. He wondered
what Mosby would tell him now. Preacher was both
the reconnoitering patrol and the combat force.

Preacher worked his way through the woods
above and behind the way station. When he came
parallel with the building, he eyed the sky again and
judged the time of day at about one o'clock. The
stage, if it was coming at all, was already late. It
usually pulled out of Red Creek and headed for
Jake's place about this time. It arrived there in time
for supper. Preacher looked again at the birds and
they had not circled lower. It was a sign, he knew,
that whatever had their interest was still alive. He'd
have to ride to the spot and check it out.

Preacher was halfway down the hill to the way
station when someone, he couldn't make out who,
staggered around the corner of the building. It was a
man and he was clutching at his chest. He looked up
and saw Preacher and raised one arm and motioned
for the gunman to move away. A moment later, he
fell face down. Preacher, armed with the Mare's Leg,
levered a shell into the chamber and started down at
a half trot and in a half crouch.

It was a sound he knew all too well. A deep,
guttural bark of a high calibre rifle. The sound was
amplified against the walls of the surrounding
canyon. Preacher dived and rolled and felt some
pain in his left shoulder as it struck a rock. A piece
of the same rock flew into the air just above
Preacher's head. He knew the gun was a Sharps,

probably a .50 calibre buffalo gun. He knew only one man in the area who carried such a weapon. Big Mike Teague.

Preacher had little idea from which direction the shot had come. It could have been from almost anywhere in the ring of woods which surrounded the way station. He did know his would-be assailant would need time to reload. He got to his feet, stayed in a crouch, and ran a zig zag pattern down the hill to the back of the station. Preacher knelt down, rolled the body of the man and found himself relieved that he didn't recognize him.

Preacher got up, pressed his back against the side of the building and worked his way around to the front. He eyed the area carefully and confirmed his suspicion that the shot had come from the woods. He moved quickly now and darted inside the station.

A man sat at a corner table at the far side of the room. He had a rifle standing against the wall next to him and a hand gun on the table in front of him. There was also a whisky bottle and a glass. Preacher considered the man. In turn, the man eyed Preacher. His mind flashed back to his past. Back to his boyhood and the day of the big shootout in his town. The day his father got so angry. He remembered the shootout and the anger and the tall man in black who carried the odd looking weapon.

Preacher moved closer, slowly. He too was remembering. The man was small, wiry, sallow cheeked but with a firm jaw and close set, ink black eyes.

"Charlie? Little Charlie Siringo?"

"It's the Widow Maker, isn't it?"

Preacher nodded, "Not the handle I prefer but I'd

guess you'd remember me best by that one."
Preacher looked around and then gestured with the barrel of the .58 calibre toward the door. "You know who our friend is?"

Charlie Siringo's face looked suddenly pained. He grimaced, downed a shot of whisky and then shook his head. "Nope. I figured he'd finally get around to me. I planned to sit here and wait him out."

"You didn't figure I could be him when I walked through that door?"

Charlie nodded. "Sure did, but I want to know who I'm shootin' at and why, if I can find out."

Preacher walked to the table. It was then he saw the blood on the floor. He set the carbine aside and knelt down. Charlie Siringo's leg was bleeding badly. The wound was dead center in the left thigh and apparently went clean through.

"It's busted.

"You'll make it Charlie, if we get the bleeding stopped."

"I'm not sure I deserve to make it." Charlie downed another shot of whisky. "I come here to do a job." He glanced at his leg. "I got bushwhacked like a damned greenhorn and let the station agent get killed and likely one or two others." He looked into Preacher's face. "Damned poor showing for a deputy Ranger with a famous daddy, ain't it."

"You're breathing," Preacher said, "and that's the best showing any man can make." He looked around behind the counter until he found a length of rope. He cut a piece. "I've got a hunch that could be a fella called Mike Teague. Mountain man and once-in-a-while bounty man." Preacher knelt again, half expecting some resistance to his efforts. He got none. "Teague is looking to get Cole Langston."

"Aren't you?" Charlie's voice broke as Preacher tightened the rope. The bleeding slowed.

"I don't know that I've got the time to do anything else to that leg right now." Preacher stood up. "The stage is due damned near anytime and things could get a little busy."

"I asked you a question."

Preacher looked down. "Yeah Charlie, I'm here to get Langston and maybe a few answers to some very perplexing questions."

"How about the Murdocks?"

"I didn't know about the Murdocks until I talked to Bill Troutman but it seems they all may belong in the same chamber pot."

"Where is Bill? When did you talk to him?"

"Later," Preacher said. He picked up the carbine and walked toward the window.

"Now, bounty killer!"

Preacher heard the cock of a rifle's hammer. He went on to the window and then he turned.

"Right now!" Charlie repeated.

Preacher turned to face Siringo but the shouts of a stage driver urging on his team caught both their ears. Charlie Siringo lowered the rifle and Preacher moved away from the window and knelt by the side of the door.

The big Concord rumbled to a stop, its wheels caked with mud, and the animals breathing hard from the strain of pulling the load through the quagmire that the road had become the previous day. Preacher peered cautiously outside. The driver dropped from the seat to the ground and looked around. He drew his pistol.

The door of the stage opened and an elderly woman half fell from the inside. A moment later, an old man followed, losing his balance and tumbling to the ground.

The driver moved slowly toward the station. "Don't see nobody around Mose, I don't like the smell of it."

Preacher watched as another man exited the coach. He wore a white collar. He helped the elderly couple up and herded them toward the building.

Preacher raised the Mare's Leg. He heard a noise just behind him. He turned and saw Charlie Siringo crawling toward him. He turned back. The man with the pistol was obviously not the driver. He cocked the gun, moved over to the Reverend and jabbed him in the ribs.

"You three go on through that door an' remember, I'll be right behind you." Mose Murdock dropped to the ground.

The roar was deafening. The big Sharps barked again and the man with the pistol stiffened, dropped his gun, staggered sideways and finally fell forward, breaking out a window. His body was draped over the sill, half in the station and half out. The elderly couple, with the Reverend pushing them, came through the door, the woman screaming and the Reverend shouting for them to get down. He saw Preacher and the gunman pointed toward the back of the room.

Charlie Siringo had reached the window on the opposite side of the door and now broke out the glass with the barrel of his rifle. He winced as he pushed himself to a sitting position. Preacher's view of the coach had been blocked by the trio of people and now he realized that Mose Murdock had dived under the stage and was taking cover on its opposite side.

"Cover me," Preacher said to Charlie. The young Ranger had no time to protest the request. Preacher rolled out of the door, came up on his feet and darted around the corner. Charlie fired two shots into the stage coach. Preacher could see Mose Murdock's legs and then he came into view. He'd darted around the back side of the Concord in hopes of reaching the station. He saw Preacher at the same time, raised his pistol and died all in one move. Preacher killed him with a single shot from the Mare's Leg.

"You alright out there?" The question came from Charlie.

"Fine, Charlie," Preacher answered. "Now stay put. You're the only gun between those folks and whoever is up on the mountain. Mose Murdock is dead. I'm going after our friend with the Sharps."

"Damn you bounty man, you come in here. You can't go. I need you in here."

Preacher didn't answer. He worked his way to the backside of the station and then made a dash for the woods. He knew the gunman was on the opposite side and would not have had the time to make the change.

Preacher reached the woods and then moved quickly along their edge back to where he'd left Cap'n. When he drew near the spot, he whistled. Cap'n appeared almost at once and Preacher moved toward him. At the same time, he heard a galloping horse across the clearing and, he figured, in the woods opposite him. Preacher mounted up, spurred Cap'n and headed in the direction of the sound.

The Tennessean used every skill he'd ever learned trying to find track but he found none that he could use. The man he believed was Mike Teague had given him the slip. He decided to head back to the way station and speak with the passengers. Only they might shed some light onto what had happened to the stage driver and who else might be headed for Red Creek station.

Preacher moved to the opposite side of the road as he headed back. He also saw the vultures still circling, lower.

Preacher promised himself that after he'd stopped at the way station, he'd ride up the trail and find out what the vultures found so interesting. One or two had drifted high and a little closer to the station. They were eyeing the dead station agent but there was too much life around yet so he knew they wouldn't come down.

Preacher started down the road to the station. He saw five horses tied up out front. "Damn!" He'd been gone nearly an hour. Those horses had to belong to whoever was coming to meet Mose Murdock. Langston? He doubted it but he was sure at least one of them would belong to Murdock's brother, Cale.

Preacher reckoned that in spite of the length of time he'd been gone, he hadn't actually been that far away. No more than half a mile. He would have heard shots had there been any. What he couldn't figure was how the five had gained entry with Charlie Siringo inside. He also knew that he couldn't sneak in.

Preacher dismounted about fifty yards from the building. He slapped Cap'n on the flank and waited until the animal was near the woods.

"You in the station," he shouted, "let's talk."

Inside, Charlie Siringo, hands and feet tied and watched over by one man, threw himself to the floor and shouted, "Preacher, watch the . . ." It was as far as he got before his guard hit him.

Two men exited the front door. At that distance, Preacher couldn't recognize either of them. He moved toward them, eyeing the windows as he did so. The body of the dead driver was still draped through the one. There was no sign of life near the other one.

The taller of the two men stepped off of the porch. He grinned. "So you're the famous J.D. Preacher." He laughed.

"Too bad we ain't got no pond around." The second man moved off the porch and distanced himself from the first man. "I'd like to see the sumbitch walk on the water." He laughed.

"We got people inside who are gonna git dead in a hurry bounty killer, unless you dump that there fancy carbine you're totin'," the second man said.

Preacher eyed the window again and then dropped the .58 calibre into the mud.

The first man walked about twenty feet and stopped. His feet came apart and he cautiously pulled the left side of his slicker back. "I'm Tige Lightner," he said, grinning."

"I've heard about you," Preacher said.

Tige laughed and glanced at the other man. "You git that, Billy. Damn! Here's the great bounty killin' Jesus hisself and he's heard o' me."

The other man moved another ten feet to his left and then stopped. Preacher saw he was carrying a low slung, hip rig.

"I heard you were a yellow backed, carpet bagging bastard."

The kid named Billy had been made a promise by Tige Lightner. He could have first crack at J.D. Preacher. Billy was William Jackson Lofton, aged nineteen. He'd killed four men in gunfights. His friends, no more than half a dozen in number, called him Billy Jack or Kid Lofton. One of the men he'd killed had been a deputy sheriff in Kansas and a fair hand with a gun. Billy Jack Lofton was not bad himself, against the average gunny.

"This one'll make ya or kill ya, Billy boy." Tige laughed and William Jackson Lofton drew his six gun.

The barrel was not quite clear of the holster when the weapon went off, a reflex signalled to his hand by an already dying brain. The shot tore most of the top of the holster away and the force spun Billy Jack all the way around. He'd been shot from the front but he ended up falling backwards. The bullet entered the bridge of his nose and tracked diagonally through his head, exiting through the rear of his lower, left side jaw bone.

Preacher had drawn from the hip and his gun was holstered before Billy Jack hit the ground. Preacher turned to face Tige.

"Pretty good Reb, pretty damned good." Tige smiled and drew. Tige Lightner was fast. A hell of a lot faster than the kid named Billy. He fired, still smiling, into a puff of smoke. His shot went over Preacher's left shoulder about six inches from the bounty man's ear. Tige's eyes got big and round.

"I," Tige swallowed and looked down, "I never . . ." He fell face down in the mud, belly shot.

Preacher checked them both and then made his way to the station. He stepped through the door and saw the elderly couple seated together at a corner table. They were eating tinned beans. He saw Charlie Siringo, his leg now bandaged, lying face down on the floor. His hands and feet were bound and he had what appeared to be quite a knot raising up on the back of his head.

"My name is Preacher," he said, speaking to the elderly couple, "and I'll escort you on to Jake's Corners." Preacher now did a half turn to his left. The Reverend sat at another table, smiling.

"Murdock," Preacher said and fired the Mare's Leg. Cale Murdock was dead instantly and his body was thrown backwards out of the chair. The shotgun he'd been holding below the table now toppled to the floor.

"My God, oh my God sir, I wanted to," the old man shook his head and looked away, ashamed that he'd lacked the courage when he needed it.

His wife looked up. "You knew?"

"By the time I came in, yes'm, I knew. Charlie there tried to warn me but it was the horses tied up outside. Two of them left deeper tracks. Three had come in with no riders. Brought here for somebody to ride out on. The driver was dead, so was Mose Murdock."

"One more horse and only one more man," the lady said. Preacher nodded.

She got to her feet and tugged at her husband's arm. He looked up. "I'm Martha and this is my husband Tom." She put her arm on his shoulder. "He's a good man, Mister Preacher. He's a brave man in his own way."

"Of course he is," Preacher said, "now ma'am if you'll revive young Charlie there and get him on his feet, I've got one more duty here and then we'll be leaving." The woman looked outside. She was clearly frightened and concerned that more men would ride in while Preacher was gone. "No need to worry, I'll be back in about five minutes."

Preacher summoned Cap'n again and rode, fast, along the stage road headed west. The vultures were still lower but the distance from the station was somewhat less than Preacher had guessed. About three quarters of a mile. As he neared the spot, he could see the form of a man along the edge of the road. He felt his throat tighten. Bill Troutman? Young Keno Harris maybe? Or Ely Kohl? Whoever it was, Preacher figured they'd been bushwhacked by the man with the Sharps.

The man was face down. Much of his back, a broad, muscular back, was an open wound. He'd been shot from the front with a high calibre weapon. He was still breathing, albeit labored. Preacher knew the wound was fatal. He looked at the face. "God! Mike Teague."

11

Nate Breed frowned. Preacher had stopped talking and was eyeing his pocket watch.

"You got someplace important to be?"

Preacher looked up and half smiled. "Yeah, as a matter of fact, I do. It won't take long and I'll be back, but it's important. It's also a couple of hours away yet."

Breed was itching to know what Preacher was doing in the City by the Bay but he was also hanging on the story the gunman had been relating to him.

"You picked a hell of a spot to leave me in suspense. You sure as hell didn't just ride back to Jake's Corners and then move on." Their eyes met for a long moment and then Breed felt compelled to add, "Did you?"

"Not hardly. What happened at Red Creek almost proved to be the beginning rather than the end of the story." Preacher took another shot of Teton Jack, shifted his position and stretched his long legs out of the open end of the booth.

"Did you get Cole Langston?"

Preacher put his head back and closed his eyes. "Langston, damn!"

12

Charlie Siringo, depressed and discouraged, nonetheless proved to be his father's son. Broken leg and all, he agreed to drive the stage from Red Creek to Jake's Corners. Preacher would have much preferred to ride hard, fast and alone to get back but Charlie's condition precluded the possibility. On top of that, the trip back brought its own ills.

Some ten miles from Red Creek, Charlie stopped the stage and fired a shotgun blast into the air. It was the first of several signals Preacher had told him to use if he ran into trouble. The bounty man seemed to materialize from out of nowhere at the sound of the gun.

Charlie Siringo was waving and pointing down the road even as Preacher came into view. Preacher didn't stop at the stage but rode in the direction Charlie was pointing. What he found disturbed him greatly. He road back to the stage.

"The horse belonged to Ely Kohl. Kohl and Keno Harris rode out together early this morning, headed for Red Creek. Obviously they never got there."

Charlie Siringo slumped onto the stage seat. He stared for a moment and then blinked and looked at Preacher. "What killed his horse?"

"Buffalo gun slug through the neck. All his gear is still on it, even his rifle."

Charlie gave Preacher a long, hard look. "Who'd you find on the road west of Red Creek?"

Preacher tried to show no sign of having an answer.

"The old woman told me you rode up there Preacher, and I saw the vultures. Who was it?"

"The man I had figured as our bushwhacker, Mike Teague. The bushwhacker took him out, too."

"Why don't you put some spurs to that stallion and get your ass back to Jake's place while there might still be somebody left to talk to." Charlie Siringo held up a hand. "That's no damn question Preacher, it's a statement. Do it! I can handle this end."

"Not when you've got no eyes in those trees you can't, Charlie. Hell, I wouldn't want you riding off and leaving me if it was the other way 'round. Let's just get moving and get back as fast as possible."

Once again, although he resented it a great deal, Charlie knew that Preacher was right.

It would have made little difference how fast Preacher had moved. Events, many of them, had already outrun him. At Jake's Corners, concern was rising. Bill Troutman's horse had returned empty saddled less than an hour after the Ranger had left. There had also been a developing dispute over legal authority. Did it belong to a deputy Ranger, Pete Hastings, or a Wells-Fargo agent, Janelle Barrett? Tension mounted too over the fate of Yanupi.

The Mogollon Rim country, little more than a speck within the two-hundred thousand square miles of western wilderness, is almost a world within a world. Its rugged grandeur offers both beauty and treachery to its infrequent visitors. One of the more common sources of the treachery is the Rim's abundance of cougar.

Yanupi hefted his rifle and tried to draw a bead on the big cat. It was futile. The animal had already mortally wounded Yanupi's horse. The Apache cursed both his bad luck and his bad judgment. He'd tethered the animal where it had little room in which to defend itself and none in which to run. Once the paint went down, the big cat scurried away. It would return later, no doubt with others of its kind, and feed.

Yanupi knew that the use of his gun would have brought him unwanted attention. He also knew he was in deep trouble without his horse. His options were slim to none, and he decided to take the course which ran the highest risk. He would continue to wait out Langston's men and try to relieve one of them of their mount. It would no doubt mean having to kill both of them and that could mean alerting Langston himself. Yanupi's decision was made however, and irrevocable. If need be, he'd sacrifice himself to kill Cole Langston. The Apache eyed the sky and smiled. "It is a good day to die," he said.

Yanupi was forced to change positions. He knew the dead horse would quickly draw scavengers, and vultures or hawks circling above him would disclose his location. He moved about a half a mile deeper into the Rim country until he found a shaded crevice. There, he could wait out Langston's men in relative safety and comfort.

The sun reached its zenith and its maximum level of misery at about the same time. It was also the time when Yanupi's keen senses first detected the sound of horses. They were moving toward him along the narrow confines of the trail. Yanupi knew they were there but he could not determine their numbers. The canyon's rocks distorted the sound as badly as the heat waves distorted the vision.

Nonetheless, Yanupi changed positions again, seeking out the fairly flat surface of an overhang. He readied his rifle and cast a final glance upward. Then, he waited. He didn't have to wait long. A horse and rider came into view, then another, then a third! Yanupi knew then that today was the day Langston himself was to meet whomever was on the incoming stage. Still, he must be sure, and then he must somehow get the information back to Jake's Corners.

Three men rode past his position. The fourth was Cole Langston. Yanupi was tempted to end everything right then. Kill Langston and die. He fought the temptation. In fact, he wanted to live. He wanted to see Langston die and he wanted his own people to accept him once more. Two more men rode behind Langston and one of them looked very familiar.

Yanupi squinted into the sun for a better look. The heat waves dissipated as the rider neared. The man very much resembled Cole Langston. Yanupi had heard the story but now he had the proof of it. This man was Cole Langston's brother. Yanupi had also heard a name associated with Langston's brother. He couldn't remember it right then. Anyway, it didn't matter. The distance between this man and the last one gave the Apache a chance. It was some forty or fifty yards. Yanupi could move quickly and quietly, kill the man, hang back and break free of the gang once it exited the Rim.

The last man in line was almost dozing in the saddle. It would make Yanupi's job easier and much less risky. He slipped from the overhang, worked his way to a rock ledge only ten or so feet above the trail. He dropped onto the horse just behind the rider. He landed perfectly and his right hand crossed in front of the man's throat and then back again. The man gurgled but there was no chance to utter a sound from his cut throat. Yanupi dumped the body off the horse, scooted into the saddle and closed a little of the distance between himself and Cole's brother.

Some twenty-five yards from the exit, Yanupi dismounted, tied his horse to a scrub bush and moved to exit. He cursed in Apache under his breath. The five riders had moved barely twenty feet from the exit. Langston was talking. All of the men looked back toward the exit. It was obvious they were looking for their companion.

Yanupi thought quickly. Perhaps he would have one chance. He looked up. The vultures were circling high. He knew they were over the spot where the cougar had killed his horse. It was on a spur trail which paralleled the main trail but dead-ended about a half mile into the Rim. If he could pull the men onto that spur trail, he could make a run for it.

Yanupi returned to his horse, mounted up and rode to the last bend before the exit. There, he fired his rifle into the air twice and then hollered. "Hey, up here, up here on the spur trail. Apache!" Yanupi was counting on several things. First, that the distance and the echo would adequately disguise his voice. Secondly, that Langston himself would want to have a look and all of the riders would follow him. "Hey," he yelled again, "Apache!"

Yanupi heard horses. The spur trail was even more narrow than the main entry trail and there was a steep, rock based strip of some twenty or more feet at its start. He could clearly discern the sounds of individual hoofbeats as horses crossed it. He counted. Five!

When he could no longer hear animals moving along the trail, Yanupi spurred his horse and rode, hell bent, out of the canyon. When he was free of it, he reined to the right. He knew a shorter route back to Jake's Corners. He hunkered down, using a length of the rein as a quirt. He slapped the mare and dug his mocassins into the animal's flanks. She bolted forward, no longer uncertain of the ground beneath.

The final gamble upon which Yanupi was resting his effort and his life was that Cole Langston would not be deterred from his own plan by the discovery of a dead horse which had belonged to an Apache warrior. Still, Yanupi felt bound, even as he rode full speed, to make certain. He reined up about a mile away and eyed the terrain. There was Spiny Backed Ridge about two miles distant which overlooked the main trail back to Jake's Corners. He turned, once again spurring the mare to full speed, and rode toward it.

Behind him, Cole and his brother, Brett Langston, sent one of their men back onto the main trail into the Rim. By the time Yanupi was headed for Spiny Backed Ridge, the Langstons knew they had been duped.

"I don't like it, little brother," Brett said to Cole.

"They may be layin' for us down there at the way station."

Cole Langston was already shaking his head, disgusted by his brother's concern. "Bullshit," he said. "Ain't no Apache gonna be workin' fer Jake Highland. He hates 'em worse'n you an' me. Besides, what we got here is a rogue brave who don't like walkin'. Hell, big cat kilt that horse. Fuckin' Apache jumped Johnny to git his."

"Yeah, mebbe. But where he'd go after?"

"Back where he came from. Ya know damned well they's plenty of Apache back in that Rim country. That's how's come I picked it."

Brett Langston remained dubious. "You don't know that for sure, little brother. You're just guessin'. Mebbe that Apache' is workin' for the army. Mebbe they got wind of us. Hell, they's plenty lookin' to find us."

"Well Brett," Cole shot back, scathingly, "If'n you want to ride out, you go ahead on. Now me, I ain't givin' the Murdock boys a goddam thing they don't earn." He grinned. "Besides, the Murdocks are gonna be down there to the way station before us. If they's a problem, it'll belong to them, not us."

Brett Langston eyed the others. They were stern faced. After all, he'd been a late comer and one or two of them had resented him at first. He knew their share of the booty would be smaller by that much. Brett shrugged. "I'm in," he said.

The Langston gang once more moved out of the Rim country and then increased their speed to a gallop to make up the time they'd lost. Now, the brothers Langston rode up front, abreast. Just behind them, two more men rode side-by-side. The fifth man rode drag.

Yanupi reached the base of the serrated ridge, eyed it carefully and spotted a stand of trees and a large boulder. It appeared to be the best spot to verify the Langstons' intentions. He nudged his horse. The animal was skittish. Yanupi tried again. The mare was reluctant to tackle more uncertain terrain.

Yanupi gained the summit of the ridge and dismounted. He left his horse in the stand of trees and climbed to the top of a boulder. As he'd figured, he had a clear view of the surrounding terrain. He spotted the four riders at once but not a fifth. As the four approached and the dust behind them settled, he saw the man riding drag. He turned, sat down on his haunches and slid down the boulder. His eyes grew large, his face contorted in pain and he rolled to his left. He'd landed squarely on his butt and atop a coiled Diamondback!

The first strike had caught him on the back of the right thigh. Now, the snake lunged at him and struck again, catching him in the left hand. Yanupi reacted as a man, any man, White or Indian. He drew his pistol, fired and killed the snake with a single shot. He knew at once the error of his act, made all the worse by the knowledge that he was likely a dead man anyhow.

He pulled the Bowie from its sheath and eyed the back of his hand. He smiled. The pain was beginning to sink in and he knew he could cut and suck poison only out of one bite. He struggled to his feet and trotted off toward his horse. He pulled both his own rifle and that of the original owner from the animal and fired a shot into the air, running the animal back down the ridge.

The Apache worked his way back up the ridge and

also a bit south at the same time. He looked up. "It is a good day to die."

By the time Yanupi reached the top of the ridge again, he could feel the effect of both bites. His hand was swelling quickly and he knew he'd soon loose its use. He was feeling giddy, almost as he did when he smoked the weed of the war pipe. The feeling would pass and turn to pain, fever, delirium and death. Those phases, Yanupi promised himself, he would not allow to happen.

The shots had thrown the Langston gang into some moments of turmoil. Uncertain of their origin and having heard both rifle and handgun, they were stalled on a course of action. After a few moments with no additional fire, Cole pointed toward the ridge. It seemed a likely haven to which they could retreat and if they had to, make a stand.

The man who'd been riding drag was now given the point. He was Farley Lofgren, a hired gun of the worst sort. Skilled beyond most men, he was completely devoid of scruples. If he could gun a man in the back or when he wasn't looking or wasn't ready, he'd do so. He saw no difference in that or in facing a man when it came time to take the credit.

He rode half way up the ridge, dismounted, pulled his rifle from its boot and started the final climb to the top of the ridge. Behind and below him, Cole and Brett Langston also dismounted and discussed the situation with which they were confronted.

"Goddamn it, Cole," Brett said, "we're ridin' into a bad thing here, bad! I say we clear out 'til we find out what's goin' on."

"An' I say we make quick work o' whoever is up there," Cole replied, pointing to the ridge, "an' then ride like hell to that way station. The Murdock boys git there first an' we won't have nothin' left."

"I ain't settin' foot near that way station 'til I know what the hell's goin' on, little brother. You understand me now. I don't ride with you 'til I know. If you can afford one less gun, you go on ahead, just like you tol' me a while ago. You go on an' ride down there but I ain't. Not 'til I know."

Cole Langston was livid. He needed his brother and his brother's gun but Brett had turned soft over the years and Cole knew there wasn't much time to argue the point.

"Alright goddamn it Brett, then you ride on right now. You ride on down to the way station an' have a look-see fer yourself an' then you ride back an' let me know what's goin' on."

The shots, three of them and all from handguns, stopped the debate. All four men looked toward the ridge but none of them said a word. If Farley rode back down in a few minutes, they'd know everything they needed to know. If he did not, they'd either have to get some fast answers or get the hell out of the territory. They waited.

Up on the ridge, the Apache Yanupi smiled and knelt down over the body of Farley Lofgren. He'd seen the gunman coming and opted to make the opportunity his last gunfight. Lofgren was as good as his reputation claimed. He was just not good enough to beat Yanupi. The rattler bites were taking their toll however, and Yanupi's time was running out fast.

The Apache worked his way down the ridge until he found Lofgren's horse. He struggled against the nausea and pain that was spreading through his sinewy body. His mind flashed to a vision of Maggie Barrett, and he thought of the child she carried. He thought of the life he'd planned for them. He pulled himself into Lofgren's saddle. He reached for the Bowie and cut the reins. He hefted a rifle into each hand; both were cocked and ready.

Down below, Cole Langston had reached the end of his patience with his brother. Cole got on his horse. "By God," he said, "I'll ride to the fuckin' way station myself an' check it out. You stay here an' take care o' whoever is on that ridge. I'll either bring back the Murdocks or I'll be back to git the rest o' ya."

He didn't wait for a response. He didn't want one. He dug spurs into the horse's side until it whinnied and reared. He jerked on the reins and cast a disparaging look at the trio of men he left behind. He rode off, fast, toward Jake's Corners.

Earlier, Yanupi had gotten a good enough look at Brett Langston to discern the resemblance and the difference between Brett and Cole. Perhaps it would have been so again except for the speed at which he now rode and the rattler's poison in his body. He intended to take Cole Langston into the world of the Great Spirit and assure himself an Apache warrior's death. He believed that was what he was about to do.

The two men left behind with Brett were the first to see the approaching rider. "Here comes Farley," one of them hollered. He'd seen the horse and paid no mind to the rider. The second man looked up. His mouth opened and closed but he couldn't say anything. Apache's petrified him. Brett Langston turned to make his own observation and drew the quickest conclusion of the lot. It was too late.

Screaming like a banshee, Yanupi rode down on the trio, firing both rifles as he did so. He was able to work the lever action on his Henry with his right hand. The left hand now lacked the strength even to hold the rifle any longer and it slipped from his grip. He fired the Henry again. The three shots had done considerable damage. One of the two men was dead, the second was wounded and Brett Langston had to dive for cover.

Yanupi wheeled his horse around, managed to lever still another shell into the Henry and started back. He fired.

At the same moment, Brett Langston fired. So did the already wounded gunny. Both shots struck Yanupi, one in his left arm, the other in the left leg. He winced, lurched in the saddle and threw the Henry at Langston as he galloped by. The rifle hit Langston in the chest, probably cracking a rib. It knocked him down. Yanupi jerked his horse in another turn and drew his pistol. His last shot with the rifle had finished the second man. Yanupi screamed the Apache war whoop and made his large charge.

Brett Langston regained his feet, whipped out his handgun and pumped five shots in Yanupi's direction. Yanupi fired his own gun into the blasts. All of Langston's shots struck the Apache and Yanupi was dead even as he hurtled through the air. He landed on an already dead Brett Langston, killed by a bullet in his brain.

Cole Langston was smiling as he rounded the final bend in the trail which led down to Jake's Corners way station. Cole was the type of man who considered being right more important than being careful. There was no one watching the road, nothing to indicate occupation of the station by the army and no real signs of any trouble. He'd known it all along, he thought to himself. He wished his brother was there so that he could bask in his victory. Cole pulled out his pocket watch. "Shit," he said, eyeing it.

The stage was due within a half hour. There was no time to go back and get the others. Cole Langston's shock over the impending arrival of the stage now turned to pleasure. He could ride in and take the place over himself. He knew Jake and he knew Jake's hands. He could handle all of them. He saw only one horse tied up out front. He reckoned it belonged to someone who had come in to meet the stage. He'd not only have his brother eating crow, he'd impress the hell out of the Murdock brothers.

He was still pondering the possibilities and, to a lesser degree, weighing the risks, when he saw Evie Highland. Cole licked his lips as he watched her walk across the corral. In the denim pants, Evie's buttocks were clearly outlined and the wasp sized waist added to the fullness of her hips. If he moved now, he'd have time to handle the men and enjoy the woman.

Cole pulled his rifle out of its scabbard, loaded it and levered a shell into the chamber. He loaded a sixth shell into his pistol. He tethered his mount out of sight and off of the trail. He worked his way to the south side of the way station, the back entrance. So far, he'd seen no one but Evie.

He moved to the back door, eased it open and stepped inside. There was a curtain separating the storage room from the kitchen. He moved up to it and was about to separate it when his rifle butt hit a stack of bean tins. Cole cursed, and Maggie Barrett screamed.

Cole Langston reacted as he always did at the first sign of trouble. He fired his gun. Maggie Barrett died instantly. Cole dropped to one knee, worked the lever on the Henry and tore the curtain from the doorway. Jake Highland's hired man, Jess Painter was just coming through the front door. Cole killed him with a bullet through the head.

Cole heard men's voices, two of them. "Shit!" What had appeared to be a deserted station seemed suddenly to be crawling with people and Cole Langston's guts were in direct proportion to the advantage he held. It had slimmed considerably and he decided it was time to pull out of Jake's Corners.

13

Some five miles from Jake's Corners, Preacher once again returned to the main road. This time it was by his own choice and he looked grim. He found Charlie Siringo up on the seat, grimacing with the pain in his leg. Swelling and infection had set in and gangrene was a real possibility if he didn't get proper treatment soon. He had solicited help in driving from the old man but the change had resulted in slower travel.

Charlie knew something was wrong the instant he saw Preacher riding up. This time there was no effort to hide or delay the truth.

"I found Bill Troutman," he said. He dismounted. "I've got to leave you. It's a gamble but it's one we'll have to take."

Charlie Siringo's eyes filled with tears. Bill Troutman had been almost a second father to him, having hunted down, arrested and helped to hang those who had instigated the lynch mob which finally had taken Toby Siringo's life.

"The sonuvabitch with the Sharps?"

Preacher nodded.

"Goddamn it, Preacher, it's your doing. If you'd have ridden out, headed back at once . . ." Charlie's voice trailed off and he shifted his position so that he could draw his gun. The old man reached out and touched him and Charlie scowled and shoved his hand away.

Preacher turned and walked back to Cap'n. He mounted up.

Charlie had his gun levelled at Preacher. Their eyes met.

"I'll kill you, Preacher, so help me God, I'll kill you."

Preacher gently spurred Cap'n, turned the big stallion and rode away. Charlie watched him through his tears and finally threw his gun into the ditch in frustration.

Cole Langston backed out of the way station, careful to keep an eye on the sides of the building. He opted to back off to the cover of the nearby woods, find a place to hide and wait out the arrival of his cronies. He could still hear the voices but he reached the woods safely and moved back through them toward the north. He'd gone no more than a hundred yards when he heard a noise behind him.

"Hold up, Langston. Don't even breathe."

Cole took the suggestion to heart when he heard a hammer being cocked.

"Drop the gunbelt."

Cole complied again, his mind racing with attempts to identify the voice.

"Turn around."

Slowly Cole Langston did as he was told once

again arid for the last time. "Jesus Christ!"

The Sharps was aimed right at Cole's head and it was the last thing Cole Langston ever saw. The Sharps roared, and Cole was dead.

Down at Jake's Corners, the little group had just found Jess Painter. Now they all froze in their tracks and heads jerked toward the sound.

Pete Hastings ran out of patience. He grabbed his rifle.

"Ranger," Jake Highland shouted, "where the hell do you think you're going?"

"To do my job, Highland. What I should have done the minute Bill Troutman's horse came back."

"You can't! It's down to you an' me an' some bushwhacker is out there pickin' us off like ducks on a pond. You go out there an' you won't be back."

"I'm going, Highland," Pete said, "an' I'll take whatever action I have to against anybody who tries to stop me."

Jake stood there helplessly and watched Pete Hastings load his rifle, his hand gun and then pull a shotgun out of Jake's gun rack. He also grabbed a second rifle, loaded it and tossed it to Jake.

"What's this for?"

"When I go out that front door, I'm making a run for the barn. You get to the back door and when I shout at you, you empty that damned rifle into the woods off there to the southeast."

"You don't expect me to hit anything, do you?"

"I expect you to do what I told you to do, Highland. Now get back there."

Jake reluctantly complied. As he entered the kitchen, he looked down and saw Janelle Barrett kneeling by her dead sister. Janelle stood up slowly and turned.

He stammered, "I'm sorry." Suddenly it dawned on him that his daughter was not in the station. "Evie," he said. "Where's Evie?"

"She ran to the barn," Janelle said, "instead of in here." The tone of Janelle's voice was one of anger.

Jake frowned. It sounded as though she was angry with Evie.

"Alright Highland, cut loose."

Jake didn't answer. He was staring at Janelle. She pushed past him.

Pete shouted again. "Damn it Highland, give me some cover."

Jake blinked, glanced again at Maggie Barrett's body and then said, "Yeah, yeah Ranger." Jake moved to the back door, pulled it open and found himself staring into the business end of a Sharps. He lived long enough to hear the weapon discharge.

Out front, Janelle had stripped off Jess Painter's rig, removed the holster from the belt and affixed it to her own. She was stripping out of her skirt when she and Pete heard the roar of the Sharps. They looked at each other but Pete moved first. He used his foot to open the front door and then he doubled into a crouch and ran, hell bent, for the barn.

Janelle heard the kitchen door open. She grabbed her skirt, the six gun and ran out the front door. As soon as she was outside, Janelle turned to her left and ran at an angle toward the west road. The way station's well was about twenty-five yards away and she tried for it. Halfway there, a shot rang out. Her head jerked and she saw Pete Hastings clutch at his chest, stagger and fall face down. She gasped, straightened and resumed her run.

Janelle reached the dubious shelter offered by the well. She crouched down behind it, frightened,

breathing heavily and her head swimming with the
piecemeal segments of the moments events. There
was a deathly calm now and Janelle peered
cautiously around the well. She suddenly realized
that there were only three people left at Jake's
Corners. Two women and a maniac with a buffalo
gun.

"A buffalo gun," she whispered aloud to herself.
She repeated the word. "Oh my God!" Janelle
recalled the action of the past thirty seconds. The
shot and Pete Hastings clutching at his chest. He'd
been shot from the front, not from behind and the
weapon had not been a buffalo gun. "Evie." She
said.

Preacher had once again stayed to the woods and
he'd made good time in spite of it. Now, he edged
down the ridge behind the way station. He'd heard
two shots. One he recognized as a Sharps. He'd seen
no sign of anyone but he moved with the caution to
which he owed his life. He eased off on Cap'n's reins
and the big stallion walked the last few feet to the
edge of the woods. Preacher reached down and
removed the .58 calibre from its boot.

Seventy-five yards from him, inside the kitchen of
the way station, the barrel of a Sharps protruded
from the window. It rocked slightly with the adjust-
ments being made to it and then it steadied.
Preacher's eyes scanned the terrain below and the
yard beyond.

A horse bolted from the corral, headed north.
Upon its back, a crouched figure. Janelle saw it.
Preacher saw it. Janelle stood up and shouted.
"Evie, you bitch!"

Preacher saw Janelle but he did not see the barrel
of the Sharps. He'd turned Cap'n so that the

animal's right side faced the way station. In that position, he could dismount and have the horse between himself and any potential antagonist. The Sharps roared. Janelle bolted for the barn. Cap'n sustained a mortal wound in the belly but his great hulk saved his owner. Preacher reeled from the animal's back and onto the ground. He scooted backwards, working the Mare's Leg as he moved and placing round after round into the wall of the way station near the kitchen window.

Preacher stopped firing. Faintly, he could hear the shouts of Charlie Siringo urging the team on toward their destination. A moment later, he heard the hoof beats of another fast moving horse. By now he had found shelter behind a large pine tree. He peered around it and he knew he was looking at Janelle Barrett riding away, to the north. He shifted to the opposite side of the tree, dropped to his belly and slithered the few yards to Cap'n's body. The big horse's lungs were rattling and a mixture of saliva and blood oozed from the corner of his mouth. He was dying, in pain. Preacher used his Bowie to cut loose his saddle bags and then edged back to the tree. He loaded the carbine, sat up, turned, fired and killed Cap'n.

Preacher reloaded the carbine, got to his feet and stood listening for the sounds of the stage. Charlie's shouts were louder, closer. The team was pulling at full bore. The gunman turned his attention back to the way station below. He had to gain entry to it and either drive the bushwhacker out or kill him. He had to do it before the stage arrived.

Preacher's mind automatically conjured up a memory of a small cabin in northern Virginia and three of his companions lying wounded in an apple orchard. Inside the cabin were two Yankee soldiers, Preacher remembered. It was the first time in the war that he'd used the old horse pistol his father had given him. He had shed his butternut field coat, loaded and primed the old weapon, gauged the distance to the cabin and then made a run for it. He saw a head bob in the window. He fired. One Yankee died. Preacher had dived as a shot rang out, just missing his head. He'd scrambled back to his feet and gained the corner of the cabin. He'd crouched low, and with record speed, reloaded the carbine. He hadn't heard the noise behind him. He got to his feet.

"You're a dead man, Reb," the Yankee soldier said. "That ol' gun is a single shot."

Preacher whirled, cocking the hammer as he turned. He'd fired. The heavy bullet tore into the man's skull. The young Tennessean winced. He swore he'd never use the gun on a man again. Times change, and so do men.

Preacher stepped into the open, leveled the Mare's Leg at the center of the kitchen door and fired. He jumped to his left, crouched and started running, working the lever action and the trigger almost simultaneously. Wood and glass flew from the back of the way station. One shot, two, three, four, five. Preacher reached the building just as the echo of his last shot died away. He could again hear the shout of Charlie Siringo and now the hoof beats of the team pulling the stage. He also heard the front door of the way station bang into the outside wall and then slam shut again.

The bounty hunter edged along the back of the building to the corner, dropped to his knee, twisted around the corner with the carbine at the ready. He saw no one. He leaped to his feet and ran to the front of the building, repeating the procedure he'd just gone through at the back. Again, he saw no one. He peered down the length of the front of the building. If there was no running across the open yard, then they had to have gone to the opposite side.

Preacher grabbed a handful of shells from his pocket and began to reload the carbine. The Sharps roared in his ears. It was as though the gun had been fired within two feet of him. Preacher's face distorted with pain and he staggered back, struggling to keep his feet. He dropped the carbine and drew his hip pistol. "Damn," he said.

Indeed, the Sharps had been discharged within two or three feet of the Tennessee gunman. The shot had been fired from inside the way station, through the corner of the building. The bullet itself missed Preacher but it drove an inch wide, four inch long splinter of wood about two and a half inches into Preacher's right thigh. The gunman then went out the back door and made the woods by keeping the station between himself and Preacher.

Even before the bloody drama had unfolded at Red Creek and then at Jake's Corners, another phase of it had already taken place. Not that it was any less bloody.

Bent on reaching Red Creek and hopefully confronting not only the Murdock brothers but also Layne Payson, Ely Kohl and Keno Harris found themselves waylayed. The man with the Sharps took out Ely's horse and Ely was rendered unconscious in his fall from the animal. Stopping only long enough to determine that Ely was still alive,

Ranger Keno Harris took up the chase, riding northwest. The man with the Sharps seemed almost magical. Numerous times, Keno cut his track but each time, he found it had been deliberately left. The bushwhacker was not the best shot Keno had ever encountered but he was clever and knew how to lure a man to him.

Keno gave up after two hours and returned to where Ely's horse had been killed. His timing could not have been worse.

"Hello Ranger." Keno had not seen or heard anyone or anything. Suddenly he was facing a small, well dressed, pleasant looking man. Keno's jaw dropped.

"Payson? Yeah, hell yeah. You're Layne Payson." Keno dismounted. He noted that Payson, who had been holding a shotgun on him, now lowered it and returned it to a special scabbard on his saddle.

"Where's Ely?" Payson turned, frowning.

"The man who owned the horse, Payson? He was knocked cold when you shot the animal. I left him here. Where the hell is he?"

Payson smiled and held up both arms, shaking his head. "Whoa Ranger. Slow down. There was no man here when I got here. I stopped to check out the horse, nothing more."

"You're a liar, Payson." Keno drew both of his pistols in a flash. The speed of his move and the man he now had under his guns amazed even him. He smiled. "You're under arrest, Payson."

The gunman's gentle demeanor and smile both vanished instantly and he turned surly and cold. "Ranger, you got no reason to arrest me but even if you think you have, I won't be taken in."

"You're a goddamn backshooter, Payson. That's

reason enough."

Payson considered the young Ranger. He knew he could kill the boy in a heartbeat. "I'm not your bushwhacker. I don't own a Sharps."

"You could have got rid of it," Keno said.

"I told you boy, I don't own a Sharps." Payson pounted to the horse. "A Sharps killed that animal and the man who did it has already done more and will keep doing it until he gets done what he came to do." Payson looked straight into Keno's eyes. Keno couldn't recall ever seeing a look like that on any man's face. "I'm here same as you, to do a job. You try to stop me and I'll kill you boy, badge or no badge."

Keno's mouth went dry. He frowned. He had a knot in his gut. He also had twin Colt pistols levelled at Layne Payson's belly. Why then did he feel clammy all over?

"Mebbe you're telling me the truth," Keno finally replied, his voice a little shaky, "and mebbe not. Either way, it's not for me to decide. Bill Troutman will decide that."

"Bill Troutman is dead," Payson said, calmly. He gestured with a nod of his head behind Keno. "Three or four miles behind you. Killed with a buffalo gun."

Keno Harris couldn't believe his ears. Reflex action consumed him and he cocked the pistols. "You turn around Payson, and you get down on all fours while I relieve you of your weapons. Then we'll find out the truth."

"I'll ride with you to Troutman's body. Show you where it is. That's all I'll do. I'm losing time, boy. I can't afford it."

"Don't call me boy anymore, Payson. I told you who I am and I told you what to do. I'm the law

Payson, and I don't have to stand up to your reputation. I've got the drop and you're going in with me. You can sit up in the saddle or ride draped over it, but you're goin'."

Layne Payson shifted his weight. The move was so slight, so well executed as to be unseen even by Keno. "I didn't come up in this country to kill Arizona Rangers and I got no quarrel with you boy, but I'll tell you one more time. I'll kill you if you try to stop me from what I came to do. I'll draw and fire and kill you before you can pull the triggers on those two cannons. You're scared o' me boy, and that's a bigger edge than havin' the drop."

Keno was thinking about J.D. Preacher and the words he'd spoken and the awe Keno held for him. Now he was facing a man with a reputation and a skill which was very likely the equal of Preacher's. Keno tried to wet his lips and swallow. He had no spit.

"Turn around, Payson," Keno said. He jabbed the barrel of his right Colt ahead just slightly.

Layne Payson had done all he could do to save Keno Harris from a premature death. He drew and fired and killed Keno before Keno could pull the trigger, just as he said he would. "I warned you boy, more'n once, I warned you."

A few miles to the west, Ely Kohl climbed a hill. He was winded.

Ely sat down. A moment later, he heard the whinny of a horse behind him. He twisted his body around, gun drawn, but he was smiling. He was certain it was Keno Harris who'd found his track and run him down. The smile faded instantly and Ely wasn't winded anymore. Even before the sound of the Sharps died, Ely Kohl died.

14

San Francisco, 1906

Preacher looked at his pocket watch and frowned. He slid out of the booth and stood up. Nate Breed's face paled.

"Damn you, Preacher! You can't leave me hanging."

Preacher smiled. "I told you, I have another appointment and it won't wait but I will be back."

He reached to his inside coat pocket. Breed had witnessed such a move before. Preacher's lightning hand moving to the inside of the frock coat. Usually when that happened, someone died. This time, no one died. The shootist produced a sheaf of papers.

"I made some notes. A kind of diary, I guess it would be. It will fill in a few other holes for you while I'm gone."

Nate looked skeptical. "You're not riding out on me again, are you?"

"You've got my word on it, Breed. I'll be back

here, likely within the hour. You'll get your story."

Nate Breed got to his feet. "I've got a gut hunch, Preacher. A gut hunch about you and being here in San Francisco. I won't give up 'til I find out."

Preacher said nothing. He just smiled and said, "See you shortly. "

Nate watched Preacher walk out, then he sat down and began to read.

15

Less than an hour after the stage arrived at Jake's way station, so did an army patrol. The man with the Sharps had gone. He disappeared along with the only other survivors of the bloody affair, Janelle Barrett and Evelyn Highland.

The army patrol had found the bodies of Langston's men and that of the Apache Yanupi. Not long thereafter, they also came upon the remains of Keno Harris and young Ely Kohl. Both Charlie Siringo and Preacher agreed to go with the patrol to the army post near Flagstaff. Charlie was placed in the infirmary for his leg wound and Preacher was up and around in a day.

The bounty man wanted to ride out of the fort and back to Tombstone. He believed Tombstone would be where he'd find Janelle, Evelyn Highland and, most likely, Layne Payson. The army wouldn't let him go however, until they got a full report of his involvement and anything else he knew. The report was made to a very interested but also very nervous

Lieutenant Colonel named John Milton Wakely.

Preacher was more than a little curious about the army's intense interest in the affair but he made his report nonetheless. That done, he bade his farewell to Charlie Siringo and headed for Tombstone. He timed his arrival for the wee hours of the morning. He didn't want to risk running into any of the remaining players in the drama until he could do so on his own terms.

"Who the hell is pounding on the goddamn—" Kate Elder threw open the door and looked up. Her mouth flew open and she stared.

"Doc around?"

Kate blinked and shook her head and stepped back. "I'm sorry, c'mon in, Preacher. I was just so surprised to see ya. We all heard you was dead."

"Not hardly."

Kate Elder shut the door, grabbed a dressing gown and threw it around her shoulders. She saw Preacher eyeing the bedroom.

"I come at a bad time."

She grinned. "Doc ain't here. I mean, he ain't even in Tombstone. He rode up Colorado way. Left about a week back." Kate walked to the table and turned up the lamp. Then, she picked up a bottle of whiskey and held it out. Suddenly she remembered. "Hell, you don't drink this rotgut. I forgot."

Preacher could see Kate was hurting. "Could you do with a shot of Teton Jack?"

She laughed, a nervous laugh. "I could do with a whole damned quart. That son of a . . ." She paused and eyed Preacher and took a deep breath. "Missouri mule wouldn't take me along. He'll be gone a month, mebbe two. That's if he comes back at all."

"He'll be back, Kate." Preacher went out and returned with his saddle bags. He opened one and broke out his last full bottle of Teton Jack. "Shall we?"

Kate smiled, rubbed her throat and nodded.

Preacher drank as much that night at one sitting as he had consumed since his one experience with being drunk. He'd been a kid back in Tennessee and spent an afternoon with one of his father's jugs of corn liquor. In spite of his over indulgence, Preacher's nerve endings were attuned to the singular goal of his profession, survival. He detected movement in the room.

"Preacher." The voice belonged to Kate Elder. She moved across the room, knelt down and sat on the edge of his bedroll. "I need you," she said, "I need you the way I needed your liquor. To forget. You're a lot like Doc."

"Then it's Doc you need," he said, sitting up, "not me."

She put her arms around his neck. Kate was a few years older than Doc or Preacher but she had a firm body and the experience to make a man feel like a man. Preacher had looked at her that way before but she was another man's woman.

"Please," Kate said, "don't make me beg. I don't want to shame myself in front of you. Please." Kate leaned down and kissed Preacher hard and full on the mouth.

He could feel her ample breasts pushing against his bare chest and the burning in his groin. At the same time, he could hear the screaming in his head. She was Doc Holliday's woman. She pulled back and Preacher got to his feet and reached for his shirt. As he put it on he turned back to her. "I can't Kate.

You're a helluva woman, but you're not mine."

Preacher moved back into his old room at the Alhambra and spent most of the next day trying to round up a dealing job. He couldn't find any takers and by day's end he had neither a job nor any answers as to why not. He knew dealers were needed.

He found an empty table at the Oriental early that evening and decided on a drink or two while he browsed through the *Epitaph*. He was engrossed in a story of a new silver find up in Colorado when he sensed the presence of someone at the table. He looked up.

"You forget your friends pretty quick, bounty man."

Preacher nodded toward an empty chair and said, "Sit, Wyatt." He folded the paper, picked up Wyatt's glass of beer, dumped it in the spitoon and refilled it with Teton Jack. "I planned on making a stop at your office tomorrow."

"After you found out you couldn't work anywhere else?"

Preacher looked puzzled but then said, "I still won't put on a tin star, if that's what you mean."

"If you're plannin' on earning your keep in Tombstone any other way, you'd better change your mind."

"What have I got Wyatt? The hydrophobia?"

"You've got yellow Preacher, accordin' to the word goin' around. Seems the stories are comin' down from Kohl's ranch and up to the fort that you didn't get anywhere near Cole Langston when you found out that Layne Payson was dogging his trail."

"Well," Preacher said, calmly, "whoever is telling

the story is telling it half right."

"How's that?"

"I never got anywhere near Cole Langston 'til he was dead. As to Layne Payson, I never even saw the man."

"What the hell did happen up there," Wyatt Earp asked.

Preacher told him, ending the story with the events of the last day at Jake's Corners.

Wyatt poured himself another shot of whiskey, downed it and then leaned back in his chair and shoved his hat back on his head. "Why the hell did you come back to Tombstone?"

"Because I figured that's where Janelle Barrett would come to." Preacher was puzzled by Wyatt's tone. It was almost as though the Marshal believed the stories he'd been hearing.

"Any special reason to think that?"

Preacher felt his hackles rising. "Yeah, one or two. She paid me some money up front for a job I didn't get done and she's got a man with a grudge and a Sharps on her trail."

"She might also figure you owe her the bounty you collected on Cole Langston since she'd know it wasn't you who took him out."

Preacher sat bolt upright. So that was the story going 'round. He'd found a man's carcass and claimed the bounty on it as his own.

"Anybody who says I did that is a liar."

"And you'll face down whoever says it," Wyatt said, "that right?"

Preacher caught a glimpse of Virgil Earp just coming through the door and he was carrying his shotgun. He looked around and then spotted Wyatt and Preacher. He didn't smile or wave, but simply headed toward the table. Preacher had a sudden feeling he was being set up.

Preacher moved carefully but he gained his feet and then he gauged the distance between himself and Virg. That done, he looked down at Wyatt. "Yeah, Marshal, I sure will. Anybody. Like I said, whoever claims that's what I did is a liar."

"Evenin' Preacher." Virg's voice didn't indicate anything wrong but neither did it show much enthusiasm for Preacher's return. Preacher considered the brothers for a moment.

"Wyatt, if you know who's spreading that story, you'd best tell me now."

"Sure I know. Got it official bounty man, over in my office."

Preacher cocked his head. "Official?"

"The U.S. Army, Preacher. They sent a telegraph cable which officially cancels the bounty on Coleman Langston and credits it collected by one J. D. Preacher, a bounty hunter. They list Langston as having been killed by party or parties unknown. Now you tell me you're gonna face down the whole damned U.S. Cavalry in Arizona?"

Preacher was dumbfounded by the revelation. He'd told the officer at the fort exactly what had happened and bounty was never mentioned. He was also angry with Wyatt.

"You been spreading the story Wyatt, why?"

Now it was Wyatt whose hackles rose and Virgil's as well. "Hold on, bounty man," Virgil said, "you got no call to make an accusation like that."

Preacher smirked. "Your brother spreads a story that I collect bounty on a stolen carcass and you get moral with me, Virgil? Go to hell."

Wyatt stepped in front of his brother. "Easy

Virg."

"This fancy gun totin' Reb don't scare me a bit, Wyatt."

"I said, back off, Virg." Wyatt's eyes had never left the tall Tennessean's face. Chairs were being moved and men were making ready to get clear what would probably be Tombstone's most legendary gunfight if it ever erupted. "I didn't spread the story," Wyatt said, "but I sure as hell resent the idea that you think I did. The army sent the same telegraph to every newspaper in the country. At least to all of them west of the Mississippi."

Preacher clenched his teeth together. He felt foolish in a way. He knew army policy but he was too close to this one and he'd let it goad him. Too many things had puzzled him of late and they were piling up to a point where they could become dangerous. Even fatal.

Preacher eyed the crowd. Each and every man in the place was tensed, ready for the shootout between the infamous Widow Maker and the brothers Earp. Preacher felt the old disgust rise up within him. The disgust he had for a civil populace who begged for good men to pin on a tin star and lay their life on the line day in and day out. The same populace who got their excitement from the life the lawman lived. Then, when it mattered, like it had to Toby Siringo, the same populace vanished into their holes.

Preacher eyed the brothers. "Virg, Wyatt," he said, "I know about army policy. I was pulling out of step."

Virg nodded. Wyatt said, "For what it's worth, Preacher, I didn't believe it but I still can't figure the commander of the southwest district makin' a claim like that if it's not true."

Preacher looked quizzical. "You still questioning the telegraph?"

Preacher shook his head. "The sender, mebbe. I never talked to the commander of the district. I talked to the lieutenant."

"Then," Wyatt said, "you'd better pay a visit to the lieutenant. Sounds like he's the one with the double tongue."

Preacher had planned to ride back north as soon as he got rested up and his leg was fully healed. First however, he had to have stake enough for some possibles and a new horse. The poker tables were his only opportunity, and then only as a player.

Preacher had over extended himself with his stake of Doc before he had ridden north. Upon his return, he found Doc had left Kate Elder broke. He staked her before he knew he couldn't work in Tombstone for a wage, unless he wanted to pin on a badge. That, J.D. Preacher would never do again.

He stayed at the tables nightly and after nearly six weeks, he was showing a profit. Cattle buyers hit town in late July and with them, high stakes games. He saw his chance to make enough to quit Tombstone and finally put to rest the stories from the army. Too, he was still wanting answers to the puzzling events which had taken him north in the first place.

Preacher had seen little of the Earp boys but he heard very disturbing stories almost daily about the feud building up between them and a family named Clanton. Just lately, Preacher had seen new gunnies riding in and most seemed to be on the Clanton payroll. Too, the Clantons seemed to have the protection of Tombstone Sheriff John Behan.

On a warm evening in early August, Preacher was in a high stakes poker game at the biggest table in the Oriental. Suddenly, two shots were fired near the front door. Everyone fell into silence when they looked up and saw Doc Holliday.

"I'm looking for J.D. Preacher," he shouted.

Preacher looked up and grinned. He excused himself from his table and got to his feet.

"Doc," Preacher said, "back here." Preacher could see Doc's hands. In one he held his pistol. In the other, his handkerchief and a small cloth sack. Doc moved through a small knot of men and it was then Preacher saw the look on Doc's face.

"You four flushin', two bit, gun slingin' sonuvabitch!" Doc hurled the cloth sack at Preacher's feet. "There's what you staked me, bounty killer. No extra." Doc jabbed his gun barrel at the poke. "It's enough to bury you." Doc holstered his gun and then jammed the kerchief into his lapel pocket.

"Doc," Preacher said, studying the little dentist and puzzled by the fact that he was certain Doc wasn't drunk, "what the hell is wrong?"

Doc spat at the floor. Now no one stood between the two men, two men decked out in black dress suits and near enough look-alikes to pass for brothers.

"Don't insult me anymore Widow Maker, by denying what Katie already told me."

The problem was suddenly crystal clear. Doc got back, probably announced to Kate that he was leaving for Colorado again soon, they quarreled, and Kate used a lie about Preacher to keep Doc with her.

Doc Holliday walked a few feet closer to Preacher.

"Widow Maker, eh? Bullshit! Katie Elder won't be no widow and now I'm not coughin' and I'm not drunk. You're called out, bounty killer."

A block and a half away, Kate Elder rushed into Marshal Wyatt Earp's office. Wyatt and Virgil were both gone. Morgan Earp sat behind the desk.

"Katie, good evenin'."

"Jesus Morgan, you gotta stop 'im, you gotta. I lied. I tol' Doc that Preacher come to the house an'—" She stopped. There was no need to finish the story.

Morgan Earp knew what the results would be. He grabbed a shotgun "The Oriental," Kate shouted. Morgan ran the entire distance.

He heard Doc's voice as he ran up to the batwing doors. Morgan pushed them both open and stepped inside. "Doc!"

Doc knew the voice. "Morgan, you either cut me down with that shotgun right now, in the back, or you put it on the table. If you don't, I'll turn around and blow your goddamn head off."

Morgan Earp was fast, hot tempered and always ready for a fight, except now. He knew Doc meant what he said. He knew that whatever Wyatt might have done didn't matter. Morg wasn't Wyatt. He tossed the shotgun on a nearby table.

"Bounty man!"

"Doc," Morgan said. It was far as he got.

"Shut up Morg, and stay out." Doc Holliday lightened the load on his left side. It was his habit just before he drew.

J.D. Preacher stood like a statue in the middle of the Oriental. He thought of two things. How close he'd once come to having to test himself against his mentor, Morgan Lake, and how he'd vowed never to place another shot. He'd done that with only one man, Jim Hickok. Both he and Hickok had sustained wounds in the shootout for Hickok had placed his shot as well. No man Preacher had known before or since had been as close to him as Jim Hickok and when Preacher's guns came out, someone died. That was Preacher's law.

The batwings flew open. "Doc, I lied. It was me tried to bed Preacher. He turned me down. He said I was Doc Holliday's woman."

Doc whirled, drew and fired. The bullet creased Kate Elder's cheek. It was a scar she would carry to the grave, marking her long after it no longer mattered as the woman of Doctor John Holliday. Doc holstered his pistol and pushed himself between Kate Elder and Morgan Earp and through the doors. He didn't want to see any of them again that night.

Inside fifteen minutes, no one would have ever known what nearly happened that night in the Oriental saloon had they not been there to see it. At Preacher's table, curiosity finally got the better of one man. "Who would have won?" he asked.

Preacher didn't look up. "No one. Doc and I are friends and one of us would have ended up lonely and the other dead."

16

Throughout the summer and into the fall of 1881, Preacher put the difficulties of his recent past behind him. Several factors made it easier for him. They included a winning streak at poker, a gradual renewal of friendship with Doc Holliday and a reduction in the rumors about him. The latter was simply brought about by the fact that Tombstone folk had something more current about which to gossip. The growing feud between the Clanton-McLaury faction and the brothers Earp was on the verge of erupting into open conflict.

The Clanton brothers and the McLaurys had gone into business together. They lauded it as a cattle operation but their ranch hands looked more like gun slingers than cow punchers. Among the recent additions were the kid named Johnny Ringo and a gray haired, menacing looking professional shootist called Juniper.

On the evening of October 18, Doc and Preacher were playing poker with three other men at a saloon and bawdy house run by Kate Elder. Kate had just introduced them to a new girl named Belle when several Clantons came in, led by Ike. He was looking for Juniper but Kate said he wasn't there. Ike called her a liar and Doc called him out. Doc started coughing and Preacher intervened, knocking Doc out with his Buntline Special. Wyatt showed up and the Clantons left.

"I appreciate what you did, Preacher, but Doc won't. He might understand if he thought I did it. He's li'ble to kill you."

"What makes you so damned sure he won't kill you, Wyatt?"

"Three things," Wyatt replied, grinning again. "Morgan, Virgil and James."

Katie looked up. "He's coming around," she said.

Wyatt turned. "Morg, help me get Doc the hell out of here."

Preacher stood at the top of the stairway and kept an eye on the McLaury-Clanton group while Wyatt and Morgan wrestled their way out of the saloon with Doc wobbling between them. He had a good sized goose egg on the back of his head and he'd be madder than a hornet when he finally came fully around.

Once they were gone, Preacher turned his attention back to the woman named Belle. Once again they eyed each other in silence and Katie Elder sensed there was more between them than she knew about.

"Room at the far end is empty," she finally said, smiling and adding, "if you two would like to get to know one another a little better."

Preacher nodded and took Belle by the arm. They were down the hall a ways when Katie hollered at them, "It's on the house. I'll let you know when the gent you're lookin' for makes an appearance." Preacher nodded.

Inside the room, Preacher poured two short drinks of Teton Jack and handed one of them to Belle. They drank.

"It's been a long time," Preacher said. "Fifteen years."

"You don't look any different to me," the woman said.

"Nor you to me."

Belle smiled. "That's a lie." She turned. "We both know it, too."

Preacher walked over, took her gently by the shoulders and turned her around. He leaned down and kissed her, firmly but gently. He pulled away.

"Remember the last time we were together. You told me you wanted me, one last time."

"I remember."

"It wasn't the last time," he said. He began unbuttoning her blouse. She didn't resist.

Belle was, in fact, JenaBelle Trotter of Sikeston, Missouri. Preacher had actually gone through the steps of formal courtship during their six month acquaintance. He'd taken up residence in the newly founded town just after he first met his mentor, Morgan Lake.

Passing himself off as a land buyer, Preacher made a daily trip to the swampy confines south of Sikeston and practiced his gun skills. Satisfied that he had honed them to the sharpest edge possible, he quit Sikeston, killed one of the men he was after in neighboring Bloomfield and then faded from the newspapers.

He had never faded from the memory of JenaBelle

Trotter. She had loved Preacher and believed he would become her husband.

Belle's flesh broke out in goose bumps at Preacher's touch. She shivered as his hands moved from the soft, rounded shoulders and down to her breasts. He tweaked the nipples and spent a few moments fondling and squeezing them. He was rock hard and ready almost instantly. There had once again been an enforced period of celibacy, made all the more tormenting by the presence of Janelle and Maggie Barrett and Evie Highland. He vowed to make up for lost time.

Belle stepped back and began to undress Preacher. He moved to the bed where he might hasten the process. Minutes later they were side-by-side and fondling each other as would a young couple who were together for the first time. They were exploring vaguely familiar territory, dusting off the cobwebs of time which shrouded pleasant memories.

Belle giggled like a schoolgirl when she felt Preacher stiffen under her ministrations on his nipples. They were one of his most sensitive and ticklish spots. Preacher retaliated with fingers which touched the sensitive skin of Belle's inner thighs.

"Oh, Preacher, good God, so many things have happened. I want to tell you."

He put a finger to her lips. "Not here, not now," he said, "it's not important."

He shifted position and slipped down until he could take the tips of her breasts between his lips. He tongued them and nibbled gently.

Belle's body suddenly went limp. She concentrated on freeing from her mind the images of face-

less men, smelling of sweat and whiskey. She
wanted to be a woman again, not a whore. If any
man could motivate her to success, J. D. Preacher
was that man.

His tongue worked over her breasts until she was
almost breathless with pleasure. Soon, all
unpleasant visions faded and Belle could see
nothing at all, hear nothing but the sound of
Preacher's breathing and feel nothing but the raw
pleasure of flesh on flesh.

Preacher moved lower and Belle's legs spread
wide to accommodate him. He kissed, licked and
stroked at the most vital and sensuous spots and he
did so with a gentleness such as Belle had not
experienced in fifteen years.

Belle's eyes blinked rapidly when she realized
Preacher had stopped. He was ready to mount her
but she wasn't ready to end their affair. She shook
her head and pushed on his bare chest until he rolled
onto his back. Belle positioned herself so that she
might return some of the pleasures she had received.

Preacher found it difficult to hold back. It had
been a long time between women and Belle's
expertise now matched her beauty. She was no
longer the daughter of a wealthy and respected
family. She was not a whore being paid to provide.
She was his.

Belle couldn't wait either. Five minutes had
brought every ounce of moisture to the surface of
every orifice on her body. She didn't even want to
wait to shift positions again. She slipped down
along Preacher's body until he could enter her. She
moaned. Her mind recalled the first time between
them and she smiled. She had been frightened of his
enormity and she had been unable to take all of him.

Even when they last made love, she could not accommodate J.D. Preacher. Perhaps, she thought, it was nothing of which to be proud but she could now and the pleasure offset the shame.

At the very peak of their passion, Belle raised up and the Tennessee gunman thrust all the way inside her. The combined effort was totally rewarding and they climaxed together in an all too short moment of total pleasure.

Both sat with their backs to the headboard and sipped Teton Jack. Neither spoke for several minutes. Belle finally broke the silence. "Don't you want to know what's happened in fifteen years?"

"I don't know," he said, looking at her, "do I Belle?"

She knew what he meant. She quietly asked herself the same thing. Did she want to know about him? She knew he still lived by the gun but she was no longer the naive little girl. That he was here, next to her, having just made love to her, should be enough.

"Will I lose you again, Preacher?"

"I'm not yours to lose Jena," he said. It was the first time he'd called her by the only name he'd known before now. She winced and then smiled, weakly.

"Who do you belong to?"

"Myself, and the times in which we live."

"Still living by Preacher's law, is that it?"

"Yes."

"And with no room to share it with someone?"

"I wouldn't ask any one to share it."

"Why do you have the right to make that decision all alone?"

"I haven't the right," he said, swinging his legs to

the floor, "that's the reason I won't ask. If I ask, then the decision must be shared." He got up and began dressing.

"No one gets close to you, do they? The last time we made love, I asked questions, you got up, dressed and left. Why? Why don't you let someone get close, Preacher? Are you afraid of hurting them?"

He smiled. It was, for J. D. Preacher, a wistful smile. "It's me I'm afraid of hurting," he said.

JenaBelle Trotter got out of bed and put on a dressing gown. She poured another drink and then turned to him. "I don't know much about Tennessee and what happened after the war but you're a cruel man, Preacher. Someone you loved died. Now, everyone else is cut out."

Preacher said nothing. He strapped on his guns and then reached for his coat. Belle walked over to him and pulled him around so that she could look into his eyes. She was determined to make a final effort to win Preacher for herself. She stared, hard, into Preacher's eyes. He didn't even blink.

JenaBelle Trotter felt a sudden chill and she recoiled. The man's eyes were black and lifeless, devoid of even a hint of the sparkle she'd once seen in them. They were, she thought, like doll's eyes. "My God," she said, "you're not the man I knew and came to love in Sikeston. You're a," she paused, stammering, groping for the right word, "an illusion. You're not real."

She turned from him, crossed the room and then turned back. "That's it! That's why no man can kill you. You're already dead, Jeremy Preacher."

Preacher left the room and sought out Katie Elder. She was smiling. A nervous smile. "Are you unhappy with my girl?"

"No one could be unhappy with her," Preacher replied. "Now Katie, tell me where Juniper is?"

Her eyes got big.

"I know you lied, and I suspect Ike Clanton knows it too."

"Juniper threatened my girl if I told anyone where he was." She turned away. "Ike came back. He's downstairs. I'm scared Doc'll wake up and be here." She turned to face Preacher again.

"Where is he, Katie? Where's Juniper? I've been hunting him."

"I sent a girl to get Wyatt," she said, "just wait, please."

"For what?" Preacher asked.

Kate didn't have an answer. She shrugged.

"Then where is he?"

"Down at the other end, back room." Kate swallowed. "Doc came around. Wyatt had to lock him up. He swears he's gonna kill Wyatt. You know Preacher, I think he might this time. I've never seen Doc that mad, not never."

"I'll make it right Kate, before I leave."

Kate looked shocked. "Leave? When Preacher?"

"Tonight, in a few minutes if the man down in that room is the Juniper I'm looking for."

"Wyatt will be here in a few minutes, wait for him, please Preacher. If it is the man you want and you kill 'im, you'll have to face Ike Clanton, McLaury an' prob'ly Pete Spence."

'I don't have time to wait," Preacher said.

Kate Elder watched the rangy gunman head down the hallway. Something had happened. Something drastic. This was not the man she'd known as Jeremy David or J.D. Preacher. This man seemed bent on killing someone or getting killed. She'd seen that in Doc but only when he was full of anger and shouting and full of the misery of his consumption. Preacher was as cold as the grave. Kate hurried down the hall and sought out Belle.

"Git on across to the Marshal's office, hurry Belle, there's about to be big trouble. For God's sake, hurry!"

Belle nodded.

JaneBelle Trotter stopped for only a few seconds at the head of the stairs. She looked in Preacher's direction but the gunman was already positioned near the door of the room Katie Elder had indicated. JenaBelle hurried down the stairs, stopping again when she saw Ike Clanton and Pete Spence moving toward her.

"Juniper," Preacher shouted, "you'd best step out here if you're the man that gunned a deputy marshal up in the Indian Territory."

"Shit," Ike Clanton said. He started for the stairway when the batwing doors came open.

Belle looked up and breathed a sigh of relief. Entering the saloon was Wyatt Earp and behind him his brother Virgin. Morgan had remained at the jail to keep an eye on Doc Holliday.

"Goddamn you Earp, the man up there works for me an' I can vouch for 'im. You can't have one o' your hired guns shoot 'im down just because of his name."

"Whether or not he gets gunned will be up to him," Wyatt said, coolly.

Virgil stepped inside and stood next to his brother. He was wielding a shotgun. He shifted his position slightly when Frank McLaury got up from the table and moved toward the group.

Everyone looked up at the sound of the opening doors. Kate Elder's face paled. Juniper had switched rooms. He was behind Preacher. "I'm the man Preacher, an' you ain't runnin' me no more."

The Earp brothers could clearly see what was happening and dared not attempt to stop it. Any movement against Juniper by either one of them would mean intervention by the trio now facing them. Ike Clanton grinned when he saw Juniper and heard the man's words. Even as he spoke, Juniper was pulling his gun.

What transpired in the next few fractions of seconds all happened too fast for the human eye to follow. When it was over, there would be a different version for every witness. Even the trained eyes of men like Wyatt and Virgil Earp widened at the speed of J. D. Preacher's movements.

He bent his knees ever so slightly as he began twisting his body to the right. At the same time, his right hand flashed to the holster which was sewn to his vest. The gun barked even before Preacher had completed his turn. Juniper's gun also fired and the bullet tore a button from Preacher's coat, it was that close.

Juniper died however, with a bullet between the eyes. He wavered for a moment and then his body did a half turn and he fell forward over the railing. He landed on a table, shattering it and his back. He didn't feel anything. He'd died instantly.

Preacher holstered his pistol and walked downstairs. He pushed past Ike Clanton and two or three steps past him, Preacher turned. "If I were you, I'd pick my hired hands with more care."

Preacher exited the saloon, followed closely by the Earps. Wyatt was surprised when he saw Preacher heading for Wyatt's office. Wyatt didn't catch up until Preacher reached the door.

"What's on your mind, Preacher?"

"Setting the record straight."

"That could be trouble, I told you that before."

"I know what you told me," Preacher said, and he reached down, opened the door and walked in. He nodded at Morgan. Virgil hurried inside. He eyed his brothers and then Wyatt shrugged.

"Turn Doc out of his cell."

Morgan nodded.

Preacher looked around until he spotted Doc Holliday's gun. He picked it up, broke the breech and checked for load. It contained six cartridges. The door to the cellblock opened and Doc came through it. He eyed the men and frowned. Preacher tossed his pistol to him. Doc wasn't ready but his reflexes were and he caught it and immediately executed a Curly Bill spin, levelling the pistol at Wyatt.

"You got the wrong man, Doc. I put you out up there, not Wyatt. He said you might take it from him, but never from me. Well, I'm here and if you've got a quarrel, let's settle it."

Wyatt stepped between the two. He looked at both and then back at Doc Holliday. "Juniper was the right man. He got behind the bounty hunter here and drew on him. Preacher killed him anyway."

Doc Holliday lowered the gun and finally holstered it. He scowled at Wyatt. "Am I supposed to be impressed?"

"I damn sure was," Wyatt said. "There was a time I had it figured you could take Preacher. Well Doc, I was wrong." Wyatt Earp moved from between the men and walked to the door, he opened it and stepped back. "Only thing I ask of you Doc, is that you do your dying outside of my office." Wyatt gestured with a movement of his head. "Out there," he said, "in the street."

Doc looked odd. None of the Earps had ever seen quite the expression Doc had on his face at that moment. He looked at each of the brothers, his good friends, and then at Preacher. He kept looking at Preacher, even as he was speaking to Wyatt Earp.

"He faster'n Frank Leslie?"

"He is."

"That makes him the best man with a gun in the whole goddamn country, doesn't it?"

"It does," Wyatt said.

"An' the sonuvabitch hit me on the goddam head, from the backside to boot." He was still looking at Preacher and now the dour expression gave way to a little grin. "How's come, bounty man?"

"I've come to like you Doc, but please don't ask me why."

Doc Holliday considered Preacher for several seconds. They were tense seconds, during which he eyed the Earp boys as well. Finally, Doc Holliday turned, walked to the deer horn hat rack, removed his hat, put it on and said, "You're the first son of a bitch that come near killing me because he liked me. I hope to hell you don't get to liking me very much more."

A moment later, all five men were laughing.

17

Preacher was taking his breakfast alone one morning a few days later when he had a visitor.

"Mind comp'ny for breakfast?"

Preacher looked up and into the face of Ned Buntline. He shoved a bite of food to one side of his mouth and said, "And if I did?"

"I'd try again at dinner time and supper time and breakfast tomorrow and so on and so on."

"Uh huh, that's what I figured. Sit then." Preacher finished off his eggs and washed them down with a swallow of coffee. He wiped his mouth and tossed the napkin on top of his plate. "What brings you back to Tombstone?"

"Several things. J.D. Preacher's collection of a bounty on a man he didn't kill." Buntline smiled and quickly qualified his words. "Or so says the army. J.D. Preacher's gunfight with a gunman named Juniper. J.D. Preacher's rumored partnership with John Holliday in a Colorado Silver mine and J.D. Preacher's linin' up with the Earp brothers against the Clanton brothers and the McLaury brothers."

"Quite a list," Preacher said, "but not too impressive for one of the most famous writers in the west. The whole damned thing is ancient history or rumor."

"Well, there is one other thing," Buntline said. "Nate Breed."

"He didn't come with you this morning?" Preacher asked.

Ned Buntline shook his head.

"Must be losing some of that famous tenacity of his."

"Not at all. He wants to meet with you tonight."

"Then," Preacher said, getting to his feet, "let him ask me himself."

Buntline stood up. "Oh, he will Preacher, he will, but he'd busy right now checking on some information about an army commander, a Major General who seems to have, shall we say, *altered* the facts a little when he made a report on a bounty payment." Ned studied Preacher's face and then smiled.

"Alright, Buntline," the gunman said, "tell him I'm baited and hooked but that doesn't mean he'll land me."

Buntline grinned and nodded.

Preacher watched the stocky little man waddle away and then he returned to his room. He couldn't help thinking that Nate Breed's efforts might hit pay dirt where his, Preacher's, had failed. What happened to Janelle Barrett and Evie Highland? Who was the bushwhacking murderer with the Sharps? What had been at stake?

Preacher heard gunshots followed by loud voices. He went to the window. Six mounted riders were lined up across Allen Street. They were facing Virgin and Morgan Earp. Preacher put on his coat, picked up the Mare's Leg and went downstairs. He walked outside.

"We're through talkin' Earp."

Preacher looked at the speaker. He was Tom McLaury.

"Your goddam brother went too far this time."

Preacher looked both ways on Allen Street. He saw Johnny Behan running toward the gathering. He stepped into the street.

Ike Clanton was on the horse nearest Preacher's position. He turned in the saddle. "You in on this, bounty man?"

Preacher didn't answer.

"I'm talkin' to you, Reb."

Virgil Earp cocked his sawed off. John Behan arrived.

"Where's Wyatt? I want Wyatt here right now. He's got some questions to answer."

"I'm here." The voice was half a block away but it was clearly Wyatt Earp's voice. All eyes turned toward it. Wyatt was particularly resplendant that evening. He'd taken his wife to a new show at the Bird Cage theater. Eddie Foy the vaudevillian was in appearance. Wyatt had on his Sunday suit, his regular rig and the special holster in which he carried the Buntline Special. He was also toting a shotgun.

No one said anything else until Wyatt came abreast of his brothers. The trio spread out. It was, Preacher thought, two to one and at that, probably favored the Earps.

"I heard you arrested my deputy, Earp. What for?"

"Suspicion of robbery."

"That's a lie Earp, a bald faced lie."

"Then Pete Spence has got nothin' to worry about when the judge gets here."

"I want bail set."

"Bail has been set already Sheriff," Wyatt said, "five-hundred dollars."

Behan reeled. He didn't have five-hundred dollars. That was five months wages.

"Damn you, Earp. He didn't do it. The only reason you accused him of it is because he arrested your no good, drunken friend Doc Holliday last spring."

That was something Preacher knew little about. It had happened while he was up north but apparently Pete Spence arrested Doc when Doc was having a bad coughing fit and had been drinking heavily. He was held for two hours until the Earps put up bail money. Ultimately, Doc was found innocent of a charge of horse theft.

"I'll put up the money," Ike Clanton said, "an' I want muh little brother outa your goddam jail, too."

Wyatt stepped forward. "Cash bail, Clanton," he said, raising the shotgun, "and Billy gets out in the morning, after he's sobered up."

"You sonofabitch! You been doggin' us long enough. I'm callin' you out."

"There'll be no gunplay here," Behan shouted.

A fourth figure emerged from the shadows and took up a spot which flanked the line of horsemen. Billy Claiborne, a youngster with a fast gun and a fast way with the ladies, was at that end. He nudged Tom McLaury.

"When you bastards take to the street tomorrow, the ball will open." Ike Clanton jerked his horse around, several others whinned as their riders turned them in the narrow and crowded street. A minute later, Allen Street looked normal again.

Preacher went back inside and moved to the bar where he ordered a shot of Teton Jack. Under a minute later, Nate Breed joined him. They moved to a table.

"You're looking fit," Nate said. "Have you eaten?"

"I spent the day sleeping," Preacher said, "but I had a good dream." Nate showed mild interest. "Dreamed my trail was being dogged by a man to whom I once made a promise and he chased me for years and finally caught up with me." Preacher was pulling Breed's leg and Breed knew it but the gunman never cracked a smile.

"What happened?" Nate asked.

"He had dinner with me and told me the debt was cancelled."

Nate leaned back and the waiter came to the table. They both ordered and then Nate Breed said, calmly, "That was some nice dream you had Preacher, but that's all it was, just a dream."

Preacher smiled. "You still want a goddamn story about me, huh?"

"Worse than ever, Preacher, and I don't intend to lose track of you again. As a matter of fact, I even have a plan to kill two birds with one stone, so to speak."

"And how's that?"

"I got some interesting information today, Preacher. I mean, I found it interesting and I guess I think you will too. Thing is, I'd almost have to trot along with you to get my share of what it's worth."

"I follow my trails all by myself Breed," Preacher

said, "you know that."

"Yeah and no exceptions, ever!"

"None Breed. Ever!"

"Might you make an exception Preacher, in exchange for some information about a certain Major General and a female Wells-Fargo agent and the daughter of way station owner and—"

Preacher banged the table top with his fist, not too hard, but it stopped Breed's chattering.

"Breed, you've outlasted my horses, most of my women, and all of the men I've gone after and haven't found. I didn't like you when I first met you. I still don't, but I do respect your tenacity. Because of that," Preacher continued, raising Breed's hope, "I've got to be completely honest with you. Nothing will change my mind about riding alone."

They considered one another.

The waiter brought the food and the two men ate about half their meals in silence. Breed finally sat back and sipped some wine. "How about your word, Preacher? When you give a man your word, how well do you keep it?"

"Always," Preacher said, wiping his mouth. He smiled. "No exceptions Breed, ever!"

"You gave me your word and you ran out."

"I didn't say *when* you'd have your story, only that you'd have it."

"Not fair, Preacher. What if something happens to one of us? Your word is broken."

"Damned good incentive to stay alive, isn't it? I'm much more safety conscious and you should ride a wide berth around trouble."

"Damn you Preacher, I want your story. When do I get it?"

"When it's over."

"Then why the hell should I help you anymore?"

Preacher smiled. "Who said you should, Breed? I didn't. But anything you do tell me is worth quite a bit."

"Like what?"

"It adds to that story you'll get one day."

Nate Breed pulled a notebook from his pocket. "Then I'll take what I can get right now. Tell me about your last gunfight."

Preacher smiled. "I haven't had it yet."

Nate Breed's face went blank and then there was a ripple of a smile across his lips which turned to a chuckle and finally full fledged laughter. He laughed so hard, tears streamed down his cheeks. Others in the Oriental saloon began to look at the two men. It was, Preacher reckoned, a combination of eased tension, too much wine and Preacher's quasi humorous evasion of Breed's query.

Finally, the young reporter regained his composure. "Here," he said, handing Preacher a page of notes. "Take it and do what you have to do. I'll catch up with you again, somewhere, sometime. I'll get my damned story." He poured some more wine. "If I were you, I wouldn't let that trail get too cold." He was pointing to the page of notes. "I've got to stick around Tombstone and see what happens between the Earps and the Clantons."

"I plan to do that myself," Preacher said.

"Yeah, I figured you had," Breed said, "but you'll change your mind."

Preacher assumed a quizzical expression. "When will I do all this, Breed?"

"Right after you read that page of notes."

18

San Francisco, 1906

Preacher kept his word and returned to the Mark Hopkins Hotel. Nate Breed was surprised but he was about to experience a whole lot of surprises. He and Preacher repaired to Breed's room. Breed broke out a bottle of Teton Jack and poured them both rather generous drinks. Also, for the first time ever, Preacher divested himself of his guns.

"Well," Nate Breed said, "I read your notes. They did fill some spaces." Breed sat in an overstuffed chair just across a coffee table from the gunman. "You did ride out of Tombstone that night, didn't you?"

"Early, very early, the next morning."

"Of course you know what happened at the O K corral."

Preacher smiled and nodded. "Is there anyone who doesn't?"

"I doubt it," Breed said, "but there are a heap

who don't know what happened to you."

Preacher shook his head. "You're still swearing up and down that there are people out there who really give a damn about my life?"

"Mebbe fewer than there were, but yeah, some. No matter. I give a damn. You're my, uh, my hobby. Anyway, you made a promise." They considered one another. "Well, Preacher, did my notes pay off?" Breed's jaw dropped when he heard the answer.

"They will. Tomorrow!"

Preacher could see stars from his room window. He knew it would be a clear morning. He was grateful. He looked at his watch. It was two-thirty and his breakfast with Nate Breed was to be at three. He had no gear now. He'd taken everything to the train depot the day before, a part of what he'd done during his brief absence from Nate.

Recalling the Tombstone days and some other events of his life had brought about a change of mind in Preacher. He would include the reporter in today's events. Events which could write the final chapter in the life of Jeremy James David Preacher.

Preacher eyed Breed when he arrived at the restaurant and said, "you look like hell, Nate."

Breed was red eyed but exuberant and made more so by Preacher's greeting. He could never remember Preacher calling him by his first name.

"You should have told me everything last night. Hell, I stayed awake trying to fill in the holes."

"I hadn't made up my mind yet," Preacher replied, "and I didn't want to make another thirty year promise."

"And now, Preacher?"

"Everything, Nate. I'll tell you everything."

"I guess it has to begin with Janelle Barrett. She was a Wells-Fargo agent just as she told me. Maggie was her sister and the Apache Yanupi's involvement was exactly as they depicted it. Janelle never gave up trying to find those responsible for the deaths of her family, including of course, Maggie."

"But where the hell did she go?"

"After one of the conspirators in the whole affair."

Nate thought back to the story Preacher had told him. Suddenly he looked up. "Jesus! Evelyn Highland?"

Preacher nodded.

"How?"

"Jake Highland's wife was the daughter of a New England horse breeder with wealth and political connections. Evie Highland went to some of the best private schools in the East and she became romantically involved with an older man during a sojourn to Washington."

"What man?"

"A cavalry officer."

Nate's eyes widened.

"Eventually achieving the rank of Major General. Corwin Halstead Armitage."

Nate Breed was writing furiously. Suddenly he stopped, shoved the notebook aside, finished his cup of coffee and looked up. "I'll write it later. The suspense is killing me." He grinned.

Preacher didn't.

"Did Janelle finally catch up, I mean, is she . . ."

"Janelle is fine. She's here in San Francisco."

"Damn! Is she responsible for you being here?"

"Yeah. So are you, in a way. It was your story

about me in that western magazine that enabled her to get in touch with me."

Nate smiled. "A happy ending. Hot damn! I've got a story with a happy ending."

"Hold it, Nate. I wouldn't write it just yet. It's not over. Janelle had all her answers many years ago. What she didn't have was proof. She was discharged from Wells-Fargo, disgraced, and more than once in considerable danger."

"Preacher, good God, that whole affair was twenty-five years ago. You, Janelle," he shrugged and smiled, "me. We were young. Who's left?"

"All of those who still matter, I'm afraid. Armitage, Evie Highland and . . ." Preacher finished his coffee and motioned for the waiter to bring more. He leaned back. He could see Nate was about to ask a question. Preacher knew it was one he was not yet prepared to answer.

"Janelle has got her proof now but she is still in danger. The danger is imminent. She cabled me to come. I did, but on the condition I hear the story before I agreed to help her. I heard it, I agreed."

"And me? She must have cabled me, too."

Preacher smiled. "You're here at my request, Nate."

Nate Breed's mind was running amuck with the many details of the earlier story Preacher had told him. He was beginning to piece together some of them for himself but he was most interested in Preacher's presence in San Francisco and the exact nature of Janelle Barrett's request.

"What's she got? Janelle, I mean. What kind of proof? Where is she, exactly. When are you meeting her?"

Preacher held up both hands in front of his face in

mock defense against the fusillade of questions Nate Breed was firing at him.

Nate's face flushed a little. He glanced down and then up again. "Not very goddamn professional sounding, was it?"

"Not very," Preacher said. "And if you're going to be in on it from now on, then it has to be done my way, no arguments."

Nate nodded.

Preacher produced three envelopes from various pockets. They were all thick and they were numbered simply, numbers 1, 2, and 3. He handed them all to Nate. Nate's fingers tightened around them, squeezing, prodding for any signs of anything besides paper. The envelope numbered 2 was hard and heavier than the others.

"Photographs?"

"Yes. Some old, some new, all revealing."

"Of what? Or who?" Nate caught himself and shook his head. "Sorry, Preacher. Habit, and a helluva lot of personal desire. I guess this is why reporters are not supposed to get involved in a story."

"I'm sure it's one reason," Preacher said, "and not too much different than my profession. Emotional involvement will get you killed in a hurry."

Nate frowned. "You got any, Preacher? Emotions, I mean. And Janelle? Have you seen her?"

"I've seen her." Preacher slipped the pocket watch from his vest, flipped open the lid, glanced at it and then put it away. He looked up. "There's no involvement, Nate. At least none which could be fatal."

"What now?"

Preacher reached into his other vest pocket and withdrew a key. He handed it to Nate. "Safe deposit box at the Marine Commerce Bank. It contains items I want you to have unless I tell you otherwise. One of them you'll get no matter what. It's as much more of what you call my story as I had time to commit to paper."

"Preacher, just what the hell . . ." Nate shook his head.

"Patience, Nate, one step at a time."

Nate nodded and then reached for his notebook.

"You won't need that right now."

Nate looked up.

"What I'm about to tell you is already written down." Preacher pointed to the key. Nate nodded. "What happens later, well, then you may want to write."

"I'm ready," Nate said, "and no more outbursts. I promise."

"We've got a little more than an hour Nate, then we go."

"We? You mean I'm to be in at the finish?"

Preacher nodded.

"The whole affair began with Major General Armitage. He was serving as Army contracts purchaser for the Arizona district. He was also in love with Evie Highland. Thing was, there was enough age difference that discretion proved to be the better part of downright desire."

"What is the difference in their ages?"

"Twenty years, give or take one or two. Armitage was about forty-five then."

Nate frowned. "Damn! He'd be near seventy now."

Preacher nodded. "Not unusual for the President

and Executive Officer of a major bank, is it?"

"Armitage? Here?"

"The Bay City Bank and Trust Company. Every penny of it financed, a whole damned empire built with stolen government gold."

"Arizona!"

"Yeah, and with Evie Highland as a partner. Armitage set up the contract in so much secrecy and with so much skill that none of his superiors even suspected anything. The gold was to be moved to the district to finance the building of two new forts and establish government operations in Phoenix."

"How much are we talking about here, Preacher?"

"Nearly six-million dollars."

"Hot damn!"

"Armitage knew that no matter how clever he was, he would never be able to actually authorize the gold's shipment until he had a contractor to move it."

"Wells-Fargo."

Preacher nodded. "He not only got the firm lined up to ship the gold, he personally supervised the route that was to be taken, how many men were to be used for security, and then got Wells-Fargo to agree to insurance coverage against loss."

"Jeezus!"

Preacher smiled, wryly. "The best laid plans." He sipped at his coffee and checked his watch again. "He'd planted a man, a former aide of his, in Wells-Fargo. At that point, Armitage and Evie stood to get three-million dollars, a fifty-fifty deal with his aide."

"He cut out his man," Nate said, smiling, "greed got him."

Preacher smiled. "You ought to take to writing

novels. That would be the typical plot. Reality was much more simple."

"No greed?"

"No greed," Preacher said. "The aide died of heart failure."

Nate chuckled.

"Time was now Armitage's worst enemy. Circumstances forced him to become a beggar and you know what they say."

"He couldn't be choosy."

"Enter Cale Murdock. He'd been working as a minor paper shuffler and Armitage's man got stuck with him."

"Things must have happened pretty fast after that."

Preacher nodded and said. "And exactly what and how, I still don't know. I'm not sure anyone does, not even Janelle."

"How'd she get involved? I mean a female agent just wasn't done. Hell, it's 1906 and it still isn't done."

"Her name was Barrett, that's why. Her kin, her daddy and brother and an uncle too, I guess. All of them were Wells-Fargo people almost from the day the company was founded."

"Armitage must have panicked."

"Never. That's what makes the man so dangerous. He ended up with his back to the wall but he never panicked. Murdock had been feeding information to Cole Langston for sometime. Minor stuff mostly," Preacher's eyebrows raised, "although by the time Janelle first contacted me, it added up to about a hundred-thousand dollars."

"Yeah, I remember the stories on the Wells-Fargo robberies."

"Anyway, Cale Murdock stumbled into the facts." Preacher smiled again and shook his head. "Armitage's old aide, training, the army. The man wrote things down. He was a damned good aide and a helluva rotten thief."

"Murdock blackmailed the good Major General."

"In a big way. He wanted shares for everybody involved and his brother busted out of Yuma prison. Armitage couldn't argue."

"Just what the hell could he do," Nate said, shaking his head with the disbelief of it all. He looked up. "He'd have to hire almost as many men as were already involved to get rid of the Langstons and the Murdocks."

"Or do it himself," Preacher said.

Nate's mouth flew open. "Do it himself?" He cocked his head and assumed an expression of total scepticism.

Preacher pointed to one of the envelopes. "It's all in there in detail but I'll give you a summary. Here in San Francisco is one of the most active and prestigious gun clubs in the country. The Antique Gun and Black Powder Assocation. Guess the name of one of its most active members?"

Nate swallowed and said, "Armitage?"

"Armitage. His skills were outstanding with rifles but most outstanding with the 1855 model Sharps Buffalo gun."

"My God! This reads better than any damned novel. He killed off anybody who might be a threat, even a minor threat, and he did it all by himself?"

"Almost. I discovered one or two bodies which had also sustained wounds inflicted by a small calibre hand gun. A Deringer most likely. Evie finished the job on more than one of 'em."

Nate Breed could hardly contain himself. "And everybody else was out for bounty. Even you. Janelle didn't tell you everything, did she?"

"Not by a longshot. Of course, she didn't know everything at that time, but she knew a lot more than she told. Me, Yanupi, Mike Teague, some of the other bounty men, were all just diversions. Janelle hoped they'd keep the Murdocks and Langstons occupied until she could nail Armitage."

"I guess the diversion part of it worked, but . . ."

"But not good enough to keep Armitage and Evie Highland from getting the job done. They've had a quarter of a century to bask in their victory."

Nate sat back and finished his coffee. He pondered the mass of information and still found it almost impossible to believe. He barely heard Preacher excuse himself to use the water closet. Nate was wondering what had happened immediately after the final showdown at Jake's Corners. Where had Evie gone, and Janelle, and Armitage himself?

Preacher returned, sat down, broke out his watch, checked the time and then pulled out the little silver flask of Teton Jack. Nate knew it was early for Preacher but he was trying to imagine the true state of the old gunman's nerves. Preacher downed a shot and returned the flask to his pocket.

"Where did they go Preacher, after Jake's Corners? Janelle and Evie and Armitage?

"Armitage had that arranged also. The Mogollon Rim."

"The Rim? How? I mean, the Apaches were sure as hell not friends with Armitage."

"Janelle can tell you the details of the chase later," Preacher said, "but she lost Evie Highland in the Rim country. Evie knew exactly where she was going. She'd been there before and everything she and Armitage needed had already been moved in, courtesy of the Apaches. Armitage had arranged for everything he'd need to deal with them. Guns, ammunition, food, clothing. Everything. Remember, he had the authority and the position."

"But he didn't have the contact, Preacher. How in the hell did he arrange the contact?"

"There's one name you've not asked me about. One more player who was little seen but very felt."

Nate frowned, thought, remembered. Suddenly the name smashed into his head with the force of a sledge. He looked straight into Preacher's eyes. "Layne Payson!"

Preacher's expression was blank. The two men stared at each other for several seconds and, for the first time Nate Breed was aware of, Preacher blinked first.

"You've got to face Layne Payson. He's the imminent danger to Janelle Barrett. He's the only obstacle between Mr. and Mrs. Corwin Armitage and justice. That's what today is about. Preacher, for Chrissakes, this is not 1880 in some God forsaken cowtown. This is San Francisco and it's 1906."

"Pier twelve," Preacher said, calmly, "at five-fifteen."

Nate dug out his own watch. "It's four forty-five," he said. He fumbled, almost dropping his watch as he tried to put it away. "Damn! Preacher, this is ridiculous. If Janelle has the proof, she can take it to the police. Let them move in and handle it."

"If she moves from where she is, Payson will kill her. Those were the plans originally. Janelle's plans. I wasn't needed or even thought about. Neither were you. Payson has been working for Armitage since the very beginning. He was Armitage's hole card. He found Janelle the day I arrived. We now have a deal."

Nate shook his head and waved his arms. "No, damn it, enough! The San Francisco police are some of the best in the world and even Layne Payson can't take them all out. Neither can Armitage."

Preacher leaned forward and took a gentle grip on Nate's lapels. "Breed, I've changed my mind about you once, don't do anything stupid to make me change it again. I haven't the time or the desire to explain why it has to be this way, but it does. I want you to understand that if you do anything at all to interfere, I'll kill you."

Nate swallowed. Their eyes met again. This time, Preacher didn't blink. Nate nodded. Preacher turned him loose and Nate sat back.

"Payson, all these years. He," Nate swallowed, "he was right here working for Armitage?"

Preacher nodded.

"God!"

"Understand, of course," Preacher said, "that Armitage and Evie didn't move to San Francisco until just a few years ago. The early years were spent elsewhere. Payson spent them hunting for Janelle Barrett. Armitage put him on a wage, a damned good wage."

"He never found her, obviously."

Preacher smiled. "Janelle went to Canada. She ultimately wound up in Alaska. She didn't do anything more about the situation until she read in the paper about Armitage founding his bank."

Nate watched Preacher down another shot of Teton Jack. He looked at his watch again and then signalled the waiter. He paid the bill and got to his feet. Nate got up. His knees felt like jelly.

"Preacher, you told me you were sixty years old. If I didn't know about you from years ago, I'd guess you a helluva lot younger, but the fact is you are sixty. Layne Payson must be mighty close to that, one way or the other. I can't imagine he's used his guns much out this way, but have you used yours?"

Preacher grinned. "You've got the longest winded way to ask a question as any man I've ever known. You want to know if I can beat Layne Payson to the draw?"

"Yeah, goddammit, I do."

"Well Nate, I'm a little curious about something myself."

"And what's that?"

"Do *you* think I can beat him?"

Nate was caught short with the question. He'd thought about some of the men Preacher had gone up against over the years and he'd often wondered about them too. He'd never really thought about Layne Payson. He only knew that as shootists went, Payson was at the top of the heap.

"Yeah Preacher, by God, I do think you can beat him." Nate smiled. "You want to know why?"

Preacher reached up and clamped his hand over Nate's mouth. "No," he said, "I don't. Not now, not ever."

Nate nodded.

They walked three blocks west and they were on the docks. Another block brought them to pier number one. The first streaks of the light of a new day were beginning to show up. Preacher stopped.

"What's wrong?"

"Nothing," Preacher said. One by one he loaded the sixth cartridge into his pistols. That done, he looked at his watch and then at the sky. "Five o'clock," he said. "Payson was right. He set the time. He said it would be dawn by then."

"Preacher, I've known you for a hell of a lot of years." Nate swallowed. "I like you," he said, "and I'd like to shake your hand."

Preacher smiled and they shook hands.

The men started walking along dockside, passing eight piers. Preacher craned his neck toward the sky again. "I got a hunch it's going to be a beautiful day."

Nate Breed winced. He had a knot in his stomach and a lump in his throat. Either one felt big enough to choke a horse. J.D. Preacher seemed as calm as Nate had ever seen him.

"I hope I can write this story the way I feel it."

Preacher thought it an odd comment but reckoned Nate was simply making conversation. "What will you call it?"

"The last gunfight."

Preacher stopped dead in his tracks. Nate was certain the gunman was angry. He locked his lips and steeled himself against the anticipated assault.

"By God, that's a hell of a title Nate, a cracker jack for sure. Yessir," Preacher said, nodding his approval, "the last gunfight." He looked down the docks. He could see the shape of a man standing by one of the piers. A short man, well groomed. He looked at Nate Breed. "It will be, you know."

Nate had seen the man too and had forgotten their subject. "What will be?"

"The last gunfight. I've got plans." Preacher looked back down the docks. The edges of the old wood were turning pink in the first rays of sun. "Either way though, it will be."

They walked on.

19

Layne Payson was dressed in a brown, broadcloth suit, white silk shirt, brown cravat and a topped with a gold flecked, satin front vest. His face was clean shaven, his nose somewhat needlelike. Payson's hair was almost pure white.

"So you're J.D. Preacher," he said. He extended his hand but Preacher declined the greeting. Payson eyed Nate Breed.

"Reporter friend of mine," Preacher said.

Layne Payson fished out his watch. It was five after five. He glanced at the sky and then the pier.

"Five more minutes, gunman," Payson said, "and we can do what we came to do." He turned back to face the Tennesseean. "I regret we didn't meet twenty years ago but nothing that is really important to men like us has changed all that much, I guess."

"I'm not a man like you, Payson," Preacher said.

Nate Breed's hand was flying across the pages. If he could have handled a gun with equal ability, neither Preacher or Payson could have beat him.

"You're a killer, pure and simple. You'd have killed Janelle Barrett if you'd caught her."

Nate Breed stopped writing and looked up. Perhaps, he thought, it will be over right now.

Payson considered Preacher. "I still will," he said, coldly. "And I'm glad you wore the appropriate clothing." He looked down at Preacher's black suit. "The mortician won't have to dress you out."

Layne Payson turned and walked out toward the end of the pier. Preacher gauged the distance at about a hundred and fifty feet. They would test one another at no more than fifty. The Tennessean cleared his mind of all thoughts about the past, the long years since he'd first met Janelle Barrett, the deal he and Doc Holliday had made involving the gunman, Layne Payson. Now, he turned every sensory perception, every nerve in his body to the task at hand. He had done it countless times before.

Nate Breed looked on while Preacher took a last shot of Teton Jack. Nate wanted to say something but even he had run out of things to say. Instead, Nate concentrated on his own job. He began looking around, writing down the details of what he saw. A ship lay at anchor a mile or so into the bay. The breeze whipped the colorful signal flags high atop the mast and then Nate saw the fleecy clouds just over the horizon. He wrote.

Layne Payson reached the end of the pier. He turned to face Preacher, checked his guns and then looked around. Nate watched him do it and wondered what was going through his mind. Nate then thought he never wanted a chance to ask him. He wanted Layne Payson to die. Payson began to walk. So did Jeremy Preacher. Nate looked around.

Odd, he thought, there were no more gulls. Moments before, the sky had been full with them, now he could not find a single gull. Nothing, no movement save for the two men.

Nate continued to jot down the things he saw. The details of the scenario would enhance the story's impact. The fleecy clouds seemed to be skimming over the blue water.

There was enough light now to silhouette the biggest of San Francisco's buildings and Nate started into a three hundred a sixty degree turn so that he might get a feel for everything at that moment. He was still puzzled by the sudden absence of birds and now he realized there were none even perched along the dock's pilings and there were no squawks.

He stopped in his turn. He reached up and rubbed his eyes. The lack of sleep was catching up with him, he decided. He could swear the top of one of the buildings was moving. He resumed his turn. Far across the narrow channel of water into part of the port, he'd seen the sun reflecting on a tin roof. Now it was gone. He thought that odd, too. The roof was on a huge warehouse and the sun's rays would be on it for several minutes.

Nate's turn was complete. Preacher and Payson were not moving anymore. He estimated the distance between them now at a little more than fifty feet. Probably sixty. He heard a low toned rumble.

Nate was disappointed that he could not somehow be between the two men. He wanted to see the draws but he knew he could not have recorded them both anyway. He glanced at his watch and then wrote:

5:12 AM Pier 12 April 18, 1906

The dull roar was no longer dull. It was loud and growing louder. Nate thought he was sick. He felt wobbly. He saw the ship at anchor. It appeared twenty feet higher than when he'd first seen it. His head jerked toward the downtown area. The building he had thought moved was not there. It had moved! He turned. He could not see Layne Payson or J.D. Preacher. He couldn't even see the pier. All three had vanished before his very eyes.

Nate was thrown from his feet and then bounced up and down on the ground as though being hazed on a college tossing blanket. His notebook slipped from his hand. He was jerked, violently, into the wooden dock. Then suddenly, there was no dock. Nate felt the cold water close around him.

Nathan Hale Breed's hands felt clammy. There was a slime beneath his fingertips. He blinked. He didn't care. He heard a squawking gull. He moved. He winced. He smiled. He was alive!

The massive wall of water which had smashed into the San Francisco docks had slammed Nate Breed into the rocks below. He was pinned there by the timbers which had once been the dock. The water retreated from the shore with almost the same force and velocity with which it had come. It carried everything with it, save that which was anchored down. Nate Breed had been anchored down by virtue of having been wedged between two pilings.

Nate had a broken left wrist and two painfull bruises on both the right and left sides of his rib cage. Aside from that, he was fine. He got to his feet and found it difficult to get his bearings. Any landmark which might have helped was gone. He looked toward the bay and felt sick. He knew there was no point to a search for Preacher.

He turned to face the city. It was engulfed in flames and smoke. "Mother of Jesus," he mumbled. It now struck home what had occurred. His first conscious thoughts were of an explosion. A ship in the horbor perhaps, or an explosives manufacturing firm. "An earthquake, my God, an earthquake has destroyed the world."

Indeed, the world Nate Breed could see at that moment was gone. The devastation was enormous. Nowhere could he look without seeing the twisted rubble that was once a building or the fire which was now finishing what the quake had left. It reminded Nate, he thought, of H.G. Wells', "War of the Worlds."

Nate ran from the docks. He didn't stop to consider where he planned to run. He was safe. Where could he go to be safer? It was, he thought, a stupid question. He had to help. Who would he help? How? He didn't see anyone. Downtown, he found life. People there were infected with Nate's affliction. They were all running. He stopped suddenly, for he saw two people who were not running. A man and a woman. They stood, side-by-side, on a window ledge five stories from the ground. The building had defied nature but everything below the couple was aflame. He watched, trancelike, as they put their arms around one another, looked into each other's eyes and then stepped off into nothingness. Nate Breed wretched.

There was no nightfall. One could read a newspaper from the light of the fires up to ten miles away. Many hundreds who survived the quake now wandered aimlessly, dazed, injured or in shock.

Rescue efforts were virtually impossible as fires spread so rapidly. Hospitals, once some of the finest in the nation, were themselves reduced to rubble and medical personnel worked out of makeshift tents.

The Governor asked for the Army to move into the area and they were placed on the same status reserved for war. The troops began to arrive as the sun went down on the 18th day of April but there was little they could do.

Nate Breed went to church.

Nathan Hale Breed ended up as one of only a handful of non resident reporters who was present at the disaster which befell San Francisco on that fateful morning. By the end of the month, much of the most gruesome work had been done. Breed's training proved valuable to authorities in that area, the final identification of the victims.

Breed's efforts began as somewhat less humanitarian than purely selfish, but he soon found himself caught up in the tragedy's individual stories. On the fifth day of May, 1906, the first list of names of those killed was pronounced official and released. Nate Breed got a copy at once. He found it unnecessary to read too far before confirming a couple of his questions.

> Anson, John T.
> Anson, Mrs. Elizabeth King
> Anson, John Taylor Jr. (Infant)
> Armitage, Corwin Halstead
> Armitage, Mrs. Evelyn Highland

Nate Breed quickly scanned the list under the letter "B". He shook his head and sat back, squeezing the bridge of his nose between his thumb and forefinger. He looked again. The name was still there.

Barrett, Janelle Elaine

Under the letter "P", Nate Breed found no familiar names. A much larger list came into his possession at mid-afternoon, however. Its heading sent a chill through him for he understood its finality, given San Francisco's condition. Most of the names were barely more than a blur to him.

MISSING PRESUMED KILLED

Payson, Layne Thomas
Preacher, Jeremy James David

Nate Breed had one final task to perform in San Francisco and one final frustration to his lifelong effort. He'd lost all of his notes and the extensive work he'd done on Preacher's life of course. The hotel where he had been a resident was totally destroyed and what little had survived the quake was lost in the ensuing fire.

The Marine Commerce Bank's location however, resulted in not only most of the building surviving but virtually all of its contents. Therein, however, was the problem. Nate had lost the key to the safe deposit box and since he could not prove a relationship between himself and J.D. Preacher, the contents remained the bank's property. Breed decided to take legal action through his employer but he knew the odds were against him.

Nate Breed quit San Francisco but he was not through with California. On June the fifth, he climbed out of the back of a horseless carriage, gave the driver a silver dollar and said, "I still prefer a stagecoach." The driver, a youth of twenty perhaps, looked at Breed with disdain. Breed smiled. He could almost hear what the young man was thinking. Stagecoach indeed! This was 1906 and horses and stagecoaches and men like Nate Breed were museum pieces. The driver pushed a lever and the vehicle, the driver had called it an automobile, rattled off down the street.

Nate walked another half a block and spotted the number on the house. It was a small, white frame structure, nothing fancy or pretentious. He was somewhat nervous. He chuckled to himself. He was still in awe of certain men and the man who purportedly lived in this house, retired now and living quietly, was one of those Breed found awesome. He steeled his resolve with a deep breath and went to the front door.

"Yes, may I help you?"

He recognized the woman at once. She was still attractive and pleasant and, Breed thought, not at all apprehensive about a stranger coming to the door. Somehow, he'd imagined such a man as the one who lived here would have to live with considerable caution and security. Perhaps, Breed thought, he had become too dramatic in his own advancing years.

"I'm sure you don't remember me, ma'am. Breed, Nate Breed."

The woman's eyes lit up and she smiled. "The young reporter. Of course I do." The smile faded however and was replaced with a bit of a frown. "I'm afraid however that you've come for nothing. My husband isn't giving interviews anymore."

"I didn't come for an interview, Missus Earp," Nate said, "I've only just come from San Francisco. I was there when the earthquake struck. I have some news for Wyatt, uh, Mister Earp."

Nate found himself more than welcome in the Earp's house and they insisted that he stay both for dinner and overnight. He was struck with Wyatt Earp's still youthful appearance. A bit more weight, perhaps a little less the board straight posture, but, Nate thought, still a man to respect and, if you were the wrong cut, feared.

- They sat in the tiny parlor after dinner.

"You still writing stories, are you?" Wyatt asked.

"Yes sir. I have several papers for which I write and now a magazine or two."

"The old days, is that still your subject?"

Nate nodded.

"Well, you'll not likely find a more exciting time to write about but the missus tells me you were up in 'Frisco when the horror struck. Terrible," Wyatt Earp said, "tragic thing."

Wyatt seemed distant for a moment, in deep thought. Then, he looked up.

"A drink, Breed?"

Nate nodded and watched Wyatt prepare two glasses with ice.

"Water or straight?" He didn't wait for an answer. Instead, he said, "You don't want water, not with this." He held up a bottle and Nate sucked in his breath. It was a bottle of Teton Jack.

"May I ask where you got that?"

Wyatt Earp grinned. "Bought it about a month back," he said, "but if I can hear between the lines, you're askin' something else and the answer is yes. J.D. Preacher got me to drinking the stuff."

They drank. The incident had somewhat cooled Nate's reason for being there.

"I know you don't give interviews anymore," Nate said, gesturing toward the kitchen, "your wife told me that but I'm curious as to how you're spending your retirement."

"Retirement? Hell, I'm not retired." Wyatt jumped up, crossed the room to a roll top desk and returned with a paper. "Read that," he said.

Nate did.

Wyatt Earp had bought into a mining claim up in Nome, Alaska. The paper was a letter from his partners wanted him to come up and take a first hand look at the property.

"Are you going, sir?"

"I, by God, am. We leave next week."

"That's great! I envy you, Mister Earp. I've not been there."

Wyatt Earp poured each of them another drink. They downed it in silence and then Wyatt leaned forward. "What brought you here, Breed?"

Nate swallowed. "It's a long story."

Wyatt picked up the bottle of Teton Jack, held it up to the light and then poured each of them another drink. "I've got one more bottle in that cabinet over there. Is it that long a story?"

Nate smiled and shook his head.

"Then let's hear it," Wyatt said.

Nate related the events of the past few months and what had finally culminated on the docks at San Francisco. He showed Wyatt the list of the dead and then the list of the missing who were presumed to be dead.

Wyatt leaned back in his easy chair and sipped at the whiskey. He was silent for several minutes and then he excused himself and went into the kitchen. Nate could hear Wyatt and his wife talking, their tone was low and he couldn't make out what they were saying. A few minutes later, he returned.

"You want another drink?"

"No sir, I think I'd better pass."

"My wife tells me I should do the same." Wyatt sat down again. "You know Breed, the night Layne Payson and Doc Holliday squared off, I pulled Holliday out of it but it didn't end there."

"I don't follow," Nate said.

"Eight years after I left Tombstone, I was contacted by Wells-Fargo. They wanted me to investigate several people who had been involved in a massive government gold theft. I'd been a pinkerton detective and then opened a private business of my own with one of my brothers." Wyatt shook his head. "I guess my marshalin' was better than my business head. We went bust finally. Anyways, it was during that time that I did my checkin' into those names."

"What happened, exactly?"

"Well, the gist of it is that I got close enough to earn myself a threat. It came from Layne Payson. The good Lord seems to watch over fools and ex-lawmen. I got out o' the business an' put the whole thing behind me. I got a passle o' threats over the years. I put more'n a few men behind bars and some of 'em had long memories but out o' the bunch, three or four o' those threats came from Payson."

"Did they ever stop?"

"Finally," Wyatt said, "after I all but vanished. Moved here and kept a real private life. Never got anymore threats or anything I thought was a threat." Wyatt frowned, got up and walked again to the roll top desk. He fished around for an envelope and finally found it. He brought it over and handed it to Nate Breed. It was a Western Union telegraph cable. "Until I got this, four days ago."

Nate Breed eyed Wyatt Earp cautiously. Four days ago? He opened the telegram and read.

> Fresno, Cal.
> 1 June 1906
>
> You'll be hearing from me again Earp. You can't escape your past.
>
> P

Nate Breed paled. He handed the message back to Wyatt Earp. "Your wife know?"

"She knows."

"She worried?"

"She was, 'til you showed up."

Nate frowned. "I have to remind you," he said, "Payson was listed only as missing and presumed dead. That doesn't mean he is and I told you what I saw, what happened out there on the pier. Hell, he could have swam to shore."

"Breed," Wyatt said, smiling, "Layne Payson seems to have you spooked." He held out the telegram again and jabbed at it with his forefinger. "P, Breed. P For Payson? Or P for Preacher?"

Epilogue

Mr. and Mrs. Wyatt Earp left for Alaska on schedule. Nate Breed lingered in Los Angeles long enough to leave behind him some information with his contacts. It was information which he hoped might one day confirm the fate of J.D. Preacher.

Breed then left the City of Angels and took a rather circuitous route back to New York. On the way, he replaced old and gathered some new information on the Tennessee gunfighter. During the next eighteen months, he collaborated with Ned Buntline on a book.

"The Life and Times of a Gunfighter"

The Story of J.D. Preacher

Nate Breed was confident of one thing. When the book was finally in print, it would certainly lure one man to him, if in fact that man was alive. Throughtout the book, Breed had made many

references to Preacher as The Widow Maker.
Preacher wouldn't take it lightly. He'd find Breed.
It was his way, it was Preacher's Law.

The End